Jessica held the doorknob so hard she winced with pain. A moment of panic seized her and held her motionless. Was that her bodyguard?

"You're obviously Jessica Kincaid."

His low, rough-sounding voice had a strange effect on her nerves. She stiffened. "And who might you be?"

"Brant Harding, your bodyguard."

Jessica swallowed, suddenly at a loss for words. The first thought that came to mind was the word *dangerous*: with his dark, brooding looks, he reminded her of a stalking panther.

Wetting her lips, she said inanely, "I wasn't expecting you."

"That's obvious."

She flushed, something she didn't do often. "Won't you come in?"

He strode into the room. Reluctantly she closed the door behind her, fighting off the insane feeling that she was sealing her doom.

MARY LYNN BAXTER

HIS TOUCH

MIRA

ISBN 1-55166-686-3

HIS TOUCH

Copyright © 2003 by Mary Lynn Baxter.

All rights reserved. Except for use in any review, the reproduction or
utilization of this work in whole or in part in any form by any electronic,
mechanical or other means, now known or hereafter invented, including
xerography, photocopying and recording, or in any information storage or
retrieval system, is forbidden without the written permission of the publisher,
MIRA Books, 225 Duncan Mill Road, Don Mills, Ontario, Canada M3B 3K9.

All characters in this book have no existence outside the imagination of the
author and have no relation whatsoever to anyone bearing the same name
or names. They are not even distantly inspired by any individual known or
unknown to the author, and all incidents are pure invention.

MIRA and the Star Colophon are trademarks used under license and registered
in Australia, New Zealand, Philippines, United States Patent and Trademark
Office and in other countries.

Visit us at www.mirabooks.com

Printed in U.S.A.

HIS TOUCH

If only that were the sum total of their lives.

One

The instant she walked into her town home, Jessica Kincaid sensed something was not quite right. She tried to mask her uneasy feelings and not let on, but her efforts didn't work. Her friend called her hand.

"What's wrong?"

Frowning, Jessica peered at Veronica Nash and forced a smile. "Why do you think something's wrong?"

Veronica's pixie features turned into a matching frown. "Because I know you, that's why. You looked spooked."

"I am," Jessica admitted with blunt honesty, deciding it was foolish to hide the truth from her friend any longer.

"Want to tell me what's going on?" Veronica asked, her tone pressing.

Jessica smothered a sigh, at the same time running her hands through her short, highlighted brown hair. "How 'bout we get comfy first and have a cup of coffee?"

"Works for me." Veronica proceeded to toss her purse on the floor, then plop down on the sofa. "Need any help?"

Jessica shook her head. "I think I can handle it."

If only that were true about the rest of her life, Jessica

thought, puttering around in her bright yellow-and-green kitchen. Once the coffee was dripping, she paused and took a deep breath.

As mayor of Dallas, Texas, one of the most up-and-coming cities in the south—in the nation, for that matter—she couldn't give in to this unexpected turn of events. She had to come up with a way to handle things herself and not involve the police.

"Sure you don't need help?"

Veronica's lively voice made Jessica move. "I'm coming. I was just woolgathering," she added, walking back into the living room with a tray.

Once they were sipping the hot coffee, Veronica's dark eyes pinned her. "So what has you so uptight? And not just tonight, either. You've been different lately."

"I'm being harassed by some nutcase."

Veronica coughed, obviously strangling on the liquid. When she sat the cup down on the coffee table, her eyes were wide and questioning. "Are you serious?" She flapped her hand impatiently. "Sorry, forget I asked that. Of course you're serious. That's not something to joke about, especially given your job."

"You're right. It's been going on for some time now."

"So why haven't the police already caught the pervert?"

Jessica hesitated, looking away from Veronica's direct stare. "Because I haven't involved them."

"That's crazy," Veronica said in a blustering tone. "They work for you, for heaven's sake."

"True, but—"

"What's the deal, then?"

"You know what the deal is, Ronnie. Ever since I

fired the police chief and suspended two popular officers, I'm not the most loved person around city hall.''

''Ah, for a second those minor points slipped my mind.'' Though her voice held a slice of humor, Veronica's features remained grave. ''But surely there's someone on the force you can depend on?''

Jessica didn't respond. Instead, she gazed around the room, her eyes settling on the items that brought her comfort: photographs of her and Porter, her deceased husband, live plants she nurtured herself, and other mementos that had personal meaning. Once she had believed that her home in an upscale part of the city was indeed her safe haven.

Unfortunately, that wasn't the case. No longer did she feel that sense of security when she walked in, that feeling of peace. In fact, she felt the opposite, as if her privacy had been totally invaded, emotionally and physically.

If only Porter were here, he would know what to do. If her husband were still alive, she wouldn't be in this precarious position to start with, she reminded herself. He would still be the mayor, and she would be the loving, supportive wife behind the scenes.

A deep sigh escaped Jessica when she felt Veronica's piercing eyes on her once again.

''I want all the gory details,'' her friend said. ''And I'm not letting you off the hook until I hear them.''

Jessica plucked at a thread on the black silk slacks covering her long, slender legs. She knew her friend meant what she said. Veronica's features were growing graver by the second.

''First off, I've been receiving phone calls on all my phones, cell included, mostly obscene. And irritating as hell. Even though I have caller ID, it's failed to identify the caller. The screen either registers Out of Area or Unknown Name.''

"Go on."

"E-mails, too. I've been unable to trace them, either. They're obviously sent from different, untraceable locations, like public libraries and Internet cafés."

"I can tell there's more."

"I'm being followed, or stalked, whatever term you want to give it."

"And you've done nothing? Good grief, Jessica, that's insane."

Jessica bit down on her full lower lip. "You're right. I can't argue with you. Still…" Her voice faded.

"No excuse will hold water, so don't waste your breath." Veronica paused, pressing her lips together. "Anything else?"

"Not so far."

Veronica gave her a look before she bounded off the sofa, walked to the fireplace and leaned against it. "What in the world is wrong with you? Your life could be in real danger—*is* in real danger. Yet you've done nothing."

"I've taken some precautions," Jessica said, her tone defensive.

"Such as?" Veronica countered, not bothering to mask her disbelief.

Jessica flushed, adding to the natural color in her cheeks. "I just kept thinking the harassment would come to an end, that whoever was behind it would get tired and move on."

"Not if he, she or they have an agenda. If someone is out to harm you, they're not likely to stop until that's accomplished."

"I did buy a gun."

"But you can't use it, right?"

"Right."

"Why am I not surprised?"

Jessica's stark blue eyes narrowed on her friend. "You're not making this any easier, you know?"

Veronica shrugged. "I know, and I'm sorry. But you're scaring the you-know-what out of me."

"I've had every intention of learning, but with things in such turmoil at the office, I just haven't had the time."

"Learning to fire a gun is fine, but you have to alert the police. You need round-the-clock protection."

Jessica shook her head. "I'm not prepared to go that far. I still think this too shall pass."

"That's just wishful thinking, and you know that."

Jessica released another pent-up sigh, her mind seeming to splinter off in a million different directions, which made her crazy. She was used to her life running according to plan and on schedule. Suddenly her well-oiled machine had careened off course, just like it had after Porter died, making her feel out of control, a feeling that didn't sit well with her.

Since her father's desertion at an early age, she had ceased to be a child. With her mother's strong, albeit bitter, influence, she had become a savvy, self-assured person who had learned to care for herself, to protect herself, especially from emotional traumas. And while she had indeed relied on Porter for many things, she had never lost that fierce sense of self and independence.

"Jessie."

Veronica's use of her pet name drew her out of her musings, and Jessica swallowed hard.

"You were thinking about Porter, weren't you?"

"Yes."

"He's been dead four years now," Veronica pointed out gently. "He can't take care of you any longer."

"He never took care of me in the sense you mean," Jessica said, feeling she had no choice but to defend herself. "He was just always there." Jessica stood. "Hold your thought. I'm going to dash upstairs for a sec. I'll be right back."

The instant she strode into her bedroom, Jessica pulled up short. She just managed to clasp her hand on her mouth to smother the gasp. A dead rose lay across her pillow. For a long moment she was too dumbstruck to move. A sick feeling settling in the pit of her stomach, she whirled and practically ran back downstairs.

"That was quick," Veronica said, the twinkle back in her eyes, then suddenly turned sober. "What happened?"

"There's...there's a dead rose on my pillow."

Without saying a word, Veronica tore toward the bedroom, then back with equal speed. "That does it. You can't afford to mess with this sicko any longer, regardless of how he got in. The fact that someone did is all that counts."

Jessica eased back onto the sofa, that sick feeling still churning her stomach. "You're right. Push has come to shove."

"So let's start by pushing the police into action. Under the circumstances, I know you're reluctant to do that, having clearly decided not to involve them. But now you have no choice."

Jessica rose again. "I'll make the call."

A short time later two officers had come and gone, with little to show for their actions. The person or per-

sons had left no trace, though they'd dusted for finger-
prints, as well as checking for method of entry. Apparently they'd jimmied the door, which had been easy due
to stupidity on her part. She'd left without setting her
alarm, something she'd often done in the past with no
consequences. This time it had been costly.

"The pervert could be any guy off the street," Veronica said. "Or it could be a direct result of you clean-
ing house at the precinct. Someone with a grudge."

Jessica reached for her coffee and took a sip, only to
make a face. The coffee was now tepid. "Possibly,
though I have my doubts," she pointed out. "I think
it's just some crazy off the streets."

"I wish I could be that sure. What about that land
deal that's been making headlines lately?"

"There's nothing there to incite an attack."

"Something has and you…we have to get to the bottom of it ASAP. Thurmon will know what to do."

Thurmon was Veronica's husband, a retired Secret
Service agent, now in business for himself as the owner
of a highly successful security firm.

"You're thinking of a bodyguard, right?"

"Absolutely, and I know who Thurmon will suggest."

"Just who might that be?" Jessica asked in a tone
tainted with sarcasm. Having someone underfoot all the
time didn't bear thinking about. This entire scenario
seemed too preposterous for words.

"Brant Harding, an old friend, who worked with
Thurmon in the Secret Service. However, convincing
Brant to take the job will be difficult."

"Then why bother?"

"Because he's the best, even better than Thurmon.
But he's become a recluse for reasons we won't go into

now. Still, there's hope, because he owes Thurmon big time—his life actually. We also have another thing in our favor. His teenage son, from whom he's estranged, lives in this area. Since Brant wants to mend fences, I'm thinking that will be our ace in the hole.''

Jessica crossed her arms over her breasts. "I don't know, Veronica. That—*he*—doesn't sound like a good idea to me.''

"You let Thurmon be the judge of that. You just sit tight while I call my better half.''

Jessica kept silent while her insides continued to churn and her thoughts reverted to that lifeless rose on the pillow. She shuddered and crossed her arms tighter.

Two

Too bad the fishing was lousy.

Today of all days. When he needed to unwind.

Brant Harding reeled in his line, then peered at the lake, noticing again how perfect the water was. Blue and spring clear, so clear he could see the colors in the polished rocks underneath. Still, he couldn't get a bite no matter what kind of bait, live or artificial, he used.

Letting out a sigh, Brant shoved his battered Stetson back and squinted up at the sun. Maybe it was too hot. Even though it was just the beginning of May, the sun had already sprouted a mean stinger.

A hot spring and summer were predicted for Arkansas and the rest of the South. So what if that messed up the fishing? He would get over it in due time, he told himself, shaping his mouth into a sarcastic twist. If only that were all he had to worry about, he'd be one lucky bastard. Only it wasn't, not by any stretch of the imagination.

Wary of where his thoughts were heading, Brant gathered his gear and made tracks for the cabin at the top of the hill that overlooked the hundred acres he'd inherited when his parents had died several years ago, killed instantly in a head-on car collision.

He'd built this place himself and knew he'd made the right decision. He'd chosen the best site on the choice land, opting for an umbrella of tall pines and oaks. He called it a cabin, but it was hardly that, though it was rustic and uncluttered. Still, it had all the amenities he or anyone else could want.

Except a woman.

Not interested.

Brant's gut tightened, and his lean, well-chiseled features hardened. Definitely not in the market. Those days were over. He'd been down the marriage road once, and that was enough to last him a lifetime. What he needed was another dog, he told himself as he walked into the cool, airy great room and tossed his hat on the back of a chair.

The interior reflected a relaxed atmosphere. Deep, rich colors, natural wood finishes and comfortable furnishings created a warm feeling.

However, something was missing. Butch, the old hound that had been with him for years, had died. Until then, he hadn't felt lonely in his isolated domain. Now he did, which didn't sit too well with him. He was here by choice not by chance. Hounds were a dime a dozen at the local pound in the nearest town, Mountain Home. Next time he went in for groceries and other supplies, he would see what he could do.

Meanwhile, he had a much more pressing and important issue to resolve—what to do about his son, Elliot. Feeling the urge for a cold beer, Brant made his way into the kitchen, an offshoot of the great room, and opened the fridge.

After downing several swigs, he peered at the clock. Five. No problem. Since his isolation, he'd made it a point not to indulge himself before late in the afternoon and then only sparingly. It would be so easy to drown his troubles in booze, but he wasn't about to fall into that trap. He'd seen too many of the guys he'd worked with do that to no good end.

Yet it felt damn good to feel the edge dull somewhat after having gone another round earlier with his ex-wife, leaving him furious and frustrated. She seemed determined to throw monkey wrenches into his plans to see his seventeen-year-old son.

Once he'd plopped down on the sofa and crossed his legs on the coffee table, Brant finished the beer, then set the bottle down. He needed a shower, but he wasn't in the mood, not when his thoughts were cluttered with his ex.

Marsha Harding Bishop knew just which strings to jerk to get him riled, especially when it came to money and their kid. Since she'd finally married the man with whom she'd had an affair and who had become more of a father to Elliot than he himself had ever been, the money issue had resolved itself. Preston Bishop owned an accounting firm and made big bucks.

More power to him.

Brant couldn't give a rip about the money. He had plenty of his own, mostly inherited from his parents, but what the hell—money was money. He didn't need much of the green stuff, anyway, not to live the way he lived. Most of it was in trust for his son, and Marsha knew that. Yet it hadn't made one whit of difference in her attitude toward him.

When he'd called and asked to speak to Elliot, she hadn't had to say a word for him to sense her hostile attitude. He'd envisioned her otherwise attractive features tightening and her slender shoulders stiffening.

"He's not here."

"Are you sure?"

That comment had turned the hostility in her voice to ice. "I don't lie, contrary to what you think."

"Come on, Marsha, who do you think you're talking to? You've lied, all right, but that's water under the bridge. I'm through arguing with you. Right now, all I care about is talking to my son."

"I told you, he's not here."

Brant controlled his rising temper with an effort. "Will you give him a message?"

Silence.

"Dammit, Marsha, when are you going to stop using Elliot as a weapon to get back at me?"

"Don't flatter yourself," she said, the ice in her voice thickening.

Again, Brant controlled his temper and words. He was treading in a current he couldn't master, at least not over the phone. He hated the damn things, anyway. He would much rather be looking her in the face when he talked to her. Maybe then she could see the sincerity laced with the desperation in his eyes.

At the moment, however, he had no recourse but to back down. "Forget it. I'll call him back later."

"Was there anything in particular you wanted?"

"Yeah," he said in a clipped tone. "I want to see him."

"I don't—"

"You might as well stop fighting me, Marsha. I've made up my mind that Elliot's going to be a part of my life."

"We'll see about that," she countered before the dial tone abused his ear.

Releasing his pent-up temper, Brant followed suit and slammed the receiver down.

Just thinking about that conversation made his blood

boil again. Damn her. Cool it, buddy, he cautioned himself, taking deep breaths. He couldn't totally blame her for the quagmire he was in with his only child. He'd gotten himself into it, and it was up to him to get out.

Trouble was, he didn't know how. He needed Marsha's help and cooperation. But apparently he was never going to get it, which meant he would have to depend on himself.

Feeling as if his insides were in a meat grinder, Brant walked onto the deck and, leaning the bulk of his weight on the handrails, stared at the lake and wooded hills beyond. The sun was beginning to set, and the picture before him was awesome. But this evening, the beauty and calmness of his sanctuary failed to soothe his seething mind and heart.

Would he be forced to pay for his sins forever?

Maybe coming here had been a mistake. Maybe he should've headed to Texas, to the Metroplex area, right off. By now he might have established a new relationship with his son instead of awkward phone conversations in between playing telephone tag.

He'd been forced into early retirement due to gunshot wounds he'd received during his long tenure as a Secret Service agent. It was while he'd been protecting the First Lady three years ago that the life-altering incident had occurred. He'd taken a bullet in the stomach and another in the right leg. Both wounds had been severe, and he'd nearly died, especially from the gut shot.

Since then, he'd become more or less a recluse, trying to recover in mind and body. But instead of healing, he found himself often lonely and discontented. Both stemmed from the burning need to bridge the growing estrangement from his son. For his own sanity, he had to find a way to become a part of Elliot's life again. A sad commentary was that he hadn't ever been the hands-on dad he should have been. Marsha's beef against him on that score was right on target.

Facing that brutal truth had been the first big hurdle he'd had to jump. Admitting he was wrong came hard for him. Since he'd come here, he'd realized where he'd gone wrong, especially when it came to Elliot.

Following his divorce from Marsha eight years ago, the breach between him and Elliot had widened. At age forty-two he had no plans to remarry and add to his family, so the need to regain his son's love and trust had become a frantic effort of the soul.

Now he feared he might have to venture away from his safe compound and uncomplicated way of life. He was reluctant to make such a bold move, since his mind still had a long way to go before recovering from the trauma it had suffered.

Yet he couldn't rule that out, though the thought made him break out in a cold sweat. He no longer sought people out for their company. He craved the space and solitude of the mountains. The thought of returning to city life with all its hustle and bustle was repugnant to him. He had to figure out a way to get Elliot here, to the cabin, for a lengthy visit.

Now that he could maneuver without a cane, he would just have to come up with a workable plan.

"What the hell?" he muttered suddenly, as the noise coming from behind finally penetrated his beleaguered senses. On striding back into the living room, he realized someone was pounding on the front door. For some reason it was locked. When had he done that?

"Hold your horses," he muttered, wondering who the hell his unwanted visitor was. He had neighbors, but they weren't close ones and rarely came calling. A chill shot through him. Had something happened to Elliot? Of course not, he rationalized. If it had, he would be the last to know.

By the time he reached the door and jerked it open, sweat saturated his forehead and upper lip.

"Knocked your dick in the dirt, didn't I, old friend?"

Brant's only response to his long-time friend Thurmon Nash's caustic comment was shocked silence.

Thurmon grinned, slapped him on the shoulder, then strode past him into the living room. There he whirled, his grin gaining strength by the second. He was tall and slightly overweight, with a bushy mustache that added to his strong features. His prematurely gray hair and blue eyes enhanced his commanding presence. Shrewd intelligence made him a friend and businessman for whom Brant had the greatest respect.

"What the hell are you doing here?" Brant demanded when he finally found his voice.

"How 'bout a cold one before we get down to the nitty gritty?"

Wordlessly Brant headed for the kitchen and returned with two beers. He handed one to Thurmon, who then made himself comfortable in the nearest leather chair.

Brant took a seat on the matching sofa. For a moment they nursed their beers in companionable silence.

"You didn't come all this way for a social call." Brant's words were a flat statement of fact.

"You're right, I didn't."

"If it's about me joining you as a partner in your security firm, I haven't changed my mind."

"I'm not here about that, though the offer still stands."

"Thanks again, but no thanks."

"Can't blame a fellow for trying."

"Is Ronnie all right?"

"Great. Blowing and going, as always."

"Still in practice with that same high-flying attorney, huh?"

"Yep. And making him a shit-load of money, too."

"When is she going to take a timeout and have a kid?"

Thurmon sighed. "It's her call. And from the way it's looking, maybe never. We're both on the career fast track and can't seem to get off."

Changing the subject, Brant said, "So unload."

Obviously choosing to ignore Brant's push to get to the point, Thurmon crossed a leg over one knee and looked around. "This is still a great place, but aren't you lonely as hell here?"

"I'm used to being alone. I was married for twelve years."

"Funny."

Brant kept his features bland.

"Don't you think you've been hiding long enough?"

That comment irritated the hell out of Brant. He hadn't seen his friend for heaven knows how long and didn't appreciate being raked over the coals for his style of living, rather than shooting the bull about things they had in common.

"I'm treading on dangerous ground, aren't I?" Thurmon asked in the growing silence.

"You read my mind."

"Are you still the same expert marksman you once were?"

Surprise raised Brant's eyebrows. "Why?"

"Just answer the question."

"Okay. Yeah, I am. As a matter of fact, I practice just about every day." He wanted to add that it whiled away some of the hours, but he didn't dare. To admit that would add fodder to Thurmon's case against him. "Why?" he asked again.

"I have a favor to ask, that's why."

Brant's guard, along with his hackles, rose. "Why do I sense I'm not going to like what's coming next?"

"Because you've became paranoid?"

Brant snorted.

Thurmon laughed, then said, "Did I mention how good it is to see you, how much I miss having your ill-tempered self around?"

"No. But I take no offense, considering the source."

Thurmon's laugh merely deepened before his features sobered once again. "Actually it's my wife who wants the favor."

"Then why didn't *she* ask? She knows my number."

"She knew I wanted an excuse to see your sorry ass."

"Veronica's not in any kind of trouble, is she?"

"Nope. But she has a friend who is."

"So? You have a security company, take care of it. I'm out of that business forever. All I care about now is mending fences with my kid."

"How's that going?"

"It's not. If Marsha had her way, I'd never see him again."

"Nothing like a woman scorned."

"Hell, she's the one who had the affair."

"After you were never home."

Brant's eyes narrowed. "You were in the same boat and Ronnie never cheated on you."

"True, but we didn't have a kid who needed his father, either."

Brant cursed, feeling Thurmon's arrow hit where it

hurt most—his heart. "That's still no excuse for what Marsha did. But like I told her, that's water under the bridge. I hold no grudges. Instead I'm moving forward and trying to fix things."

"I'm about to give you that opportunity."

"How's that?" Brant's voice overflowed with suspicion. He didn't trust his friend as far as he could throw him.

"By getting you back to Texas."

"Ah, so that's where this is going? Figures."

"Veronica's friend needs a bodyguard, and you're the best I have to offer."

"Are you deaf? I just told you I don't do that anymore. But then, you knew that before you came all this way."

Thurmon leaned forward. "First off, you owe me. And while I never intended to remind you of the fact that I saved your life, I'm doing it now."

"That's hitting below the belt."

"I know, and I'm sorry. But you also know how I feel about Ronnie. I'll do anything I can to keep her happy. And she wants you to help her friend, so here I am."

"Tightening the screws," Brant said, barely suppressing his fury at being shoved into a corner with no way out.

"I wouldn't do this if it weren't of utmost importance."

"Somehow that doesn't loosen the screws any," Brant responded tightly.

"If you help me out, you'll be doing yourself a favor, as well. You'll be close to Elliot and can mend those fences close up instead of from afar."

Brant rose. "You're a blackmailing SOB."

Thurmon seemed to take no offense at the harsh words. "You'll thank me, my friend. You wait and see."

God, Brant hoped so. But he was afraid, something he could never let Thurmon or anyone else know. Yet he was even more frightened of never seeing his son again. So whether he liked it or not, the die had been cast.

Brant sat back down. "So what's the problem?"

Three

Jessica sat at her desk in her office at city hall, her mind in an uproar. She had so many items on her agenda she didn't know where to start. As a result, she simply *hadn't* started. Instead she'd poured herself a second cup of coffee and was drinking it at leisure, something she rarely did.

Today, however, was going to be an especially difficult one, and she needed extra fuel to help her get through it. First off, she had a meeting scheduled with Councilmember Lance Saxon, her biggest adversary regarding the current brouhahas with the police and over the land annexation.

The bottom line was that Saxon didn't like her personally or professionally. She suspected his disfavor stemmed from the fact that she was a woman. He couldn't seem to surmount that hurdle and deal with her accordingly. He'd never said as much, of course—he had more political savvy than that. Still, she sensed his feelings. Like Porter, she had an uncanny knack for reading people.

Saxon was also outspoken and adversarial. Often she was capable of putting him in his place without losing her dignity or her professionalism, but there were times when he pushed her too far and felt the sting of her tongue.

She hoped this morning she could maintain her cool professionalism and make him understand once and for all her actions concerning the chief and the land. Since the controversy had occurred, Saxon had managed to swing several other councilmembers over to his side.

Not a good thing.

Jessica sighed, then took another sip of her coffee, letting her gaze wander around the room. Nice. Soothing. Smart. Those were the words that jumped to mind as her eyes touched on the mint-green and gold tapestry-covered chairs, the tall, full plants placed just right for the sunlight to perform its magic, and the artwork that adorned the wall, gathered from her trips abroad with Porter.

At the moment her office felt more secure than her home, as the office hadn't been invaded by her nemesis. Jessica shivered, her thoughts reverting to her conversation with Veronica last evening and the decision she had made.

All morning she'd been regretting giving Veronica the green light on the bodyguard gig. Given more time, surely she could work through this situation on her own. On the other hand, the rose incident had frightened her to the core.

Someone hated her.

Enough to *kill* her?

Jessica gripped the cup so tightly she could see her knuckles turn white. She wouldn't let this pervert win, dammit. She wouldn't. Even if it meant having a stranger invade her life for a while. She could cope with that. But could the council? Should she even tell them?

Under the circumstances, what choice did she have? To date, the only one besides Veronica who knew about the threats was her assistant, Tony Eason, and even he didn't know about this latest one. She dreaded telling him for more reasons than one.

"You're here awfully early."

"Ah, good morning," Jessica said to the short but stout young man who all but fluttered into her room, dressed outlandishly, as usual. He had on a brightly flowered tie and salmon-colored sports coat. She winced inwardly at the combination but didn't let on. "I was just thinking about you."

Tony Eason smiled while shoving his small wire-rimmed glasses closer to the bridge of his nose. Once he'd removed his hand, his gray-green eyes peered into hers, something he always did, as if gauging her mood for the day.

He was single, in his early thirties, efficient and precise as a prim schoolteacher. The buzz around city hall was that Tony was gay. She discouraged and disapproved of such gossip when it pertained to anyone, but especially Tony. He was completely dedicated to her and the job, and she couldn't imagine what she would do without him, and his sex life was no one's business but his own.

"So how was your evening?"

"You don't want to know."

"Uh-oh, what happened?"

"More of the same, only worse."

Tony perched on the edge of her large desk, placing the folders he was carrying on his lap. "This has gone on far too long."

"I know."

"So what happened?"

Jessica filled him in, leaving nothing out.

"Lord a mercy, we've...*you've* got to do something."

"I am." She told him then about Veronica and Thurmon's friend.

"Mmm." Tony rubbed his smooth chin. "A bodyguard. Not a bad idea. I should've already thought of that."

"How do you think the council will react?"

"They'll be concerned."

"Or tell me I deserve it."

Tony lifted a sooty brow, too perfect to belong to a man. "Saxon, perhaps, but he's a pompous you-know-what."

Jessica smiled. "He thinks he's right and I'm wrong. That's his prerogative."

"I don't think you could please the man no matter what you did."

Jessica smoothed a pleat on her coral Ralph Lauren slacks that had a matching jacket hanging on the coatrack. She had purposely dressed in what she referred to as high style. Although her outfit was tailored, it was also very feminine. Even though she worked in a man's world, she never wanted to join that world. She was content with herself as a woman and what she'd accomplished.

"Porter would know how to handle Saxon," she finally said, more for her benefit than Tony's.

"If your husband were still mayor, there wouldn't be anything to handle."

"So you also think it's me?"

"Sure do. He can't get over the fact that a woman is running the city. I bet he chokes on that every meal. Pleasant thought, isn't it?"

Jessica almost smiled. "Shame on you."

"Ah, forget him." Tony gestured with a hand. "Even

if he doesn't come around to your way of thinking, the others will. The city has too much to lose.''

"We'll see. But never forget how much influence Saxon wields or how much money he has. Both are synonymous with power.''

"I'm betting on you.''

"In any event, I'm going to send each member a letter explaining what's going on, especially since I'm getting a bodyguard.''

"That's probably smart.'' Tony paused. "So when's this bodyguard supposed to come on duty?''

"I'm not sure. Could be any time now, I suppose. Thurmon and Veronica are in charge of the arrangements.''

"Meanwhile, do you think it's wise for you to be alone? I can always bunk on your sofa.''

"Absolutely not, even though I appreciate the offer.'' Jessica's full lips thinned. "I'm not about to let this maniac totally rule my life.''

"You'll be careful, though, won't you?''

Jessica heard the anxiety in Tony's voice and realized how foolhardy she must sound. Last night's incident, in particular, was not something to be taken lightly. Still, it was hard to admit she needed anyone. She'd grown so used to taking care of herself that she resented the loss of that God-given right.

"I promise I won't take any unnecessary chances. But I'm sure Veronica and Thurmon will see that I don't, so you can rest easy.''

"Good.'' Tony stood, then peered at his watch. "Since it's almost time for Saxon's appointment, I'll let these files slide until later.''

"Not if they're important.''

"Nothing that can't wait until after he leaves.'' Tony

paused, his features becoming solemn and pinched. "There is one more thing. I debated about telling you."

"Don't ever do that." Jessica came as close to snapping at him as she ever had. "What is it?"

"Dale Lipton. He's thrown his hat back into the mayoral ring."

Jessica groaned out loud. "That's not good news."

"And Saxon will be backing him. Count on it."

"Oh, I know. Lipton and Saxon are not only good friends but business partners of sorts, or so I've heard."

"No problem. You've got class and smarts. They have neither." He massaged the top of his head. "Besides, you've already trounced Lipton once. You can do it again."

"I won't give in or up without a fight. Last election, he fought low and dirty."

"But you didn't, and that's why you beat him."

Tony grinned at the same time his glasses slipped down on his nose, making him look like a figure out of a comic magazine, especially as a twig of unruly hair was sticking up from the crown of his head. But she didn't dare say a word. He would have a fit if he knew his hair was mussed.

"As soon as things in the office and in my personal life settle, we'll find a new chief, then I'll get started on my reelection plans."

"I have several people in mind to manage the next one. Well-qualified people."

"Good. We'll get together on that soon."

Tony headed toward the door. "Oh, something else."

"What?"

"Since the council okayed that Zurich mayoral conference, does that mean I'm to make plans for you to attend?"

"Of course. It's a chance I'd be foolish to pass up."

"Well, with all this mess going on, I wasn't sure."

Jessica didn't hesitate. "Now you are."

"Great. I'll buzz personally when Saxon arrives."

"Thanks," Jessica said with a downturn of her mouth.

Tony's lips twitched. "Any time."

Once she was alone, Jessica stood, walked into her bathroom and trashed her cold coffee. But instead of heading back to her desk and tackling the phone messages and mounds of paperwork, she went to the window and stared at the Dallas skyline.

Lovely city. Lovely time of the year. Her favorite, in fact. The flowers and trees were in full bloom. Everything looked and smelled fresh, especially after a cleansing rain shower like the one they'd had last night.

Now the sun was shining. Maybe that was a good omen.

She needed that. Since Porter's death, she had made her career her life in an effort to soak up the loneliness that oftentimes haunted her. She knew she had been a good mayor. She had made things happen for the city— good things. She definitely earned more money than she was paid rather than being paid more than she earned.

Her goal was to continue to be the best, most conscientious mayor she could be, then seek reelection, a prospect that no longer loomed brightly. But it would, as soon as she rode out the current political storm. Because she felt so justified concerning her bold actions, she was determined to remain strong and unbending in her decisions.

The chips would just have to fall where they would.

Her buzzing phone jolted her back to the moment at

hand. She crossed to the desk and pressed the button. "Yes."

"Mr. Saxon's here."

"Send him in." Jessica walked to the coatrack and slipped into her jacket just as the door opened and Saxon strode in.

"Morning, Mrs. Kincaid."

He rarely showed her the respect of her title, which didn't bother her. It merely showed how unprofessional and insulting he could be when it suited him. Today was apparently one of those days.

"Good morning," she forced herself to say as politely as possible. "It's nice to see you again."

"I hope you'll still feel that way after I leave," he countered with his usual bluntness.

She ignored that and asked him to sit down.

Lance Saxon was of average height, with a balding head and jowls that shook when he made any kind of sudden movement. The circumference of his middle was also noticeable, indicating that he lived the good life to the max.

He took a seat, but by the time she sat behind her desk, he was standing again, seeming to tower over her, his nostrils flaring.

Keeping her emotions in check, Jessica smiled, then asked, "So what's on your mind?"

"Oh, I think you know. But for starters, I insist you reinstate the police chief."

Thirty minutes later Lance Saxon strode out of her office, but not before stopping, turning and firing off one more verbal round. "Rest assured, you won't get away with your actions, Mrs. Kincaid."

Though her legs were less than steady, Jessica had

forced herself to follow him to the door with another smile plastered on her face. Now that he was actually leaving her office, her hand circled the knob so hard she experienced a wince of pain.

That was when she saw *him*.

Standing in her outer office, staring at her. A moment of panic seized her and held her motionless. Had her nemesis managed to get... No. The pervert harassing her wouldn't look like this man.

Was that her bodyguard?

Most likely, she assured herself, feeling her stomach unknot. As far as she knew, she didn't have any more appointments until after lunch. Where was Tony? Not at his desk, unfortunately.

"You're obviously Jessica Kincaid."

His low, rather rough-sounding voice had a strange effect on her nerves. She stiffened. "And who might you be?"

"Brant Harding, your bodyguard." His lips twitched, as if he would have loved to smile, only his lips wouldn't cooperate.

Jessica swallowed, suddenly at a loss for words. She didn't know what she'd expected, but it wasn't the likes of this man. For some crazy reason, she felt an instant visceral response. The first thought that came to mind was the word dangerous; with his dark, brooding looks, he reminded her of a stalking panther.

No man had ever struck her with such animal force, leaving her more than a little disconcerted.

Wetting her lips, she said inanely, "I wasn't expecting you."

"That's obvious."

She flushed, something she didn't do often. "Won't you come in?"

He strode into the room. Reluctantly she closed the door behind her, fighting off the insane feeling that she was sealing her doom.

Four

Jessica sensed Brant Harding was as uncomfortable with the situation as she was. It didn't take any brain-power to figure that out. So why had he come? And why didn't she just send him on his way? Good questions, but with no good answers.

"Shall we get down to business?"

Although his tone was not exactly brusque, it touched on it. "I have no problem with that," she said, feeling her temper rise, which was totally out of character for her. It took a lot to rile her, but there was something about this man that set her on edge. As the seconds ticked on, that edge seemed to sharpen.

Why hadn't she asked Veronica more about him when she'd had the chance? She kicked herself mentally for that oversight. At the time, however, she had assumed he was an older man, the Saxon type, perhaps, with a bald spot on the top of his head. Well, he certainly wasn't old—early to mid-forties, she gauged. Nor did he have a bald spot.

Shifting her thoughts abruptly, Jessica turned and made her way into her office proper.

Brant didn't sit down, but then, she didn't invite him to, either. Briefly their eyes met before both looked away.

However, Jessica didn't have to stare at him to know

what he looked like. The image of his tall, well-honed body dressed in a pair of casual slacks, sports shirt and boots was imprinted on her mind. He seemed to dominate her office, and it wasn't small, either. It was the man himself. He exuded that kind of power and authority.

No wonder he was a crackerjack agent. Still, that didn't excuse his curt behavior. Without having to be told, she knew no one had been able to make him show up here—favor or no favor. She imagined Brant Harding did his own thing, in his own time.

Handsome? No. His features, which were etched with an almost bitter overtone, were too strong for that. Noticeable? Oh, yes. His thick dark hair was entwined with silver and appeared like it wanted to curl, which merely added to its richness. And his dark eyes were surrounded by thick sooty lashes, lashes that most women would kill for, herself included.

A living, breathing work of art was what he was.

Clearing her throat and hoping she'd successfully maintained her composure, Jessica jerked her mind back on track. Remembering her manners, she offered him a cup of coffee.

"No, thanks. But I would like to know who that guy was and what he meant by his parting shot."

He was also a man who came straight to the point, Jessica noted. A man who apparently didn't believe in wasting words.

"His name is Lance Saxon, and he's a councilmember."

"He's obviously not happy with some of your latest decisions."

"That's an understatement. He's by far my biggest critic."

"Is it because of the police stink?"

"So you know about that."

He shrugged his shoulders, which were the width of a fullback's. "Thurmon told me you'd cleaned house."

"I wouldn't go that far. What I did was relieve the chief of his duties, along with two officers whom I put on suspension."

Dark eyebrows quirked. "Sounds pretty drastic to me, but I'm sure you had your reasons."

God, he was irritating. "Evidence was uncovered that the officers were on the take and the chief knew it but did nothing. In addition, there was strong evidence of police brutality, not just in one incident but several. The same officers were involved each time."

Jessica paused and drew a clear breath. "Pending further investigation, I thought it best for the city that I take such a bold move."

"So everything is well documented."

"I have folders filled with complaints," Jessica said.

"So you do indeed have your guns loaded."

"That seems to surprise you," she responded in a testy tone, having difficulty hiding her growing irritation. "Or maybe it's that you don't approve."

He lifted his eyebrows. "It doesn't matter what I think."

"You're right, it doesn't."

Brant's eyes narrowed. "It's what the council thinks that matters."

"If I were a m—" Jessica broke off, choking on the word *man*.

Brant finished the sentence for her. "If you were a man, you might have more support, right?"

"That's right," she said, unable to suppress the bitterness that sometimes caught her unawares. "I suppose you feel the same way." Not that she gave a damn.

Again he seemed a bit shocked at her directness, though his tone was even and unruffled. "Actually, I don't have an opinion one way or the other."

"Good," she muttered, turning away from his intense gaze.

"Not all on the council are on your side, I take it."

Jessica faced him again. "Saxon especially, like I said. He's determined to make me reinstate the chief and the officers, then make a public apology."

"And you intend to fight him?"

"To the end. I did what I felt was right, but only after I carefully weighed all the evidence. And consequences. Trust me, it wasn't an easy decision. And in the long run, it could cost me dearly."

"Your job." A blunt statement of fact.

"Yes."

"Do you think Saxon might be behind the threats toward you?"

Jessica was taken aback. "Of course not. He's a pillar of the community, plus he's one of the wealthiest men in the city."

"So?"

She stiffened. "So I don't think it's Saxon. He's pompous and everything that goes with that, but he's no fool."

"That remains to be seen."

Jessica tightened her lips. Talking to him was like constantly bumping into a brick wall.

"What else is going on in your professional life that might generate this kind of menace?"

"There's a big land deal pending," she said, following a deep sigh. "More to the point, there's a huge tract of land I'm trying to annex into the city. In fact, I thought I had all the loose ends tied and knotted, that it was a done deal, only I've suddenly encountered severe opposition.''

"Such as?"

"Industry. One of the major land owners, who's actually a friend of mine, has been approached by a worldwide industrial company. This company wants to build a plant on part of the land. As it stands now, the community where it's located has a much cheaper tax rate than the city of Dallas.''

"If you get your way, then the company might want to move elsewhere.''

"Most likely they will.''

"Which will screw the owners out of a mega deal.'' Brant rubbed his chin. "Not a great scenario.''

"There's more, I'm afraid,'' Jessica added. "The other portion of the land is being developed for garden homes. A polling firm was hired to question the interested parties. The community won hands down, citing city taxes again.''

"Sounds like another hornet's nest.''

"Maybe.'' Jessica stiffened. "Nonetheless, I'm going to fight them on it.''

"Is the council behind you?"

"I'm not sure.''

"Could anyone connected with the land project be responsible for the threats?''

"I have no idea, though my first thought would be no.''

Brant rubbed his jaw. "What about your friend?''

"Curtis Riley? Absolutely not.'' This time she was empathic.

His eyes drilled her. "How do you know?''

"I just know," she said with cold emphasis.

"Okay, how 'bout your personal life?"

Jessica bristled. "That's not an issue."

"At this point, Mrs. Kincaid, everything's an issue." He gave her a hard stare. "And everyone."

"Not as far as I'm concerned."

The air suddenly crackled with suppressed hostility.

"Look, if I'm going to do my job effectively," Brant said, his slightly curled lip registering his impatience, "you have to be forthcoming."

"Need I remind you it's not your job yet?" The words were out before she could stop them. Now it was too late to recall them. In that moment the already charged atmosphere seemed to heighten another degree.

"Fine." Brant pushed away from the wall where he'd been leaning. "When you decide, I'll be at the Nashes' house."

"I'll be in touch."

Brant turned at the door, his eyes narrowed to slits. "You have twenty-four hours to make up your mind, then I'm out of here."

The moment she was alone, Jessica's entire body wilted. She hadn't realized she'd been so uptight until then. Biting down on her lower lip, she walked back to her desk and sat down.

Brant Harding had the potential to rev up her nerves as much or more than the threats against her. The idea of having him invade her life was unthinkable. Where did that leave her?

Back at square one.

He had told Thurmon this was crazy, that he wasn't the right man for the job. Since he'd met the woman, he knew that for a fact. Thank God her clear dislike of him had gotten him off the hook.

She wasn't about to hire him.

Even so, he thought as he sat in his car in his friends' driveway, he wasn't looking forward to conveying the news to them. If he weren't careful, the whole episode could turn around and bite him on the ass. The monkey had to rest on Jessica's back. But whether she would assume that responsibility remained to be seen.

That was her problem, not his.

He might as well get out and get his chore over with. Yet he didn't budge. Instead he took his cell phone out of his pocket with every intention of calling his son. Then it dawned on him that Elliot was probably still in school. Or was school out? Hell, he didn't even know what his kid was up to. All the more reason why he needed to hang around, he reminded himself, bitterness swelling inside.

But working for that uptight broad was not the answer.

She might be a looker as well as a mover and a shaker, with that lovely face, short tousled hair that moved when she did, and those long, shapely legs, and thin, well-curved body. Too much for him to handle. He would be the first to admit that, and he didn't feel the least bit shamed by it.

A cold fish under a warm designer outfit.

That had been his initial reaction and that hadn't changed. Hell to work for, too, he would bet. Spoiled, used to having her own way. Nah, he didn't need that extra headache. Thurmon would just have to find someone in his firm who would suit her needs. He wished them the best of luck.

Come morning, he was hauling ass back to Arkansas.

In just the small amount of time he'd been in the city, his stomach had been knotted. He despised crowds and concrete. He'd had enough of both.

Once he was back on his own turf, he would have to start working on another plan for patching things up with his son. Just because this arrangement hadn't panned out didn't mean he'd lost his determination. He would merely have to take another tack.

Moments later, Brant was inside the Nash house, sitting at the kitchen table watching Veronica whip up a bowl of chicken salad for sandwiches. A tray of cheese and fruit was already on the table, along with three choices of bread.

"As you guessed, Thurmon had to run to the office and handle a problem," she said, turning and smiling at him.

"Figures."

"You of all people should understand that," she said, adding to her smile.

"It's been a long time, but yeah, I understand. It goes with the territory."

"I'm still not used to it, though. I don't think I'll ever be."

"But you've hung in."

She obviously picked up on the bitterness in his tone, because her animated features sobered. "Are you still smarting from Marsha's betrayal?"

"No. We should never have married to begin with. The part I regret is Elliot."

"Have you spoken to him yet, let him know you're in town?"

He heaved a sigh. "I almost called a few minutes ago, but I didn't know if he was in school or not."

"I don't think it's quite out yet, but close. Anyway,

you'll have plenty of time now that you're back for a while." She paused. "Which brings us to the reason you're sitting here. How did your meeting with Jessica go?"

Brant didn't flinch, though he picked up on the anxious note in her voice. "It didn't."

"What does that mean?" Veronica's voice rose a level.

"I don't think your friend was impressed with me."

"That's crazy. You're the best at this kind of thing."

"You'll have to take that up with her."

"Exactly what did she say?"

"That she'd call me. I told her she had twenty-four hours to make up her mind. But I think it's already made up."

"Oh dear," Veronica said, gnawing on her lower lip. "You can't desert her, Brant. You just can't."

"Hey, she's the one who's making that call, not me. I asked some questions she didn't want to answer, and that seemed to be that."

"She's a very private person. Her job forces her to be."

"I can respect that, but at the same time, when your life's in danger, you have to make adjustments." He toyed with a fork. "She apparently hasn't reached that conclusion yet. Until she does..." He let his voice trail off, but Veronica got his drift.

"I'm really worried about her. She's so damned independent, yet she misses depending on Porter."

"What happened to him?"

"He died of a heart attack. He was twenty-five years older than she was. I know what you're thinking, but it worked for them."

"Whatever."

Veronica eased down in the chair across from him. "Promise me you won't give up. Not until I've talked to her again, anyway. Thurmon, too."

Brant blew out his breath. He hated feeling trapped in the middle of a situation he couldn't control. Granted, he wanted to help his friends, to do right by them. At the same time, he had to look out for his own best interest.

And watching over Jessica Kincaid was not in his best interest. Still, he had given her a deadline, and he intended to honor that. "All I can promise is to wait for her call."

Veronica toyed with her lip. "She can be really stubborn."

"If I get the green light, I'll do my best."

"Fair enough," Veronica said, looking slightly relieved. "Maybe she'll come to her senses."

He doubted that, but he kept his mouth shut.

Five

"Sure you don't want me to bunk on the sofa?"

"Thanks again, Tony, but no." Jessica softened her words with a smile. "You escorted me this evening and made sure I got home. That's more than enough."

He made his familiar hand gesture. "I wouldn't have it any other way. If you need me or the police, don't hesitate to call. There are a lot of officers who are still backing you."

Jessica's features turned pensive. "I wish I could be sure of that. Sometimes I feel like daggers are being thrown at me. Sort of paranoid, I know, but—" She broke off with a small shrug.

"Trust me," Tony said in an adamant tone, "that's not the case. You did the right thing. Don't forget that."

"Thanks for those encouraging words." Jessica smiled. "I needed them. Thanks again, and I'll see you in the morning."

"I'm not leaving until I check the house."

A few minutes later Jessica bolted the door behind Tony and headed to her bedroom for a quick shower. She'd had a soaking bath before going to the art exhibit, but for some unexplainable reason, she felt the need for a hot shower. Maybe it would calm her fractured nerves.

She hadn't said anything to Tony, but during her meanderings through the exhibit she'd felt certain she was being followed, as if evil eyes and footsteps followed every step she took. Of course, she hadn't been able to spot anyone who appeared out of the ordinary. But that hadn't meant anything; when it came to stalkers, she would be easy to fool.

All the more reason why you need protection, she told herself.

Thrusting that unwanted thought aside, Jessica peeled off her silk black dress and hung it up. That was when the phone rang. She froze, chills running through her. But after checking the caller ID, she breathed a relief of sorts.

It was her stepson. Since it was late, his calling couldn't be good news. This wasn't the first time he'd pulled such a stunt, either. "Hello, Roy," she said as pleasantly as possible.

"Where have you been?"

Jessica squelched her tart reply, not up to having a verbal slinging match with him. She already had too much friction and discord in her life to add him to the list. "At a charity function, doing my job."

"Look, I want to come over."

"Now?"

"Yes, now."

"No, Roy, you can't. It's too late."

"It's only eleven o'clock, for chrissake."

"That's late for me."

"Make an exception."

"Is something wrong?" Perhaps this time there was a legitimate reason for his call, not just one of his pleas for extra money.

"Yeah, there's a lot wrong. I want my money."

Jessica sighed silently, turning a deaf ear to the desperate note she heard in his voice. He was up to his same old tricks, and she refused to be hoodwinked again.

"I don't want you here," Jessica stressed, though she hid her anger. "So don't waste your time."

"I'm coming anyway."

"Go ahead," she said in the same tone, though she firmed it up a bit. "But I won't let you in, and if you cause a ruckus, I'll call the police or someone else in the complex will."

"Dammit, Jessica—"

"You can damn me all you want, Roy, but I'm not going to talk to you in person tonight."

"You can go to hell."

With that, he slammed the phone down in her ear. Wearily, Jessica eased down on the bed and ran her hands back and forth though her thick hair.

She didn't know when her relationship with Roy had begun deteriorating. Yes, she did: soon after Porter died and Roy found out she'd been made executor of his trust fund. When the will was probated, Roy had been sure he would get his inheritance in one lump sum. Porter had made sure that hadn't happened, which had stirred bad feelings.

Still, Roy had moved in with her for a few months, trying to get on his feet after starting a new job. Then he moved out. She guessed the only reason that brief time together had worked was because he was never there, so they had rarely seen one another.

Apparently, though, his animosity toward her had been silently festering and she hadn't realized it. Porter had never taken the time to discuss his will. She had assumed she would inherit her share and Roy his, with no strings attached to either. Well, there had been strings attached, all right, and Roy had never forgiven his dad for what he saw as a betrayal. He hadn't forgiven her, either, for not relinquishing her hold over his money.

Too bad. Roy would just have to continue to live within his means instead of outside them. After all, he was thirty-three years old, with a responsible job at a respected computer firm, making good money. And he wasn't married. She couldn't imagine why he was always broke.

Booze, she suspected. Or worse.

But that wasn't her problem. *He* wasn't her problem, and she refused to let herself worry about him. While she would help him, *had* helped him, she refused to further indulge his taste for the high life. If she did, he would soon be broke.

Holding to that thought, Jessica got up and finished undressing, then stepped into the shower. Shortly afterward she climbed into bed, but sleep eluded her.

Tossing back the sheet, she crossed to the computer and reached for the switch, only to hesitate. Then, furious with herself for letting her nemesis win, she clicked it on. If there were any messages from him, she would have to face them sooner or later.

She had several messages, the last one from her cowardly enemy. Gritting her teeth, she forced herself to read the words.

You Stink-Ass Bitch. You're Not Much Longer For This World.

Another threat. Sick to her stomach, Jessica shut down the computer and began pacing the floor. Brant Harding? Was he the answer? The only answer? Just thinking about him and his strong appeal made her uneasy, though certainly in a different way. Yet she had to admit, there was also something about him that made her feel safe and secure. Her instincts told her he would take care of her.

Or did that feeling stem from something else—a more basic instinct?

Shrugging that absurd thought aside, Jessica paused in her thoughts and in her pacing. It was just that she felt so alone, so incredibly lonely. So frightened. Maybe if she and Porter had had a child... What was wrong with her? Her husband hadn't wanted another child, nor had she. She had never thought of herself in terms of motherhood, anyway, probably because her own mother hadn't set all that great an example.

Jessica's eyes darted to the picture of her mother, father, sister and herself that she kept on the secretary in her bedroom, the only picture still in existence of them as a family. She had hidden this one from her mother's vicious rampage. She had never figured out why, since that time in her life had been one of the most painful.

Even now, just thinking about that fateful day when she'd learned her father had abandoned them, her breathing turned labored and the room spun. Time had never softened that blow.

She had been barely seven years old and had walked into the kitchen one summer morning to eat breakfast. Her mother had been sitting at the table, sobbing.

"Mommy, what's wrong?" she had asked, racing up to her.

"Your father's gone, that's what," Opal had spat. "The sorry coward just walked out, leaving nothing behind but this lousy note." She held it up, then proceeded to rip the paper into tiny pieces.

"Don't cry," Jessica pleaded. "He'll be back. He's just gone to work."

"No, he hasn't!" Opal cried again, then, grabbing her, shook her until her teeth banged together. "Don't you understand? He's gone forever."

"No," she whimpered, after her mother turned her loose, though her little heart was beating so hard she found it difficult to speak. "He loves us. He wouldn't do that." Huge tears spilled from her eyes and soaked her cheeks.

"He hates us!" Opal cried, her features twisted with bitterness. "Don't you ever forget that. And don't ever mention his name again. As far as I'm concerned, he's dead. You hear that? He's dead."

Fearing her mother was going to grab her again, Jessica stepped out of harm's way, whirled and ran to her room, where she cried until she couldn't cry anymore. Then she got up and went to the window that overlooked the front yard. She stood there all day and night waiting for her daddy to come back home.

He never did.

From then on, her life was never the same. Her mother changed, turned into a mistrusting, bitter woman who continually bad-mouthed men, instilling in both her girls how important it was for them to stand on their own, never to trust or depend on a man for anything, especially their livelihood.

Jessica had taken that lesson to heart, rarely ever dating until she went to college. Even then, she had only one serious relationship, which failed when she refused to marry the boy.

Only after she graduated from law school and began practicing law had she dated anyone else seriously, and that was Porter. That had been a giant step for her.

Scar tissue covered a portion of her heart. And every so often thoughts of her mother and that awful day would prick that tissue and reopen the wound. She would hemorrhage from the heart again.

Like now. Feeling the wetness on her face, Jessica grabbed a tissue out of the box. This weak display of emotions would never do. The tears resulted from the havoc she was going through, mainly the threats against her.

Once that was fixed, her life would surely revert to normal. So how was she going to stop the menace? Simple. Do what she should already have done.

With a resigned sigh, Jessica reached for the phone and punched out the Nashes' phone number, praying she wasn't making a big mistake.

Six

He would rather have a root canal than be confined indoors, doing what he'd sworn he would never do again. Brant thought he had learned long ago never to say never. He guessed he hadn't.

He could look for a scapegoat all he wanted, but there wasn't any. He had no one to blame but himself for letting his conscience overrule his sound judgment. A cynical smile altered his lips.

Face it, Harding, you don't have a conscience.

He had lost that years ago. Yet something was sure as hell playing pull and tug with his insides or he wouldn't be in this predicament. His son. He was that something. If it hadn't been for Elliot, he wouldn't have fallen victim to Thurmon's arm twisting in the first place.

But dammit, wallowing in self-pity wasn't going to do any good or change one thing. Besides, it wasn't like him to look back. Maybe that had to do with the fact that he was a trained marksman whose eyes were always ahead, on the target.

He admitted that part of his ill humor stemmed from the improbability of the situation that had again sneaked up on him and bitten him in the rear.

He really hadn't expected her to call. In fact he'd been stunned. After their encounter the day before, he'd figured he would be making plans to see Elliot, then return to Arkansas.

Brant wondered what happened to make her change her mind. When she'd called the Nashes' house and told him he had the job, she had asked him to meet her at her office the following morning. Early.

He was there at the appointed time. He suspected she was, too, alone behind closed doors. Not a good idea. Brant peered at his watch just as the door to her office opened and Jessica walked out.

"Thank you for coming, Mr. Harding," she said in her cool, polite manner.

It was obvious she wasn't any happier with the situation today than yesterday. She wasn't happy with him or what he represented, that was the bottom line. Too bad. She got the entire package, whether she wanted it or not.

"I'm willing to make this as painless as possible for both of us," he responded in the same tone.

An uneasy silence fell between them.

Her assistant picked that moment to breeze in, and she introduced him. The young man was dressed so comically it was all Brant could do to keep a straight face. And smiles didn't come easy to him. Still, that bow tie and black-and-white shoes he had on should've been outlawed in the work place. On second thought, they should have been outlawed, period.

He shrugged inwardly. As long as Eason was competent and Jessica was comfortable with him, Brant couldn't care less. The guy's mode of dress was the least of his concerns.

"I know we need to talk, to lay some ground rules," she said, "but it'll have to wait." Pausing, she glanced back into her office. "I have a full agenda today," she added awkwardly, obviously having difficulty dealing with this abrupt change in her life—a stranger invading it.

For a moment Brant felt a pinch of sympathy for her. But it passed just as quickly. He wasn't about to develop feelings for her one way or the other. As soon as he nailed whoever was behind this menace, he would be gone. Until then, he would have to suck it up, the same as she would.

"No problem. If you need me, I'll be here."

"Where?"

He picked up on the panic in her voice, and his lips twisted. "Wherever you want."

"Surely not in my office proper."

This time her tone was so strained it came out a raspy whisper. For some reason that small change added to her attractiveness. Realizing his thoughts had betrayed him, Brant mentally shook himself.

"Not unless you want me there," he said, knowing damn well she didn't.

"No," she countered quickly. "Here in the reception area will be fine." Her gaze shifted to a stack of magazines. "Maybe you can keep occupied."

"Don't worry about me. Waiting and watching is what I do."

She visibly let go of a breath. "Fine, then."

Once she was back at her desk, Tony turned to him. "Please bear with her." His eyes were anxious. "It'll take her a while to get use to this drastic change." He paused and touched his plastered-down hair. "But I'm glad you're around. This person who's after her apparently means business."

Brant was instantly on the alert. "Has something else happened?"

"Yes," Tony said almost in a hushed tone. "In case she doesn't mention it to you, ask her about the e-mail she received last night."

Ah, so that was what had made her call him. She'd gotten scared. Good. She was wising up. This pervert could end up harming her. No longer. The sicko would have to go through him to get to her.

"Thanks for the tip."

Tony nodded, then went into Jessica's office and shut the door.

Although it had been a long day, it hadn't been boring—too much activity. He'd been busy handling traffic. There had been a steady stream of people in and out of Jessica's office all day. Millie, her girl Friday, had identified them beforehand, as if sensing Brant would have stopped them otherwise.

In addition, he'd touched base with Thurmon a couple of times, though they hadn't been able to talk much. But then, there really wasn't anything to talk about, since he hadn't had time alone with Jessica to talk over the situation. His instincts told him she'd planned her day that way.

Maybe not. Maybe he wasn't being fair. He had to hand it to her; she was one busy lady, with her fingers in every pie in the city, which could be what had landed her in the jam to begin with. She had royally pissed off someone, that was for sure.

Now, as the work day came to an end, Brant leaned against the wall and crisscrossed his arms over his chest. The office had finally emptied, leaving Jessica alone. She suddenly appeared in his line of vision. She looked weary. Or maybe concerned was a better word.

What was on her mind? Him, probably, he told himself with his usual cynicism. What to do with him after they left here. Well, he wasn't jumping through hoops over spending the evening alone with her, either. But that was part of the job, occasionally one of the hazards. In this case, it was definitely the latter.

He hadn't meant to stare at her as she moved about her office, but in spite of himself, his gaze held steady. Just for a moment he indulged himself. No doubt she was an eye grabber. A classy one at that.

Great profile.

Great hair, too, the blond highlights looking like streaks of sunlight every time she moved her head.

And those legs. They seemed to go on forever beneath the skirt of her suit, another designer one, he bet.

And her breasts. He couldn't ignore them. Never. Through the silk blouse, he was privy to just a hint of their upright fullness. She chose that moment to stretch, thrusting those breasts front and center, her nipples pushing against the silk. Brant's breath caught in his throat.

Muttering an oath, he was about to jerk his eyes away when she caught them with her own. For a second it was as if he'd been shocked with a sudden jab of electricity.

Muttering another curse, he was the first to look away. Then he strode to the window and stared below at the beehive of activity. Traffic was bumper-to-bumper. What was he doing here? His worst nightmare. He fought to get control of his runaway emotions, which were telling him to bolt.

Why did she have to be such a looker? Why couldn't she have been as homely as a mule eating briars through a picket fence? Luck of the draw. And the draw hadn't been in his favor.

He hadn't felt the need or the desire to get laid in a long time. He couldn't allow himself to entertain that thought now. His son was the only thing he should be concerned with, certainly not his sexual needs.

And when and if he scratched that itch in his groin, it wouldn't be with the likes of Jessica Kincaid, who lived in a different world from him, worlds that would never mesh in a million years. That aside, he simply wasn't interested.

Marriage hadn't agreed with him. Still, he wasn't sorry he'd bitten that bullet. Otherwise, he wouldn't have Elliot. Thinking about his son miraculously refocused him. He peered at his watch, thinking this might be a good time to try to reach Elliot. He had just flipped his cell phone open when she appeared in the door.

He swung around. She stood at a distance, a hint of a frown on her face.

"I'm about ready to call it a day."

He cleared his throat. "I'm ready when you are."

"I'll only be a few minutes."

"No problem. Your time is mine."

She didn't respond, though she hesitated for a minuscule second before walking back into her domain, her narrow derriere filling out her skirt to perfection.

Brant's lips thinned into a pencil straight line.

"Does she always work this late?"

Wesley Stokes glared at his partner, Dick Wells, who occupied the seat beside him in his pickup, then curled his lips, showing off crooked, tobacco-stained teeth. "How the hell would I know?"

Wells shrugged narrow shoulders that matched his slight build and dark, clean-cut features. "Thought maybe you might have checked out her schedule."

They had been sitting across the street from the city hall parking lot waiting for Jessica to leave. So far, she hadn't made an appearance, and it was nearly six thirty.

Stokes' glare harshened as he shifted his tall, beefy body in the seat so as to get a better look at his partner. "Hey, we're in this together, right? Or have you conveniently forgotten that?"

"You know I haven't," Wells snapped.

"Then why didn't you take care of it?"

"I've had other stuff on my mind," Wells muttered.

"If you think you're alone, think again." Stokes' tone was filled with contempt.

"Jan's been raising old billy about me being on suspension," Wells admitted almost reluctantly. "I've been spending most of my time trying to calm her down. She walks around wringing her hands, convinced we're going to be living on the street in our car."

Stokes snorted. "To hell with that nonsense. I told my old lady to keep her mouth shut or I'd shut it for her."

"I can't get by with that," Wells said, down-in-the-mouth.

"Sure you could. You just don't have the balls. If you'd backhand her a time or two, she'd straighten up. With a busted lip, she'd find it damn hard to nag."

Wells cut him a look. "You're a real bastard, Stokes. Did anyone ever tell you that?"

"Most likely, though I didn't pay 'em no mind. I do what I have to to keep the peace in the family. When you got four kids making demands all the time, you run a tight ship."

"I've got two kids myself, but I'd never hit my wife."

"You might before we get out of this jam," Stokes

pointed out bluntly. "So don't be taking that holier-than-thou attitude with me."

Wells frowned. "Don't you think the mayor will be forced to back down?"

Stokes snorted again, this time louder. "So far, Gaston Forrester hasn't been able to budge her."

Forrester was the interim chief, who had sworn he was on their side and who had promised to speak a good word on their behalf.

"That's what worries me," Wells said, following a deep sigh. "Absolutely nothing seems to be shaping up in our favor."

"Which is why we have to take matters in our own hands and try and talk some sense into the hardheaded bitch."

Wells shook his head, his frown darkening his features. "What if that tactic backfires?"

"Then we'll move to plan B."

"And what is plan B?"

Stokes grunted. "Dunno. At least not yet."

Wells rolled his eyes. "Great."

Stokes' beefy hand tightened around the steering wheel. "You know, your attitude's really pissing me off."

"Sorry," Wells retorted. "It's just that I'm scared shitless that we may lose our jobs permanently."

"Not if I have my way, we won't," Stokes declared. "Trust me, I'm not going to take her poking her nose in where it doesn't belong. It's high-time someone convinced her she doesn't have balls and can't hold her own with those of us who do."

"I hope you're right, because my family is running out of money fast."

Stokes laughed bitterly. "Lucky you. We've been out. We were broke before I got suspended."

"If only you hadn't smacked the guy that one last time, we—"

"Cut that crap," Stokes interrupted, his voice shaking with anger. "You were right there with me, so you don't have the right to start squealing like a stuck pig."

"Still, I wouldn't have beat him half to death."

"Well, you ain't me, and as senior partner, that was my call. Besides, with a do-good mayor running the department, thugs are going to take over the city. That's why those of us working the streets have to take charge."

When Wells would have responded, Stokes sat up straighter in the seat. "Dammit, man, she's almost to her car and here we sit." He slapped Wells on the arm. "Come on, let's haul ass before she does."

Seven

"I want you to ride with me."

Jessica paused midway to her vehicle and peered up at Brant, but not before slipping on her sunglasses, hiding her amazement. "Whatever for?"

A muscle worked in Brant's jaw, indicating he was not pleased at being questioned. He had a lot to learn about her. Ride home with him? Why, that was crazy. So was his overbearing manner, a flaw she refused to overlook.

She knew he was used to people asking how high when he said jump, especially since he'd worked for the White House. However, her situation was a far cry from Pennsylvania Avenue, and she didn't intend to be told what to do at every turn.

"For safety reasons," Brant said into the tense silence. "But then, you ought to know that."

She ignored those pointed words. "What about my car?"

"I'll see to that later."

"I'll pass, thank you."

His jaw worked harder, which told her he was furious. Seconds passed while they stared at each other, as though waiting to see who backed down first.

"I'll follow you," Brant said through tight lips. "But

I insist you take me to my vehicle, since it's parked across the lot.''

"Oh, for heaven's sake, surely that's not necessary?"

"Do you intend to take issue with everything I suggest?"

Though his harsh bluntness took her slightly aback, she held her ground. "Look, there's no one around. I'll be okay."

"Fine, I'll get my car. It's just over there. Meanwhile, don't move. Stay where I can see you."

Fuming inwardly at his high-handed treatment of her, Jessica had her hand on the door handle when she heard her name.

"Mayor, wait up."

Jessica whirled around and stiffened. Wesley Stokes and Dick Wells seemed to have come out of nowhere and were making their way at a rapid clip toward her. Had they seen Brant? More to the point, had Brant seen them?

Of course he had, which undoubtedly had sent his fury up another notch.

Although she was not afraid of the two suspended cops, she felt her own fury mount. It took a lot of nerve on their part to approach her in the parking lot. But then, she wasn't surprised. It was poor judgment calls like this that had landed them in trouble in the first place. This latest move certainly wouldn't help matters.

"Sorry to approach you like this," Dick Wells said without hesitation, though the rest of his entire manner was indeed hesitant. For an instant she almost felt sorry for him. But only for an instant. Of the two men, Wells had a possibility of holding on to his job, but only if she could get him out from under Stokes' influence.

Stokes was one tough renegade cop, who required close scrutiny.

"What do you want?" Jessica demanded before either of them could come any closer.

"We'd like our jobs back, ma'am," Wells continued in a humble tone, his eyes veering off in another direction.

Stokes didn't have that problem, Jessica noticed. His eyes pinned her as if she was a worm under a knife. If she weren't mistaken, he'd been drinking. What a disgusting man.

"This is not the time or place for such a discussion."

"Well, just when is a good time?" Stokes said in a demanding tone.

"With your attitude, never, Mr. Stokes."

His face flushed and his eyes flared. "You think you're—"

Jessica backed up, only to hit the side of her car.

"Take a hike, both of you," Brant ordered in a cold, steely voice. "Now!"

Both men stared at Brant as if trying to decide if he was someone to be reckoned with. Apparently they thought so, for they turned without another word and strode off.

Jessica refused to look at Brant. She didn't have to. *I told you so* would be written in every line of his face.

"Get in," he snapped, opening the door for her. "I'll be right behind you."

Silently she got behind the wheel, feeling like a child who had been reprimanded, a feeling she abhorred and wouldn't tolerate. But now was not the time to have a confrontation with Brant. Her home would suffice.

Twenty minutes later, she drove into her garage.

Once they were inside, he didn't waste any time. "Who were those guys?"

She told him.

He gave her a hard stare. "Do you realize they could have harmed you?"

"No. They might be stupid, but not that stupid."

"Are you always this mule-headed?"

Jessica didn't flinch. "Yes."

For an instant she thought she saw a flash of humor in his eyes. That couldn't be. If this man ever smiled, his face would probably crack. What had she gotten herself into?

"Well, someone's out to harm you, Mrs. Kincaid, and it could very well be one or both of them. If I were betting, I'd say the big one, the one who was looming over you, wouldn't think twice about doing whatever it took to get his job back."

"That's Wesley Stokes. If I have my way, he'll be off the force permanently."

"I think he knows that, which is all the more reason why he's been elevated to the top of the suspect list."

Jessica frowned. "It's possible, of course. But I doubt he has the intelligence to pull off the threats. Dick Wells might be a different story. I know he's computer savvy." She paused and took a deep breath, already so tired of this situation she could scream. But that wouldn't do anything. She simply had to get through these bumpy spots in the road, then maybe she could get on with her life.

"His computer expertise sends up a red flag," Brant said. "As far as the Stokes character goes, I wouldn't put anything past him. He's street smart, the most dangerous kind of smarts."

"I'm sure you're right," she admitted on a sigh.

"Good. So from now on, when I suggest something—anything—that's in your best interest, I expect you to do it."

She threw her head back to look at him. "I'm not a child, Mr. Harding. And I resent being treated like one."

"Then I think we're both wasting our time."

A hostile silence descended over the room.

"You mean there can't be a happy medium?"

"Not with me. If I'm to do my job, then it's my way or no way." He paused as if to let those words sink in.

Damn his stubbornness. More to the point, who did he think he was? It wasn't too late to fire him. It was on the tip of her tongue to do just that, but the words stuck in her throat. "Look, maybe we should postpone this discussion for another time. It's been a long day for both of us."

Brant shrugged his shoulders. "It's your call. Tell me where I can bunk in for the night, then I suggest you give what I just told you serious thought."

"Follow me," she said through tight lips.

A short time later, Jessica was still harboring ill will toward her unwanted houseguest. She had taken a hot bath, hoping to relieve her tension and chaotic thoughts, to no avail. If anything, she was more agitated than ever. Just his presence was responsible.

After she was in her robe, it dawned on her that she hadn't had anything to eat, nor had he. The thought of food was as unappetizing as going downstairs and running into him, but she wondered if he was hungry. Manners should have prodded her to tell him he was welcome to use the kitchen.

Too late now. Anyway, she wasn't sure she could

have uttered those words. What an impossible situation. Her gaze went to the computer, but she dared not boot it up for fear of what she would read. She would have loved to e-mail Veronica, but she couldn't deal with anything else this evening.

When the phone rang, whether it was her land line or her cell, her instinct was to answer it. But unless she knew for sure who the caller was, she wouldn't do it. Life was definitely too short to live like this.

All the more reason not to relieve Brant Harding of his duties.

Following their earlier conversation, she'd had every intention of doing just that, deciding she definitely couldn't subject herself to such an invasion into her privacy. And while the thought remained tempting, her sound judgment once again came to her rescue. If she refused Brant's help, she would be doing herself a grave injustice.

After all, this was indeed a dangerous game she was playing. And before the game came to an end, the stakes could escalate even more.

Jeopardizing her very life.

The ringing of her cell phone jarred her from her thoughts. Only after the caller ID registered a familiar number did relief wash through her.

"Hey," she said.

"So how are things going, friend?"

"You don't want to know." Jessica eased onto the bed, then propped her head on a stack of pillows.

"Uh-oh," Veronica said. "Not so good, huh?"

"I was just about to call you."

"More harassment, I'm assuming."

"That and—" She broke off, deciding not to blurt out her feelings concerning Brant.

"Go on," Veronica urged in a seemingly innocent tone.

Jessica wasn't fooled for a second. She would bet her friend either knew exactly what was going on or had a pretty good idea. "I don't want to do this," Jessica admitted at last.

"I know you don't, but what choice do you have?"

"Isn't there someone else in Thurmon's office who could do the job?"

Silence hummed through the line.

"Not as well as Brant." Veronica sighed. "Do you just not like him or what?"

Jessica was reluctant to admit that, fearing it might lead to much more probing questions, questions she wasn't prepared to answer. Yet she had no intention of lying to her friend, not now, not ever.

"For some reason, he just rubs me the wrong way."

Veronica chuckled. "That doesn't surprise me."

"Then why on earth did Thurmon pick him?"

"He's told you already. Brant's the best at what he does. And since you're my dearest friend, I'm determined that you have the best."

Jessica sighed. "While I love you dearly for your care and concern, I'm just not sure I can handle his strong personality."

"You're one to be talking. I can see why you two would butt heads."

"It's just that he's so…" Jessica's voice faded as she realized how whiny and childish she must sound. Veronica, of all people, shouldn't have to bear the brunt of her dilemma.

"Bossy and strong-willed? Was that what you were going to say?"

"Yes."

"Look, you'll get adjusted, but not in one day. You're expecting too much, too soon."

"You're right, I know. Still…" Again Jessica's voice faded, while her frustration rose.

"Still nothing. Just chill and go with the flow. It'll all work out, maybe much sooner than expected. If Brant's as good as my better half says, and I have no reason to believe otherwise, he'll find the jerk who's dealing you all this misery and deal him some misery of his own."

Jessica blew out her breath.

"Where's Brant now?"

"In the downstairs guest room."

"So…out of sight, out of mind?"

"Right."

"Look, you can face this mess again tomorrow. To-night you need to get some sleep, knowing you're in safe hands."

"I'll do my best."

"Good. Let me hear from you." Veronica paused with a chuckle. "Don't be too hard on the poor guy, okay?"

In spite of herself, Jessica smiled. "I'll get you for that."

"Later then."

After she replaced her phone in its case, Jessica's good humor fled. Somehow, she would endure. That was what she'd done all her life, and her inner strength wouldn't fail her now.

Clinging to that thought, she turned over and closed her eyes.

Eight

He hadn't wanted to take Thurmon up on his offer, but he had. Desperation had been the driving force. Marsha had given him the runaround long enough. He still hadn't seen or talked to his son, because every time he called, he either didn't get an answer or his ex-wife picked up. He'd had enough.

So when Thurmon had told him he would cover for him with Jessica that afternoon, he'd said okay. Brant's features twisted. He knew Jessica wouldn't be upset. On the contrary, she would be relieved.

They had been together for several days now. And while those days had been uneventful as far as threats went, the tension between them had continued to mount.

He was damned if he did and damned if he didn't. He sensed that she flat out didn't like him and wasn't comfortable with him under her roof. Well, he felt the same way, only he was careful not to let that show. He'd been trained not to reveal his emotions while on the job.

However, with Jessica Kincaid, that was hard to do. He was too damn aware of her as a woman. That was the problem. Her perfume drove him nuts. Everything about her drove him nuts. When she walked into a room, it seemed to come alive. She had that type of infectious personality. Laughter would ring from her office one moment, and the next she would ream someone out for not doing his duty.

She was definitely a contradiction, which made her all the more exciting. But though he admired her professionalism and her personality, most of the time he wanted to throttle her.

Jessica wasn't into rules and regulations. Unless she set them. He'd learned that. He'd also learned she was fearless. He still wasn't convinced she realized just how much danger was lurking around her, especially now that the pervert had backed off for a few days. That unpredictability was unnerving.

Not as unnerving as Jessica herself. What he had to keep in mind was that she might as well be the First Lady. That was how off-limits she was to him. Not that he wanted it any other way, he assured himself quickly. He didn't, though it made him more uneasy with each passing day that his awareness of her only seemed to be heightening.

Was it only yesterday that he'd found his eyes locked on her breasts when she'd thrown her head back and laughed? When it had dawned on him what he was doing, he'd jerked his gaze away and let loose an expletive.

He'd been alone too long, he guessed. That was the only feasible explanation he could come up with for his unorthodox behavior. Maybe this torture would end sooner rather than later, so he could get back to *his* life.

But not before he spent time with his kid.

Which was why he was sitting across the street from Elliot's house on the off chance he might catch him when he came home from school, then talk to him face-to-face. Brant knew it was a long shot, but he had to do something. He'd thought about waiting at the school, but since he didn't even know what kind of car Elliot drove, it would be like hunting a needle in a haystack.

He had no idea if Marsha had been relaying his phone messages to Elliot or not. Brant suspected she hadn't, though he couldn't swear to it.

His son knew he was in town and had his cell number. So far, Elliot had made no effort to contact him. Brant rubbed the back of his neck, then peered at his watch.

Was this opportunity going to be wasted after all? Time was getting away from him, and he hadn't made any headway. If only he could grab his boy and they could head back to Arkansas for a couple of weeks together. He would teach him how to fish, hunt and garden.

Brant almost laughed at that last thought. Elliot would probably think he'd lost his mind. Most kids would, and Brant suspected his own wouldn't be any different.

His urge to laugh suddenly dried up. His son was seventeen, and he didn't know anything about him, what he liked to do, what he liked to eat, what he dreamed about.

Nothing.

Brant gripped the steering wheel with his strong, tanned hands and squeezed. God, if only he could undo the sins of the past, what a difference it would make in his life. Unfortunately that was not the way things worked.

His screw-ups had started a long time ago. When Marsha had divorced him, Elliot had been nine. Most of those nine years, he'd been gone. And afterward— well, he rarely ever saw his kid. In a nutshell, he'd never known his son—not as a baby, a toddler, an adolescent or a teenager.

Brant's gut twisted, and sweat dotted his upper lip. Somehow, he had to rectify that. He didn't think he could live with himself if he didn't. He glanced at his watch again, trying to temper his growing anxiety. Rarely did anything shake him. For the most part he was steady as a rock, or had been before he was shot. Since then, he'd had to work just to keep body and soul together. That was another reason why he hadn't wanted an assignment.

He didn't feel he was ready. But when Thurmon put the squeeze on him, he hadn't had much choice. At least it gave him the opportunity to see his son, an opportunity he wouldn't have had otherwise.

"Damn," Brant muttered, lurching upright.

While he'd been deep in thought, Elliot had driven up and was getting out of his Mustang. For a second paralysis seemed to hold Brant in his seat. His eyes feasted on the one human who was part of himself. Pride rose in him. Even from this distance, he could see what a good-looking young man Elliot had become. Tall and strapping, just like he'd been at that age, with the same profile. His hair, however, was light brown, like his mother's.

Forcing himself to move, Brant jumped out of his vehicle and crossed the street. "Elliot, wait up."

His son whirled and stared at him wide-eyed; then his dark eyes narrowed and his lips thinned. Brant's heart faltered as he thought Elliot was going to turn his back on him.

"Hello, son," Brant forced himself to say before his own nerve failed.

"Hi," Elliot muttered, shifting his gaze.

"I hope you don't mind me stopping by," Brant said, hearing the awkwardness in his voice and hating it.

Elliot shrugged. "Whatever."

Brant strove for a decent breath. This was going to be even harder than he'd anticipated—for both of them. He was sweating like he'd been chopping logs at the cabin, and it wasn't even hot.

"You know I'm going to be close by for a while."

"Yeah, right."

Brant refused to be defeated. "I thought maybe we might get together soon, maybe go out to dinner."

"Whatever," Elliot said again, finally looking at him.

The pain and confusion mirrored in his son's eyes almost brought Brant to his knees. What if he couldn't fix their broken relationship? What if the gulf was too wide to breach? No. He wouldn't think like that. He would make things work. Whatever it took.

Now that he'd seen his son, no way was he leaving, even if Jessica Kincaid fired his ass tomorrow.

"Look, Elliot, I want a chance to make things right between us."

Elliot's eyes flared. "Why?"

"Because you're my son." *And because I love you.* But for some reason those words stuck in Brant's throat. "I want us to get to know one another. I want to find out what you're up to, where you plan to go to school." He broke off. "Stuff like that."

Elliot's mouth took a bitter turn. "Don't you think it's a little late?"

Brant ignored his sarcasm and kept his voice calm. "No, I don't."

"You never cared before."

"I always cared, Elliot," he said with patience. "It's

just that—'' Brant broke off, refusing to make any more excuses for the way he'd treated his son.

"Look, you're right on target with your contempt of me. I'll admit that. And I know saying I'm sorry won't do the trick. Instead, I want to show you.'' He paused, trying to gauge Elliot's reaction, only he couldn't. His features were as blank as a stone wall. "So what do you say?'' Brant pressed. "You have any free time?''

"I'll call you,'' Elliot said, pawing at the ground with the toe of his left running shoe.

That wasn't the answer Brant wanted, so his initial response was to say no, to set a time and place right then. Beg, if necessary. But he held his tongue. If he pushed, he sensed Elliot would push back. Get further away. At least Elliot hadn't told him to get lost. And while that was a mere crumb, he was grateful for it.

"Calling me will work,'' Brant said at last, blowing out his pent-up breath. "That'll work just fine.''

Elliot nodded, shoving both hands down in the pockets of his jeans and not responding.

"You have my cell number, right?'' Brant asked. He felt foolish, but he was loathe to end the conversation. Just being near his son gave him a new lease on life.

"Elliot?''

Brant froze. Marsha. He hadn't even known she was home, but then, he hadn't cared. When he'd darted up the driveway, he'd had tunnel vision. Everything else had fled his mind. Now, looking up and seeing his ex-wife standing outside the front door brought reality home with a bitter jolt.

She hadn't changed much in the years since their divorce, except that her hair was more frosted, probably to cover up the fact that she was getting older and grayer. Perhaps she'd put on a bit more weight as well.

Yet she was still attractive in an ordinary sort of way. She was short and curvy, with a reserved manner.

Her main goal in life had been to marry and have a home and children. She had resented his job from the get-go, mainly because he'd been away from home so much. Back then, he'd blamed her for that, throwing it back in her face how much she liked to spend the money he made.

So many mistakes. But losing her was not one of them, except that it had affected Elliot and their relationship. Still, he didn't have anyone to blame for that but himself, certainly not Marsha, although she had done everything in her power to keep that wedge between them.

His downfall had been letting her get away with it. No longer. He was ready to fight.

"Hello, Marsha," he said into the growing, hostile silence.

"What are you doing here?" she demanded, her eyes pinging from him to Elliot, concern knitting her brows.

Elliot, in turn, kept looking down, as though he wished he were anywhere but there or that he could simply disappear. Brant didn't blame him. His son had been caught in the middle his entire life.

That was also about to stop.

"I came to see Elliot." *Since you obviously haven't bothered to give him my messages.* Like so many other words, they remained unspoken.

"I can see that," she retorted.

"We're planning a time to get together for dinner."

"I didn't say that," Elliot countered with defiance in his tone.

Brant clamped down on his emotions. "Well, I'm hopeful that will be the case."

"Elliot, come on inside," Marsha said. "I'm sure you have some homework."

For a minute his son looked as if he wanted to argue, which was another crumb Brant snatched. But then Elliot muttered something under his breath, strode up the steps and slammed the door behind him.

"Thanks, Marsha. I really appreciate that."

"No one gave you permission to come here."

"Dammit, I don't need permission to see my son, certainly not from you."

"Ah, so now you've decided to become the model parent," she spat, her tone as nasty as her features.

"That's right. I made that promise to myself. I also promised I wasn't going to have a verbal slinging match with you about Elliot."

"What about Elliot?" she flared back.

"What about him?"

"He has no say-so in this. Right now, he's a happy, normal young man who has a father. And it's not you." Marsha paused, as though giving him time to digest that thought. "It's Preston. He's taken your place in Elliot's life."

Those harsh words cut like she'd taken a knife and slashed his heart to pieces. Yet Brant never so much as flinched. "No matter what has happened in the past, Elliot is my son. And no matter how much you wish that weren't true, it is."

"I'll continue to fight you."

"That's your prerogative. But I'm not giving up unless it comes from Elliot. You can hate me all you want, but I'm asking you not to let your hate spill over to our son."

"Stay away from here, Brant."

"For god's sake, Marsha, you're being unreasonable.

Why not let Elliot make some choices on his own? He's certainly old enough.''

"Because I don't trust you not to hurt him again," she said, her voice shaking with anger. "He's suffered enough at your hands."

"I swear to you, that won't happen," Brant said in a soft tone. "And while I might have done some unpardonable things in your eyes, I've never lied to you."

"Somehow I take little comfort in that."

"Can't we just please reach a truce, for Elliot's sake?"

"I'm making no promises, Brant, either way. I'll talk to Preston."

Brant clamped down on his lip so hard to stop his retort that he tasted blood. "You do that, but it's not going to change things. Meanwhile, leave the boy alone. Use me as a whipping boy all you want, but don't stand Elliot beside me. He deserves better."

"And you can go to hell."

"Thank you very much, but I've been there for some years now."

For once Marsha didn't seem to have a comeback. Instead, she let out a deep sigh, then said bitterly, "I doubt I'll have much to say about it, anyway. As much as I hate to admit it, Elliot's as stubborn as you when he makes up his mind."

"Then let him make it up." Brant stopped short of pleading.

"I told you, I'm making no promises." With that she turned and flounced back into the house.

Brant remained rooted to the spot, feeling much like he had the day he'd gotten shot in the gut. Numb all over. That was when he noticed Elliot standing at the window, peering out, his face pinched in sadness.

Pain, as lethal as the strongest narcotic, shot through Brant's system, almost sending him to his knees. Dejected, he turned and walked back to his vehicle.

Nine

The situation had worsened. Jessica didn't think she would ever adjust to having another man in the house, especially a stranger. She kept telling herself something was terribly askew when one had to have a bodyguard.

The reality of that was appalling. Determined to reroute her thoughts, she opened the French doors onto the small balcony and stepped outside. Evening was settling in, and the temperature was quite pleasant. Soon, however, the heat from the brutal blast of summer would hit Texas with a vengeance, the Dallas area in particular, with very little rain to ease the pain.

Still, she wouldn't want to live anywhere else. This lovely, high-profile city was home, the place where she lived and worked, the most important thing in her life, the reason she climbed out of bed each morning. Since she had lost Porter, she'd had to refocus, though not a lot. Without children, it was logical and easy to focus on their careers—his more than hers, as she was the backbone behind him, or so he'd told her many times.

The pain of losing Porter had subsided, thank goodness. Time had taken care of that. Now she could think of him with fond, sweet memories that were to be cherished at moments like these, when she was down-and-out. A bird sang merrily in a nearby oak tree that draped over her small deck. The oak's thick foliage served as an umbrella against the sun during the heat of the day.

Jessica heard a sound and leaned over the railing slightly, peering down. Immediately, her heart almost stopped beating. Someone was there. She leaned farther, but whoever it was had gone.

Brant? Had he been outside? Or had her imagination been playing tricks on her? Instead of thinking about *him*, she forced herself to peruse the vibrant annuals, their colors bursting from the various pots spaced around the area. But her thoughts refused to cooperate. Then she heard that sound again.

With her heart thumping at an even faster rate, Jessica moved slightly, then peered down once again. Brant in the flesh. Her breath caught, and every nerve in her body jumped to high alert.

He stood unmoving with his hand shoved into his pocket, staring into the twilight. Instead of the slacks he'd worn today, he was dressed in jeans and a T-shirt. Not sloppy, but definitely comfortable.

Jessica swallowed hard, feeling her heartbeat move from her chest to her throat, where it seemed to pound without mercy. She was behaving like an idiot, like someone totally out of control. She fought to remove her gaze. Nothing doing. It was like her eyes had been welded to him, embracing everything about him, from his tanned muscled arms to his powerful thighs. It hit her suddenly what the problem was: he was simply too male to suit her.

A dose of trouble wrapped in a sexy package.

She wondered how he perceived her, especially when those eyes seemed to touch every part of her body when he looked at her.

Jessica shivered.

That was when he turned and looked up. In the remaining light, their gazes met and held. Her cheeks blazed, and her mouth went dry. Words she would ordinarily have no problem speaking jammed in her throat.

This would never do.

"Nice evening," he commented, then raked his long fingers through his dark hair.

His voice had just enough harsh strength in it to further assault her senses. She couldn't tell if he was being sarcastic or if he really meant it. It wasn't important. It wouldn't be wise to enter into a light, bantering conversation with him. Ever. That in itself would be asking for trouble. Strictly business. The less she knew about him, the better off she would be. He, on the contrary, seemed to think everything about her life should be an open book.

But this mess she'd gotten herself into for whatever reason wasn't his fault. She had to remember that and not take her mounting frustrations out on him.

She didn't know much about him. But she knew enough to realize he didn't take orders nearly as well as he gave them.

"It's lovely," she finally forced herself to say, though she barely got the words past her dry lips.

He didn't respond for a second, but he didn't stop looking at her, either. "Hopefully we'll nail the bastard and I'll be out of here ASAP."

Jessica flushed at his uncanny ability to read her mind. "I hope so, too," she responded, not about to apologize for anything, including her attitude.

"Try and get some sleep," he said, following another moment of strained silence.

"Do you need anything?" She hadn't planned on

continuing the conversation, but a myriad of hidden emotions seemed to be driving her to say meaningless, irrational things.

"I'm fine. You don't need to concern yourself about me."

Something in his tone further irritated her. "I'm not," she said coldly. "It's just that you *are* in my home."

His lips turned into a smirk of sorts. "Trust me, I'm aware of that."

Her flush deepened. "Good night."

She didn't know what his response was to her abrupt words or departure. Moreover, she didn't care. If that conversation was anything to judge by, this was going to be a worse ordeal than she'd first imagined.

Only after she was back in the sanctuary of her room did Jessica breathe a clear breath. As Brant had said, she could hope it wouldn't take long to find the pervert, then both of them would be out of their misery.

Although she wasn't sleepy in the least, Jessica slipped out of her clothes. That was when her stomach rumbled and she realized she was hungry. She supposed she could wander downstairs and grab a quick snack. Or not. She might cross paths with Brant again.

So what if she did?

If not tonight, then certainly in the morning and all during the day, she reminded herself, slipping into a caftan. Still, she didn't move toward the door. Instead, she grabbed a folder out of her briefcase and headed for her desk, where she turned on the computer.

Her first instinct was to check her e-mail, but, as usual these days, she hesitated, choosing to finish her work first. If she had a frightening or degrading message, it would upset her and detour her concentration.

If only the phone would cooperate. As if compelled by the same magnet that had drawn her to Brant, her gaze sought the beige instrument. In the process her eyes caught on Porter's picture, which sat beside it. For a moment a wave a despair washed through her.

How dear and gentle he had been, and how she missed him, despite the fact that passion had never really figured in their relationship. Even though she'd shared his bed, he had never stirred the embers of her emotions. Oftentimes she'd wondered if she was capable of feeling such stirrings. Having been reared to distrust men, she'd been a virgin when she'd married Porter.

Because of that, her husband had treated her like a fragile piece of porcelain in bed. Out of the bedroom, however, he'd treated her like an equal, which had become the strength and underpinnings of their solid marriage. It had been through him that she had overcome so much pain, making her strong-willed and resilient, strengths she knew would get her through this latest ordeal.

Yet when she'd told her mother she was getting married and to whom, Opal Cannon had been outraged.

"Have you lost your mind?" she'd asked, a frown adding unflattering years to her otherwise unlined face.

Jessica had stiffened. "That's a hurtful thing to say."

"I don't care," Opal declared with a sweep of her pudgy hand. "I thought I'd done a better job of rearing you than that."

"Oh, Mother," Jessica said, her tone brimming with sadness. "I wish you could let go of the past. What Daddy did has almost ruined your life."

"And you're about to do the same thing."

Jessica shook her head adamantly. "Not all men are

like Daddy. Contrary to what you think, some have sticking power.''

Opal's frown deepened. "And you think Porter does?''

"Without question.''

"What about that son of his?''

Jessica stiffened. "What about him?''

"If you think he's going to put you before that kid, think again. You'll always be second.''

"I don't think so.''

"Even if he hated his own flesh and blood, you're still making a big mistake. Why, he's old enough to be your father, for heaven's sake.''

"That's all right.''

"Is that what you're looking for, huh? Someone to take his place?''

"Of course not. How can you say that?''

"Because that's what it looks like from the outside. You're a successful attorney with a bright future in front of you, with the sky as the limit.''

"Marrying Porter's not going to change that.''

"That's what you think," Opal countered scornfully. "Before you know it, you'll be dancing to his tune.'' She paused, her breathing becoming more labored by the second. "What about your desire to go into politics?''

"He'll support me.''

"Dream on, honey." Opal's tone was tainted with bitterness. "He has political aspirations of his own, if I'm not mistaken.''

Jessica crossed her arms over her chest as if seeking protection from the sharp blows of her mother's criticism. "That he does, and I'll support him one hundred percent. If need be, mine can wait.''

Opal threw up her hands. "For all the headway I'm making, I might as well be talking to a brick wall. You're as obstinate as that sorry daddy of yours."

Jessica winced visibly. It seemed her mother took delight in taking her own hurt and anger out on her just because she'd been close to her father and had even been willing to forgive and forget, if only Farrell had made the effort to make amends before his death. Of course, he hadn't, which made the pain of his rejection that much harder to bear. But she had managed. Unlike her mother, she'd moved on and grieved over the loss of her dad, silently, in the darkest corner of her heart.

"I'm sorry you feel that way, Mother. However, I'm not asking your permission to marry Porter."

"Then what are you asking?"

"Your blessings, actually."

"I'm sorry, but I can't give them."

That cut to the core. "What happens when Joan decides to get married? Will she be subjected to the same lecture?"

"No because she won't make that mistake. She has better sense."

"Sure, Mother," Jessica responded, making an effort to hide her smile and her disdain. Her younger sister had had numerous boyfriends, a fact that she'd hidden from their mother. One day, though, Joan would meet Mr. Right and marry him. Jessica would be curious to see her mother's reaction to her favorite child's rebellion.

"You go ahead and take the leap," Opal said into the silence. "But mark my words, you'll be sorry."

Needless to say, she and her sister both had defied Opal, and both marriages had been successful. Joan, fortunately, was still married, with three children whom

Opal doted on. As for herself, she had never been able to completely forgive or forget her mother's hurtful words or hostile attitude.

Suddenly the phone rang. The caller ID identified her mother's number. Was that mental telepathy or what? She hadn't heard from Opal Cannon in over a month, something that wasn't out of the ordinary.

Since her mother had remarried—a shock in itself, considering her attitude toward men—and moved to Florida, she and Opal had drifted further apart.

"Jessica?"

"I'm here, Mother."

"I was just thinking about you," Opal said in the hesitant tone that was usual when she spoke to her elder daughter. "So I decided to call."

"I was thinking about you, too, actually."

"Oh."

Jessica heard the surprise in Opal's voice and felt the old sting of guilt. Her mother had tried throughout the years to patch things up between them, but it never quite worked. Jessica had decided long ago that the blame rested equally between them, which lessened her penchant for beating up on herself.

"Are you and Chris all right?" Chris was Opal's husband, a good man and a good provider, for which Jessica was thankful. Long after her father had deserted them, leaving her mother to support two young children on a teacher's salary, Opal's resentment had continued to fester. She had sworn she hated men and would never have another.

She'd vowed to make it on her own. That endeavor had been difficult, especially financially. Yet Opal had done remarkably well. It was in the emotional arena that she had failed.

"We're fine," Opal acknowledged into the silence. "How 'bout you?"

"All right," she lied. "Busy as usual. I'm about to jump-start my bid for reelection."

"That's a plus. But are you sure everything's all right? I read where you're embroiled in a controversy, something to do with the police force, if I recall."

Jessica smothered a sigh. "Your recall is on target. The investigation is still ongoing, but it's nothing I can't handle."

"Well, you were always the strong one in the family."

Jessica thought she heard a note_ of envy in her mother's voice, but maybe she was mistaken. Anyway, it didn't matter. Her mother's opinion, good or bad, had ceased to sway her one way or the other.

Sad but true.

"When are you coming to Florida?"

"Oh, Mother, I have no idea." She wanted to invite Opal to visit her, but right now was not a good time. Her mother's presence would only complicate things, not help.

"Is there perhaps another man in your life?"

Brant Harding's face suddenly came to mind. Horrified, Jessica gripped the receiver until she had no feeling left in her hand. "Absolutely not."

"It wouldn't hurt, you know," Opal said in a slightly offended tone. "Porter was more of a father than a husband. Now that I've married Chris, I know what it's like to have a real man and a real marriage."

"As I've said before," Jessica told her in a tight voice, "I'm happy for you. But I'm not interested in remarrying—now or ever."

"Whatever." Opal's tone was resigned. "Joan and the kids send their love."

"Give them mine, too. Look, as soon as things settle here, I'll try to get to Florida."

"We'd all love that." Opal's voice had perked up considerably. "We'll talk again soon. Meanwhile, you take care."

"You, too."

Once the receiver was back in place, it hit home one more time that no "I love yous" had been exchanged. An even sadder fact.

She was grateful for the sudden noise that pulled her out of her reverie. Realizing it was her stomach rebelling once again, Jessica decided to raid the kitchen or she could forget about sleeping. Besides, she figured by now he was in his room asleep.

Wrong.

The instant she entered the kitchen, she pulled up short, her eyes widening.

Brant.

Her pulse rate soared. He was kneeling, his back to her, rummaging through the cabinets. That in itself was no big deal. Like her, he was apparently hungry. The big deal was the way he was dressed.

Only in jeans, which rode low on his waist.

Her gasp must have alerted him that he was no longer alone. He turned slowly, and for the second time that evening, their eyes met and held.

Ten

Sparks.

No, actually, her insides felt like rockets erupting on the Fourth of July. This kind of reaction to Brant had to stop. Somehow she had to maintain control when she was around him. The constant awareness of him as a man was wearing thin.

Discipline. It boiled down to that. Nothing more complicated than that.

Only it was.

The way she reacted to him in a physical sense made it very complicated. She couldn't get past this absurd need to *touch* him. Jessica felt her face flame. For heaven's sake, how could she feel this way about a man almost as frightening, in his way, as the pervert interfering in her life?

"Hello again," Brant finally said, relieving the smothering silence while rising slowly to his feet.

Jessica swallowed and forced herself to smile, though she knew it fell far short of genuine. "Are you looking for something to eat?"

She might as well cut to the chase so she could get back to her room. But for the moment it appeared she would have to carry on a cordial conversation whether she wanted to or not.

"Actually, I was looking for a lightbulb, then I was

going to make some coffee.'' He paused, massaging his slightly shadowed chin. "I hope you don't mind.''

She gave him an incredulous stare. "Not about the coffee, certainly. But why on earth are you looking for a bulb?''

"The light's out in the small hallway next to my room.''

His room?

Jessica swallowed the hysteria bubbling in the back of her throat. "I know it is. But it's not the bulb. Something's wrong with the electrical system, and I just haven't had it fixed.''

"No problem. I can take care of it. I'm a whiz at that kind of work. I wired my entire cabin.''

She couldn't believe they were having this conversation. "That's not your job.''

"I know, but I don't mind.'' He paused and angled his head. "Unless you do, that is.''

"Not at all,'' she said lightly. It suddenly dawned on her that underneath her caftan, she was nude. Could he tell?

"Why don't I make the coffee?'' he said, once again breaking the silence.

Jessica shook her head, venturing farther into the room, suddenly feeling like a stranger in her own house. Renewed resentment welled up inside her. She curled her nails into the palms of her hands, wincing against the sting of the pain.

"I'll do it, but thanks, anyway,'' she said, sounding out of breath.

He shouldn't be here. More to the point, he shouldn't look so damn manly and attractive, *half naked,* standing in front of her. In all fairness, bare chested hardly qualified as naked. Still, he should have on more than a ragged pair of jeans and no shoes.

Maybe at the root of her dismay was the fact he exhibited what she'd always envisioned as the perfect male "bod." Hairy chested, but not too much hair. Tanned skin. Flat abs. Muscled, but not too muscled. Even the scar that jig-jagged down one side before disappearing beneath the waistline didn't detract. In fact, it made him appear that much more rugged and manly.

In a nutshell, perfect.

And he acted like nothing out of the ordinary was happening, that it was his God-given right to parade around her home as he pleased, dressed any way he pleased. That galled her. It should have occurred to him that she just might appear unexpectedly.

Apparently that was no big deal to him.

Or was it all an act? Was he as cool and comfortable as he appeared, or was he as rattled inside as she was? For some perverse reason, she hoped for the latter, which was ludicrous, of course. She didn't want him to think about her except as just another assignment. That way *he* would remain objective and in control at all times.

The perfect bodyguard.

"Is something wrong?"

Jessica moved her tongue against the back of her teeth. "No, why do you ask?"

He shrugged his wide shoulders. "You're just standing there, not saying anything. If you resent me being in your kitchen, all you have to do is tell me."

Jessica stiffened, but she forced her voice to remain calm and cordial. "You have to eat."

"So do you," he said roughly.

"I wasn't hungry earlier."

He sighed visibly and peered at her through knowing eyes which sent color surging into her face. Averting her gaze, she went about the task of making coffee.

"Mmm, that smells good," he said, cutting a glance at her.

"You never answered my question," she said, ignoring the tightening in her chest, latching on to a cup.

His eyebrows raised. "What question?"

"Whether you were hungry or not."

"Are you offering anything?"

Another surge of color stung her face, and she gritted her teeth. Innocent enough, so why did it sound so suggestive? She had to get a grip. "Soup and salad."

He thought for a moment. "The soup."

"Have a seat and I'll heat it."

She felt his eyes on her from start to finish. She wondered if he could see through the thin material of her caftan. If so, he was having a field day. Just the thought made her pulses hammer. Still, she managed to get through the ordeal without dropping or spilling anything. Under the circumstances, that was a miracle.

It had been so long since she'd had a man in the house, watching her putter in the kitchen, or anywhere else for that matter, that she had forgotten what it was like.

"Need any help?"

"No, I'm fine," she said without turning around.

"I could've scrounged something up on my own."

This time she faced him, two bowls of soup in her hands. He stood and reached for them. Only after she was seated across from him did she answer. "It's okay. I didn't...don't mind."

He was silent while eating. Suddenly she felt his gaze

on her, a question in his eyes. "Aren't you going to eat?"

Jessica lowered her head, mortified that she'd been caught staring. Although she'd made the soup from scratch the other day and knew it was good, the thought of eating it now almost turned her stomach. His presence had taken her appetite.

"Man, that was good," Brant said, after draining his bowl and pushing it away.

"There's more. All I have to do is heat it."

He rubbed his stomach, which instantly drew her eyes. "Thanks, but no thanks. I'm full as a tick on a fat dog."

Unwittingly that corny analogy made her laugh. "I'm glad you enjoyed it."

"Did you make it?"

"I did."

His eyebrows shot up.

"You're surprised," she said, slightly miffed and letting it show.

"Actually, I am. I never would have pegged you as the domestic type."

She knew she should have let that barb slide and moved on to more secure ground. But the remark rankled, and she spoke before she weighed the consequences. "Oh, and just what type am I?"

This time he smiled, though it never reached his dark, brooding eyes. Still, it changed his demeanor, easing the strain on his face and adding to his appeal.

"I didn't mean that as an insult, though you apparently took it that way."

"It doesn't matter," she said, dodging his piercing gaze and clamping down on her anger.

He sighed. "Are you always this sensitive, or is it just me?"

"It's everything," she admitted honestly. "Especially right now."

His lips thinned. "I know what you mean."

Jessica stood and removed their bowls. She had sat still as long as she could, especially in front of him. "I have dessert, also," she added from in front of the sink, purposely changing the subject.

"I'll pass. I've had enough, especially since it's so late."

She swung around. "With that in mind, I think it's time I tried to get some sleep."

"Not so fast."

She paused in her tracks. "Excuse me?"

The room suddenly vibrated with suppressed tension.

"Look, we have to talk," he said, rubbing the back of his neck.

She released a shallow breath. "I don't think this is the time."

"I do," he countered, the roughness back in his voice.

"Talk about what?" she asked, her tone filled with suspicion.

"Scheduling, for starters."

Jessica knitted her brows. If that was all, she could handle that. She told him about the upcoming week.

"I don't want you ever going anywhere by yourself."

She gave him an astounded look, her sense of relief fading. "That's not possible."

"Oh, I think it is."

"Do you plan on literally dogging every step I take?" she demanded. "Surely not?"

"Absolutely. That's what you're paying me big bucks to do."

"If that's the case, maybe we should end this right now."

A closed look came over his face before he stood. Then he lifted his shoulders in that nonchalant shrug of his. "It's no skin off my back, Mrs. Kincaid. It's your life that's been threatened. If you say stay, I'll stay. If you say go, I'll go."

Although there was a definite period at the end of the sentence, she realized the subject was not finished. And that was no accident, either. He was deliberately trying to frighten her without spelling out the possible consequences of her decision. The worst part about his ploy was that it worked. It also fueled her growing agitation.

She'd been called many things, but stupid wasn't one of them. If she wanted to put this nasty, disruptive part of her life behind her, she had to set her mind and abide by rules she didn't agree with.

Why her? she wanted to ask. But she refrained. Not only wasn't she stupid, she wasn't a whiner, either. Still, in all his years as a public servant, Porter had never encountered a situation even close to this one. What was the difference? Perhaps it was the fact that she was a woman, perceived as an easy target.

"So what's it going to be?" Brant demanded with obvious impatience.

Unable to meet his steely gaze another second, Jessica shifted her eyes and groped for composure, something that heretofore had been second nature to her.

Not around him, unfortunately.

"I'll play by your rules as long as I can."

"Wise choice." He paused. "If it's any consolation, I'm not thrilled with this arrangement myself."

She held steady. "I'm aware of that." There was something else she was aware of, too. She wasn't going to let him dog her every step; he would have to keep his distance for the sake of her privacy, both professionally and personally. Some lines she would not tolerate him crossing. If he couldn't accept that, then she would tell him to leave and not look back.

"So are you already having second thoughts?" he asked with an unmasked smirk.

"No," she declared tightly.

"Look, I won't deny that we'll clash, both being as strong-willed as we are. But for this to work, we have to find some common ground. Agreed?"

"Agreed," she said wearily, toying with her lower lip.

Suddenly there was a softening of his features as his eyes seemed to home in on the moist lip she had been gnawing. Or was that intimate softening another figment of her imagination? Brant was a hard one to read, even for her, and she took pride in her intuitiveness.

"Good night, then," he said, that rough edge back in his voice. "Call if you need me."

Jessica nodded, then turned and left the room before she shuddered in front of him, his words ringing in her ears.

Call if you need me.

God forbid *that* should ever happen.

Eleven

Roy Kincaid strode out of the bath into the bedroom and stared at the young woman splayed across the bed sound asleep. The light from the two lamps allowed him to peruse her painfully thin body.

He could see her protruding hip bones under her heavily tanned skin, skin that had been burned in swimming pools and tanning booths to the extreme, almost to a crisp in several instances. Her dark hair was in almost the same sad shape. It was short and choppy and looked baked, though he had no clue how that had happened. He only knew that women were always messing with their hair, if nothing else changing the color.

He didn't know why he let Dottie hang on, disrupting his life with her constant whining about what she needed and wanted. More to the point, what she expected from him.

Money. And drugs.

With her, the two went hand in hand. But he had no gripe coming; he put up with her on a daily basis. In fact, she'd practically moved into his apartment since she'd gotten in the bad habit of bouncing from job to job.

In a way she was attractive, or could be, if she would take the time to fix herself up. But she apparently couldn't care less, even though she worked as a girl

Friday in an office building. All Dottie cared about was having enough pot or coke on hand to satisfy her growing hunger for the stuff. He had to be careful; he was close to sinking into that same dark hole. Maybe he was already there.

So what? He enjoyed the hell out of the way drugs made him feel. The powder never failed to pep him up when he was feeling down-and-out, and it gave him the courage to face his mundane job as a sales representative for a computer company, a position he felt certain wasn't good enough for his high-minded stepmother.

A grin spread across Roy's lean face. She thought he ought to be some mucky-muck rich attorney, like herself, someone who ran in her circles and who wouldn't be an embarrassment to his father's memory. Roy's grin spread, taking the edge off the gauntness of his own features.

His dad was probably rolling over in his grave at the mess Roy had made of his life. But it was *his* life, and if he chose to mess it up, so be it. Now that his old man was dead and he'd gotten a taste of freedom the past four years, he'd finally made peace with himself.

As long as he had drugs.

Roy's gaze settled on the bag of coke sitting on the table, just waiting for him and Dottie to snort it. They had partaken far into the night, then screwed their brains out into the wee hours of the morning. Now it was time for him to get to work. Maybe he wouldn't go. Hell, he hadn't missed in a while. If the boss fired him, he didn't care.

He'd found this job. He would find another one if he had to. The only problem was, his drugs and his money were getting frighteningly low. Dottie was to blame. She couldn't hold on to either. When his trust check was cut every month, it didn't take long for it to disappear. By the time he paid his rent and bought drugs, it was gone.

Roy's gaze remained on the bag of white powder. When that was empty, there wouldn't be money to buy more. He was flat broke. It was only the middle of the month, and nothing would be coming in until the first, nearly three weeks away.

Roy's insides rebelled, and he felt himself panic. For a second he thought he might be sick. Out of money; out of drugs. It was that simple. Only it wasn't simple. It was damned complicated, especially since he didn't have free access to the money his old man had left him. To all intents and purposes it was his mother's money, to be exact.

His panic suddenly turned into blinding anger. The bitch. How dare his stepmother think she could continue to jerk him around like he was a puppet on a string? Some way, somehow, he had to get control of that trust fund. She had to relent, dammit. So far, though, when it came to budging her, he'd slammed into a brick wall.

He should blame his old man for not trusting him. And he did. But since Porter had given that bitch power over his money until he was thirty-five, two years from now, he was at her mercy.

At first, when he'd run short of cash for whatever reason, Jessica had given permission for extra. The last few months, however, she had outright refused.

Her refusal to see him the other night had pissed him off royally. He had no intention of letting her get away with it anymore. He'd lost count of the times they had fought verbally over his trust. In his mind, the conversations never seemed to change.

"It's your money," was always her comeback. "I

never said otherwise. But this is the way your father set up the trust, and I have to abide by it. And even if I wanted to, I couldn't change it."

"Don't be too sure of that," he'd retaliated. "Nothing in this world is ever set in stone. Laws are broken every day. You ought to know that, you being a lawyer and all."

"Do whatever you have to," Jessica responded, "but it won't change things. I'm not backing down, nor is the bank. Look, Roy, you and I have always gotten along. I loved your dad, and because I loved him, I also loved you. And I still do."

"Hogwash."

"Think what you like, but your attitude doesn't change anything. My hands are tied. You're just going to have to learn to live within your means, like other responsible working Americans."

"We'll see about that. I'll get that money. It's just a matter of time."

And it was. Unfortunately for him, time and coke were synonymous. When the coke was gone, he was in trouble. His trust was his only hope. He had no place else to turn. He was already in debt to a friend of his. Big-time debt.

Jessica would come through. It was just a matter of time. In the end, she wouldn't best him. She might see him as the stupid stepson, but he wasn't. Far from it. Sweat popped out on Roy's forehead, and he let an expletive fly.

"Something the matter, honey?"

Roy swung around. Dottie Walters was propped up in bed, the covers tossed back, displaying her nude body. He felt himself harden, which was a miracle, considering the amount of time they'd spent screwing. But he wasn't complaining. Lately, after they'd been using for several days straight, he hadn't been able to get it up, something that scared him shitless.

He could do without drugs if he had to, but he damn sure couldn't do without his dick.

"Roy?"

"I was just thinking," he muttered.

"About me?"

Another selfish bitch. "Not this time."

"Then why's your dick harder than a baseball bat?"

Having been caught red-handed, he grinned. "Even though you're too skinny, baby, you still have what it takes."

"You're one to be talking about being skinny," she muttered petulantly. "You're right there with me."

He shrugged, not interested in discussing their bodies. He had much more important things on his mind.

"How 'bout snorting a little more before we get up, along with one more good lay?"

"Can't," Roy said, though his gaze rested on the powder with longing. "Gotta go to work."

She quirked a finger at him, the nail painted with chipped hot-pink polish. "To hell with work. We've got some serious business to take care of first."

"I told you no," he said in a hateful tone. "What is there about that word you don't understand?"

She made a face. "You can be mean when you want to."

"Then go shack up with someone else."

Tears welled up in her makeup-streaked eyes. "You don't mean that, do you?"

"No, not now. But if you continue to piss me off…" Roy let the words trail off. She got the message, though. She stopped whining. "Get up and get dressed."

"When can we use again?" she asked, her tone tentative.

"Tonight. And nothing in between, you hear me?"

The tears returned. "You mean I can't—"

"No, dammit, you can't," he interrupted. "That's all the stuff we have left."

"You'll get some more. I'm not worried."

"It's not that simple. I'm out of money."

"Then go to see your stepmother, our mayor."

The way she said that last word made him think Dottie had just stepped into something nasty. "Shut up and get dressed. You're beginning to get on my nerves again."

Wordlessly Dottie did as she was told. Once she had disappeared into the bathroom, he put on his clothes, not caring if they were rumpled or not. Right now, he didn't care about anything but returning to the coke on the table and forgetting the world existed.

"Get the lead out of your ass, Dottie. We gotta go."

She'd been behind closed doors for over an hour. Brant didn't mind that. He knew exactly where she was and who she was with, several women from the Dallas Beautification League. He had no idea when the meeting would end, but that didn't matter, either.

He had nothing but time.

"Would you like another cup of coffee, sir?"

Brant leveled his gaze on Millie Ford, the young receptionist who occupied the desk in the outer office, and who served as gofer for both the mayor and her assistant, Tony.

"No thanks, Millie. I'm about to float away as it is."

For some reason, she colored, as though embarrassed he was giving her his full attention. He almost smiled, thinking how innocent she appeared, much like he envisioned his son, though she was a few years older than Elliot. Still, the innocence was refreshing, something that was rare these days.

"If you change your mind," she added hesitantly, "I'll be glad to get you another cup."

"I know you will, and I appreciate it." Brant made himself smile in order to put her at ease. He sensed she was uncomfortable with him being underfoot. From time to time he would catch her peering at him from under thick lashes, as though she was trying to come to terms with the sudden and drastic change in the office. Just another in a long line of many, he figured cynically.

Realizing her questioning eyes were still on him, he added, "You don't have to wait on me. If I want something, I'll get it myself."

Millie's flush deepened; then she said in a rushed voice, "I don't mind."

When he didn't respond, she ducked her head and went back to work. If his presence made her nervous, she would just have to get over it. Dismissing the girl from his mind, Brant turned his attention back to the window, shoving his hands into his pockets. That was when he saw Thurmon walking across the parking lot, heading into the building.

By damn, for once luck was smiling on him. Talking to his friend had been high on his priority list. After returning to his room last evening, he'd wanted to call Thurmon. He'd actually picked up the phone a half-dozen times, only to slam it back down. He'd never liked discussing something important on the phone. Better face-to-face, though what he had to tell Thurmon wouldn't set well with him no matter how he presented the news.

"Hey, good buddy."

Thurmon's low, rumbling voice forced Brant back around. Before he could respond, his friend was speaking to Millie, who was blushing again.

"You're the last person I expected to see running around loose," Brant said after Millie's head dipped again.

"That's what happens when you work for yourself, my friend."

Brant ignored that pointed statement and asked, "To what do I owe this honor?"

Thurmon chuckled. When he did, every part of his huge body shook. For a second Brant was envious. This was a man who had it all—good sex, good money, good food, and good booze. Now that he was no longer a slave to the Secret Service, he had managed to get his life back.

Damn shame he couldn't say the same.

"Why that sour look on your face?" Thurmon demanded, walking closer.

"Feeling a pinch of envy," Brant admitted. Then, seeing the confused look on Thurmon's face, he waved his hand. "Forget it."

"Is there anywhere we can talk?" Thurmon asked.

Brant nodded. "The coffee area." He gestured toward a small room adjacent to where they were.

Once they had their coffee and were seated at the small table, Brant made sure he was facing the door to Jessica's office. She wasn't about to make a move without him knowing it.

"Jessica's behind closed doors, I take it."

"Right," Brant said. "I know what you're thinking, but don't say it."

Thurmon chuckled again. "Not to worry. I'd rather stick my bare hand in a hornets' nest."

"Funny."

A twinkle appeared in Thurmon's eyes. "Jessie's being her usual hardheaded self, huh?"

Brant snorted. "That's an understatement. In fact, I almost took a hike last night."

Thurmon's good humor fled. "You damn well better not."

"My gut instinct tells me that's what will eventually happen."

"Hell, man, you gave your word. Since when doesn't that mean anything to you?"

Anger rose in Brant, but he clamped down on it. He didn't want to end up at cross purposes with his lifelong friend. Not now, not ever, especially over a woman who didn't mean Jackshit to him. Still, he had to make Thurmon understand what he was up against with her.

He didn't belong here. Didn't want to be here. Being around Jessica was like living in high-alert mode. He'd been there and done that.

"She's much too headstrong to adhere to rules and regulations," Brant finally said, picking up on Thurmon's growing agitation. "But I suspect you knew that."

Thurmon had the grace to look sheepish. "Of course I knew it. She and Veronica have been friends forever, like you and me." He paused, his features brightening. "Doesn't it help that she's mighty easy on the eye?"

Brant scowled, even though he silently agreed with Thurmon. Jessica's image sprang to mind, the way she'd looked as she'd paraded around the kitchen last evening in nothing but a slinky caftan that left little to the imagination. No doubt about it, she was blessed with more curves than a mountain road.

Suddenly Brant felt the heat rise in his own body and cursed inwardly.

"Okay, so she's attractive," he forced himself to say in a nonchalant voice. "But beautiful women are a dime a dozen."

This time Thurmon scowled. "Don't you get horny as hell, alone in those hills?"

Brant's features darkened. "Mind your own damn business."

Thurmon merely laughed, then sobered. "The most important reason for hanging around is your son. Don't forget that."

Brant laughed without humor. "My friend, that's probably the only reason I haven't taken a hike. Otherwise, I would've found another way to repay my debt."

"Such as join my firm, perhaps?"

"No, not as a partner or anything else."

"I won't take no for an answer. Not yet, anyway. Elliot might yet soften your hardened heart."

Although Thurmon had a teasing note in his voice, Brant knew he wasn't teasing. He was dead serious. Rather than argue with him about something that was off-limits, Brant changed the subject. "I need you to do something for me. It concerns Jessica."

Thurmon quickly reverted to all business. "Shoot."

Brant told him about Jessica's confrontation with the two cops, Stokes and Wells. "I want you to get me everything you can on those two guys."

"You don't have to ask twice. I'm just glad we finally have suspects." He stood, then slapped Brant on the back. "You've still got what it takes, my friend."

"Don't give me credit yet. It's much too soon."

Thurmon walked to the door. "Stay in touch."

"Oh, you bet I will. But since I can't leave Jessica, you're going to have to do the legwork."

Thurmon's face wrinkled in a grin. "Jessica, huh?"

"Get the hell out of here before I throw you out."

"Whether you ever admit this or not, you're doing what you do best."

"Don't push your luck," Brant responded in a dark voice.

Thurmon left, but not before his grin spread across his face.

Damn him, Brant thought. Damn this entire situation.

Twelve

"Have you checked your day planner yet?"

Jessica ran a hand through her hair while giving Tony an exasperated look. "Yes."

"I don't know why you consented to see that man," Tony said, flitting around the office, first snatching a dead leaf off a plant, then disposing of their empty coffee cups. "He's a pain in the rear."

Jessica sighed. "I know, but he's a friend."

"Just because you've gone out to dinner with him doesn't—"

Jessica gave him a startled look. "How did you know that?"

"It's my business to know your business."

Jessica had to smile. "All right, so we've gone out several times. However, this meeting is strictly business."

"No doubt, since he's got his shorts all in a wad about that land deal." Tony's eyes were questioning.

"I'm not going to back down, if that's what you're thinking."

"I was just testing your temperature. That guy's got a big mouth, and from what I understand, he's been using it behind your back to influence some of the councilmembers."

"Let him talk. When the time comes, I think I'll have

the votes needed to annex the land even with the dissenters. Curtis has waited too late.''

"Let us pray,'' Tony said, rolling his eyes. He paused for a moment, his face sobering. "Mind if I ask you something personal?''

Another smile teased Jessica's lips. "Does it matter? You'll ask it anyway.''

A grin filled Tony's face, causing his glasses to slip lower on his nose. Jessica swore that one of these days they were going to simply fall off. She often wondered if he really needed them, as they never seemed to be in place.

"Uh, how are things working out with what's-his-name in there?'' Tony's tone was low and conspiratorial as his head bobbed in the direction of the outer office.

It took Jessica a minute to regroup, to get her mind off Tony's inane glasses. But maybe her stalling tactic was a cover. She would have liked to make any discussion of Brant taboo, but she couldn't. He was a reality she had to deal with. She couldn't pretend he wasn't hovering outside her door, nor could her staff.

For now, he was attached to her. Unwittingly her heart raced, especially when she cut her glance in his direction. He was standing at the window, hands in his pockets, appearing totally relaxed, as though he didn't have anything better to do.

Relaxed he wasn't, and he had plenty to do—watch her every move. If only she could figure out what made him different, made him so viscerally noticeable. It certainly wasn't the way he dressed. No one could accuse him of stepping off the pages of *GQ* magazine. As usual, he had on an ordinary pair of casual slacks and a sports shirt open at the neck.

This morning his hair appeared still damp, like it had

been sprinkled with dewdrops, or else the sun was shining on it at just the right angle. While it was a tad too long and slightly mussed, that didn't bother her.

His smell was his own, too, if that made any sense, something she had never associated with Porter. When he'd walked into a room, nothing had popped. With Brant, all her senses sprang to life, a feeling that continually unnerved her.

And thinking about him, staring at him, was becoming a bad habit.

A dangerous habit.

"Jessica?"

"Sorry," she said in a halting tone. "It's okay. He's okay."

Tony harrumphed. "Right."

"What else do you want me to say?"

Tony sighed. "Nothing really. I'm glad you have someone looking out after you. It's just that he's so…" He wrinkled his nose, then lowered his voice even more. "So manly."

Jessica merely shook her head and forced herself not to smile. "That he is. And a nuisance to boot." The instant she'd said those words, she wished she could retract them. They were both to blame for the volatile chemistry between them.

"Oh, really," Tony said curiously. "Why?"

"Forget I said that." Jessica's tone was abrupt.

"Actually I can't think of anything worse than having a stranger underfoot, especially one with an attitude. But if he can find the creep who's making your life miserable, then it'll be worth the aggravation."

Jessica peered at her watch. "Curtis should be here any minute now, and I need to get my mind in order."

"You want me to stay?" Tony asked, suddenly all business.

"No. I can handle him."

"Well, if you can't, you can always call in the one-man cavalry." Tony once again nodded toward Brant.

Jessica stared at him pointedly.

"I know that look, and I'm going. I'll be working on next week's schedule, and from the way it's shaping up, you're going to be on the run."

Jessica didn't respond. Instead she focused her attention on the folder in front of her, which was filled with numerous documents concerning the pending land deal, only to be interrupted by Millie's buzz.

"Mr. Riley's here."

"Thanks, Millie. Send him in." Standing, Jessica smoothed the skirt of her short linen suit, wishing she hadn't worn linen, since it wrinkled so badly. But the vibrant orange and magenta colors gave her a much-needed lift.

By the time Curtis strode in, she was no longer behind her desk. Instead she stood in the center of the room, a fixed smile in place.

"Hey, it's great to see you," he said, smiling broadly and extending his hand.

Jessica clasped it briefly. Curtis was as sure of himself as she was, though she never perceived herself as being cocky. But he was, at least in her opinion. He had dark copper-colored hair and brown eyes. A handsome combination. And he used both to get what he wanted, which was money and power.

And her.

He'd hinted on more than one occasion that he would like for them to be more than just friends, but she wasn't interested, never had been. There was something about him besides his cockiness that rubbed her the wrong way. Perhaps it was his condescending attitude, especially around women in business—her in particular.

With them at cross-purposes over the land annexation, that attitude seemed to have worsened. Now, however, Curtis was all flowers and smiles.

"You're looking gorgeous, as always," he said warmly, his eyes perusing her with the same enthusiasm as his tone.

"Thank you," she said with cool politeness. "You're looking good yourself."

While he took a seat in front of her desk, she walked over and closed the door, purposely not meeting Brant's eyes. She knew he wouldn't approve of that move, but she didn't care.

"Would you like some coffee?"

"No, thanks. What I would like to know is who's that guy hanging around your outer office?"

"Why do you ask?"

A flash of anger appeared in his eyes. "He stopped me and all but frisked me, that's why."

Oh, dear. "He's my bodyguard."

Curtis gave her an incredulous look. "You've got to be kidding me."

"I wish I were."

His features sobered. "What the hell's going on?"

Jessica gave him as much information as she deemed suitable. Actually, just the bare facts.

"Well, I'll be damned."

She didn't say anything.

"Do you think it's someone on the police force?"

"I have no idea."

He rubbed a baby-smooth chin. "With your high-profile image, it could be any nut off the street who's taken a disliking to you.''

''Could be,'' Jessica said, hedging on purpose.

''Somehow the thought of him in your house isn't very comforting, either.''

''Let's change the subject, shall we?'' she responded in a chilly tone. ''And get down to business?''

Curtis shrugged slender shoulders in a suit she knew had been tailor-made, something Brant would never have considered. Appalled that her mind seemed to be stuck on *him,* Jessica forced herself back to the matter at hand.

''So you know why I'm here,'' Curtis replied in a confident tone.

''To try and talk me out of pressing for the annexation.''

''Exactly.''

''Then I might as well save you the trouble. I'm not prepared to change my mind.''

His features darkened momentarily, then cleared. ''I still think you owe me the courtesy of hearing my side.''

I don't owe you a damn thing. Jessica smiled. ''I think I've heard your side—more than once.''

Curtis' lips flattened. ''The city can do without the land. You've got more than enough revenue coming in to meet the city's needs.''

''We're a growing city, one of the fastest growing in the country. There's never enough money.''

''Then get it from somewhere else,'' Curtis said. ''This manufacturing park that wants to build on my property will benefit the metroplex even if it doesn't get one dime of property tax money, Jessica. Think about it. Most of the employees, especially the bigwigs, will live in the city. They'll be paying taxes on their personal property.''

''That's not the same, and you know it.''

Curtis stood, his eyes narrowing on her. ''Why won't you listen to reason?''

''I'm not the only one who thinks this move is the right one.''

''Are you sure you have a majority on the council?''

''If I don't, I will.''

Curtis' chest swelled. ''Don't be too sure of that. I won't deny I'm going all out to convince them otherwise, to gather votes for my side.''

''Your ploy won't work,'' Jessica said with a show of confidence she was far from feeling. But if she didn't appear confident, then Curtis would walk all over her. She couldn't allow that. She was just as determined to win as he was.

''I guess we'll just have to see, won't we?'' Curtis' tone shook with suppressed anger.

Jessica didn't give an inch and was even able to manage a cool smile. ''I guess so.''

Curtis' mouth worked for a few seconds. ''I can't believe you're doing this,'' he said harshly, before lowering his voice. ''Dammit, Jessica, I thought we had something going, that—''

Jessica's raised hand interrupted him. ''You know better than that, Curtis. I've never given you any reason to think we were anything other than friends.''

''That's not true.''

''Oh, but it is true. If you choose to deny that to yourself, then it's your problem, not mine.''

Anger flared in his eyes. ''You're turning out to be a big disappointment. Selfishness and political ambitions are masking the soft, feminine woman I know is under that hard veneer you're displaying.''

Jessica was appalled at his assumption and said as much. "You don't have any clue about me personally. We've only had the most casual of dates, none of which allowed you insight into my private life."

The anger in his eyes flared again. "I won't let you nix this deal. I have too much riding on it. Besides, I've—"

Curtis stopped midsentence, as though he thought better of what he was about to say, which fed her curiosity. He had sounded almost desperate. Had he perhaps made promises he couldn't keep? She didn't ask, because she really didn't care. If he had done something irresponsible, he would just have to suffer the consequences.

"Ah, hell, forget it," Curtis muttered.

"I already have."

He waited a few heartbeats, then closed the distance between them, both his features and his tone softening. "Hey, I don't want to argue with you. I'd much rather make love to you."

Jessica's eyes widened, and she sucked in her breath just as he lifted a finger and caressed the side of her cheek. It was when she jerked away that she noticed that the door was cracked and Brant was moving fast, his face as dark as a thundercloud.

For a few seconds, fury stole her voice. "Don't ever touch me again." Out of the corner of one eye, she noticed Brant had stopped at the door, short of coming in.

Still, his presence added more firepower to an already explosive situation.

Curtis' laugh evolved into a sneer. "For now, I'll

indulge you in your little power play, but not for long. Just so you'll know, I'm not a patient man.''

With that he wheeled and headed for the door that Brant held wide-open for him. With a set jaw and stiff body, Curtis strode out.

Once he had disappeared, Brant didn't waste any time in demanding, ''What was that all about?''

''He's the one who doesn't want the land deal to go through.''

''Does he mean anything to you?''

Though that personal question struck another nerve, she answered it. ''No.''

''Then why did he think he could touch you?''

Jessica sucked in her breath again, now furious at Brant. ''I have no idea.''

A smirk crossed Brant's lips, which further inflamed her fury. Before she could make a suitable comeback, however, he went on, ''Have you considered pretty boy a suspect?''

''No,'' she said again.

''Well, you should,'' Brant said flatly.

''That's absurd.''

''Look, dammit, nothing's absurd, and everyone is a suspect. I thought we had that understood.''

Thirteen

"Hey, friend, how's it going?"

"It's going."

Veronica hesitated for several heartbeats. "Obviously not well or you wouldn't sound so down in the dumps." She paused. "It's Brant, right?"

"Along with work."

"I was hoping you two would've come to grips with the situation, worked things out by now." She paused again with a deep sigh. "Apparently I've been living in a dream world."

"What you are, my friend, is indulging in wishful thinking," Jessica replied. "But if that makes you feel better, then go ahead."

"Okay, so you and Brant are not a match made in heaven. No matter, you have no option but to keep him around until this idiot is caught. Speaking of the creep, what's the latest?"

"He seems to be lying low, for whatever reason. However, I can't back that up with proof. I haven't checked my personal e-mail in several days. I'm chicken. I'll admit that, but..." Jessica's words faded. She was so tired of talking about her personal quandary, she didn't know what to do.

"Maybe he's dropped dead." Veronica chuckled at her own flippant statement.

"I wouldn't be that lucky."

"You never know. Anyway, promise you won't do anything reckless or stupid, like send Brant packing?"

"I won't—can't—promise that."

As if Veronica had picked up on the stubborn note in Jessica's tone, she didn't push or waste any more time. "Look, I'm not going to keep you. But I can't say I like leaving things on such shaky ground. I'd love for us to get together for lunch this week. You have any free time?"

Jessica quickly reviewed her day-planner in her head. "Tomorrow is a day from hell. The following one looks better, if I remember correctly. I can let you know in the morning."

"Any day this week will suit me, so it's your decision. Believe it or not, I'm not tied up in court."

"Then you're on for sure. And thanks for calling, Ronnie," Jessica added in a subdued tone. "Thanks even more for caring."

"Stop thanking me. You'd do the same for me. So go to bed and get some beauty rest."

"What's that?"

Veronica's chuckle preceded the sound of the dial tone, leaving Jessica feeling better than she'd felt when she'd answered the phone, although she'd known it was her friend.

That quick call had come around ten. Now it was twelve, and her eyes were still wide-open. She had to get some sleep. Maybe she would take something that would force her to sleep. Tomorrow was indeed a hard day, meeting after meeting, both in and out of the office. She had told Tony a while back to poll the city's staff and the councilmembers about the possibility of holding a weekend retreat to discuss how the city's needs fit into budget considerations for the next fiscal year. To date, the retreat hadn't been confirmed, but she trusted that it would be and that word of that would come tomorrow, as well.

If only she could keep her thoughts off Curtis' unsettling visit. She disliked dissension, but of late, it seemed to shadow her. On this issue, however, she refused to take the blame. Curtis was the one who had set the tone, who had drawn a line in the sand, forcing them on opposite sides.

One good thing to come out of the verbal altercation was that she'd seen his true colors. Underneath that charming facade was someone who had no qualms about getting nasty when crossed.

And she *had* crossed him. And would continue to do so. She had meant it when she told him she would fight him, even if court proved the only method of settling things. Of course, she had no idea what position the council as a whole would take on such a controversial move, but she had to think they would back her.

Time would tell. Meanwhile, she had to focus her mind on other issues. Despite all the seething controversy behind the scenes, personally and professionally, up-front things were definitely happening—productive things, too. While she couldn't take all the credit, she could take some.

There was talk of another big company coming to Dallas, an issue she had thought was dead. Apparently that wasn't the case. The idea had seemingly been resurrected, which thrilled her.

Another reason for the retreat. If she were to pull off that coup as well as the pending land annexation, she would be in the catbird seat when it came to reelection, or so she hoped. But nothing was a sure thing in this world; she knew that from experience—from lots of hard knocks. Still, she had no intention of losing her positive outlook or enthusiasm for her work.

So what if I have a bodyguard following my every step?

She could handle that, too, she assured herself staunchly. Suddenly Jessica laughed in the darkness, the sound of her own laughter sounding almost diabolical. Who was she kidding? She wasn't handling it. She was barely holding body and soul together.

And she suspected Brant wasn't faring much better. For some reason that no longer made her feel better. She had no idea if he'd contacted his son or how things were on that score. He continued to stick straight to business, a tactic she admired. Yet she couldn't help being curious about him, about the man who was sharing her home and her life.

Thinking of the latter made her yearn to get hers back. And her *home*. If he hadn't had to set up residence here, she would find this whole bizarre situation much more tolerable. As it was…

Stop it, Jessica told herself. She had to stop dwelling on him and his presence. If not, the wear and tear on her would start to interfere with her work. She couldn't allow that.

Suddenly she tensed, her thoughts stopping cold. Had she heard something? She stiffened, even stopped breathing for several moments, and listened. All quiet, except for the air-conditioning unit clicking on.

Finally she released her breath and eased her head back onto the pillow, not even realizing she'd lifted it. Her eyes sought the clock. One. Paranoia. That was what she was experiencing. Forcing herself to relax, she closed her eyes and began counting sheep, silly, but oftentimes effective.

Jessica made it to fifty. That was when she heard the sound again. She sucked in her breath and listened. A door creaking? Was that what she'd heard? At this juncture, it didn't matter. Whether she'd actually heard something or not was no longer the point.

Something was amiss. She didn't know what, but she couldn't lie there another second pretending her paranoia wasn't making her a basket case.

Brant?

Was it him moving around the house?

If not, then someone else?

Her mouth turned dry, and her pulse rate dropped.

Had he heard the intruder?

If there was one.

Let it be, she told herself. If someone had managed to get inside again, she should trust Brant to take care of him. After all, that was what he'd been hired to do, what he was *trained* to do. But what if he was a heavy sleeper who didn't hear night sounds, valid or otherwise? She didn't know anything about him, much less his sleeping habits, for crying out loud.

One thing she did know, her mind was once again becoming her own worst enemy.

"To hell with this," she muttered, slinging back the sheet and scrambling out of bed.

Since the night-light was on in the bath, it allowed her to see through the shadows. Her eyes scanned the room. No one lurked in those shadows, which gave her confidence to reach for her robe, slip it on. Still, she didn't move, because her legs had all the consistency of melted butter.

Coward.

It was probably nothing except her overactive imagination. Even so, she might as well investigate and get it over with. Otherwise, she would just continue to stew and not get any rest. More important, if someone *had* gotten inside...

Jessica shut that thought down and made her way to the door, which she very cautiously opened, noticing her palms were so clammy that they threatened to slip off the knob. In addition, her heart was banging like a gong against her ribs.

Once the door was open enough for her to get through, she met nothing but inky-blackness. Pausing, she drew a shuddering breath and held it, casting her eyes to the right, then to the left. She couldn't see a blessed thing.

Tiny baby steps brought her out into the hallway. Once there, she turned left. At the time she didn't know why she chose that route. Maybe because it was in the direction of the stairs and Brant.

She had taken only three steps when she bumped into something.

A person.

Warm but solid.

Her scream froze in her throat as strong arms locked around her upper arms.

"Dammit, Jessica!"

Brant.

Thank God. His minty breath and distinctive scent enveloped her like a cocoon.

She went limp, suddenly too weak with relief to stand on her own power. Her instant capitulation seemed to catch him by surprise, for he muttered another expletive, then grasped her tighter and closer.

Seconds passed and neither moved, their hearts beating in sync. Then Jessica's paralysis broke and she began shaking uncontrollably, teeth and all.

"Hey, it's okay," he whispered against her ear, his warm breath sending shivers of a different kind through her body. "Nothing's going to happen to you."

"Is someone—"

"No," he interrupted, his lips remaining close to her ear, heightening her awareness of him. "I've checked every square inch of the premises, and all's clear. No one has broken in, and no one will as long as I'm here."

Despite his steely tone and take-charge attitude, Jessica couldn't stop shaking. Her body seemed to have a will of its own.

"Don't," he pleaded in a guttural tone. "You're fine. Trust me."

Strangely, in this instance, she did. So why couldn't she take charge of her body, respond to his reassurance, and pull away?

Because I like feeling his warm arms around me, like having his hard body molded against mine.

Those forbidden thoughts evoked a muted cry from deep within.

"Jessica, please, don't."

He sounded in as much agony as she was. That was what brought her eyes up. Having adjusted to the darkness, she could finally see his face. That was when she realized it was so near hers, another blast of his warm breath caressing her face.

In that moment, and for the second time, their breathing ceased, and his moist lips closed over hers in a hot, almost desperate kiss. As if anticipating the inevitable, her lips were wet and pliant, giving him license to do what he wanted.

He took full advantage.

His tongue flicked through the seam between her lips, and she moaned, locking her arms around his neck, as much for support as anything else. Heat spread through her body like wildfire, a totally new experience for her.

Porter had never brought on this kind of havoc or this kind of irresponsible response.

Jessica wanted to pull away, to stop this insanity, but she was powerless against the sweet-savage onslaught. A heavy weakness invaded her limbs, rendering her useless, while his teeth nibbled, then sucked, on her top lip before moving to the lower one.

With each bold move, he seemed to devour her, spreading that fire throughout her system, lust making her wet and aching.

As if he sensed this, he cupped her buttocks and pressed his extended flesh against her. Even through their clothes, she felt that impressive bulge as though they were naked.

She clung tighter, drunk on him, on what he was doing to her.

He groaned, then moved her hips in a circular motion. "Brant!"

It was her cry that brought him back to reality, that brutally ended the adhering of their lips and bodies. Cursing more than ever, Brant thrust her away from him. Then, without looking at her, he turned his back and strode down the hall.

Somehow Jessica managed the short walk back to her room. Once inside, she leaned against the closed door for support, drawing long breaths, shaking all over. That was when she realized with a sinking heart that their relationship had taken yet another turn.

Definitely in the wrong direction.

Fourteen

He should be sorry. Moreover, he should have told her he was sorry. Only thing was, he wasn't. At least not for kissing her, if you could call it that, he reminded himself. What had happened between them had been more than a mere meeting of the lips. For a moment he had practically feasted on her, eaten her up. Her lips had the taste and feel of honey, sweet and adhering.

Good Lord.

On second thought, feeling his erection still pressing against his zipper, he *was* sorry all right—sorry that he worked for her. The fact that his body ached from unfulfilled need was bad enough. But the most unpardonable of sins was crossing that professional line. Tonight was the first time he'd ever done anything so *un*professional in all his years as a Secret Service agent.

So why tonight, when his mind should have been focused one hundred percent on the job and not on the person who'd hired him? Brant crossed to the French doors, opened them and walked outside. The muggy air hit him in the face, but at least he could breathe.

With his thoughts running amuck, he'd felt claustrophobic. But then, he'd felt that way ever since he'd come back to civilization.

Brant let go of a harsh breath, thinking he probably wouldn't have to worry about his job come morning.

Most likely Mrs. Jessica Kincaid would fire his ass, and he didn't blame her. A humorless smile tugged at his lips. Hell, he'd never kissed a woman he didn't call by her first name.

Stranger things had happened, he was sure, but not to him. Brant's callused hands circled the railing. He maintained that firm grip until he felt his fingers go numb. Letting go, he merely propped his hip against the hard metal. He ought to go inside and try to get some sleep, but he knew the effort would be fruitless. So why bother?

Besides, he didn't require much sleep. At the height of his career, he'd learned to do without it and function just fine. It hadn't taken him long to get back into that mold. Some things, he guessed, never stopped being second nature.

Except his ability to do the job.

He questioned that now, especially in light of the stupid stunt he'd just pulled. Yet no matter how deep he dug into his conscience, he found no sign of repentance. Not good, Harding, he told himself savagely. He'd screwed up. And not to learn from that would be heading down a slippery slope indeed.

Although he didn't think this goon harassing her would turn out to be a serial killer, not by any stretch of the imagination, he still had to be reckoned with and treated as carefully as if he was one. With all the craziness in society these days, you never knew when someone you least expected would turn out to be deranged.

That was why everyone who came in contact with Jessica was suspect. And it was his job to find him or her or them.

Not to maul his own client.

"Hell," Brant muttered, wishing he smoked.

Thurmon would have his head on a platter. But then, his friend would probably never know. He doubted if Jessica would say anything to Veronica, either. Like him, she was probably having a hard time accepting what had happened between them. Besides, she was such a private person, rigid and cold.

That latter thought brought a bitter laugh to the surface.

Outside, maybe, but inside, she was hot and pliant.

And her smell. It was her own. She smelled like she'd been dipped in a tub of wild roses and her skin had soaked up the scent, more erotic and breath-catching than the most exotic of perfumes.

The instant she had bumped into him and he'd encircled her with his arms, he'd known he was in trouble. It was as if her entire body had gone on alert, especially her nipples. Right off, he'd felt them poke his chest. After that, his blood had heated and his control eroded.

And when her lips, so ready and willing, met him kiss for kiss, he'd ached to lift that flimsy thing she had on, haul her up around his waist and ram his hard penis high into her warmth.

Just thinking about that made him break out in a cold, needy sweat. Until now he'd managed to put sex and the thought of it on the back burner, and had been relatively content knowing that along with sex came responsibility and commitment.

He wasn't prepared for either.

Still, he was going to be hard-pressed to keep his hands off Jessica Kincaid. After having tasted of that forbidden fruit, he craved more, bigger and juicier bites.

Another bitter laugh erupted. Like he'd already figured, he expected his walking papers first thing in the

morning. If that happened, then it was for the best, since
he knew it was going to be damn near impossible to
ignore her as a woman.

But if she didn't send him packing, then he would
honor his word, tie a knot in his libido, strap a rein on
his hands and do the job he'd been hired to do.

That was the only way he could live with himself.
With that reassuring thought in mind, Brant trudged
back inside. Fully clothed, he flopped down on the bed
and stared at the ceiling.

Until the wee hours of the morning.

"Hi, Brant," Veronica said, giving him a brief hug.

"Hey, yourself." Brant half smiled. "You're looking
great, as always."

"You're full of it, but it's nice to hear."

Jessica felt his eyes rest on her briefly before he said
in his low, remote tone, "You two have a nice lunch.
I'll just do my thing."

"Will do," Veronica said, facing Jessica. "Come on,
our table's ready."

Wordlessly Jessica followed Veronica and the waiter,
who showed them to a corner table in the atrium room,
where greenery and flowers dominated the area, making
her feel as if she were dining in an open garden.

"What a neat place," Veronica said, her eyes flitting
from one thing to another. "How come we've never
been here before?"

"I think it's fairly new," Jessica replied. "But I've
heard a lot of good things about it, so I wanted to try
it."

"If the food's as good as the decor, we'll be in luck."

"We'll soon find out."

They took a few minutes to peruse the menus, then

gave their drink and salad orders to the waitress. Once they were alone, Jessica tried to force herself to relax, but it was hard. She was conscious of Brant's hovering presence, though when she glanced around, he was no-where to be seen. But she knew he was watching her every move along with everyone else's, which, given the latest circumstances, should have been reassuring.

It wasn't.

"Chill, friend." Veronica's gaze was piercing, though humor lurked there. "You look like you're about to jump out of your skin."

"Do I?" Jessica wasn't sure she could pull off her innocent act, but it was worth a try, anyway. She wasn't about to tell Veronica about her reckless behavior the night before, something that had been both shocking and exciting. Even now, she couldn't look at Brant without turning breathless and wondering what would have happened if he hadn't stopped.

Dear Lord, was she that emotionally starved?

"Yes, you do," Veronica was saying. "So don't pull that innocent crap on me."

Jessica smiled wryly. "Were you always such a bully?"

"Only when necessary."

"Uh, sorry, I guess my mind was on the latest." She hated lying, but under the circumstances, it was war-ranted.

Veronica frowned. "Latest what? Incident?"

"I received another threatening e-mail."

"Damn, just when we thought the pervert might've dropped off the face of the earth."

"I hadn't checked my home e-mail in days, but I knew it was stacking up." Jessica paused with a shrug.

"So I really had no choice. Besides, I'm trying not to let this psycho totally rule my life."

"I can imagine Brant's reaction."

Jessica shifted uncomfortably. "I haven't told him yet."

"And just why not?"

Jessica was saved from answering by the waitress delivering their salads.

"Butter for your bread?" Veronica asked, pushing the hot loaf and cup of butter toward her."

Jessica shook her head. "I'll pass."

"It wouldn't hurt you to put a little fat on those skinny bones, my friend." Ronnie grinned, helping herself to a healthy chunk of bread, then slathering it with butter. "Now me, I don't mind adding a little padding to the south end, nor does Thurmon. He just says there's more to love."

Jessica rolled her eyes. "You're a long way from being overweight."

"Compared to you, I'm a heavyweight."

"I'm just not that hungry. I'd rather have my salad than fill up on bread, though it does smell delicious."

"Mmm, it is."

Jessica lifted her glass filled with peach iced tea, to Ronnie. Their glasses clicked as they simultaneously said, "To friends."

Then they focused their attention on the food. For a while they munched in silence, though Jessica knew her reprieve was short-lived. Her friend was gunning for her and wouldn't mince any words, a trait she was guilty of, as well. Perhaps that was why they had remained such good friends. Neither was afraid to speak her mind.

"So why haven't you told Brant?" Veronica demanded bluntly once the waitress had cleared the table, leaving flavored coffee for dessert.

"I haven't had a chance," Jessica said, her tone hedging.

Ronnie's eyebrows rose. "What about this morning? You two do occupy the same house, right?"

"Sarcasm doesn't become you."

"Fudging the truth doesn't become *you*."

Jessica pressed her lips together, accepting the fact she was between a rock and a hard place. Getting out of it without divulging her secret would take some fast dancing.

"I'm waiting, and not very patiently, either," Veronica said.

"Look, I'm having a real problem adjusting to Brant taking care of me and my business."

"I can certainly understand that in light of your love of independence. Still, that doesn't excuse you. Brant should be privy to everything that goes on, especially when it comes to your problem, which is the reason he's here."

"You don't need to remind me of that."

Veronica threw up her hands in a dramatic way, regardless of any curious onlookers. "You're making absolutely no sense, and that's not like you. You, of all people, who's such a stickler for detail. And I think this is a very important detail."

Ronnie leaned her head back, narrowing her eyes. "Something's going on that you haven't told me. I can feel it deep in my bones. Yep, you're definitely hiding something."

Jessica forced herself not to take the bait. But it was hard, when she suddenly felt the urge to blurt out that

Brant had kissed her last night and that she had enjoyed every minute of it and hadn't wanted him to stop.

Her breath caught as she realized that she had actually admitted that seamy fact to herself. But she still couldn't tell Veronica. She didn't dare.

"You're just tapping into that overactive imagination of yours," Jessica said. "I'm still having trouble adjusting to this drastic change in my life. As you say, I've always been independent to a fault, something that never bothered Porter. Actually, he encouraged it."

"But you will show the e-mail to Brant?"

"Of course."

Veronica gave her another long stare, then shrugged. "You two haven't had words, have you?" she pressed. "From what I know of Brant, he's about as headstrong and obstinate as you."

"Definitely not a match made in heaven." *More like hell*, Jessica added silently, thoughts of last night reigniting her senses.

"Well, at least he doesn't turn you on."

"What?" Jessica gasped in an appalled tone.

"You heard me. I'd be hard-pressed not to jump his bones if I weren't happily married."

Jessica gave her an astonished look. "You're crazy."

"You're blind."

"You're pushing your luck, my friend. When would I have time for a relationship?"

"You'd have to make time, something you're not prepared to do. Don't worry. I know Brant's not your cup of tea. I was just teasing about him. I know how hard all this has been for you, and I'm really concerned first and foremost for your safety and second for your sanity."

Veronica paused and took a sip of her iced latte. "I

also know having someone shadow your every move has got to be horrible. Just think of how the First Family must feel. They're constantly living in a fishbowl.''

''And that's not for me. I have to have freedom to think and do as I please.''

''You will again soon, I promise.'' Veronica reached out and squeezed Jessica's hand. ''Brant will make this all go away, one way or the other. Thurmon keeps reassuring me he's the best at this kind of thing, though I've noticed a difference in him since he took those bullets.''

''Was it really bad?''

''Awful. He almost died. Any time you're gut-shot, you're in trouble.''

''Well, he seems to have bounced back.''

Veronica frowned. ''Not entirely. According to Thurmon, Brant's reflexes aren't as sharp as they used to be. The bullet in his leg is the reason for that. Yet all in all, he's still a crackerjack agent and shouldn't have been forced into retirement. He got a dirty deal.''

''I'm sorry about that. I'm also sorry about his problems with his son.''

Veronica sighed. ''That's another whole ball of wax. I could strangle Marsha.''

''His ex-wife?''

Veronica nodded in the affirmative. ''She's a selfish whiner, always has been and always will be. She's using Elliot to punish Brant for doing his job, a job he had when he married her.''

''Maybe they'll work it out.''

''He deserves better. One of these days, I hope he can put his bitterness behind him and learn to trust again. Then maybe he'll find a woman who appreciates him for who and what he is. Despite his aloof, brooding nature, he's a straight up kind of guy.''

Jessica barely heard the last accolade for dwelling on the idea of him finding another woman to love. Then it hit her what she was thinking. The very idea that she could be jealous of another woman in Brant's life was ludicrous.

Veronica suddenly interrupted her thoughts.

''Oops, I've got to run. I have a nail appointment in twenty minutes. If I'm late for that, I'll be late getting back to the office, too.''

''Me too. I'm swamped with work.''

They rose together; then Veronica reached out and gave her a brief hug. ''You will cooperate with Brant, won't you?''

''Yes, Ronnie, you know I will,'' Jessica said, holding on to her patience.

Veronica's features cleared, and she smiled broadly. ''Good girl.''

''I hope she pulls your nails out one by one.''

Veronica laughed out loud. ''You'll thank me one of these days for being an interfering broad.''

''That remains to be seen,'' Jessica responded, trying not to smile.

''Come on, let's get Brant.''

Jessica turned and saw that he was weaving his way toward them. Her stomach plunged to her knees when she realized anew how very dangerous this man was to her vulnerable heart.

Fifteen

He was nervous.

Brant felt perspiration pop out on his upper lip and forehead, an absurd reaction, considering the circumstances. He was having dinner with his own son. Why would he be sweating that?

Because the stakes were so high.

First off, he'd been damn lucky he was getting to see Elliot alone for any length of time. The opportunity had arisen when Veronica had invited Jessica for dinner this evening. Thurmon had said he would be around to keep an eye on Jessica.

Still, Brant didn't feel good about leaving her, especially after she'd shown him the e-mail she'd received the last evening.

I'm Still Around, Bitch.

After he'd read that, his blood pressure had shot up. Jessica had said very little. Nonetheless, he'd known how she had felt.

"Is this ever going to end?" she'd asked in a tight voice.

"Since the bastard's e-mails are from Internet cafés, libraries and no telling where else, they're hard to trace. Same goes for the cell calls. This guy's a tough nut to crack. And Thurmon's solely responsible for physically tracking him down, since I'm tied down.''

She must have heard the frustration in his voice, because she'd frowned. ''I've already told you, you don't have to be with me every second.''

''Yes, I do, unless you're with Thurmon and Veronica.''

She hadn't said another word, but that wasn't unusual. Since that heated kiss, she'd avoided speaking to or looking at him as much as possible. What a messy situation, and he blamed himself. He'd taken distinct advantage of her and needed his rear kicked. Thinking that crackpot had broken into her place again, she'd been frightened out of her wits. Fear had made her vulnerable and susceptible.

Susceptible to a lowlife like himself.

While Brant couldn't change what had happened, he could make damn sure he didn't step across that professional line again.

That was when she'd told him she was having dinner at the Nashes', then disappeared behind closed doors at her office. He'd immediately called Thurmon. During that conversation, he'd asked about the cops, Wells and Stokes.

''My men haven't reported anything out of the ordinary.''

''Have you gotten a file together on them yet?''

''Pretty much, and it's Dick Wells who's definitely the computer nerd.''

''So focus in on him.''

''Consider it done.''

''Also, run a check on Curtis Riley.''

''Riley? Surely you don't think—''

''Just take care of it, okay? I'll explain later.'' Of

course, he had no intention of explaining anything, because he couldn't. He just knew he didn't like the cocky sonofabitch, and he didn't trust him, either.

"You're the boss."

Brant snorted. "I wish."

"Don't worry, Jessie will be in good hands this evening."

"I'm not worried."

"The hell you aren't."

When Brant let that pass, Thurmon continued. "Spend the evening with Elliot and stop fretting like you're going through menopause."

"Good thing I'm not looking into your baby blues right now," Brant responded in a scathing tone.

Thurmon laughed.

"I've decided it's not easy being a dad."

"But you are. And there's no time like now for starting the rebuilding process," Thurmon said, the laughter no longer in evidence.

"I know, and believe me, I'm grateful."

"So good luck."

He would need more than luck, Brant had told himself later when he was getting ready to go pick up Elliot.

When he'd first called his son, the boy had been reluctant to commit. Finally, though, he'd said yes, but only after Brant had refused to take no for an answer.

For the better part of the afternoon, Brant had been rehearsing what he was going to say, but nothing he'd come up with sounded right, so he'd scrapped that idea. He would just have to go with his gut and hope he didn't screw things up more than they already were.

Now, as he waited for Elliot in the driveway of his home, he wiped the sweat off his brow. About that time his son appeared. What a good-looking kid, Brant thought again, pride swelling his chest.

He was smart, too. According to Marsha, however, his grades weren't as good as he was capable of. But then, what boy's his age were? Most of them were more interested in sniffing girls than information in books.

He couldn't say anything. He'd been guilty of the same thing, until he realized push had come to shove and if he wanted to amount to a hill of beans, he'd better start cracking the books. He had confidence Elliot would do the same.

By the time his son got in the car, Brant's heart was pounding with both excitement and trepidation. He wanted to reach out and hug him, but he quelled that urge, sensing right off that Elliot wouldn't take kindly to that.

Tread softly, he warned himself. It's been a long time.

"You're looking good, son," Brant said instead, trying to lighten his tone as well as the suddenly tension-filled atmosphere.

"Thanks," Elliot muttered, a sullen twist to his mouth.

Ignoring his son's terse reply, Brant went on. "So where do you want to eat? I have no idea what's in town."

Elliot shrugged his shoulders, football shoulders, like Brant's own. Yet he didn't even know if his son played that sport—or any other, for that matter. That truth pinched. Pinched hard.

"C'mon," Brant said, casting a quick glance at Elliot's profile. "I know you're bound to have a favorite."

Elliot shrugged again, then said, "Okay, let's go to

Little Joe's Mexican place. It's kind of a dump, though.''

Brant grinned, then shoved the car in Reverse. ''Sounds like my kind of place. Just tell me where it is.''

''Want me to drive?''

Brant didn't hesitate. Anything that would warm his son to him. ''Sure thing. Come on.''

A few minutes later, Elliot looked at him out of wide, slightly dazed eyes. ''Man, this mother handles great.''

Brant smiled, while secretly breathing a sigh of relief. If it took a 4-wheel-drive SUV to help clear the animosity between them, then so be it.

Twenty minutes later found them in a booth in a typical Mexican restaurant that wasn't quite a dump but close to it. However, it was spotlessly clean, Brant noticed, and probably had melt-in-your-mouth food.

''I'm hungry,'' Brant commented into the growing silence. ''How 'bout you?''

Elliot looked up from the menu. ''Uh, sorta.''

Now that they were out of the truck, Elliot's face had grown sullen again, and that wary look had returned to his eyes. Maybe they should have just ridden around and forgotten eating. Brant dreaded these long periods of almost hostile silence. Too, he hated having to dig every word out of his son. But if that was what it took to start the healing process, he would dig.

Almost immediately, they gave their orders to a gum-chewing waitress. Once she had shuffled off, Brant reached for his iced tea, all the while watching Elliot, groping for something to say that would trigger a positive response.

He knew better than to depend on Elliot to take the

conversational ball and run with it. That wasn't going to happen.

"So how are things?" Brant asked inanely.

Elliot frowned. "What do you care?"

Brant counted to ten. "I care a lot, and you know it."

"I don't think so."

"Look, if you want me to grovel and say I'm sorry for the past, then I'll do it."

Elliot's tan took on a flush, and his eyes turned fierce. "Hey, you cut out on us, remember?"

Not true. That's your mom's line of crap. "Maybe I did, but I'm back now, and I want to make things up to you."

"How?" Elliot asked, a sneer in his tone.

"By seeing you as often as possible and sharing your life."

"Why, just so you can leave again?" Elliot demanded in a petulant note.

The waitress brought their food, which forced Brant to swallow his comeback. Not a bad thing, considering he was holding on to both the truth and his patience by a mere thread.

They ate in silence, especially Elliot, who wolfed his food down like the growing teenager he was. Brant wasn't hungry, the strong, hot mix of the enchilada dinner suddenly turning his stomach. Or maybe it was his son's attitude that had nixed his appetite.

But hanging on to his patience at all costs was a necessary evil. He had to keep in mind that his son was still a kid, and an immature one at that, thanks to his mother's protective coddling. He had to accept that fact and work around it, whether he liked it or not.

He certainly hadn't stepped into this commitment

wearing rose-colored glasses. Nor had he expected a bed of roses. Going in, he'd known the score and the stakes. He'd just hoped that when they were together one-on-one the damage wouldn't be as bad as he'd thought. Unfortunately it was worse, much to his acute disappointment.

"I don't intend to leave again, son," Brant said at last, easing his plate away.

If Elliot picked up on the fact that his father had barely touched his dinner, he chose to ignore it. Probably just didn't care.

"Whatever."

"Are you involved in any kind of sports?"

"Football, though I'm not on the starting team."

"That's a goal you can work toward."

"Yeah, I guess."

Brant went another route. "There's never a time when I didn't think about you, Elliot, and wish we could be together."

"That's not what Mom says."

Brant swallowed his anger. "Let's leave your mom and her feelings out of this. She's happily married to another man, and I'm glad. I want you and me to be a family."

"I just don't understand why you had to go."

"Son—"

"Stop calling me that," Elliot said, his teeth clenched and his eyes sparking. "Preston's my dad."

Brant winced. "I'm glad you feel that way about him. But I'm your dad, too. No matter how you feel about me, that's not going to change. And I'm not going away again."

"Yeah, right."

"I mean it, Elliot."

"So have you moved here?" The jut of his chin and his tone were both belligerent.

Brant hesitated, momentarily feeling as if he'd just had the wind knocked out of him. "No, but you can come to Arkansas anytime. You'd love my cabin there. The hunting and fishing are great."

Elliot made a face. "Not interested."

Brant expelled a sigh. "That's fine. We could do whatever you wanted, then. You name it."

"Mom wouldn't let me go."

"Oh, I think she would."

"You don't know Mom. She hates you." Elliot's eyes were challenging.

Brant winced again. Damn Marsha for slandering him in front of Elliot, something he would never have done. And the crux of the matter? He was bitter, too, especially when she had booted him out.

If Elliot knew the truth, would it make a difference? He would never know, because he had no intention of telling him. The truth would just belittle his mother, even though Marsha had certainly had a hand in their disastrous marriage. Yet he wasn't about to fight old battles again. Anyway, he didn't give a damn about Marsha, except when it pertained to their son.

And she couldn't stop him from seeing the boy.

Only Elliot could do that, even though by law he had visitation rights. And he'd never missed one child support payment.

"What did I do wrong?"

It took Brant a moment to jerk his mind back to the present. But when he did and realized what Elliot had said, he felt like a knife had been plunged into his heart. There had been such deep pain in his son's tone.

Fighting the urge to grab Elliot and hold him close, Brant said in a low, firm tone, "Look at me."

When Elliot didn't respond, he added, hearing his own desperation, "Please."

Elliot complied, though Brant knew he wasn't happy.

"What happened between your mother and me was never your fault, never anything you did. If nothing else is settled this evening, you have to understand that. You have to *know* that." Brant paused, struggling to keep his head above imaginary water when he felt like he was drowning.

Elliot still didn't respond, though Brant sensed he was listening.

"I loved you then and I love you now. I'm just sorry I didn't tell you that sooner."

"So? Now you've told me."

Not the words Brant wanted to hear, but he had to face facts as they were and move on. He wasn't giving up.

"Can we do this again?" Brant asked, his desperation deepening.

"I dunno."

"I'll call, okay?"

"Suit yourself."

"Let's get out of here," Brant said, trying to cover his own pain.

Once Elliot had disappeared inside the house, he drove off, wondering why the car in front of him was blurry. That was when Brant realized his eyes were filled with tears.

Maybe he had a conscience after all.

Sixteen

"So how do you think we stand?"

Curtis Riley felt the color drain from his face.

"Not good, huh?" Adam Foley muttered, his thin upper lip drawn so tight it almost disappeared.

Anxiety took another chunk out of Curtis' gut. He hated admitting he had failed to accomplish what he'd promised, a fact that didn't bode well for all parties involved.

He and Adam, the plant guru, had agreed to meet for breakfast at a diner in the small town near the tract of land in question. They had just polished off a healthy meal of bacon, eggs, grits and biscuits. Now that mountain of food lay on Curtis' stomach, threatening to sour.

"Dammit, Riley, good, bad or bloody indifferent, you've got to tell me."

Curtis fingered the top of his coffee cup that was now empty, then looked up. "You guessed it. It's not good."

Adam let an expletive fly, then took a drink of his own coffee, only to curse again as he put the cup back in the saucer.

Even with a scowl on his face, Adam was a good-looking man. Medium height, with an abundance of curly brown hair except on the crown, where no hair existed at all. It was as though he'd cut a perfect circle out of the top of his head. Yet that small imperfection didn't detract from his self-confidence. He was young, cocky and hyper—a mover and shaker.

And his corporation wanted this land. Badly.

Almost as badly as Curtis wanted them to have it. Just the thought of making a deal with such a huge manufacturing company made him salivate at the benefit to his pocketbook. He would be on Easy Street for the rest of his life.

That was why he couldn't let Jessica Kincaid and her pigheadedness mess this up.

"Might as well spit out the bad news. All of it." Adam entered the silence with a clipped tone.

"The mayor's still hell-bent on annexing the land into the city."

"I thought you two were chummy enough that you could derail that?"

Curtis gritted his teeth. "I thought so, too."

"What happened?"

Curtis looked away, then back at his companion, whose features were now pinched in fury.

"Stop stalling, dammit."

Curtis swallowed hard, grappling for a way to appease Adam. He saw none. "Apparently I read her wrong," he admitted truthfully.

"Then change her mind."

Curtis laughed. "You don't know this lady. On the outside, she's as lovely as anyone you'd ever want to look at, and ultrafeminine, too. But underneath, she's tougher than nails, a lot tougher than her deceased husband."

"What you're telling me is that you can't get into her panties."

Curtis flushed, though more with anger than embarrassment, disliking Adam's crude sarcasm. "Not at the moment."

"Then you'll just have to come up with another plan to make her see reason."

Adam made it sound so simple, but he didn't know Jessica. "I'm working on it."

"Any ideas?" Adam pressed, picking up his spoon and clicking the side of his cup.

The sound grated on Curtis' nerves, adding to his agitation, if that were possible. At the moment he felt so frustrated, he wanted to toss the whole thing. He squelched that ridiculous notion. He'd gone too far to chuck it now. Besides, Adam would ruin him financially and any other way he could.

The bigwigs Adam worked for didn't take too kindly to being thwarted. And they wanted that tract of land— and not in the city, either. He had promised they would have it. Now he was in jeopardy of having that promise crammed back down his throat. Suddenly Curtis almost strangled on his own fury.

Damn Jessica and her tough stance.

"I asked if you had any ideas."

Adam's tone had turned a bit nasty. Curtis figured he'd best do some fast tap dancing if he even wanted to survive this meeting. "Yes. I already have something in place."

"Care to share that something?"

Curtis shrugged, as if his piss factor were at its lowest level. "Not at this point. However, I feel confident about my endeavors."

Adam leaned forward, his eyes becoming beady. "What about your partner? What does he have to say about all this?"

"He's letting me take care of it."

"Maybe I ought to talk to him."

Curtis stiffened. "That's not necessary. Hell, don't you think I want this deal to happen as much as you do?"

"Then get results. My company's tired of mollycoddling that woman."

"So am I."

"Then do something about it and do it soon, before she gets the majority of the council on her side."

"Right now the council's split, thanks to my behind-the-scene dealings."

"Split won't cut it."

"I know," Curtis said, losing his patience. "I told you, I have a plan in place."

"Are you sure you don't need help from your partner?" Adam demanded as though determined not to let that ride.

"No, I told you I was handling this."

His partner was his elderly uncle, for whom he was responsible, an uncle whose mind was not what it used to be. Uncle Selman, in his condition, was useless. The fact he was in that shape made closing this deal all the more important.

When his uncle died, other nephews were bound to jump in and try to tie up Selman's will, which in turn would tie up the property. Curtis wasn't about to let that happen. Right now, he had the old man's permission and the power of attorney to sell the land.

"Maybe I ought to have a go at the mayor." Adam lifted a renegade eyebrow. "Would that bother you?"

"Not in the way you mean. It's just that I don't think it would do any good." Curtis refrained from giving his reason, but it was simple. If Adam Foley came on to

Jessica like gangbusters, she would only dig her heels in deeper.

His uncle always told him you could accomplish more with honey than with vinegar. With Jessica, that was definitely the case. Too, he sensed Jessica wasn't interested in developing a personal relationship with anyone, so Adam's "charm" would be wasted.

"Well, then handle it—and soon, too," Adam said into the silence. "Otherwise we'll be forced to look elsewhere for a site for our manufacturing park. The company's ready to make a move, and if you can't swing a deal, then we'll find someone who can." He paused. "Do I make myself clear?"

"Absolutely," Curtis said tersely, shifting uncomfortably, feeling as though his balls were in a nut grinder.

Adam stood. "Just keep in mind that my patience is wearing thin."

"You've also made that clear."

"I guess we're on the same page, then."

Adam turned and walked out, leaving Curtis behind with the check and his seething anger.

Jessica Kincaid might not know it yet, but she'd met her match. The sooner she found that out for real, the better off she would be.

"I don't know where you got that, but it was damn good."

Jessica gave him a lame smile. "I'm glad you enjoyed it."

"Was this another of your culinary endeavors?"

Brant's baiting, if that was his intention, fell on deaf ears. Her forced smile gathered strength as she said with fake sweetness, "Yes, it is."

A twinkle appeared in his eyes, like he knew he'd ticked her off. ''Well, it tasted damn good, and I was damn hungry.'' Having said that, he pushed his plate aside and reached for his glass of iced tea.

The fact that he was hungry was an understatement, Jessica thought, as he'd consumed two chicken salad sandwiches, along with a generous helping of coleslaw.

Since it had been such a long day, she'd had no intention of inviting him to share her evening meal, certain he wouldn't want to, anyway. However, after she had changed into something more comfortable and wandered into the kitchen, guilt had worked on her until she'd made the offer. Once she'd asked, she had crossed her fingers he wouldn't accept. Much to her chagrin, he had. Quickly, too.

And like the last meal they had shared, tension had been thicker than the humidity outside. Several times Jessica had felt his gaze leveled on her, bringing unwanted heat to her face.

She knew his mind was on the same thing hers was—that kiss—especially when she'd felt his eyes linger too long on her lips before moving to her breasts, where her nipples poked against the material of her lounging outfit. But then, just being in the same room with him brought on that reaction.

Insane.

Insane or not, he affected her like that, and she no longer bothered to deny it, at least to herself. Still, this desperate hunger, this overpowering need for something she'd never desired before, frightened her.

And she was no closer to understanding why than she had been in the beginning.

He appeared tired, the lines in his face more pronounced than usual. And he needed another shave, which made him look more uncivilized and menacing than usual.

He had changed into a pair of faded jeans and a T-shirt. She wondered if he had anything on under those jeans. God, she couldn't keep this up. Jessica bit down on her lower lip, then shifted her gaze. He must never know what was going through her mind.

"Have you received any more e-mails?"

His thick-edged voice jolted her mind back into focus. She looked at him with what she hoped was a bland face. "Not today, though I haven't checked yet."

"Let me know."

"You'll be the second." She paused. "Have you made any progress?"

He sighed. "I'm still waiting on Thurmon."

"I know he's not dragging his heels, but…" Jessica's voice faded as she was careful not to sound critical of her best friend's husband.

"He isn't, though it does appear that way. But gathering information on people is not as easy as it sounds, even with computers." Brant stood abruptly and began gathering their dishes.

"I'll take care of that."

"No, you won't," he said. Then, as if he realized his tone was heavy-handed, he added, "Clearing the dishes is the least I can do."

"I'd really rather do it myself." If you don't mind, she almost added, then thought better of it. She didn't care if he minded or not. The reality of him taking over her kitchen was not something she was prepared to tolerate.

Couldn't tolerate, for her own protection.

"Fine," he said, his tone growing more harsh.

After setting the dishes on the counter, he reached for

the pitcher of tea and refilled his glass. When he would have poured her some more, she placed her hand over the top of her glass. "Enough for me. I probably won't sleep as it is."

He replaced the pitcher, then sat back down. Jessica had thought her rejection of his help would have sent him to his room like a kid who had been scolded by his parents. Well, he was no kid, and apparently her scolding had rolled off him like water off a metal roof.

"Have you heard any more from Riley?"

His question took her aback. "What makes you ask that?"

Brant didn't hesitate. "He's a man with a mission. And you two do have a relationship."

That last statement fired her temper. "We don't have a 'relationship,' as you put it."

"So he's not going to get his way."

"No, not if I have mine, that is."

"It'll be interesting to see if his threat escalates as a result of your unmovable position."

"You'll never convince me Curtis is behind this menace."

"I guess it's a good thing I'm around to be objective."

"Guess it is," she retorted.

A stiff silence ensued while Brant took a drink of his tea. The mundane gesture brought her eyes to his long, tapered fingers, which had just the right amount of hairs sprinkled on them. She wondered what they would feel like on a woman's bare flesh.

On *her* flesh.

Jessica's heart plummeted to somewhere around her toes, and it was all she could do not to get up and rush out of the room. She was thinking like some streetwalker.

She didn't need sex.

She didn't *want* sex.

She didn't want anything from this man, not even his protection.

"Let's go back to your husband," Brant said, once again pulling her attention back to him.

"What about Porter?" she asked in a resigned voice.

"Did your husband have any enemies?"

"None that I'm aware of. So you can forget about going down that path."

Brant shrugged. "You never know till you ask."

"My husband was loved by everyone in this city," she said, feeling on the defensive. She wouldn't let him attack Porter or demean him in any way.

"Lucky man."

She tensed. "How are things with your son?" Now why on earth had she asked that? Maybe it was because he was grilling her and he deserved some of his own medicine. "Look, forget I asked that." Her tone was unsteady.

"Because you don't care?" His unreadable eyes were pinning her.

She released a slow breath. "Because it's none of my business."

"I'm not making much headway," he volunteered, as though her last statement hadn't penetrated.

Jessica knew better. Nothing escaped this man. He seemed all knowing and all seeing.

"I'm sorry," she said, for lack of anything better to say.

"Yeah, me too."

"Maybe things will change."

He grimaced. "They have to." He didn't say anything else for a moment, then went on, "In some ways, you're fortunate not to have kids."

"That was my choice."

"They sure know how to step on your heart."

"And your pocketbook."

"You sound like you know about that from experience."

"I've dealt with my husband's son. Money's all he thinks about."

"I guess you're lucky he doesn't come around."

She picked up on the despondency in his tone and for a second was tempted to reach out and touch him, to try to comfort him. As if he sensed that, he caught her eyes.

Heat leaped between them.

Brant cleared his throat, then said in a thick voice, "About the other night—"

Suddenly the doorbell chimed. Both seemed to freeze.

A frown formed a vee between Brant's brows. "Expecting company?" he asked harshly, obviously unhappy at the interruption.

Jessica felt the panic that had flared inside her immediately subside. The other night's episode wasn't something she wanted to discuss with him, especially not now, not when she was feeling so vulnerable. "No," she said tersely.

"Let me get it."

"No," she said again.

Brant's features darkened. "Don't forget to ask who it is before you open the door."

"That goes without saying," she said in a cutting tone. "Give me credit for having *some* sense."

"It's not you I worry about, Mrs. Kincaid."

Feeling sufficiently chastised, Jessica got up, skirted past him and made her way to the front door. After peering though the spy hole, she breathed easier, then opened the door.

Big mistake. Roy stumbled past her, his eyes glazed. He was either drunk or high.

"Who the hell are you?" he demanded, almost diving headlong into Brant, who was blocking the way into the living room.

"I might ask you the same thing," he responded in a calm but deadly tone, his eyes swinging to Jessica.

"It's Roy, my stepson."

Brant's features turned to stone.

Seventeen

"What do you want, Roy?" Jessica asked, the door still open.

Roy, looking like hell, blinked his eyes between Brant and her. "I want to talk to you," he slurred, trying to steady his gaze on her.

"Since you're obviously not in any condition to talk, I suggest we make it another time."

"I second that suggestion," Brant put in, holding staunch to his position, his arms folded across his chest.

Jessica gritted her teeth as she flung Brant a look. The last thing she wanted was a confrontation between the two men. But if Roy didn't leave, that was exactly what would happen. She realized her stepson wasn't drunk but high on drugs. Dangerously high, she suspected.

In this condition, he didn't even resemble himself. He had lost more weight than he could spare, making him appear ill. His color wasn't good, either. His skin was pasty, and his eyes—well, besides being glazed to the point of bugging out, they were red with dark circles under them.

He was a wreck. Such a shame, too. When he was himself, Roy was a nice-looking young man, tall, with jade-green eyes and dark blond hair. His only drawback was that his full lower lip often protruded, reminding her of a petulant child. Also, his manner in general left something to be desired. If he didn't get his way, he could be abrupt and surly.

Though Porter had been tough when necessary, Jessica had always thought he let his son run roughshod over him. But she'd kept that thought hidden and her mouth shut. As long as Roy didn't interfere in her and Porter's business, she hadn't cared.

With Porter gone, Roy had targeted her for his greediness, then tried to use her for a whipping boy when she didn't dance to his tune.

Jessica clung to the knob, then finally shut the door after Roy showed no signs of leaving on his own. She just hoped Brant wouldn't say anything else, adding more gasoline to an already raging fire. Still, she realized her stepson couldn't stay, especially if he held on to that nasty attitude.

Roy suddenly switched his scrutiny back to Brant. "Get lost."

Jessica's breath caught, robbing her of an instant comeback. She didn't have to worry. Brant didn't need any help from her. He was perfectly willing to take on the likes of Roy.

"Say what you have to say, then leave," Brant told him in a firm but easy tone.

Jessica wasn't fooled. Nothing about Brant was easy. He was on high alert himself, ready to pounce like an angry panther at a moment's notice. But not on her stepson, for god's sake. Surely it wouldn't come to that.

No wonder he had made an excellent Secret Service agent, Jessica told herself. He didn't miss a thing. His eyes moved at all times, even though his body remained still as a piece of stone.

Jessica shuddered inwardly, fearing the situation was

about to get worse, if the snarl on Roy's face was any indication. Under the influence of drugs, he was apparently feeling his oats, thinking he could say and do anything he pleased.

"I don't know who you are," Roy said in a sneering tone, while his gaze, filled with disdain, traveled up and down Brant's lean frame. "But I bet I can guess." He snickered. "Her lover, right?"

Jessica dared not look at Brant, though she felt color invade her face. "Roy, please—"

He went on as though she hadn't spoken, his bleary eyes holding fast on Brant. "I want to speak to my stepmother alone. So get lost."

Jessica turned to Brant. "Maybe it *would* be better if I talked to him alone."

"I'm not going anywhere."

Brant hadn't raised his voice or moved an unnecessary muscle.

Jessica opened her mouth, only to close it. Now was not the time to argue with him. That would also aggravate the already highly charged atmosphere, something she couldn't afford to do.

Refocusing her attention on Roy, she said, "I'm listening."

"Got anything to drink?"

Great. Just great. Jessica's gaze rested on Brant for just a second. He wasn't looking at her, however. His eyes were narrowed on Roy, as if just waiting for him to make one wrong move. Just one.

"No, I don't," Jessica finally said, forcing her attention back on her stepson.

Roy laughed, an unnatural laugh that sent chills feathering down her spine. "You're lying. My old man always had booze on hand. I betcha it's still here."

"You've had enough of whatever it is you're drinking or using." This time Jessica's tone brooked no argument.

Roy laughed again, cocking his head toward Brant. "Wonder what dear old Dad would say about lover boy here. Wonder if he'd approve of you having such a stud in your bed after his shriveled up old body."

Jessica gasped, feeling a new invasion of color flood her face, wanting suddenly to throttle Roy or stuff a sock in his mouth, anything to shut him up. "Enough," she snapped, her eyes sparking. "You're in no condition to be here." She continued to keep her eyes off Brant. "You need to go home and sleep this off before you get into real trouble."

"Ah, don't sweat it, Mama dear, I'm gonna be just fine." Roy's slurred words were as insulting as his tone. "Why, I'm feeling finer than I've ever felt, except for one thing."

"And what is that?" Jessica demanded tersely. She knew, but she also knew if he didn't have his say, he would never leave on his own.

"Money. I'm broke, but then, you knew that."

Jessica curled her hands together and squeezed. "It's not time for your monthly—"

"Allowance," Roy broke in with a harsh sneer. "Was that what you were about to say?"

"If that's the way you choose to phrase it, then so be it."

Roy bared his teeth. "Listen here, you bitch, I want some more money, and I want it now."

"If keeping those teeth is a top priority, then I suggest you watch your mouth."

Oh, dear, Jessica thought, her heart upping its beat. Brant's voice was no longer easy but cold and hard. He had also moved nearer to her, his closeness enveloping her with a feeling of safety and well being.

Only not for long. As soon as Roy was gone, that closeness would overwhelm her, make her heart beat out of sync and that funny feeling invade her stomach. Make her crazy with a longing she didn't want to feel.

Now, though, she was glad to have him there, fearing her stepson for the first time ever, which was not a good feeling.

"And I suggest you go to hell," Roy slurred, blinking several times at Brant.

"I'm not going to give you any more money, Roy," Jessica said quietly.

Roy's face contorted and his voice shook. "You...you have to. I can't wait until the first of the month."

"You have no choice." Though her heart was breaking for him and the state he was in, she had to use tough love. If she gave in now, she would only enhance his problem. Without money, he couldn't buy more drugs. Unless he used more drastic measures. She shut that thought down, not even wanting to contemplate it.

"For chrissake, Jessica, don't you have a heart?"

"Yes, that's why I'm not indulging you or your habit."

"Sell the boat. That way you won't have to dip into the trust. You hate the damn thing, anyway."

She felt Brant's questioning eyes on her. She ignored him and went on. "That's not the answer, Roy." She paused and drew a shuddering breath. "If you want to talk about treatment, that's a different matter. I'd gladly sell the boat and whatever else it would take to cure you."

He laughed again, that ugly, unnatural laugh she'd

come to abhor. "Treatment. That's crazy. I've just been to a party, having fun. But that's something you wouldn't know anything about—having fun, that is."

"Go home, Roy, and sleep it off," Jessica said wearily, sensing Brant's growing impatience for this whole sick scenario. Roy was beyond reasoning with; she was merely wasting her time and her breath.

"Not until you give me some money, you bitch." He leaned toward Jessica.

That was when Brant moved behind Roy, grabbed him by the collar and literally lifted him off the floor.

"Get your hands off me, you bastard!" the younger man yelped, kicking his legs and struggling like a crazy man.

All for naught. Brant might as well have grabbed a pussycat by the neck for all the effort it took to hold Roy. Though she had suspected Brant was strong, she'd had no idea he was capable of lifting a grown man and immobilizing him in such a manner.

Would this man never cease to amaze her?

Wordlessly Brant opened the door, shoved Roy out, then slammed it shut. "I should've done that from the get-go."

Trembling, Jessica wrapped her arms around herself. "I know I should thank you, but somehow..."

He held up his hand, his deep-set eyes appraising her with disturbing intensity. "It's okay. You're upset, which is understandable. But there's nothing else you can do for Roy, at least not tonight. You might as well try to get some sleep."

With a sob in her throat, Jessica nodded, turned, then made her way to her room, knowing his eyes were tracking her every step.

* * *

The night air was suffocating; the humidity caused her gown and matching robe to stick to her skin. Yet she was loath to go back inside. She couldn't stand the confines of her room. Despite the busy day ahead of her tomorrow, she hadn't even tried to sleep, knowing the effort would be futile.

She couldn't shut her mind down. She felt as if she was on one of those dizzying rides at the fair that continuously went in circles. Even her stomach heaved. Although she took a deep breath, Jessica failed to pull any air through her lungs. None existed. It was one of those cloyingly steamy Texas nights movie moguls tried to depict in movies but rarely could.

A night for lovers.

A night to be naked.

A night for forbidden passion.

With those scorching thoughts came the image of Brant, standing naked in front of her, his shaft hot and extended.

Waiting.

For her.

Touch me, please, came his silent plea.

Jessica's knees buckled, and if it hadn't been for the railing, she would have crumpled to the cement. Oh, dear Lord, she cried inwardly, where had such thoughts come from? They had never haunted her until...

Brant.

He was to blame. But why him? Why this particular man? Why not countless other men who had tried to worm their way into her life and into her pants? With them, she'd never even been tempted.

Jessica clung to the railing, unable to ignore the wetness that pooled between her thighs. She knew it wasn't from the temperature but rather from her erotic and vivid picture of touching him *there,* then him leading her to the bed, where he thrust himself inside her, making her come over and over.

To her shame, she didn't even know if she'd ever had an orgasm.

Or maybe that was what she was experiencing now, this knee-buckling sensation that was reducing her limbs to putty and making her breathing come in short spurts.

Suddenly Jessica forced her wobbly legs to move back inside. The blast of the air-conditioning hit her in the face like a splash of cold water. It didn't help. She couldn't remain there. She had to get out, away from the room, away from the bed, away from the computer.

Away from herself.

Fleeing, she made her way to the kitchen. There she poured glass of milk, then warmed it, hoping something in her stomach would calm her. With glass in hand, she strode into the living room, only to pull up short, so short the milk splashed on her robe, leaving a wet spot at the side of one breast.

She gasped.

At that moment Brant uncoiled his frame and stood. Their eyes locked instantly.

Out of the frying pan, into the fire, Jessica thought inanely, reaching for anything that even resembled sanity as she'd once known it.

"Sorry," Brant muttered, his gaze unabashedly targeting the wet spot on her robe and lingering.

As she felt her pulse take an unwanted leap of excitement, Jessica's hand automatically went to her throat, and she stared at him out of apprehensive eyes.

After several beats of shocked silence, he made another apology. "Didn't mean to frighten you."

"Well, you did."

"Are you okay?"

"No," she replied in a small voice.

"Are you still upset over Roy, or did you get another e-mail?" His tone had hardened.

She shook her head no, finding speech difficult. *At least he had all his clothes on.* Hysteria was close to bubbling up the back of her throat.

"Jessica?"

"It's...Roy," she finally got out. *And you.* Terrified he might read her thoughts, she lowered her head.

"I should've known," he added on a harsh note.

"I've never seen him like that."

Another silence, awkward and heavy, fell between them.

"Look," Brant said, his voice taking on an even harsher edge. "I know I'm the last person you want to talk to right now, so I'll get out of your way and let you drink your milk in peace."

She couldn't figure out if his mouth was curved in a smile or a smirk. No matter. She sat down, her eyes tracking him to the door. "Don't go." Although she knew she'd spoken those words, she didn't know where they had come from. Perhaps from the depths of her soul. But she didn't want to retract them. She slowly released her breath. "Please." That last word was barely audible.

Fool, have you no shame?

Brant paused midstride and swung around, his shuttered expression effectively masking whatever thoughts might be churning in his head.

"Are you sure?" he asked in a low, raspy voice.

"I'm sure."

He walked to the closest chair across from her and

sat down, once again pinning her with that disturbing gaze. "You look like you've had it."

Jessica worried with her lower lip. "I'm worried about Roy."

"He's in way over his head."

"Cocaine, right?"

"Hooked."

Jessica shook her head. "That's something I never expected out of him. I'm glad Porter's not here to witness this."

"I'm sure you are," he said in a noncommittal voice.

"I hope you never have to face this situation with your son."

Brant leaned his head to one side and didn't speak for a moment. "Me too. But you never know."

"I have no idea what to do about Roy, how to handle him."

"Like you said, he needs help, but he isn't about to get it."

"There's got to be something I can do," Jessica said on a plaintive note. "I just can't sit back and watch him destroy himself and his life."

"Yes, you can."

Her eyes widened. "How can you say that?"

"He's a grown man, Jessica."

The use of her given name was like a shot of added adrenaline through her system. Somehow it put them on another level, a more intimate one. As if he noticed, too, he swore under his breath, then shifted his gaze.

"There just has to be a solution," she said, purposely switching her thoughts.

"There is. Face the fact that your stepson has a problem, a problem that only he can solve." Brant paused, as if for effect, then continued. "You also have to know he's a walking time bomb."

"Meaning?"

"Meaning he's not only a threat to himself but to you, as well." As if he sensed her chaotic feelings and her growing dilemma, he suddenly relaxed his stiff guard and softened his voice. "I have no choice but to add him to the suspect list."

Jessica's initial response was to deny that, to make him understand that no way would Roy actually harm her, despite his abusive manner. Yet the words wouldn't come, her instinct telling her she couldn't discount what Brant had said, that it had merit.

"God, what a mess," she said in a forlorn voice.

He didn't respond, though his eyes meshed with hers again. Fear of another kind followed in the wake of a heartbeat. No longer could she deny the heightened sexual tension that crackled between them.

That kiss, in the dark.

That was what this awareness was all about. The heat behind his eyes told her as much, making her feel hot and breathless. And alarmed. It would be so easy to give in to those flaring emotions, to fling herself into his arms.

One wrong move on her part or his and she would do just that.

Then what?

"We can't keep ignoring it."

Her heart turned over. "Ignoring what?"

His expression told her he didn't buy her innocent act, but he didn't call her hand. "That kiss."

Kisses. She wanted to correct him but didn't.

"It's forever there. We have to deal with it."

"I don't think that's a good idea."

"Well, I do," he said flatly.

Jessica swallowed hard, then waited.

"I was out of line. What's your excuse?" Brant let go of an expletive. "That also was out of line. I took advantage of both you and the situation that night."

Her gaze drifted before returning to his tight features. "Only because I let you," she whispered.

His features twisted. "The gentlemanly thing would be to say I'm sorry."

"Only you're not." That statement was barely audible.

"I'm sorry, all right. But not sorry I kissed you."

Jessica was clutching the arms of the chair for imaginary support as she felt an unsteady tremor in her knees.

"Which gives you every right to boot my ass," he added bitterly.

"Suppose we just forget it?"

His eyes nailed her. "Can you?"

"Yes," she lied.

"Then so can I."

Another silence fell between them, a mocking silence, Jessica thought, hysteria once again close to the surface.

Brant abruptly cleared his throat at the same time as he rose to his feet. "I'm going to bed." He peered down at her, his eyes dark and hungry. "I'll see you in the morning."

She drew a trembling breath and peered up at him.

"Don't," he rasped, "or I won't walk out of here."

She shifted tear-filled eyes, though it took every ounce of strength she had. Yet when he walked out, she nursed an empty sense of abandonment.

And hated herself.

Eighteen

Thurmon tugged on his mustache as he closely eyed Brant. "What's with you?"

Brant pretended ignorance. "I don't know what you're talking about."

"Bull." Thurmon's eyes darted to the right and then to the left, as though making sure no one was paying attention to them. Then, leaning nearer Brant, he added, "Bullshit."

Brant grinned.

He and Thurmon were in Tony's office, which was within seeing distance of Jessica's, though she was behind closed doors in a meeting. Thurmon had called and said they needed to meet, a meeting that was long overdue to Brant's way of thinking.

He was eager to get something going, anything that would move things along. He felt like nothing was getting done, that the search for the pervert was moving at a snail's pace.

Having to depend on someone else to gather information was the pits, even if it was his friend and former cohort, who was as sharp and capable as he was himself. Still, there was a difference. He would much rather have been out in the field than stuck inside.

Maybe if he'd been stuck with someone other than Jessica, then...

"You'd like to kick my ass, wouldn't you?"

Thurmon's blunt question took Brant aback for a second. Then he grinned again, briefly. "Now that you mention it, yeah, I would."

"I know you hate being cooped up, that it's making you crazy." Thurmon's eyes drilled him from below bushy brows. "Yet I sense there's more to your agitation than that."

Brant sipped his coffee, trying to sort through his thoughts. He had no intention of telling Thurmon about the knife edge he was walking when it came to Jessica, how he'd already breached the unwritten code of conduct.

Thurmon wouldn't be shocked. The hell he wouldn't, Brant corrected mentally. He wouldn't be at all happy with that lapse in judgment. Frankly Brant wasn't, either. Furthermore, he was at a loss as to how to handle the increasingly volatile situation.

"I know things still aren't right between you and Elliot."

Thurmon was fishing, which was okay. Brant knew his friend took full responsibility for him being there, in a situation he loathed. Maybe it wouldn't be much longer until they were all out of their misery.

Yet he still couldn't leave, Brant reminded himself, not until his relationship with Elliot took a turn for the better. He blew out a harsh breath.

"Before we get down to the nitty gritty on Jessie, what's the latest you've heard from Elliot?" Thurmon pushed.

"I haven't heard from him at all. Not since dinner."

"That's partly why you're out of sorts."

"I just thought it would be so much easier."

170 Mary Lynn Baxter

"No, you didn't. You knew you had your work cut out for you."

Brant rubbed his neck. "He blames himself for the divorce. Go figure that."

"From what little I know about kids, that's pretty normal."

"I guess so, though I wasn't expecting it." Brant didn't bother to mask the bleak despair that was gnawing at him. "If you could've seen the look on that kid's face and heard the pain in his voice..."

"Knocked your dick in the dirt, I would imagine," Thurmon said in a deep, sympathetic tone.

"I tried to explain without going into any sordid details." Brant's face turned grim. "But hell, what do you say to a kid who thinks his mother walks on water?"

"Man, that's a tough one. I couldn't begin to advise you there."

"Ah, it'll all work out," Brant said in a frustrated tone. "It just has to. I'll never forgive myself if it doesn't." He paused. "I just should've been there more."

"Hell, man, you were making a living."

"Still, if I had known how unhappy Marsha was, I—"

"What would you have done?" Thurmon interrupted, disgust coloring his voice. "She was always unhappy, or at least that's the way I read her. And she made you damned unhappy right along with her."

"Marriage made in heaven," Brant quipped sarcastically.

"In hell's more like it."

"Enough about me," Brant said caustically. He peered at his watch. "I suspect Jessica will be out of her meeting shortly."

Thurmon's lips twitched. "Jessica, huh?"

"Go to hell."

Thurmon pitched his head back and laughed. "Ah, so you two *are* getting along, after all."

"Not worth a shit, actually," Brant muttered darkly.

Thurmon's laughter died. "Want to explain?"

"She wishes I would go away. It's as simple as that."

"And you feel the same way."

"Yeah, I do."

"I was hoping—" Thurmon broke off, then flung his body back in the chair. "Hell, you don't want to know what I'm thinking."

In spite of himself, Brant smiled. "Probably not."

"Just stop beating up on yourself, okay?"

"Good advice, and I suggest you do the same."

"Then you're not deserting?"

Brant picked up on the still-anxious note in Thurmon's voice and forced himself to reassure his friend. "No, I'm not deserting anyone. But I can't promise she won't boot me out."

"Dammit, Brant, you haven't gone and done anything stupid, have you?" Thurmon's eyes were fierce. "Something you're hell-bent on hiding?"

When Brant dwelled on the evening he'd kicked her stepson out the door, his insides knotted. It had been that damp spot on her breast that had done it, that had shot his temperature up and caused an instant erection.

He had ached to put his lips against that spot. Who was he kidding? With little prompting, he would have jerked her into his arms, eased her down on the floor or table—hell, it didn't matter—and buried himself in her, then ridden her hard.

Brant shifted in the chair, hoping to ease the sudden discomfort between his legs.

"Did you hear what I said?"

Brant cleared his throat. "Uh, yes. And the answer is no, I didn't do anything you need to know about. So you can get your shorts out of a wad. I'll get the job done, and so will she. Speaking of job, anything new on those cops?"

Thurmon seemed to immediately relax. "They're both in debt up to their eyeballs, which makes a man desperate."

"And desperate men take desperate measures." Brant shoved back his chair and crossed one long leg over the other. "Are they tailing Jessica?"

"Not that we know of. Actually they've been sticking pretty close to home. Except for a couple of times."

"Oh?" Brant leaned forward.

"They've met with the assistant chief. According to our source, Gaston Forrester will get the nod from the council as the new chief. Has Jessica said anything to you about that?"

"No, but you can bet I'll say something to her," Brant said. "Especially since it appears they're plotting against her."

Thurmon massaged his chin before moving to his mustache. "She might not know what Forrester's up to."

"If not, then she should."

"I'm assuming the e-mails and phone calls are still coming?"

"But erratically, which I find strange," Brant said in a thoughtful tone. "It's almost like the sicko gets side-tracked or something."

"Well, as long as the bastard doesn't get back in the house."

"He'll have to walk over me," Brant said with deadly coldness.

"That's why you're there."

"What about Riley?" Just saying his name irritated Brant. Even if the man wasn't guilty of anything, he would like to smash his face.

Thurmon raised his eyebrows. "You don't like him, do you?"

"Nope."

"Me either. Never did. And so far, he appears as clean as a sterilized needle."

"I still want him watched," Brant said, his eyes hard. "Also, add her stepson to the list."

"Roy? When did he get to be a problem?"

"Since he got on drugs."

"I'll be a sonofabitch."

Brant told him about the episode at the house.

When he finished, Thurmon shook his head. "You're right. He *does* bear watching."

"Jessica's a bit vulnerable where he's concerned, and that worries me." Brant frowned. "If he doesn't get some help or some money soon, Roy-boy's going to topple over the edge."

"That's why you're there, good buddy, to see that he doesn't take Jessie with him."

"On the other hand," Brant said in a faraway tone, "we may not be on the right track at all. It could just be some off-the-street pervert with an ax to grind who strikes out of the blue at random."

Thurmon looked at his watch, then got to his feet. "I don't think so, and neither do you. But I'll be in touch, and you do the same. I've got to get back to the office before no telling what happens."

Brant stood, as well.

"Keep in mind that any time you need to see Elliot, I'll cover for you."

"Thanks. I'd love to be able to take you up on that offer."

"Hope you do. Later, then."

Brant nodded, and after Thurmon was gone, he turned toward Jessica's office. The door was still closed. He drew in a slow breath, then let it out, his mind spinning.

Jessica was worn-out.

The ladies from the beautification committee never seemed to know when enough was enough. If Tony didn't stop scheduling her meetings one on top of the other, she was going to strangle him. However, she knew he was doing the best he could. There was so much to get done and not enough hours in the day.

The budget was top priority. She had been working on it herself, but remained hopeful for the retreat. Getting the staff's input was of paramount importance to her. Money. That was the holdup. The council had to approve funding for such an endeavor, even though it was just for one day.

Now, however, Jessica had regrouped, switched her thoughts in a totally different direction. Her elderly friend and strongest supporter was due any minute. She simply adored Willie Baker. Since Porter's death, he had transferred his loyalty to her.

She couldn't wait to see him, certain he'd asked for an appointment because he'd heard about the threats against her and wanted to offer his help, which was typical of him. Too, she hoped he would continue to back her reelection efforts with money.

Heretofore, he'd been adamant about contributing

heavily to both Porter's and her coffers. Plus, he was someone whose advice she always heeded. When it came to politics, she trusted Willie as much as she had Porter.

She couldn't imagine not having his support.

Jessica had just finished replenishing her lipstick when Millie announced his arrival. He strode in with a smile on his round face, though she noticed it lacked its usual warmth.

Thinking her imagination was overacting again, Jessica gave him a brilliant smile and hugged him. "Oh, Willie, it's so good to see you."

"Likewise, girlie," he said, huffing and puffing as usual.

He was short and overweight for what there was of his height. However, there was nothing short about his smile or generous-hearted nature. They were as big as his frame.

"How about some coffee?" Jessica asked, motioning for him to sit down.

"Sara's put me on the unleaded stuff. You don't by chance have that?"

Jessica's face fell. "No, but I bet I could scrounge some up."

"Don't bother. I've already had my quota for the day." He paused, his cataract-clouded eyes appraising her. "What's this about a bodyguard? What in the Sam hill's going on?"

"So you haven't heard?"

"Heard what?" he demanded, on the alert.

Jessica filled him in on the details.

"Well, I'll be damned," Willie said, clearly agitated. "I can't believe you've managed to keep that out of the news."

"I have Tony to thank for that."

"And you have no idea who's behind it?"

"We have our suspicions, but no tangible proof as yet."

"Well, that fellow out there seems perfectly capable of handling anything." Willie's eyes twinkled. "He grilled me good and proper."

Dismayed, Jessica apologized. "I'm sorry about that, Willie. I didn't have time to tell him hands off on you." She frowned. "He has a tendency to be a bit pushy."

"Not to worry, my dear. That means he's doing his job."

"I guess," Jessica said in an evasive tone. She had to be so careful not to let her emotions show when Brant was mentioned. Her reaction to him still remained a mystery, and she would be mortified if anyone picked up on it.

"So tell me what brings you here." Jessica smiled. "I'd like to think you just wanted to say hello and discuss my reelection campaign. You know how I depend on you for advice."

"Actually, I wanted to talk to you, but not about your campaign."

An uneasy feeling caused her stomach to bottom out. It wasn't what he'd said so much as the way he'd said it. "What's on your mind?"

"I want you to rethink your position on this land deal, my dear. And perhaps the fired chief, as well."

Jessica's eyes widened. "You don't approve?"

"No, I don't," he replied bluntly. "And I think you're severely crippling your chances of reelection if you don't back off."

Feeling as if she'd just been blindsided, Jessica clenched her hands at her sides and fought for composure.

Nineteen

Roy was nervous.

Maybe that was because he wasn't high. Yet at the same time, he was also wired. He'd been out of drugs for days. That little twit he shacked up with had used them all while he'd been busting his ass trying to make a dime.

If she hadn't been such a wild woman in the sack, he would have dumped her a long time ago.

Roy blinked several times, and finally his eyes adjusted to the figure in front of him. He blinked again, surprised to see that the man looked like an average, decent guy.

For some reason he hadn't expected his contact to look normal. Guess he'd seen too many movies, Roy told himself with a sneer.

He narrowed his eyes a bit more as he approached the man, who stood solemn-faced and unmoving. On closer observation, he was actually nice looking, could have been any Joe Blow walking down the street. Youngish, with dark hair and eyes, there was nothing outstanding about him except his clothes. They appeared tailor-made to fit his slight frame.

However, one thing was different. His eyes; they set him apart. They were as cold and empty as a dead man's. Roy shivered inwardly, his steps faltering.

Roy had no idea who he was or anything else about him. His girl had set up the meeting, having told him she knew someone who would sell them all the drugs they wanted, and at a discounted price.

Since he was so desperate, Roy chose to believe her. Sober as he was now, he figured there had to be a catch. When something seemed too good to be true, it usually was. Still, he had kept the meeting, and so had the man, which couldn't be all bad.

They had agreed to meet at dusk, outside an office complex at the edge of a middle-class section of the city, another thing that surprised Roy. He'd expected some clandestine gathering in a shady motel.

Whatever this guy had going, he apparently wasn't intimidated by the law. A cynical smile separated Roy's lips. Maybe he had the right cops in his pocket. Frankly he didn't give a rip either way. All he wanted was drugs, then he would be on his merry way.

Problem was, he didn't have any money.

Damn Jessica, he thought again, feeling his rage build and sweat ooze from every orifice. He would get that bitch yet. It was just a matter of time. Right now, though, he had to dismiss the wicked stepmother from his mind and try to make a deal when he didn't have anything to deal with.

He'd pulled off other miracles. Why not this one? This time, however, he was playing in a much bigger league. If he messed up with this guy and his cohorts, he might end up dead.

On the other hand, what's-his-face just might be a Lone Ranger dealing on his own. He would soon see. Push had come to shove.

"You Kincaid?" the man asked.

Make no mistake, Roy cautioned himself; the man's tone was as dead as his eyes. "And you are?"

"Never mind. Names don't matter."

Roy shrugged. "So they don't."

"Let's see the cash."

"Uh, let's see the goods," Roy countered in a bluffing tone, feeling his stomach sour.

The man reached in his pocket and pulled out a bag of white powder, then put it back in.

Roy licked his lips, already tasting the magic stuff on his tongue. Suddenly he was grateful for Dottie and glad he hadn't dumped her. After all, she'd introduced him to this new way of life. Now he didn't know how he'd faced each day without the coke. He couldn't face many more, that was for sure. That was also the problem. He had to have a fix or he would go berserk.

"The money."

"Isn't Dottie your friend?"

The guy's face hardened even more. "Have you got the cash or not?"

"Dottie said you'd be willing to—"

The man suddenly grabbed Roy by the shirt, jerking him forward. Roy panicked, much the same as he had the night Jessica's stud had manhandled him. Dammit, he was getting tired of being treated like he was dim-witted scum.

"I said, where's the money?"

"Okay, okay," Roy wheezed. "Let me go."

The guy let him go, all right, so hard that Roy stumbled back, barely able to hold himself upright. Then and there, he swore he would join a gym and start lifting weights. He was tired of being shoved around. It was time he learned to do some shoving of his own.

"I've asked twice about the money. Don't make me ask again."

"I...don't have any."

It happened so fast, Roy didn't see it coming. The man hit him in the mouth, splitting his lip.

Terrified, Roy cried out, before lifting his hand and using it to stop the flow of blood.

"Next time I'll beat the living hell out of you, you piece of garbage. This isn't a game we're playing."

"Look—"

The man inched closer.

Roy shook all over.

The man poked him in the chest. "No, you look. Next time, if there is a next time, the price doubles."

"Please," Roy all but squealed. "Don't do this. I have a trust fund that's worth thousands. When I get my hands on it, I'll—"

The man shoved him out of the way. "Go fuck yourself, sonny boy."

Why did she have to have on a short skirt? Of all days, when they were confined to a limo.

Alone.

With her legs so exposed.

Long, graceful legs that ended with heeled sandals and vividly painted toenails.

It was all he could do to keep his hands to himself.

Brant swallowed, then turned and gazed out the highly tinted window, but he couldn't see a damn thing. The imprint of those incredible legs blurred everything else.

Not only were her legs driving him nuts, but her entire face and body seemed lovelier than usual, affected him more than usual, if that were possible. If he didn't gain control soon, he would get a hard-on. Then where would he be?

Pissed off in a world of hurt.

Nothing had changed. *She* remained off-limits. He could look, but he sure couldn't touch. He'd made that fatal mistake once, and he wouldn't do so again.

They had been to a Chamber of Commerce luncheon, where she'd been the featured speaker. He was certain that was why she'd dressed up more than usual, looked so spiffy. The cream-colored suit was silk, with a vee neck that hinted at the creamy fullness of her breasts underneath. A small diamond stud shone from each delicate earlobe. A watch and bracelet circled her wrists.

Classy. And elegant.

She'd done great speech-wise, too, even held his attention. But then, that was no special feat when *she* was all he thought about anyway.

Or maybe it was because they were closed up together which forced her up front and in his face. God, he hated tight places, not that the limo was that—far from it. Yet he might as well have been crammed in a tiny, dark hole, with her pressed against him.

Brant shifted positions in the plush seat. What if she spied his hard-on? He dared not check his crotch. To hell with it, he fumed inwardly. She had to know she turned him on.

Besides, she wasn't completely innocent. He had noticed her eyes on him plenty of times with the same intensity.

That was what was on his mind when he looked at her now, thinking once again how lovely her eyes were, how expressive. Yet he couldn't read them this moment, at least not the secrets hidden behind the sea-blue color.

"I enjoyed your speech," he said, forcing himself to break the smothering silence.

She seemed surprised, yet she smiled. "Really?"

He kind of smiled, too. "Really."

"Bet you can't tell me the theme."

"How to motivate yourself."

She grinned for real. "Ah, so you did listen."

He angled his head. "You look good, too." Now why had he added that? Hadn't he just warned himself about getting personal?

Although added color tinged her face, she didn't seem to take offense. "Thanks," she said.

He heard the breathlessness in her voice and realized she was as uptight as he was.

"What did you and Thurmon talk about?" she asked, suddenly putting things back on a steady footing.

"You."

Her colored deepened. "You love antagonizing me, don't you?"

"Sorry."

"No, you're not."

He cut her a sharp glance.

"I don't think you've ever been sorry about much, if anything, in your life."

"That's where you're wrong, lady."

Her lips tightened at the harshness in his tone, but when she spoke again, her tone matched his. "Back to my question. Did Thurmon have any information? As you know, we haven't had any time to talk."

He swallowed a sigh, not really wanting to talk now. "Not anything concrete against the cops, unfortunately."

"I guess that's good. Or maybe it isn't."

"He's still monitoring Riley, and now your stepson."

Jessica gave him a troubled look. "I just wish this would all end."

"It will," he said grimly. "But apparently not as soon as we'd both like. This pervert's pretty smart, knows how to cover his tracks."

"Since he hasn't really tried to hurt me, physically, I mean, maybe he won't. Maybe I could—"

"Forget it," Brant interrupted. "That's not going to happen. The second you let your guard down, he'll strike. Count on it."

"It all seems so...so overdramatized."

He gave a cynical smile. "Read any newspapers lately?"

"You don't have to be insulting. I get the point."

"Just so we continue to understand each other."

Her eyes were sparking and her lips were wet. Suddenly he wanted to grab her and kiss the fire out of her, hoping to knock some sense into her. She was much too brave for her own good.

She turned away. That was when his cell rang. Frowning, he answered it, his heart plummeting. It was Marsha.

A few minutes later, he shut it off, white-faced.

"Something wrong?" Jessica asked, genuine concern mirrored in her eyes.

"That was my ex-wife, Marsha."

"And?" she pressed gently.

He shouldn't have let her get by with probing, but he did, especially since he was tied to her apron strings, dammit. "It's about Elliot," he bit out.

"He's all right, isn't he?"

"Maybe and maybe not. You can't tell with Marsha. She has a tendency to blow things out of proportion when it comes to Elliot. Anyhow, he hasn't come home from ball practice. She thinks he's hanging out with this guy who's on drugs.''

Brant paused, feeling like he'd been sucker-punched in the gut. ''She's blaming me for his rebellion, said he wouldn't have done anything like that before I hit town. Now, supposedly he's confused and out of sorts.''

''Do you know where he is?''

Brant's eyes narrowed. ''She told me the address, like I could do something about it.'' His tone was bitter, and he knew it. But he didn't care. As always, when his son needed him, he wasn't available.

''But you can.''

At first what she said didn't register; then it hit him. ''What did you say?''

''I said, you can do something.''

''What?''

''Go there. Right now. In the limo.''

''You'd do that?'' His tone was incredulous.

''Of course,'' she all but snapped. ''If your son's in trouble, then you need to see about him. It's that simple.''

He knew he must look like an idiot with his mouth gaping. But he was more than a little taken aback by her generous offer. She didn't owe him diddly squat. Except maybe a kick in the nuts.

She leaned forward and knocked on the closed window. ''Howard, please take us to this address.''

A few minutes later, the limo pulled up in front of a large brick home in an affluent neighborhood. Brant reached for the door handle, only to stop when he felt a soft hand on his arm. His heart took a dive. But instead of looking at her, he peered down at the hand, aching to place his over that fragile flesh.

That was when she withdrew it, sucking in an audible breath. He raised his eyes and met hers.

Tension crackled.

"Be gentle," she cautioned.

He merely grunted, then got out. Five minutes later he was back with Elliot, who climbed into the limo in front of him. For what seemed an interminable amount of time, silence reigned supreme.

Then Brant said in a clipped tone, "Jessica Kincaid, my son, Elliot."

"Are these your wheels?" Elliot asked in an awed voice, his hostility having momentarily disappeared.

Jessica's lips twitched. "As long as I'm mayor."

"Wow! This is cool."

Brant bit back his retort, deciding to cut Elliot some slack, especially in front of Jessica. Time would come soon enough to bring him back to the real world.

With a thud, too.

Twenty

Jessica frowned at her assistant. "I'm not sure I can handle that right now."

They were in her office behind closed doors, with Tony trying to get her day started in the right direction, a hard task of late. Her consciousness of Brant on the other side of the door, and the seething awareness that connected them, kept her on edge.

"I'm not sure you have much choice," Tony finally replied, also frowning. "If you're going to run for re-election..."

"You know I want to," she said with more sharpness than she intended. But she felt overwhelmed. Maybe embattled was a better word, like she was being shot at from all directions and couldn't dodge the bullets fast enough.

"I'm sorry if I seem pushy," Tony added, fingering his tie, which had fish swimming all over it. "But time is of the essence here."

Jessica barely heard him; her mind was on his attire. The tie was bad enough, but the lavender coat—well, there simply weren't words to describe the combination. Sometimes she wondered what planet Tony hailed from. At least he kept the place livened up, Jessica thought fondly.

When she remained quiet, he continued. "Of course

you're right. You've had more on your plate lately than you could possibly eat.''

"That's one way of putting it.''

"I'm assuming the e-mails and phone calls are still coming.''

"In spurts, actually, which is a strange thing. I began to relax and think maybe the sick scenario's ended, then it starts up again.''

"Thank heavens for the he-man outside.'' Tony made a face, flapping his hand. "I don't think anyone will try and physically harm you with him around.''

The way Tony said *him* forced another weak smile from her. "You're right about that, which is comforting.'' Liar, her conscience mimicked. There was nothing comforting about Brant or his presence. Her life had taken a ninety-degree turn, and she was grasping to get it back on track.

"I know how set you are on having the retreat,'' Tony said, changing the subject.

Jessica brightened. "And?''

"It's pretty much a done deal, but only for the one day.''

"That's a relief. I firmly believe all the city staff should have input on the budget.''

"I'm with you on that. Let's just hope everyone minds their manners.''

"Not to worry,'' Jessica said with confidence. "Let me look over the agenda when you get the time and place finalized.''

"You'll be the first to see it.''

Jessica fell silent for a moment, then said in a concerned tone, "I wish you'd been here yesterday, when Willie Baker came to see me.''

"I'm sorry I wasn't. I really like Willie. He's one of

my favorite people. In fact, he's at the top of my call list about the reelection campaign.''

"Nix that.''

Tony looked stunned. "The call or the campaign?''

Jessica gave him a pointed look. "Both for now.''

"I don't understand. Willie's your staunchest supporter and always has been.''

Jessica sighed and toyed with her hair. "He's not happy with me.''

Tony's expressive eyes opened wider than usual.

"He's against both the land annexation and the firing of Joe Mayfield.''

"You've got to be kidding? Why would he care one way or the other?''

"That's exactly what I asked him.'' And she had, immediately after he'd dropped his bombshell. She probably wouldn't have been quite as blunt if she hadn't been so shocked.

"So...?'' Tony's features were pinched with displeasure.

"I think some of his buddies on the council have gotten to him.''

"So he hedged?'' Tony asked in his blunt fashion.

"The bottom line was that I'm becoming far too controversial, that I've made a lot of people angry.''

"Well, I've never heard such...'' Tony said, his voice reaching a high pitch. "Who does that old fart—''

"Tony,'' she interrupted sternly.

He reddened. "Sorry. It's just that he's kicking you while you're down, and that makes me furious.''

"I appreciate your loyalty.''

He shrugged. "Let's blow him off.''

"How? Without Willie—'' Jessica broke off with a

shudder. "He's always been my backbone, especially when it comes to money."

"We'll just have to get the money elsewhere."

"Under the circumstances, that's not going to be easy."

"Are you sorry you fired the chief?" Tony asked suddenly.

"No, of course not."

"What about the land? Are your convictions still strong on that?"

"Absolutely."

"Then he either backs you or he doesn't."

Jessica suppressed the urge to hug him. "Thanks, Tony. I needed your special brand of logic."

"What did he say when you told him you weren't backing down?"

"Only that I needed to stop and think, to maybe reconsider, at least on the chief, that Porter would never have rattled so many cages at one time."

"You're right, someone's gotten to him. Lucky he's not on the council."

"Well, J. D. Wymon is, and he's another one who's easily swayed."

"Maybe he's stronger than you think."

"Maybe, but I doubt it."

"I just don't understand that, especially since he and Porter were such good friends."

"I guess we'll just have to wait and see what happens."

"As far as Willie's concerned, I believe he'll come around. If not…"

Tony left the rest of the sentence unsaid, but Jessica knew what he meant. Like he'd already said, they would have to raise money some other way. It could be done, or so she hoped.

She didn't kid herself, though. Without Willie's backing, she would have problems getting reelected. Still, she wasn't prepared to back down on her decisions, even if they did end up costing her the mayorship.

But the thought of that happening was shattering. After all, her job was all she had.

"Are you okay with this?" Tony asked in a strained tone. "I know Willie's attitude was another blow you didn't need."

"I'll recover," Jessica said with forced assurance. "Now, let's go over the day's agenda."

Thirty minutes later, they were finished. When Tony opened the door, Brant was directly in her line of vision. For a second she indulged herself again, letting her hungry eyes linger on him.

Perhaps if she hadn't met his son, seen the remorse in Brant's eyes when he'd looked at Elliot, keeping her distance would have been easier. After having met the kid, she somehow felt part of their lives.

And she'd actually liked Elliot, felt sorry for him. It was obvious he adored his dad, though he wouldn't admit that to himself or to Brant. That adoration was returned, but Brant masked his feelings well, too. As a result, the trip to Elliot's house had been carried out in a cold and uncomfortable silence.

It was only after Brant returned to the limo that he'd said anything.

"Look, thanks again for the favor." His voice had been low and rough, sounding as though the words were pulled out of him.

"Any time," she'd responded lightly.

She'd felt his eyes on her. "He despises me, you know."

That broke her heart. "Oh, Brant, that's not true." The fact that she'd used his given name gave her pause. Nonetheless, she took a deep breath and went on. "Actually he cares a great deal about you."

He snorted.

"He's just confused and angry with life right now."

"I wish I could believe that. But Marsha has—"

Brant broke off, tightening his lips. She sensed he didn't want to badmouth his ex, at least not in front of her, and she respected that. Yet he couldn't continue to think Elliot hated him.

"Elliot's not on anything, is he?" Jessica asked hesitantly, fearing she had already overstepped her bounds.

"No, at least I don't think so. He's obviously pulling these stunts to get back at me."

She sighed. "You can't give up. He's such a fine boy."

"Yeah, he is," Brant said with pride.

"He looks like you."

He fired her another quick glance, probing. "You think so?"

"You know that. All you have to do is look at him, then in the mirror."

Brant shrugged, that brooding look falling over his face again. "If you hadn't told me to take it easy, no telling what I would've said to him. But I took your advice and told him we'd talk later."

His eyes were probing again as if he was remembering her hand on his arm, the touch of flesh against flesh. That old breathless feeling almost smothered her, completely robbing her of a coherent response.

"I think he liked you."

A safety net. She grabbed it. "I hope so. I liked him, and I'd love to see him again."

Brant seemed surprised by that. Yet he was quick to say, "Maybe we could arrange that." His eyes were on her lips.

Jessica swallowed, not daring to look at him again for fear of what would happen.

Muttering a sudden curse, Brant had effectively shattered the moment.

Suddenly the phone rang and shattered her memory, yanking her thoughts back to the present. Sighing, Jessica lifted the receiver.

Her day had started.

"So what do you think, Chief?"

Gaston Forrester, interim chief, rubbed his chin. "Don't you think you're putting the cart before the horse?"

"Naw," Wesley Stokes said, displaying his dirty, crooked teeth with a smile. "I'm sure in the end you'll get the nod."

"I agree," Dick Wells added in an eager voice, his head bobbing up and down.

Forrester massaged his girth. "I'm not. I'm thinking our mayor has other ideas."

"Screw her," Wesley said viciously.

"I'll pass, thank you," Forrester said with a smirk. "She's one cold piece of work."

"Don't you mean ass?" Wells asked with a snicker.

His companions shot him a glance. "Not bad for a virgin," Stokes said, then laughed crudely.

Wells gave him a go-to-hell look.

The men had decided to meet at Forrester's hunting cabin, southeast of Dallas in the piney woods, where

2 Get FREE BOOKS!

Hurry!

Return this card promptly to GET 2 FREE BOOKS & A FREE GIFT!

The Best of the Best ™

YES! Please send me the 2 FREE "The Best of the Best" books and FREE gift for which I qualify. I understand that I am under no obligation to purchase anything further, as explained on the back and on the opposite page.

385 MDL DRSU   185 MDL DRSQ

FIRST NAME	LAST NAME

ADDRESS

APT.#   CITY

STATE/PROV.   ZIP/POSTAL CODE

The Best of the Best™ — Here's How it Works:

Accepting your 2 free books and gift places you under no obligation to buy anything. You may keep the books and gift and return the shipping statement marked "cancel." If you do not cancel, about a month later we will send you 4 additional books and bill you just $4.74 each in the U.S., or $5.24 each in Canada, plus 25¢ shipping & handling per book and applicable taxes if any.* That's the complete price and — compared to cover prices starting from $5.99 each in the U.S. and $6.99 each in Canada — it's quite a bargain! You may cancel at any time, but if you choose to continue, every month we'll send you 4 more books, which you may either purchase at the discount price or return to us and cancel your subscription.

*Terms and prices subject to change without notice. Sales tax applicable in N.Y. Canadian residents will be charged applicable provincial taxes and GST. Credit or Debit balances in a customer's account(s) may be offset by any other outstanding balance owed by or to the customer.

If offer card is missing write to: The Best of the Best, 3010 Walden Ave., P.O. Box 1867, Buffalo, NY 14240-1867

BUSINESS REPLY MAIL

FIRST-CLASS MAIL   PERMIT NO. 717-003   BUFFALO NY

POSTAGE WILL BE PAID BY ADDRESSEE

THE BEST OF THE BEST
3010 WALDEN AVE
PO BOX 1867
BUFFALO NY 14240-9952

NO POSTAGE
NECESSARY
IF MAILED
IN THE
UNITED STATES

they could discuss a strategy for getting them off suspension. They had been drinking beer since midafternoon. Now they were grilling chicken legs and sausages.

"If you don't get the job, my ass is grass," Stokes said, taking a gulp of beer, then swiping the remains off his mouth with the back of a hairy hand.

"Trust me, I'm doing everything I can to suck up to the bitch," Forrester said. "Though I'm not sure it's going to do me any good."

"She doesn't have the final say," Wells added. "Keep that in mind."

"But she sure as hell swung enough clout to get Joe fired."

"And to put us on suspension," Stokes ground out.

"My point, gentlemen," Forrester said, getting up and stoking the fire.

"No matter, seems to me you have every right to put us back on duty," Wells said in a glum tone.

Forrester cut him a look. "Not until I'm appointed officially. Right now, she's more or less running the force." Forrester paused and reached for another beer, popping the top. "Trust me, we're not the only ones she's pissed off. Rumor has it she's been getting threats against her."

"Couldn't happen to a nicer person," Stokes said, following a healthy belch.

Forrester's gray eyes narrowed. "You two wouldn't know anything about that, would you?" He held up his hand. "On second thought, if you do, I don't want to know anything about it. I have to remain as pure as the driven snow."

"We're behind you all the way," Stokes responded. Wells smiled and raised his thumb.

"Which means no one can ever know we met, now or any other time." Forrester's features hardened. "You got that?"

Both men nodded vigorously.

"My only hope is to rack up points with the council behind her back. And with her twat-deep in this land controversy and everything else going on, she won't survive the shitstorm."

"For us, the timing couldn't be more perfect," Wesley said. "Kick her while she's down is what you're saying."

"And make sure she doesn't get back up." Forrester smiled a cunning smile. "That way we'll all win."

Wesley tossed his empty can and dug in the cooler for another beer. "Wouldn't it be justice if she got canned?"

"Works for me," Forrester mused, giving both men a pointed look.

They raised their cans in unison and grinned.

Twenty-one

A Saturday at home.

Several weeks ago that would have thrilled Jessica. But that was before the threats and Brant. In all fairness, though, the day hadn't been too bad. Surely that didn't mean she might be getting used to having *him* underfoot.

Still, Brant hadn't bothered her as much as she'd thought. She'd lazed around in her room, worked awhile, then taken care of some chores in the house, all without a threatening call or e-mail.

Actually she'd seen little of Brant. He'd remained outside most of the day, puttering with her plants on the deck and in the yard, even though she had a lawn service. She shouldn't have been surprised that he was a master at gardening as well as electric work. Each day, it seemed, another facet of his personality unfolded. But then, she shouldn't have expected otherwise. This man was an entity unto himself.

Now it was late afternoon, and her conscience was goading her to prepare dinner. But the thought of sharing another intimate meal with him was as frightening as it was intoxicating. As she walked downstairs into the living room, she remained in a quandary as to what to do. A ringing phone distracted her. It was Roy.

"I don't think that's a good idea," she said when he asked to see her.

"Look, I'm sorry I made a fool of myself the other night."

Jessica wasn't sure she believed him. However, she couldn't judge his sincerity, at least not on the phone.

"So could we please meet and talk?"

A pleading note was clearly in his tone, and she hated having to say no to him. Yet she didn't want to go through what she had the other night, and she had no way of knowing whether he was setting her up again or not.

She spoke her mind. "Frankly I don't trust you."

Roy didn't say anything for a moment. "I just want to apologize."

"I'll accept it now, on the phone."

"I'd rather it be in person. I made an ass—uh, excuse me, fool—out of myself the other night."

"That you did," Jessica responded without guilt, smiling ironically at his attempt to nullify his behavior.

"All the more reason why we need to make up. How 'bout I take you to dinner?"

"When?" she asked, stalling. Regardless of when he had in mind, she wasn't going. But she was reluctant to come right out and say that. Why, she didn't know. Perhaps because of Porter. He had loved Roy and wanted him to be happy.

"What about now?"

"It's a bit early for dinner."

A silence.

"Look, Jessica, I know you don't like me, but—"

"I'd rather not go into that over the phone, either," she interrupted, her sigh audible. "I—"

"That's just an excuse," he cut in sarcastically.

"Why don't you just come right out and admit you aren't going, that you don't want to?"

"All right, I'm not going and I don't want to," Jessica said, calling his bluff.

"You're determined not to make this easy." Roy's tone had grown hostile again. "Well, that's just fine with me. I'm tired of sucking up to you and your lofty ideals, anyway. I want what's coming to me, dammit, and I intend to have it."

With that, he slammed the phone down in her ear.

Biting down on her lower lip, Jessica made her way toward the kitchen, then realized Brant was standing in the room. She gave a start, having thought he was still outside. Obviously not, as he'd apparently just showered. His hair was still damp and looked as though he'd combed it with his fingers, giving him a primitive look. Raw desire weakened her.

She looked away, then back. "I wish you wouldn't sneak up on me," she lashed out, realizing she was taking her anger out on Brant.

He slightly elevated his eyebrows. "Who was that?" he asked, ignoring her outburst of temper.

Mollified, but not about to apologize, she said, "Roy."

"I figured as much."

"How long have you been there?"

He didn't so much as flinch under her accusing gaze. "Long enough."

She relaxed suddenly. Why take her personal and professional frustrations out on him? Her obsession with him was *her* problem to work through. He was just doing his job; if spying was part of it, then so be it. But she didn't have to like it. In fact, she didn't like it at all. She never knew when he was going to just show up. If he didn't disturb her so much, she guessed that wouldn't matter, because she wouldn't react in such a volatile manner.

At the moment, his gaze was aloof, as though he couldn't care less about her or anything else. Damn him.

"What did he want? More money?"

"I'm sure. But his excuse for calling was to take me to dinner so he could apologize in person for the other night."

"Sure."

"That's exactly what I thought, and I told him so."

"Wasn't he ever told no?"

"I have no idea," she said defensively and coolly, feeling the need to protect Porter. She didn't want Brant to think Porter hadn't been a good father. Besides, he didn't have any room to criticize. Look at the mess he'd made with his own son.

As if he read her thoughts, Brant said, "Forget I said that."

"I have."

"Just so you'll know, Roy-boy's gone up a notch on my hit list. He's intelligent, something Stokes and Wells aren't. He's also computer literate and pissed off, which makes him extremely dangerous."

Jessica waved a hand. "Look, since nothing life threatening has happened, I'm about convinced that whoever's behind this is simply trying to scare me or distract me."

"Like I told you, you can't know that for sure. This idiot could turn on a second's notice and up the ante."

Jessica jutted her chin. "I just don't see that happening. Since I haven't changed my modus operandi, he's apparently losing interest."

"Is there a bottom line to this?"

She felt her face flush and hated that he could do that to her. "No."

"Good, because I'm not going anywhere." Brant's eyes burned into her, upping her heartbeat.

Desperate to ease the tension, she said the first thing that came to mind. "Are you hungry?"

"Yes, what if I treat you?"

"Take me out?"

"No."

She blinked. "No?"

A sudden twinkle appeared in his eyes. "Make you dinner here."

"Oh, I don't think—" The thought of him rummaging around in her kitchen, like he belonged there, was more disconcerting than ever.

"That's your problem," he told her. "You think too much. Just say yes."

His logic was so simple, so *frustrating*. Yet it was hard to argue with. She camouflaged a smile, but his all-seeing eyes didn't miss it, because his own lips twitched. Getting chummy would not be smart, she warned herself. It would merely add fuel to the already heightened sexual awareness that continually smoldered between them.

Still, it would be nice to be catered to. It had been a long time.

"So what do you say?"

"Oh, all right," she said with more ungraciousness than she intended.

Brant grinned briefly. "I won't disappoint. I'm a mean chef."

She rolled her eyes. "What can I do?"

"*Nada.* Just relax and go on about your business."

"You have no idea where anything is in the kitchen."

"Not to worry. I'll find what I need."

"I really don't want—"

"Hey, lighten up. I won't break your prized china or anything else, for that matter." Humor still lurked in his eyes.

Knowing she was defeated, she threw up her hands. "Fine. I'll do the cleanup detail."

"I clean as I go. Now, do you have any preference? On food, that is."

Actually the thought of eating anything right now was nauseating, but Jessica hid that thought. She would try to be a good sport about this, though it would be hard. Porter used to cook all the time, but there had been nothing threatening about him.

Brant winked suddenly. "I'll call when it's ready."

Ignoring her heightened pulse rate, she said in a thin tone, "Suit yourself."

She was midway up the stairs when the doorbell chimed. Frowning, she turned and made her way back down. Brant was standing in the entrance to the kitchen, a question mark in his eyes.

"I wasn't expecting company," she said.

He was all business once again. Gone was the charmer of a moment ago. "It's probably Roy."

"Oh, I don't think he'd chance taking you on again."

"He would if he was high. He'd do anything."

Jessica didn't respond. Instead she made her way toward the foyer, then peered through the peephole, prepared not to open it if it were indeed her stepson.

It wasn't Roy, though it was someone almost as annoying. She opened the door, a plastic smile in place. "Hello, Curtis."

He grinned, looking as polished and confident as ever as he crossed the threshold, all but thrusting a huge bouquet of flowers into her hands. "Pretty flowers for a pretty lady."

His flattery was a bit much—gagging, actually—though Jessica held on to her smile and said agreeably enough, "How lovely. Thank you."

"Peace offering," he commented almost sheepishly.

"Oh?" Jessica hugged the flowers to her chest, her mind churning. She didn't want him here, but now that he was inside, there was little she could do, short of being blatantly rude. Why hadn't he called first?

Although she didn't shift her gaze, she figured Brant was lurking, if not visible. Apparently Curtis hadn't seen him, or she suspected he wouldn't be so jovial.

"Are you free this evening?"

"Did you want to discuss business?" If he were going to apologize for his rudeness the other day, then she would be more receptive to him staying, in spite of Brant preparing dinner. Having Curtis come around to her side in the land deal would improve her day considerably.

"No. Actually, I wanted to take you to dinner."

"Maybe another time," she said, smiling. Three dinner invitations in one day. And from three different men. Lucky woman? Or cursed?

"Have you eaten?" Curtis asked bluntly.

This time she slid her eyes toward the kitchen. To her relief, Brant still hadn't appeared. "No, I haven't, but—"

"So you have no excuse," Curtis pressed, taking the liberty of removing the flowers from her arms and placing them on the foyer table. "Those can wait until later."

Talk about taking over and making himself at home. Suddenly she wanted to tell him to get out of her house and leave her alone. She couldn't count on Brant to remain behind the scenes for much longer.

Showing none of her teeming emotions, Jessica settled for the lesser of the two evils. "Why don't we do dinner another time and settle for drinks now?"

"Whatever, just as long as I'm with you."

Not at all pleased with those personal words or the warm look in his eyes, she walked into the living room and gestured for him to be seated. "What would you like to drink?"

He told her, and once she'd served him, she went after the flowers. "Excuse me for a moment while I take care of these."

"Don't bother with them right now. Sit and relax and let's enjoy our drinks."

"After I tend to the flowers," she said with polite firmness.

Curtis shrugged. "By the way, where's your watchdog?" He chuckled. "I hope he's in his cage."

Ignoring that insulting comment, Jessica made her way into the kitchen, dreading the encounter with Brant. She had no idea what to expect, didn't even want to contemplate.

"It's Curtis Riley," she said unnecessarily, noticing that he had already prepared a delicious salad and was now starting the main meal, which looked like some kind of Chinese stir-fry. Suddenly she was hungry and didn't want to miss out on the treat.

"I know. Want me to get rid of him?"

Her lips tightened at his high-handedness. "No."

"So are you going to invite him to dinner?"

She couldn't tell if he was being sarcastic or not, but

she rather thought he was. "Would you like for me to?" she asked, meeting his gaze, deliberately trying to provoke him, then quickly wishing she hadn't.

Something unidentifiable flashed in his eyes, but it disturbed her, nonetheless. Playing any kind of game with Brant could turn out to be more serious than the threats, much more serious than entertaining Curtis. She'd best keep that in mind.

"No, that's not my intention. However, I'm not going to toss him out on his ear. I need his support if I can get it." She busied herself getting a vase and attending to the flowers.

"That's your call," Brant said in a curt tone, turning his back on her, and an intriguing back it was, too. She stood there for a moment, then, groaning inwardly, walked out, vase in hand.

Curtis was sipping on his drink. Seeing her, he placed it on the coffee table and smiled warmly. "I wanted to make sure our disagreement had left no hard feelings. I wouldn't want anything to come between us."

Jessica was taken aback, and she didn't bother to disguise it. "There was never anything between us, Curtis." She placed emphasis on the words "between us."

The warmth disappeared from his eyes, though his smile remained intact. "We could change that." As if realizing she hadn't sat down, he stood and stepped toward her.

She forced herself not to back up. "I don't think so, especially not as long as we remain on opposite sides of the fence."

He sighed. "We could make this all go away if you'd just listen to reason."

Though there was no rancor in his tone, Jessica knew this conversation had taken a downward turn. Now was the time to get rid of him, before heated words were voiced. She hadn't changed her mind about the annexation, and apparently neither had he.

Nothing would be accomplished by him staying.

Without saying anything, she pivoted on her heel and walked toward the front door. He followed suit, but with reluctance, she was sure. His entire face had tightened.

"I guess this wasn't such a good idea after all." His bold gaze traveled over her. "Despite what you think, I care about you."

"Curtis, please, this isn't the time."

"Apparently not for this, either, but I don't give a damn."

Before she realized his intention, he grabbed her and placed his lips on hers. For a second she was too stunned to react. Then, when she would have shoved him away, he let her go, his eyes triumphant.

"I'll call," he said in an arrogant tone, opening the door, then walking out.

Jessica stood there for the longest time, her mind swirling.

"I thought you said there was nothing between you two."

The sound of Brant's voice brought her widened eyes around to him. His features were cast in stone. Her heart faltered under his fury. He'd witnessed the kiss. "There *isn't* anything between us," she stressed savagely.

"Really? You didn't seem to object to him mauling you," he pointed out, his eyes narrowed to slits as he strode toward her, not stopping until he was within touching distance.

With nowhere to go except against the wall, Jessica remained still as a statue, battling her own fury. How dare he? "He wasn't mauling me."

"That's the way it looked to me."

"I'm going to bed," she said tersely.

"What about dinner?"

"I'm not hungry."

His eyes were dark and smoldering. "Well, I damn sure am. But not for food."

With that, he reached for her and buried his lips into hers. This time every bone in her body melted as his mouth and tongue turned into weapons that weakened her knees and drove the very air from her lungs.

While his hand kneaded her breast, tugging on the nipple, he drew her lower lip between his teeth and feasted on it until wet heat pooled between her legs. Moaning, she tilted her head to better accommodate him, then dug her fingernails into his shoulders, reveling in the havoc he was creating inside her.

Then he tore his mouth away. "I couldn't let you go to bed with the taste of another man on your lips."

Twenty-two

He peered in the mirror and groaned. He looked like he'd been on a ten-day binge. God, he wished he had, Brant thought as he rubbed his jawline, checking for any whiskers he might have missed. He felt none; at least he'd done a decent job of shaving.

Giving his reflection a sardonic smile, he turned away and finished dressing. Lucky for him Jessica had decided not to go into the office this morning.

He'd needed the extra time to pull himself back together. He hadn't slept a wink. He'd lain awake all night thinking about her, about the stupid stunt he'd pulled. Again.

So much for self-denial.

Full-blown jealousy had been responsible. When Curtis Riley had grabbed Jessica and kissed her, it had triggered his rage. Instead of breathing deeply and letting his temper cool, he'd acted on impulse.

At least she hadn't slapped him, having definitely been a willing participant in that second adventure down Forbidden Lane. She'd been as caught up in the fiery kiss as he'd been. In fact, they had made love to each other with their lips.

He hardened just thinking about how hers had teased, toyed, cajoled until they were both close to losing control.

Sweet heaven, he had to stop thinking about her or the top of his head was going to come off. Not to mention his dick. It was as hot and hard as a branding iron.

He was in one of the most damnable situations of his life and he had no idea what to do about it. Do *without* it, his conscience whispered. *Put your libido on ice and leave it there.*

Brant's eyes fell on the phone. As an act of desperation, he lifted it and punched out his ex's number. Maybe talking to his son would put things back in perspective.

So lost in thought was he that when Elliot actually answered, he was speechless for a second. "Hello, son," finally stumbled out of his mouth.

"Hello," Elliot muttered.

Would his son's attitude toward him ever improve? He was beginning to get damned discouraged there, as well. But in defense of himself, he hadn't had much time to cultivate their relationship since he'd gotten here. He couldn't be in two places at once. And he couldn't forsake Jessica. Her need of him was the reason he was able to talk to and see Elliot at all. He guessed he should be grateful for that.

But under the present circumstances, any credit to her came with a high price.

"I'm just calling to see how it's going, what you're up to." Brant knew that must have sounded corny to Elliot. But what else was there to say to a son who wished he would just disappear? He had to take baby steps when he wanted to take giant ones, but patience had never been his strong suit.

"I'm trying to find a job, only Mom doesn't want me to work."

At least Elliot hadn't hung up in his ear. Another

crumb. "Why is that?" he asked, but he knew. Damn Marsha. Didn't she understand how important summer jobs were to kids?

"She's afraid it'll interfere with ball."

"Will it?" Brant knew Elliot was involved in the summer teen league, which would certainly enhance his chances of getting a scholarship. If Elliot had a stellar summer, that was. Yet with or without a scholarship, his son could go to any college he preferred. He had the money to send him. He knew how important it was for Elliot to excel in sports, something worthwhile that would keep him out of trouble.

"Nah, not if I find the right kind of job."

"Maybe I could help."

"How?"

He was making more progress, even if it might be in the way of a disguised bribe of sorts. Elliot's voice had definitely come alive. "I'll talk to a friend, see if he has anything at his security agency you might do."

"Cool!"

"Don't get your hopes up, not until I've talked to him. Also, there's your mother."

"What about her?" Elliot's tone had become defensive again.

"She has to approve."

"Then I'm dead in the water."

"Not necessarily. Let's just see what happens. Speaking of your mother, I hope you haven't upset her any more by hanging around with that guy, Jerry what's-his-name."

"No, thanks to you and Mom," Elliot responded in a glum tone. "Jerry told me to stay away from him, said he didn't need my family's shit."

Rather than open that can of worms on the phone,

Brant took another tack. "When can we get together again, maybe take in a baseball game?" If anything would rekindle Elliot's interest, that just might.

"Dunno."

Brant swallowed a sigh. Talking to kids nowadays was like pulling wisdom teeth. "I'll check the Ranger schedule and let you know."

"Okay."

Another crumb. "Good. I'll also get to work on the job possibilities."

"You'll talk to Mom?" Elliot's tone was both hopeful and leery.

"Both of us will, if it comes to that," Brant stressed, wishing now he'd kept his mouth shut until he'd talked to Thurmon. However, he felt certain he could persuade his friend to find something for Elliot to do, even if he had to create a summer position.

When Elliot didn't respond, he added, "I'll call you soon, son. Meanwhile, take care." He wanted to add, "And stay out of trouble," but he refrained. Elliot heard enough of that from Marsha.

Once the dial tone buzzed in his ear, Brant slowly replaced the receiver and rubbed his chin, fighting the urge to jump in his vehicle and go see his son, his job be damned. But he couldn't do that and live with himself. Even though the situation with Jessica was like walking in a field of land mines, he wouldn't desert her.

If only he didn't feel so trapped. He had hoped that by now the claustrophobic feeling would have lessened, but it hadn't. The city and his situation held him hostage. He resented that loss of freedom.

Correction. He actually resented Jessica and her hold over him more. She'd scrambled his brain, not to mention his libido. He was a mess, and his hands were tied.

He couldn't leave her, and he couldn't touch her. Rock and a hard place.

His dick was the rock, and she was the hard place.

He didn't see anything changing any time soon, either. His work with the Secret Service had kept him on the move, while working for Jessica was oftentimes as slow as watching paint dry, especially when she was behind closed doors all day. Those times were the hardest for him, drove him the craziest. Gave him too much time to think. About Elliot. About *her.*

But unless Thurmon was there, he dared not turn his back on her, even though nothing really traumatic had befallen her. Yet. Until the guy was behind bars, it would be foolhardy of all parties to lower their guards. Just as he kept stressing to Jessica, that was when this kind of sicko moved in for the kill.

He was determined that wouldn't happen on his watch.

Now, however, he had to force his head back on straight and do his job. His eyes wandered to the table in his bedroom where he'd put Jessica's monthly schedule. It was crammed full of speaking engagements and appointments, both in and out of the office. The only controversial thing on it had been the parade downtown. Jessica was to serve as the grand marshal.

"I don't think that's a good idea," he'd told her when she'd given him the agenda.

"You know how I feel. I'm not going to let this jerk rule my life."

"Flaunting yourself could give that jerk the opportunity he needs," he'd flared back.

She hadn't budged. "I'm not going to change my plans."

"Even if I insist?"

She bowed her shoulders. "Are you? Insisting, I mean?"

"Dammit, Jessica, you're too stubborn for your own good."

"Is that a no?"

He rolled his eyes and cursed. "That's a yes, actually. I want you to cancel. I expect you to cancel."

They had glared at one another, two immovable objects.

"I'll consider it," she said in a lofty tone, a tone that had grated to the point that he'd barely been able to keep his hands off her.

However, she'd said no more, and he'd had to be content with that. But if he was still running the show then, she wouldn't get in that parade car. Right now, though, he had to see that she got to her office on time.

Brant glanced at his watch as he put it on, realizing it was time to shove off. At noon she was due to speak to a group at a renovated hotel in the heart of downtown Dallas. First, however, she was going to the office.

He paused at the door, his features grim. He had no idea what he was going to say after last night's stunt. Nothing, he told himself.

What was there to say?

Holding to perfection, Jessica had been a smashing success as the keynote speaker for the Ladies of Distinction luncheon. The participants, including Jessica, had been dressed to the hilt. But more than the simple linen suit she had on, it had been the way she'd handled herself.

She had once again electrified her audience. When she smiled and spoke in that southern drawl of hers, she'd had the participants hanging on to every word.

He'd remained at the back, perusing the audience as well as her. He knew he would never tire of looking at her. *Or tasting her.*

Finally, though, the speech had ended along with the meeting. Now they were weaving their way through the post-lunch hour crowd. Jessica had opted to walk the few blocks back to the office, despite the climbing heat.

"I need the exercise," she told him, exiting the building.

"It's going to be hotter than hell out there on the sidewalk, especially this time of day."

"I won't melt." She cut him a sideways glance. "Will you?"

He shrugged. "You're the boss."

"Since when?"

He smiled, which seemed to lighten the moment and make her less uptight. That alone made it harder for him to keep his libido on ice. He could deal with her better when she was pissed at him.

Swallowing a curse, Brant forced his concentration on the people around them, making sure no one appeared threatening.

They walked in silence for a while, weaving their way in and out and around the window shoppers and the people returning to work after lunch.

"By the way, you gave another stellar performance."

She cut him a glance, though her sunglasses hid her eyes. "I did my best."

He quirked an eyebrow. "You had the audience eating out of your hand. You must have known that."

Additional color tinged her cheeks. "I'm never that confident."

"Could have fooled me." Then, realizing how his

remark might have come off, he went on. "I meant that as a compliment."

"Thanks. That's nice to hear from an objective source."

Mmm. An objective source. He'd been called a lot of things, but that was a new one. "I wouldn't bet on that," he muttered, more to himself than to her.

But she apparently heard him, because the color in her cheeks deepened. Or maybe it was the heat staining them a deeper pink. "Brant—"

"Come on," he said brusquely. "Let's get across the street while we can."

Taking him at his word, she somehow managed to get a few feet ahead of him. That was when it happened, the second after she stepped onto the opposite side of the street.

Later, he had no idea what made him look up. Fate? Premonition? Training? Not important. All that was important was that he saw the chunk of concrete come hurtling down out of nowhere.

"Jessica!"

He recognized the sound of his own voice as he dived toward her, feeling his bad leg trying to buckle. Blind panic and sheer willpower came to his rescue and kept him upright. With superhuman effort, he managed to shove her out of the way just in the nick of time. Then his leg collapsed, and they both slammed onto the sidewalk.

Jessica screamed.

Twenty-three

He knew he hadn't been ready to take on another job. He had tried to tell Thurmon, but he hadn't listened. Now his worst fears had nearly come to pass. Sweat drenched him. As fast as he wiped it off his face and neck, it returned.

Get a grip, Harding, he told himself. She was okay, only a few scratches and bruises to show for the horror that had befallen her. She hadn't even needed to go to the hospital, although he'd wanted to take her, had insisted. That insistence had gone in one ear and out the other.

"Please, Brant, I just want to go home."

"Dammit, Jessica."

"Please." Her voice had broken.

For a second, he hadn't known what to do. Then he'd given in, knowing she feared the gossip a trip to the hospital would garner. He figured the media would get hold of it anyway, though that hadn't been the time to remind her of that.

Once home, she'd headed straight to her room, showered, tended the scrape on her knee, then gone to bed. He'd just gotten out of the shower himself, and put on his comfortable cutoffs and T-shirt.

He wiped another bout of sweat off his forehead, then rubbed the back of his neck. But the image of what had happened wouldn't go away. While the foiled attempt on the First Lady's life had been a nightmare, this was worse.

And it hadn't been an accident, either. Brant had been sure of that even before Thurmon and a couple of detectives had backed him up. Granted, there had been construction around the area—hell, the whole world seemed to be under reconstruction. But atop that particular building, nothing had been going on. That building's renovations had taken place the previous year.

Someone had been watching and had deliberately dropped that block of cement with the clear intention of harming Jessica. And that someone had almost succeeded, thanks to his bum knee.

Icy rage charged through him when he thought of that. At the time, blind panic had seized him when he'd felt his knee give way. He'd been terrified he wouldn't reach Jessica in time.

He almost hadn't.

One second later and she might have been crushed.

"Jessica, are you all right?" he'd asked in a strangled voice, frantic the impact of the hot pavement and his own strong body landing on top of her might have broken multiple bones.

She hadn't spoken until they had untangled themselves and he'd helped her to her feet. "I'm...okay," she stammered in a dazed voice.

"Are you sure?" His eyes scanned her entire body, looking for protruding bones and nasty scrapes. A hole in her panty hose exposing a skinned knee was the only visible damage.

"I'm...sure."

"Come on, let's get out of here." That was when he

realized they were surrounded by a group of well-meaning people, clamoring to help.

After thanking them, he'd called the limo driver from his cell and had him pick them up. Once Jessica was safely inside, he'd called the police. Soon the site was teeming with officers. He answered the questions since he was the one who had witnessed the incident. Jessica had had no idea anything out of the ordinary was going on until he'd zoomed at her from behind.

Now Brant was waiting to hear from both the detectives and Thurmon to see if any evidence had surfaced from passersby or from the top of the building. He would settle for a gum wrapper if it would help nail the son of a bitch.

The incident had put a whole new spin on things. As he'd feared, the psycho had finally struck. If that block of cement had hit her... Brant refused to let his mind go there. It hadn't, and that was what he had to cling to.

Small comfort, he thought with disdain, despising his own weakness. Damn Thurmon and damn himself. He'd known his knee had a penchant for failing him at unexpected times. He should have used that to convince Thurmon to let him off the hook.

Maybe he'd been out to prove something to himself. Well, he'd proved it, all right. His inadequacies had almost cost Jessica her life. And because that life had been in his hands, he took full responsibility.

That's why you have to leave.

Failure. He hated that word, hated what it represented. But that was exactly what he was—a failure. A pretty damn miserable one, at that. He was washed up as both a bodyguard and as a father.

Unwilling to dredge up painful thoughts of his son

and determined to run from them, he used Jessica as an excuse. He had to reassure himself that she was indeed all right. Ignoring the wrenching in his gut and refusing to ask why, he strode to the door. The ringing of his cell phone stopped him.

It was Thurmon.

"Nothing," his friend said without preamble.

"Damn."

"The roof was clean as a whistle."

"You didn't take the cops' word on that, I hope," Brant said.

"You know better than to ask that." Thurmon sounded offended.

"Sorry, just had to be sure."

"How is she?"

"Shaken, I'm sure, though we really haven't talked."

Thurmon's sigh rattled through the line. "Does Veronica need to come over? She's been waiting for Jessica to call, but she hasn't."

"Physically, she's fine. Emotionally, I don't know."

"Well, call if you need us."

Tell him, a voice urged. *Tell him you're hauling ass ASAP.* "Count on it. Oh, and keep your men on this. Something might turn up yet."

"Not to worry. Between us, we'll get that bastard."

"Up the pressure on those two cops. This has their names written all over it."

"Consider it done."

Once the conversation was terminated, Brant pursed his lips and made his way to Jessica's room. Surprisingly her door was cracked, which was in his favor. What wasn't in his favor was that she was awake. The French doors were open, and she was out on the balcony.

His steps faltered, along with his breath. He didn't want to leave her. The thought tore at his insides. Even from behind, she was sexy as hell, especially since he could see through the gossamer material of her gown.

He clenched and unclenched his fists, his eyes feasting on her narrow waist, then moving downward to her rounded buttocks, the cheeks so delicately and perfectly separated.

His zipper pinched. Hard.

He winced, barely controlling the urge to close the distance between them, circle that delectable frame with his arms, inhale her scent, then nuzzle her neck before nibbling that creamy flesh.

"Jessica," he said instead, not wanting to frighten her. She'd endured enough trauma for one day.

She swung around. Tears glistened in her eyes. He groaned inwardly. Great. Just great. He could take almost anything from a woman except tears. They got to him every time. Especially Jessica's. They cut to the core.

"I'm sorry," he said lamely, cursing himself for what had turned out to be a screwball idea. He shouldn't be here. His presence would merely add insult to injury. "I didn't mean to intrude. It's just that—" His voice failed him. "Oh, hell, I just wanted to make sure you were all right. I wasn't convinced," he finished on that same lame note.

Though she didn't remove her gaze, she folded her arms across her chest as if to shield herself from his eyes. Too late. His gaze had already homed in on the pointed thrust of her nipples.

His zipper pinched again. Harder.

Brant fought for a decent breath. "Is there anything you need?"

"I'm...okay."

Liar, he wanted to shout, but he didn't. As it was, the tension was as draining as the humidity outside.

"Did you find out anything?" she asked softly, her composure wrapped around her as tightly as her arms.

This woman had all the right stuff, no doubt about it. She had never whined or complained about her narrow escape.

"No, not yet," he finally managed to get out. "Whoever pulled that stunt left no trace."

"You were right," she responded, a slight tremor in her voice. "He's either getting braver or more desperate."

"Both, I would imagine." Brant forced himself to stay put. But it was hard. It was one of the hardest things he'd ever done. "I also suspect time's running out."

"What happens next?"

"Find the son of a bitch," Brant said harshly. "And put him out of his misery."

"Thanks for checking on me." Jessica took a breath, pulling her lower lip between her teeth.

Brant steeled himself not to react to that sexy gesture, though his insides quivered like Jell-O. "You're welcome."

The tautness in her was hard to disguise. "Good... night," she whispered at last.

He cleared his throat. "There's something else."

A question flared in those grave eyes.

"I put you in jeopardy today, so I'm leaving." He knew he had been unnecessarily blunt, but that was the only way he could handle it. "Thurmon will find a replacement."

Her expression was incredulous and anxious. "I don't understand. You...saved my life."

"Just barely," he confessed bitterly. "My leg gave way, and I almost didn't get to you in time."

"But you did, and that's what counts."

"No, that's not what counts," Brant stressed in that same harsh tone. "Next time I might not make it, and it could cost you dearly. Your life. I can't take that chance."

"Isn't that my call?"

"Not this time," Brant said wearily.

"I disagree," she said with renewed strength in her tone.

"Jessica, please, don't argue. I've made my decision, and it's non-negotiable." He hadn't expected this sudden curve. Emotionally he wasn't prepared for it. Considering the circumstances, he'd figured she would gladly hand him his walking papers.

"You...want to go?" she asked, the tremor back.

He groaned openly. "No, dammit, I don't, but—"

"Then stay." A tear broke loose and trickled down her face.

He groaned at the same time that two long strides closed the distance between them.

Later, he didn't know which one of them made the first move. All he knew was that his arms were coiled around her trembling body and his face was buried in her sweet-smelling hair.

Then, wordlessly, they lifted their heads and stared at each other, the atmosphere so charged that Brant felt an imminent explosion. Of the heart.

"Jessica..." His voice, filled with agony, dwindled to nothing. What was there to say, anyway? Wasn't this what he'd wanted since he first saw her? To hold her? To taste her?

To make love to her?

"Kiss me," she whispered, her breath caressing his lips.

He groaned again and sought her mouth, angling his head to make their lips a perfect fit. Once their tongues united, then warred, breathing became impossible. Finally he dragged his mouth off hers, leaving her lips parted and succulent.

Then, deliberately and boldly, and without shielding his yearning for her, he eased the straps of her gown off her shoulders, completely exposing her breasts. The cloudless, moonlit night allowed him the privilege of basking in the beauty of her naked flesh.

His breath deserted him.

He ached to touch.

Not yet, he warned himself.

Savor the moment.

Then, slowly and with more boldness, he eased the material further down until it pooled at her feet. This time she sucked in her breath and stared wild-eyed at him.

Perfection.

No other word fit.

"Touch me," she pleaded, reaching for his hand and placing it on one full breast.

His blood thundered through his body as his callused palm surrounded that soft flesh. It was only when his fingers made their way downward that she swayed toward him.

Unable to restrain himself a second longer, Brant lifted her and carried her to the bed. Then he rapidly disposed of his clothes. When she saw his hard, distended penis, a look of sudden shock crossed her face.

"I won't hurt you," he said in a broken tone, kneeling on the bed beside her.

"I know," she said in a like tone. "It's just that—"

"Now it's your turn to touch me," he rasped, taking her hand and placing it on him.

Her eyes widened still further while her thumb massaged the tender end of his shaft. He was dying from the sweet pain of that gesture, but still he held back, wanting her to be sure this was what she wanted.

"Love me."

Those words, spoken in a broken whisper, were all Brant needed. He sank his lips onto hers once again, drinking greedily. Still, that wasn't enough to quench his lust. Leaving her mouth, his lips roamed at will until they reached the curls nestled at the juncture of her thighs.

When he parted them and eased a finger inside her, she cried out and bolted. "Did I hurt you?" he asked anxiously, stilling that finger.

"No," she said wildly. "I've...never—"

He didn't give her time to finish. Instead he bent his head and thrust his tongue in that same spot. Her hips bolted higher; then she began to thrash about the bed. Only after she climaxed did he rise above her and push himself inside her, which was no easy feat.

She was tight.

Glove tight.

But hot.

"Don't stop, please!" she cried, reaching for him.

He thrust further, riding her hard and fast. Only after her cries mixed with his did he collapse on top of her, burying his lips against her damp neck.

And listened to her muted sobs.

Twenty-four

Jessica's heart raced. At first she didn't know why. Something was not quite right. A feeling of sudden terror gripped her, leaving her weak. She gazed around the room before her eyes settled on the bed, on the rumpled sheets next to her.

She fell back against the pillow, filled with both relief and another kind of terror. At least no one had invaded her premises again. Only Brant. Her every nerve tensed. And he was leaving. Panic filled her.

No. Please, he couldn't go, not like this, not like a thief in the night. Suddenly the immediate hammer of panic subsided as she convinced herself he hadn't left her alone in the house. Yet she dreaded what would follow, what was inevitable.

He would leave.

Brant was not a man who made idle threats or promises. In the moments before they had both tasted the forbidden fruit of each other's body, she recalled the look of agony on his face, heard the contempt for himself in his voice. He blamed himself for that awful day yesterday.

And what an awful day it had been, too, though she'd been oblivious to the menace until it had happened. Her body went rigid. What if he hadn't been behind her, hadn't looked up and seen the falling chunk of cement? She might have been dead or seriously maimed for life.

He had truly saved her life. She just had to reassure him of that. She refused to let him leave thinking he hadn't done his job. Yet she was loathe to face him, especially after last night.

Last night. The most incredible night of her life.

A sense of awe came over her that was followed by a sense of shame. Dear Lord, she couldn't believe how she had thrown caution and sound judgment aside and indulged in a sexual marathon. She had never let herself go to that extent. With anyone.

Porter jumped to mind, deepening her shame. He had never had free rein over her body. She had always held that part of herself aloof. Yet he had never made such demands, either, never touched her in the places Brant had touched her.

Secret places. *Forbidden places.*

Not to Brant. She hadn't known she was capable of such passionate abandonment. Her mother had instilled in her that she should always hold herself at a distance, never let a man get too close to her or use her for anything, especially as a sexual toy.

Sexual toy.

Jessica felt color blister her cheeks. Was that how Brant saw her? That was exactly what she'd been last night. Her mind struggled for a reason, an excuse, something that would justify letting him make her come with his mouth. More than once, too.

What had made her behave so brazenly? The heat of the moment? Relief at being alive after the attempt on her life? The emotional upheavals of late? Her attraction to him? None. All cop-outs. The simple truth was that she had wanted him.

So maybe it wouldn't be the worst case scenario if he did leave. Like he'd said, Thurmon would replace him. Shivers shook her body. Automatically she reached for the sheet and draped it over her nude body. But the shivers wouldn't go away.

The truth was, she couldn't bear the thought of him forsaking her. Better the devil she knew than the one she didn't.

Unable to remain with only her tortured thoughts for company, Jessica tossed back the cover and, with a heavy heart, headed toward the bathroom. On her way, she glanced out the window and noticed dawn was breaking.

A new day. New opportunities. *A fresh start?*

She was in the process of turning on the shower when she heard her cell phone ring. A frown marred her brows. Who would be calling her this early? Tony? Veronica? Or the pervert?

Jessica padded back into her room, grabbed the phone. After recognizing the city's main number, she gave a puzzled frown, then answered it. The loud music that assaulted her ears was bad enough, but the lyrics of the rap song were loud and vulgar.

And threatening.

Her blood turned to ice as the color drained from her face. Dropping the cell, she sank onto the side of the bed, fear and disgust lumped together in her stomach.

Just when she'd thought her situation couldn't get worse.

The shower felt good, except that it washed away Jessica's personal scent as well as the scent of their lovemaking. Brant's hands stilled on the soap. An emotion he couldn't begin to identify weakened him for seconds on end.

He wondered if Jessica was awake and going through the same gut-wrenching. Or perhaps she was still curled up in bed, her lovely limbs all loose and pliant, an image that suddenly made him hard again.

An even more enticing vision was of her in the shower. He would love to be washing *her,* exploring those magnificent curves, lathering them with soap, then shoving her wet and slippery body back against the tiled wall, hoisting her up and taking her on the spot.

Brant cursed, telling himself that he couldn't possibly be hungry for her again. He'd lost count of the times he'd been inside her or loved her with his mouth and tongue. Enough to satisfy any man, he told himself.

Only he still wanted her, dammit.

Insanity had consumed him, robbed him of the ability to make rational decisions, which strengthened his case for leaving, his physical inadequacies aside.

Don't you mean deserting her?

Feeling his agitation build despite the soothing effects of the hot water pounding his skin, Brant shut off the shower and climbed out. Would his conscience truly allow him to desert her?

Yes, if he thought it was in her best interest. But was it? Witnessing the sheer panic in her eyes and face, hearing it in her cracked voice, had cut him to the quick, had made him have second thoughts.

Too, he'd never backed down from a challenge, and he saw this sicko as just that. His determination to best the man was palpable. Yet he no longer had the physical tools to pull that off; his leg giving out on him bore testimony to that.

So where did that leave him?

If he took the gamble and stayed, he might further jeopardize her, though the real problem, the knock-'em-in-the-gut kind of thing, was his feelings for her. If he gave in to them, whatever the hell they were, she would break his heart.

A permanent relationship with her was out of the question for obvious reasons. His only true goal in life was to regain the love and respect of his son, then return to his life of solitude where his nerves were no longer frayed. And Jessica had her own goals, goals that didn't include him. She thrived on the limelight of her career, city life and people.

He abhorred all three. He'd been there and done that. That type of existence no longer interested him.

But after tasting her body, he didn't know if he had the courage to walk away, not that he would ever get the opportunity to touch her again even if he stayed. Still, he wasn't a quitter, and she had asked him to stay.

The time it took him to dress didn't lessen his anxiety about seeing her. Perhaps he wouldn't have to worry. If her fears were as real as his, then she might have changed her mind. Maybe now she wanted him to go.

His ultimate fate as her bodyguard would have been taken out of his hands. He could live with that. Couldn't he? After slapping some cologne on his face, he peered at his watch. Too early to make his appearance.

His eyes shifted to the phone and his thoughts to Thurmon. Without wasting any more time, he picked it up and called his friend.

"Hey, anything new?" he asked, knowing full well there wasn't.

Thurmon saw through his bluff. "Not that I'm aware of, but I'm sure you know that."

Brant let that slide. "I just wanted to remind you not

to leave this up to the cops. You know what a mess Jessica's stirred up in the precinct. That will work against her now.''

Thurmon was quiet for a moment; then, in a slightly irritated tone, he said, ''You've already told me that. You don't sound like yourself. It's not Jessie, is it?''

''I haven't seen her this morning,'' Brant said in a hedging tone, guilt stabbing at him for having taken advantage of her at another vulnerable time. ''But you know how closemouthed she is,'' he added, for lack of anything else to say.

''Do I ever, and so does Ronnie.'' Thurmon paused, then asked bluntly, ''What's this call really about? I know you, and something's wrong.''

''I told her I couldn't do this anymore, that you should replace me.''

''Dammit to hell,'' Thurmon snapped. ''That's not going to happen.''

''It's her call, Thurmon,'' Brant said, certain that she would be glad to see the last of him at this point.

That fact seemed to stop him momentarily. ''If you'd quit wallowing in self-pity long enough, the truth would be obvious. She didn't get hurt, because you saved her life.''

''Luck, pure dumb luck,'' Brant lashed back.

''Whatever. It doesn't matter. I'm asking you not to bail out, not when things are heating up. To replace you now wouldn't be in her best interest. Doesn't that mean anything to you?''

More than you'll ever know, my friend, which is the problem. ''Of course it does, but ultimately it's Jessica's decision.''

''Let me know,'' Thurmon said, his disgust obvious.

''I have a favor to ask of you,'' Brant said.

"You have more balls than you've got brains."

Brant laughed without mirth. "Maybe that's why we get along so well."

"So let's have it. What do you want?"

"Will you give Elliot a summer job?"

A moment of silence followed.

"I can do that," Thurmon replied at length. "But not for you. For the kid."

Brant's laughter was genuine this time, though he knew Thurmon was scowling. "Thanks, old buddy. I'll let Elliot know."

"You're a real son of a bitch."

"No one knows that better than me," Brant muttered. "Keep in touch."

"Yeah," Thurmon muttered darkly before all but slamming down the receiver.

Seconds later, Brant punched in Marsha's number. He hoped his son was at home and he didn't have to leave a message. He couldn't wait to tell Elliot the good news. Maybe a job would be the turning point in their relationship. Right now, he was grabbing at any straw he could find.

"Hello?" Elliot said at the other end of the line.

"Hey, it's your dad."

"Hello," Elliot repeated, without nearly as much enthusiasm.

Still, Brant felt a sense of pride at his son's deep-sounding voice. At seventeen, he was no longer a kid, but rather a young man on the threshold of his life. And to think he'd missed so much of that life.

"I have some good news for you."

"What?"

"My friend's agreed to put you to work."

"Super!"

"So you like that idea, huh?" Brant asked, feeling like he'd just won a million dollars.

"Wait'll I tell Mom."

"Whoa. That's not the way to handle this. It's your mother's call. You explain the job to her and how it won't interfere with practice, then see what she says. I bet she'll agree."

"What if she doesn't?"

"Let's think positive, okay?"

"I'll give it my best shot."

"Good. When I find out more details, I'll get back to you, or Mr. Nash will."

"Super!" Elliot exclaimed again, then hung up.

Brant stared at the empty receiver for a moment, wishing Elliot had at least said, "Thank you, Dad." Maybe he was expecting too much too soon. Thanks of some sort would come later, when things were on a better footing. He couldn't lose his faith or his patience.

While that conversation with Elliot had been a shot to his ailing heart, he still had to face Jessica and what had transpired between them, figuring that would more than likely sour the remainder of his morning, if not his day.

Thinking the time was decent enough to approach her, Brant walked out of his room. He checked the living room first, then the kitchen. She wasn't in either place, which meant she was still in her room. Surely she was dressed and ready, though maybe not. She'd suffered yesterday from more than one source, he reminded himself bleakly.

He reached her door and found it cracked. That was the only reason he deemed it appropriate to intrude. He knocked, then cracked the door even wider. That was when he saw her, sitting on the side of the bed, shaking and pale, looking as though she'd been sucker-punched in the stomach.

The sicko had struck again.

Fear, infused with outrage, heightened Brant's adrenaline. Yet for a moment, he couldn't seem to move. Then he strode toward her and knelt beside her. "Jessica, what happened?"

She held the cell phone out to him, disgustingly vulgar music pouring out of it.

He slammed it shut and stood motionless, too furious to move.

She lifted her traumatized eyes to him. "Promise you won't leave."

Twenty-five

Jessica was behind closed doors, and he was at his usual station in the outer office. From all appearances, nothing had changed. Only it had, though nothing had been discussed.

Unspoken words and thoughts simmered below the surface. Sooner or later, though, they were going to have to face their volatile relationship and come to terms with it.

Since he hadn't left.

Her earnest plea had obliterated his defenses, gotten to him on the gut level. When he'd found Jessica sitting on her bed that morning, she had seemed at a loss, helpless, totally out of character for her. She was the bravest and most together woman Brant had ever known.

But the sick chain of events had begun to take its toll. He had seen signs of her cracking on the way to work, and even now. He still couldn't get the image of her face out of his mind.

That rap music blasting out of her cell phone had been a shock, frightening and demeaning, the lyrics dealing with sex and death. While that lowlife way of getting to her hadn't shocked him, it had her.

She wasn't used to dealing with the scumbags of the world. But he was. That was why he'd sworn then and there to protect her as best he could. Yet he was having a tough time adjusting to the softening of his hard edges. Since he'd become a recluse, he'd turned into a self-absorbed cynic, his only vulnerability his desperate desire to make things right with Elliot.

At the moment, however, his son seemed easier to handle than Jessica. When he'd told her he wouldn't desert her until the pervert was apprehended and behind bars, her relief had been obvious, something he'd almost cautioned her against.

He wasn't a safety net.

And, having tasted her body, he wasn't sure he could stay away from her. "I thought you'd be eager to send me packing," he'd told her.

After last night.

Though he didn't speak those words, she wasn't rattled to the point she didn't get what he meant. Her gaze didn't waver. "I need you."

No one had ever said those words to him, certainly not Marsha. He groaned inwardly at the added pressure. Yet it was all he could do not to sweep her in his arms again, hold her and promise he would never let anyone hurt her. Ever. But he didn't. He had the good sense to hold himself in check, realizing in the heat of frustration and lust that that was a promise he couldn't keep.

"I'll do my best," he said in a strained voice. "But about last night…"

Jessica shifted her gaze, the color still absent from her face. "It should never have happened."

"Then you're sorry," he said, his mouth twisting along with his heart. He didn't know what he'd expected. His fantasy, of course, would have been an eagerness for a repeat performance.

But her aloof, practical approach was the right one.

For both of them. Otherwise... He didn't dare go down that path.

She was looking at him again, anyway, having just wet her lips, lips stained with some kind of berry color that gave them a sexy, just-bitten look. His nerves tingled, the heat of last night returning with a vengeance.

"Don't," she whispered.

"Don't what?" he asked deliberately, trying to rile her and not liking himself for doing it.

"Look at me like that."

He cursed, then said in a low, husky voice, "What do you expect?"

Jessica licked those stained lips again, seemingly at a loss as to how to deal with the situation. Deal with him.

Brant dragged a deep breath through his lungs, his eyes darkening. "Look, we have to talk."

"You're right, we do," she said softly. "Only later."

He wondered now if she had really meant what she'd said or if she'd just bought herself some time. Eventually this would all end, and he *would* be gone.

Suddenly brushing aside that thought, Brant made his way into the lounging area and helped himself to a cup of coffee. He was about to return to the main area when Millie appeared at the door.

"Excuse me, sir, but there's a lady to see you." Her tone was uncertain, and her eyes kept darting around the room, as though searching for something that would take her gaze off him.

Brant frowned his surprise. "To see me?"

"Yes, sir."

He wanted to question her further but declined. Apparently she was uncomfortable enough with having to come get him, though he'd thought she'd gotten over her intimidation of him. Guess not.

"Thanks, I'll be right there," he said, giving her a weak smile.

She nodded, a curious light suddenly appearing in her eyes, which made him down the remainder of his coffee in one swallow. The instant he walked into the other room and saw her, he pulled up short.

"Marsha, what the—" He broke off abruptly, realizing Millie was at her desk. And though her head was bowed, she could hear every word.

"I need to talk to you."

Elliot. Brant's chest tightened. Had something happened to him? Or had she merely come to take him to task in person over what he might or might not have done?

"I thought about calling," she said into the silence.

That was when he noticed her heaving chest and the tears welling up in her eyes. *Something was wrong.* His heart bottomed out. Terribly wrong, or she wouldn't be here. To have thought otherwise was crazy. She despised him and would go to any lengths not to see him.

On closer observation, he noticed her face was devoid of makeup and splotchy. Her frosted hair was in total disarray. He'd never seen her look so frazzled.

He forced himself not to panic. "Let's go out in the hall." He turned to Millie then and added, "I'll be outside." Left unsaid was, if Mrs. Kincaid should need me.

"Yes, sir," she replied, her eyes more curious than ever.

Luck was on his side; the hallway was quiet, a miracle, as this place was usually a beehive of activity. He suspected his luck wouldn't last long.

"Elliot's missing," she said without preamble.

His stomach bottomed out again. "Missing? What the hell does that mean?"

"Don't you dare holler at me." She was close to hysterics.

"I wasn't hollering at you, Marsha," he said, forcing himself to remain calm while trying to cope with her anxiety and his own temper. "Please, just tell me."

"I don't know where Elliot is."

"Is that your way of saying he didn't come home last night?"

"That's exactly what I'm saying."

"Did you call the police?"

"Yes, but they said there was nothing they could do until more time had elapsed."

"Why didn't you call me sooner?"

"I figured he was with you."

Brant almost lost it. "With me? Dammit, Marsha, you know better than that."

She laughed bitterly. "Oh, but I don't."

How did one reason with someone who was so totally unreasonable? But why was he surprised? This was the type of thing that had split them, ended their marriage. When she got something lodged in her head, she refused to let it go, to admit that she might be wrong. Making that worse was her mistrust of him.

But then, he'd given her reason for that, not that he'd ever been unfaithful to her, because he hadn't, except with his time and his emotions, which was almost as detrimental. He'd spent far more time at work than he had at home. As far as his emotions went—well, she'd never even tapped them, not like Jessica….

Shutting that thought off before it could take root, Brant forced himself to maintain a cool head. "I would never take him without your knowledge, nor would I allow him to play us against each other. How could you even think that?''

"Because I don't know you anymore, Brant." Her eyes flashed. "In fact, I never knew you."

"Look, can't we keep us out of this and just concentrate on our son?"

"Since you've been back, he's been a different person. Moody, mixed up."

"You've made that quite plain already. But that's not the issue here. Did anything out of the ordinary happen yesterday?"

She laughed another hysterical laugh. "The call about a job. Have you forgotten that?"

"Of course I haven't," he snapped in spite of himself. "What does that have to do with him missing?"

"I told him no, that he couldn't take it."

Brant controlled the anger that tore loose inside him and expelled a ragged breath. "Why? Because of me?"

"Absolutely not. It would interfere with him playing ball and getting a scholarship."

"So you two had a fight?" Brant asked, resisting the urge to shake her, to make her see that she was using Elliot to punish him.

Marsha bowed her shoulders and shook her head. "There was nothing to fight about, actually. I simply told him he couldn't take the job, and so did his fa—"

"Preston is not his father," Brant interrupted, not about to let that slide. It cut too deeply.

Marsha tightened her lips. "If you had any decency about you, you'd—"

"I'd what?" he interrupted again in a harsh tone, realizing he'd sunk to her level and brought personalities into this when he'd jumped all over her for the same thing. "Look, that's not important right now. I'll find him. Don't worry."

Marsha's eyes burned with hatred. "Still the fixer. Just pick up the phone and make a call, and *voilà*, the world's all perfect once again."

Brant decided not to let that barb slide, either. "Isn't that why you're here? So I can fix it?"

Brant had known that she was bitter and full of hatred toward him, but not to this extent. Time had done nothing to heal the wounds he'd apparently inflicted on her heart. While he would take some of the past regrets to the grave with him, he had moved on. As far as she was concerned, he never thought about her except as Elliot's mother.

Any other emotion was long dead. Too bad for her she hadn't been able to bury their dead marriage and move on, too.

"Yes," she finally admitted through clenched teeth. "Then I hope you have the decency—"

"Don't go there, Marsha, because it's not going to happen. I want Elliot back in my life, and I intend to do everything in my power to make that happen."

"Damn you, Brant Harding. Damn you."

"I'm sorry you feel that way, but he's my son, too. And no matter how much you wish that weren't so, it is. Having said that, know that when I find him, I'll bring him home where he belongs."

She made an unladylike sound.

Ignoring her, Brant continued. "I'm not trying to take Elliot away from you. Never that. I just want to be a part of his life, as well. Why is that so hard for you to understand and accept?"

He hadn't talked to her with any civility in so long, he hadn't known he was capable. But he was frightened, more frightened than he would ever admit to her. The thought of Elliot, in his vulnerable state, turning to drugs or alcohol was a horror he didn't want to contemplate, but he had no choice.

All the more reason to find him. Now.

"Because you don't deserve a place in his life. You deserted us, you bastard. For that you should have to pay as long as you breathe."

Brant rubbed his neck, desperate for words that would break through the cement wall of hostility surrounding her. Then, sensing that his efforts were futile and with time being of the essence, he told himself to screw it. Marsha would have to come to terms with him and Elliot in her own way. Like it or not.

"Go home and wait. Meanwhile, I'll find him."

"How? You're tied to the mayor's apron strings."

"Don't you worry about the how," he countered coldly. "I'll do it."

"And when you do, don't mollycoddle him."

Nearly choking on his fury, Brant counted to ten. "I'll be in touch."

Twenty-six

"I wish you would do what you're supposed to be doing."

Brant swung around, irritation as well as worry mirrored in his eyes. "I am. I'm here with you, doing my job."

Jessica sighed, rearranging her feet under her on the sofa. She had eased her sandals off for comfort, knowing this was going to be a long evening. "I'll be all right, Brant," she said gently. "The woman you left to take care of me did just fine."

"I know, but I still needed to check back, especially since it's getting dark."

"No, you didn't. You should've stayed with Thurmon until your son was found. That's more important than baby-sitting me."

"You're both important. And if something happened to you—"

Though he left the sentence unfinished, she knew what he was about to say.

"I wouldn't blame you."

He gave her a bitter smile. "You wouldn't have to. I'd blame myself."

"God, you're stubborn."

Brant raised his eyebrows. "*You're* calling *me* stubborn?"

Jessica let go of a weary sigh. "Look, I don't want to argue with you."

"Then don't."

"It's not that simple, so don't try and make it that way."

Brant stared at her for a moment longer, his dark eyes unreadable. Jessica rubbed a tender spot at her temple. Another mess. One she prayed would end much quicker than hers.

Since Brant had come into her office and told her his son was missing, she had canceled the remainder of her appointments for the day, despite his objections. Then she'd picked up the phone and called the acting chief, giving him the go ahead to search for Elliot.

Brant, of course, had called Thurmon, who'd joined the search. So far, there had been no sign of Elliot. None of his friends seemed to know his whereabouts, either, which made the situation more puzzling and harrowing.

They had finally left the office and returned to her town home. Once the female security guard arrived, Brant had joined Thurmon. And she had waited. The hours had dragged, at least for her, though Brant had thoughtfully kept her briefed by phone.

Since his return, he'd been on the phone, constantly in touch with both his ex-wife and Thurmon. But neither Thurmon and his crew nor the detectives had anything to show for their endeavors.

She had prepared dinner for herself and Brant, though neither one of them had eaten enough to justify her efforts. But she couldn't just do nothing. She hadn't wanted to leave Brant to go through this trauma alone, though she was sure he would rather do just that.

Gazing at him now, she saw that his features were tight and unyielding. She shuddered to think of Elliot's

fate when he was found, though she hoped Brant would
be as gentle as possible under the circumstances.

So as not to give him more reason to worry, she had
pretended to stay busy, having brought a pile of work
home with her. She'd perused Tony's agenda for the
still-pending budget retreat, along with the latest information on a proposed interstate, but her mind hadn't
been focused.

For a while she'd even worked on her speech for the
women's conference in Lugano, Switzerland, since
she'd just received her agenda. She hadn't as yet taken
Brant into her confidence about it. No matter. He
wouldn't be going with her. There was no need. She
would be safe out of the country. Once she was on the
plane, he could have his life back, at least for a few
days, and hopefully spend some quality time with his
son.

If he was found.

The thought that he wouldn't be didn't bear contem-
plating. Yet she couldn't stamp out the crazy notion that
if something dangerous had befallen Elliot, it was because of her. What if he'd been kidnapped as a pawn
to get back at her for hiring Brant? More bizarre things
had happened, she reminded herself.

Suddenly Jessica rubbed her arms, feeling as though
her skin was crawling.

As if sensing her distress, Brant whipped around, his
eyes narrowed. "I don't want you to worry about this.
You have enough on your plate as it is."

"Well, I'm worried."

"I know we'll find him and that he'll be okay."

"I know that, too." Jessica frowned. "Still—" She
broke off, having no intention of divulging her cocka-
mamie idea.

"What?" Brant demanded, quick on the uptake.

"Nothing."

"Jessica, let's have it," he pressed in a gritty voice.

She knew he wouldn't let her be until she confided in him. "Do you think his disappearance could have anything to do with me?"

Brant's look was incredulous. "Why would you think that?"

She conveyed her fears.

His features immediately softened. "Hey, trust me, Elliot's little stunt is to get back at his mother for not letting him work. And me for coming back into his life. He's one mixed-up kid right now."

"So you really think that's what this is all about?"

"Absolutely. He's pushing the envelope to the limit, so to speak."

"But where is he?" Jessica ached for him, sensing that underneath his calm demeanor was a man in agony. How could he not be? But he would never let on. He was that kind of man. "If you weren't tied down, you—"

"Don't," he cut in. "If Elliot's not found soon, I'll leave you with my replacement. But for the moment, Thurmon's in charge."

"Don't forget about the detectives. They're also in the hunt."

"Which I appreciate," he said, his gaze softening on her.

Color flooded her face as she went limp inside. God, this man had some kind of hold on her. It was mind-boggling. "I know you do," she murmured into the sudden and awkward silence.

If only she could comfort him. She wanted to put her arms around him, assure him that his son would be found soon and that he was all right. But she had no reassurance of either. Besides, he wouldn't take too kindly to her sympathy.

In so many ways they remained far apart. Even though their bodies had connected in hot passion, their minds had never connected on any level.

"Did you hear from the pervert today?" Brant asked, facing her again, his eyes hooded.

"Not so far, thank goodness."

"The day's not over," Brant pointed out cynically.

"I keep thinking he'll get tired and give up. After all, it's been two weeks, and I haven't changed my position on either of the hot issues."

"After that building incident, he's not giving up." Brant's tone was hard again. "Count on it. He's just biding his time, waiting for another opportunity."

"I can't understand why he's doing this, what he hopes to accomplish. I'm not going to change my mind. Surely he's figured that out by now."

"Whoever's behind this is either demented or so desperate that he's lost all reasoning power."

"I still don't think Roy or Curtis is responsible. Or the cops, either, for that matter."

"Well, I'm still not ruling anyone out," Brant said flatly. "But it could be someone off the street, someone you've never laid eyes on, who has an ax to grind for whatever reason."

"So the beat goes on," Jessica responded bleakly.

"Until the bastard's behind bars."

"With me leaving the country, maybe—"

"What did you say?"

His tone was as cutting as his eyes.

She stiffened, resenting his reaction. "I haven't told you, but I've been asked to speak at a women's mayoral conference in Switzerland the week after next.'' Before he could respond, she gave him the particulars.

''Don't you think you should've discussed that with me?'' Brant's anger was obvious.

She was taken aback. ''No, since you're not going.''

He laughed with dark humor. ''Oh, yes I am. Where you go, I go.''

''That's crazy. Once I leave the city, I won't be in any danger.''

''You know that for sure?''

Under his logical scrutiny, her confidence wavered. ''As sure as one can ever be about anything,'' she lashed back impatiently, sensing that her opportunity to put some much-needed distance between them was in jeopardy.

''Which translates into no.''

''I don't agree.''

Another silence fell over the room as their eyes clashed and held.

''Look, we'll discuss this another time, okay?'' she said, averting her gaze.

''There's nothing to discuss.''

Jessica bit back a scathing retort because of the present situation. If Elliot hadn't been missing, she would have taken their argument to closure, since she was in no doubt that she would come out the winner. But he didn't need to be distracted by something so trivial as her travel agenda, certainly not when even his best efforts would not override her determination.

Some things were nonnegotiable, and this was one of them.

''I think I'll go up and call Veronica,'' she said, hoping to diffuse the antagonistic environment.

A nod was his only response.

Once upstairs, in the sanctity of her own room, Jessica breathed without restriction, realizing how tense and uptight she was in Brant's presence. The fact that she saw no end in sight to his presence or her situation depressed her. But only for a moment. Things could be worse, she reminded herself, forcing her spirits to lift.

And a dose of Veronica could cheer her up when nothing else could.

"I'm so glad you called," Veronica said. "I've been dying to talk to you."

"You could've called me," Jessica replied, pointing out the obvious.

"Hey, I figured you were behind closed doors tending to business."

"Actually, I'm at home. With Brant."

Veronica didn't try to disguise her astonishment. "I thought he was with Thurmon, that Sue was—"

"She was," Jessica interrupted. "But Brant's with me now, although I'm sure Sue's still around."

"I see."

Veronica didn't see, but she wasn't about to give her friend any room for speculation. "Brant won't be around for much longer. He just wanted to check on things here."

"I'm just holding my breath the kid's all right, that he hasn't gone and done something stupid."

"Like what?" Jessica asked, her fear mounting. After all, Veronica knew Elliot a lot better than she did. Having met him only once, she couldn't make any kind of judgment call. Still, she'd liked him on the spot and knew it would be tragic if he had gotten into trouble with drugs or whatever else kids got into these days.

"Drugs are the worst case scenario, of course," Veronica said, "but there are other things I refuse to dwell on. I just feel sorry for Brant. I'm sure Marsha is giving him bloody hell over this.''

"He hasn't confided in me about that, of course, but from what I do know, I think you're right.''

"She's a first-class bitch.''

"That's too bad.''

"I can understand why Brant never wanted to go home. She's one of those whiny, clingy types who wants a man who'll cater to her every whim.''

"Oh, dear.''

"Anyway, he's rid of her now.''

"Not really,'' Jessica pointed out. "Elliot will always link them.''

"You're right, which makes it a blessing that Brant has no interest in remarrying.''

For a reason Jessica wouldn't care to explore, she found that flat statement disconcerting. She couldn't care less about Brant's personal life now or later. When he walked out of her life at the end of this madness, she would never see him again. That was the way she wanted it, the way it had to be, regardless of the sizzling desire that had fused their bodies in mindless passion.

Shifting her thoughts, Jessica said in a slightly breathless tone, "I just wished this hadn't happened, especially when he's tied to me.''

"The kid will turn up.''

"It's just that I feel so helpless. I wish he'd forget about me.''

"After that block of cement nearly hit you, just be glad that he's taking his job so seriously.''

Too seriously, Jessica was tempted to say, only she didn't. Now was not the time to unload any more problems on Veronica. Besides, she still wanted to keep her private life private.

"Oops, gotta run. The niece and nephew are staying with me, and they're at it again."

Jessica chuckled. "Give Jeff and Jennifer a hug for me."

"Hug, my foot. If they don't stop tormenting each other, I'm going to tan their little backsides."

"Yeah, right," Jessica said with another chuckle. "I'll talk to you later."

Once the conversation ended, so did her good humor. Thinking perhaps Brant might have heard something, she made her way back downstairs. She had just stepped into the living area when the doorbell rang. Freezing, she stared at Brant, who was already in motion, heading toward the door.

Jessica followed him, her heart in her throat, afraid to speculate as to who was standing on the other side. If it was Curtis or Roy, she wouldn't let him in. A worst case scenario was that it was Thurmon or the detectives with bad news. Stop thinking negative thoughts, she told herself. It took no more effort to think on the positive side.

Brant looked through the peephole, then made an unrecognizable sound, as if he was strangling. He jerked open the door while Jessica held her breath.

Elliot was standing on the porch.

Twenty-seven

For several moments no one moved, no one spoke. It was as if all three of them were frozen in some kind of time warp.

"Son," Brant finally said, sounding like he'd just gotten over a siege of laryngitis. He didn't know whether to grab Elliot and hug him, or shake him. Right now, he ached to do both.

Instead he cleared his throat, then stepped aside, making a motioning gesture with his hand. "Come on in."

Jessica was standing adjacent to him, her eyes wide with shock. No more shocked than he was, Brant thought. The last place he would have expected his son to turn up was on Jessica's doorstep. He hadn't even known Elliot knew where she lived. But that minor detail wasn't important. He was here and safe, and that was all that counted.

"Is this okay with you?" Brant asked in a low tone, seeking Jessica's eyes and holding them.

"Of course," she all but snapped, as though insulted he felt the need to ask.

"Thanks," he muttered, then focused his attention back on his son, who was hovering inside the door, his hands crammed into the pockets of his jeans, looking terribly uncomfortable. And guilty.

However, Brant had no intention of lambasting Elliot

for this antic, at least not in front of Jessica. Maybe not period. A kid that left home, for whatever reason, had problems. He needed counseling, not condemnation, at least not from him, an absentee father who was trying to rehabilitate their relationship.

Still, he had made both Brant and his mother frantic, and he couldn't be allowed to totally get away with his conduct. He was old enough and responsible enough to be held accountable for his actions.

"Elliot, why don't you sit down," Jessica suggested in a tentative voice, destroying the silence, "while I get you something to drink."

"Thanks," Elliot mumbled, pawing the carpet with the end of his big Nike, still not looking at Brant.

"What would you like? Coke or iced tea?" Jessica asked, that tentativeness still in her voice.

"Uh, Coke's okay."

Without saying anything else, Jessica made her way toward the kitchen. Once she was gone, Brant said, "Sit down, Elliot. I'm not going to chew you up and spit you out."

Elliot's head came up, a relieved look on his face.

"At least not just yet," Brant added.

The boy's relief visibly and quickly dissolved. "Mom's pissed, isn't she?"

Brant ignored his choice of verbs and said, "What do you think?"

"She's pissed." Elliot remained standing, angling his head. "You are, too, right?"

"Let's say we were more concerned than anything else." Brant paused, expelling a breath, feeling like he was walking on bloody eggshells and hating every minute of it. He wished he had better parenting skills, that he knew how to handle this volatile situation without making matters worse.

"Mom wouldn't let me work," Elliot muttered as he slumped into the chair, a sullen look falling over his thin features.

"That's no reason to scare her to death."

"I know."

"Where have you been?"

"At Kyle's parents' cabin."

Brant had no idea where that was, but it didn't matter. "Did Kyle take you?"

Elliot nodded.

"Did his parents know?"

"I'm sure Kyle didn't tell them," Elliot said, "but they wouldn't have cared."

"Oh, I bet they would have if they had known the circumstances."

"Uh, right," Elliot muttered, lowering his head.

Brant wished he'd been the one who had talked to Kyle. Thurmon had done that, while he'd checked with some of Elliot's other friends whose names and addresses Marsha had given him.

Jessica chose that moment to walk in with a tray holding two glasses of Coke, a small plate of sandwiches, and cookies.

"I thought you might be hungry," she said by way of explanation.

Brant felt awful, feeling he was imposing on her. He shot her a grateful look, then said to Elliot, "What do you say?"

"Thanks, Mrs. Kincaid."

"Are you hungry?" Jessica asked.

"Sorta."

"Good."

She didn't sit down. Instead, Brant felt her gaze on him. He met those lovely, expressive eyes, losing himself in them for a second, before shaking himself and returning to the real world.

"Look, I'll go to my room and let you two work this out alone."

"Don't go," Brant said impulsively, knowing his eyes were pleading as they remained on hers.

He had clearly put her on the spot, he could tell by the slight frown drawing her brows together. "Oh, I don't think—"

"Please." He didn't want to appear as though he were begging, but he thought maybe her presence would keep him from doing something, saying something, to further alienate his kid.

He had no idea why Elliot had chosen to come to him. But he was both delighted and suspicious, and he refused to let Elliot play him and Marsha against each other.

"All right," Jessica said at last, giving Elliot a small smile before sitting on the sofa.

For a moment silence dominated while Elliot drank his Coke and munched on the sandwiches. "Man, these are good."

"Damn," Brant muttered, lunging out of his chair and reaching for his cell phone. "I haven't called your mother or Thurmon." He paused. "I'll be right back."

He hated to leave Jessica stranded with Elliot, but maybe that wouldn't be all bad. Elliot seemed to like her, and vice versa. Anyhow, he didn't want to call Marsha in front of his son, knowing the fireworks would erupt. She would be worse than pissed.

He was right.

"You mean he's there, with you, at that...that woman's house?"

"Yes," he said through tight lips, trying to keep his voice down, thinking maybe she would get the hint and do the same. Hers was barely a decibel below a shrill.

"You bring him home right now, you hear?"

"I want to talk to him first."

"No! I'm the one who should do that. Just wait till I get my hands on him."

"Dammit, Marsha, get hold of yourself and calm down. He's all right, for God's sake. That should be more important than reaming him out."

"Don't you dare lecture me on how to raise my child."

Brant's nerves were on the verge of snapping. "I promise I'll bring him home shortly. Right now, he's eating."

"What did he say?" Marsha demanded, her voice quivering with anger.

"Not much yet. He just got here."

"You're responsible for this," she bit out. "If you hadn't come back—"

"I'll call you when we're on our way," Brant cut in. "Right now, I have to call Thurmon and let him know."

Without saying anything else, he hung up. Once he'd informed Thurmon and the detectives, he made his way back into the living room, feeling like he'd been gutted.

Brant paused at the door, taking in the scene before him. Jessica and Elliot were deep in conversation. His son seemed as comfortable with Jessica as he was in a pair of holey tennis shoes.

Damn, who would ever have thought it? What kind of magic did she have? Whatever it was, he wanted it.

For a second, envy churned through him. If only he had that kind of easy relationship with Elliot, what a joy that would be. Then his envy turned to remorse. After all, he had only himself to blame.

Now, however, he had another chance, and he wasn't about to squander this one.

As if he sensed his dad had come back into the room, Elliot clammed up, then swung around, an uneasy look on his face.

Silently, Brant took a seat. "Your mom wants you home."

"Figures," Elliot muttered darkly.

"Is there anything you'd like to tell me?" Brant asked as gently as he could. "Like what you hoped to accomplish by pulling this stunt?"

Elliot thought for a moment, then shrugged. "I'm tired of Mom trying to run my life."

How did one respond to that? "Look, son, just because your mom disagrees with you, that doesn't mean you can run away and hide. You know better than that."

Elliot paled, his lips thinning. "She should let me work. Can't you make her?"

So much for his lecture, Brant thought, watching Jessica's eyes widen while he searched for something suitable to say. "No, son, I can't make her do anything, and you know that. But what I do know is you owe her an apology for putting her through hell."

"She hates you, you know."

He heard Jessica suck in her breath and knew she was appalled; he wished she weren't party to this conversation. "This is not about me and your mother, Elliot," Brant stressed. "It's about you."

"So she grounds me? That's nothing new."

''Just keep in mind that she loves you very much and wants only what's best for you. And so do I.''

''Then why can't I work?''

''Isn't ball important to you, too?'' Brant was struggling for the right words to defuse this explosive situation. He felt like a miserable failure, that nothing he said made any sense, much less got through to his son.

'''Course it is, but I can do both.''

''Not if she doesn't want you to,'' Brant pointed out as gently and patiently as he could.

Elliot lunged off the sofa, clenching and unclenching his fists, his eyes firing. ''Why does she always get her way?'' His voice rose, while his features turned fierce. ''Why can't you have a say?'' Tears now blurred his vision. He swiped at them angrily. ''You keep telling me I'm your son.''

Without thinking, Brant shot off the sofa and grabbed Elliot. Seconds later, they both stiffened as if shell-shocked by the sudden move. Afterward, Brant hadn't known his intentions, whether he was going to shake Elliot or hug him.

All he knew was that his kid's pain was simply too much to endure.

''You are my son,'' Brant stressed, raising his head and searching for air. His gaze landed on Jessica. Her eyes were filled with tears; his heart wrenched another notch.

That was when he realized he was crushing his son against his chest as though he would never let him go. And God, he didn't want to. ''Did you hear what I said, Elliot?'' He heard the panicked note in his own voice while fighting back tears. ''You *are* my son. Nothing will ever change that.''

For several more heartbeats, Elliot let him hold him.

Then he pushed himself away. "Take me home," he said in a dull voice.

Jessica told herself she shouldn't wait for him. She should go to her room. He wouldn't want to see her or anyone else when he got back. But her heart had over-ruled her head, and she had remained downstairs.

Even though they had exchanged few words, she wasn't alone. Sue, the security lady, was with her again and wouldn't leave until Brant returned. At the moment she was out front, smoking.

Jessica was puttering in the kitchen when she heard the front door open. Thinking it was Sue, she remained where she was.

"Jessica?"

Her pulse leaped, and the tray she held trembled slightly, though she didn't put it down. Brant hadn't eaten, nor had she. She wasn't hungry, and she figured he wasn't, either, but they both needed a little some-thing in their stomachs. Chicken salad, crackers and fruit should suffice.

"Jessica," he said again.

She heard the question in his voice, and the eager-ness. Or had she just imagined the latter? Clutching the tray, she went into the living room, where she gave a start. He looked like he'd been whipped mentally.

Her first reaction was to drop the tray, dive into his arms and comfort him. But she couldn't do that. She couldn't get any more emotionally involved with this man than she already was. It was bad enough that she'd given her body to him with such foolish abandon. But to give her emotions, as well, would be suicidal.

Still, that session with his son had touched her deeply, that poignant exchange between father and son.

She hoped with every fiber of her being that it was the beginning of a fresh start for both of them.

Yet she feared she was too optimistic, especially after Elliot had all but lunged out of Brant's arms, demanding to be taken home.

"It will all work out," she said lamely, when Brant continued to just stand there, as if he didn't know what else to do.

"I doubt that," he responded wearily, but with a harsh edge to his voice.

"Are you hungry?"

"Yes, but I'm not sure I can eat."

Standing there, even in his low-spirited state, he looked disturbingly attractive. The sight of him never failed to take her breath.

"Thanks for the offer, anyway," he said, pulling her out of her thoughts.

Jessica nodded, then placed the tray on the coffee table and eased into the nearest chair.

Brant walked to the fireplace and stood with his head down for a moment, then turned around. "Elliot didn't say a word all the way to his house."

"I'm sorry. I was hoping things—" She broke off under the torment she saw in his eyes. If only she knew what to say and do, but she was at a loss. She could only listen if he wanted to talk.

"I'm sure Marsha's giving him the devil even as we speak, which will only make it harder for Elliot and me to patch things up."

"You can't stop trying, regardless."

"Oh, I know that, but Elliot's right. His mother hates me, and as a result, she can be vicious."

"Surely she'll back off now that this has happened," Jessica said cautiously. "This has to have shaken her."

He sneered. ''Don't count on it.''

''All the more reason why you should be there for Elliot.''

''Meaning?''

Color suffused her face. ''Meaning, while I'm in Zurich, you'll be able to spend quality time with him.''

''Exactly when do you leave?''

''That doesn't matter,'' Jessica said. ''You're not going with me.''

''Yes, I am.''

''No, you're not. I'm going alone.''

A muscle jerked in his jaw. ''If you do, then I won't be here when you get back.''

Twenty-eight

Jessica's head ached, not subtly, either, but like a pounding gong. She didn't see it getting any better any time soon either, not as long as several vocal members of the city council remained in her office.

At the moment Lance Saxon was in Chuck Hanson's face, reading him the riot act for not supporting his position. "What we need to do," Saxon was expounding, "is simply hire Joe Mayfield back and be done with it."

"God forbid," Hanson fired back. "What's wrong with Gaston Forrester, the interim? He's doing a bang-up job."

"Horse puckey," Saxon countered, scrunching his face in distaste. "He can't hold a candle to Mayfield."

It was all Jessica could do not to shout at them to grow up and stop badgering each other like spoiled brats. She also wanted to remind them that she was in the room, that she did exist and was actually running the city whether they liked it or not.

She did neither. She remained behind her desk and let them continue haranguing each other.

There were three others present, tipping the table against her by one vote, though this was not an official meeting, so no items were actually coming to a vote. She had met with the five of them out of courtesy.

However, this type of renegade gathering not only alarmed her but raised her ire, as well. Supposedly these particular members had been mulling over questions on various issues and wanted answers from her in a more relaxed atmosphere. With Lance Saxon involved, however, she should have known the session wouldn't be cordial, much less relaxing. Regardless of what she wanted, Saxon was against it.

She didn't understand his acute dislike of her, unless he had political aspirations of his own and feared her forceful stance on important issues would somehow tarnish him and hurt his endeavors to seek office. Of course, that was just speculation on her part, with nothing concrete to base it on. Still, something had him out for her blood.

No matter, she still had no intention of changing her mind about Chief Mayfield or the land deal. Unless the council overruled her.

And they had yet to take the final vote.

The only plus for her was that no one objected to the budget retreat. As soon as she returned from Europe, that would be her next big project. Maybe getting their minds on the budget would get them off the other controversies surrounding her.

"Mayor."

The use of her title drew her attention to J. D. Wymon, Porter's old friend, on whom she had always counted. But as she'd told Tony, he had become wishy-washy of late, suggesting someone had put pressure on him. Maybe she was about to find out.

He was a shy but kind man whom Jessica thought was also the most intelligent member on the council. "Yes, J.D.?" she asked with a genuine smile.

"The plant manager approached me personally," he

said in a steady tone, "and outlined his concerns about building on land that was part of the city proper." He paused and shifted his feet, as though uncomfortable with what he was about to say. "Curtis Riley was with him. I have to tell you, they're two unhappy men who are determined this issue won't pass."

"I couldn't agree more," Saxon put in. "You and I have discussed—"

"I have the floor right now, Lance," J.D. interjected without so much as looking at Saxon. "If you don't mind, that is."

Although Saxon didn't have a comeback, he was not happy, Jessica thought, seeing the flush that appeared on his cheeks.

"I'm aware of their concerns, J.D.," Jessica said in a calm voice. "I've spoken to Curtis myself." More than once, she wanted to add, but didn't.

J.D. rubbed his scrawny chin. "The way I see it, if we don't annex the land, we still win, still benefit from the windfall. The people who live in Merrick will utilize the city to its fullest by shopping and so forth."

"I'm sure you're right," Jessica said, "but the company won't be paying city taxes, which would be a big shot in the arm for our economy for years to come." Her eyes touched on each of the members. "That's been my position from day one."

"And you don't see it changing?" J.D. asked in a somber tone.

"No, I don't."

"I have to tell you up front, Mayor," Saxon said, taking the floor once again, "I'm going to continue my campaign against it. I'm like J.D. Why tick off a big corporation to the extent that they'll opt to move elsewhere, out of this area entirely? Then no one will benefit.''

''I think they're bluffing, Lance. And if they're not, then something else will be done with the land.''

His eyes slanted along with his lips. ''You're willing to take that gamble?''

''Yes, I am.''

''Well, I'm not.''

A silence followed his harsh declaration.

Another councilman, Tiny Conner, who was anything but tiny, stood. He was huge, weighing in at close to three hundred and fifty pounds, she suspected, but his height, well over six feet, helped distribute that excess weight. ''I know you've informed us by letter that you're being harassed and that's the purpose of the bodyguard. But if you don't mind, I think an update on the situation is in order.''

While the change of subject was a godsend, she had hoped this particular one wouldn't come up. She should have known better, especially in such a small, confined meeting. Still, it was something she wasn't comfortable discussing with the council. If she knew whether the threats were job related or personal, she might be more forthcoming.

''Unfortunately the culprit hasn't been apprehended as yet.''

''That incident downtown was a very serious matter,'' Tiny pointed out, concern darkening his ruddy complexion.

''Rest assured, my work isn't suffering as a result.''

''We never thought that at all,'' Avery Bates chimed in, the only member who had heretofore kept his silence. ''It's just that we're concerned about your welfare, Mayor.''

"I appreciate that, and will keep you informed."

"You've apparently made a vicious enemy, Mayor," Saxon said, a glint in his eye.

And you're delighted, too, she told herself. "It looks that way, though it could be just some crackpot off the street who really has no agenda, political or otherwise."

Byford Downs spoke up. "If there's anything we can do, you let us know."

There were nods from the rest of the group except Saxon. He didn't move a muscle, though that glint increased in his eye. She fought the urge to slap the pompous know-it-all, suddenly wondering if he was behind the menace.

Brushing that thought aside as ridiculous, she smiled at the entire group, then said, "As you well know, I respect all of you and your opinions. At the same time, I'm counting on you to respect mine."

Before Saxon or anyone else could go off on another tangent, Jessica went on. "I have interviews set up next week for the chief's job. Meanwhile, we'll continue to see how Gaston Forrester performs."

Although she heard Saxon's snort, she ignored it. "As far as the land deal goes, I guess that will ultimately depend on the way the council votes."

Another member, Tilford Jennings, stood, then faced the others. "I think we've taken up enough of the mayor's time for one afternoon." He paused with a sarcastic smile. "I know you've taken up enough of mine."

They all chuckled.

Tilford shoved back his chair. "So let's get out of here."

"Thank you all for coming," Jessica said graciously,

shaking hands with each of them, even Saxon, who all but glared at her.

Whatever his motive, he was a bump in the road she could do without.

Once they were gone, Tony stuck his head in. "Sorry I was out when they bombarded you. How did you make out against Saxon?"

"I held my own, but it was all I could do not to put my fist in his mouth."

Tony grinned. "You don't have to wait on my permission."

Jessica didn't respond. She merely rubbed her sore head.

"Why don't you and he-man outside call it a day and head for the house? You look exhausted."

The fact that he never used Brant's name always conjured up a smile, regardless of her mood. This afternoon was no exception. "I'm sure he-man won't object," she said lightly.

Her cell phone rang. For a second her entire body tensed; then she forced the tension to evaporate. She had changed her number again, which meant this was a friendly call. Flipping the lid, she placed it against her ear.

"Bitch," a coarse voice whispered. "I'm counting down."

White-faced, she slammed the phone closed.

"That bastard!" Tony spat, his hands fluttering. "You'd think with all the modern technology they've got, the law would've nailed him by now." He paused. "Want me to get he-man?"

"I'll tell him later," Jessica said in an unsteady voice.

Tony hesitated. "What about Zurich? Do you think you should still go?"

She gave him an incredulous look. "Of course. I'll be out of harm's way for sure, at least for a while."

"He *is* going with you, right?"

"It appears I have no choice," she said with mixed emotions.

"I'll check on room arrangements ASAP."

"Thanks," she murmured.

"Anything come up in the meeting that I need to know about?" Tony asked, changing the subject, as if sensing her mood.

"Nothing's changed. Some still support me and some don't. So I guess we'll see how it all comes out in the next big meeting."

"Okay, then," he said, turning and waving his hand behind him. "See you in the morning."

He shut the door, which blocked out Brant, though she was conscious he was there. Always. Now it appeared she wasn't going to get any reprieve from him at all. She'd pinned her hopes on the European trip to do just that, but in light of his ultimatum, she'd changed her mind.

When he'd issued it, she'd been too taken aback to respond right off. Then, when she'd regrouped, she'd been tempted to call his bluff.

"I mean it, Jessica," he'd stressed, his grating voice shattering the silence.

Her chin had jutted. "I still think I'll be fine on my own."

He hadn't responded. He'd simply stared at her, his features set in stone.

"Oh, all right. Have it your own way."

Later, she didn't know why she'd capitulated. Maybe

it was a niggling fear for her own safety or maybe it was something much more basic, the fear of him actually walking out of her life, the most lethal fear of all.

Pulling her thoughts off him, Jessica made preparations to shut down for the day. She had grabbed her purse when Brant appeared in the doorway.

"I heard your cell," he said without preamble, his gaze unwavering on her.

"It was him," she admitted, that unsteady note back in her voice.

Brant let an expletive fly. "I hope you're finally convinced you shouldn't leave home without me."

His attempt at dark humor fell on deaf ears. "What choice do I have?"

Twenty-nine

The Alps were magnificent. Gazing at them from the plane and now on the ground, Jessica was in awe of the never-ending beauty that surrounded her. In her travels with Porter, somehow they had missed Switzerland. She had always regretted that, thinking she might not get the chance to travel again.

Now she was here, though she still couldn't believe it. Not with Porter, though, and not alone, as she'd intended. Brant, looking altogether irresistible in a pair of slacks and a sports jacket that called attention to his lean, muscular frame, seemed completely at ease. But then, he'd been a world traveler and could seemingly adapt to anything.

Even baby-sitting her.

Jessica tried not to dwell on the indisputable fact that he would be with her throughout the duration of the conference. Why, she still didn't know. There had been no problems thus far. The flight had taken off and arrived on time, and no suspicious-looking characters had been seen lurking about.

A week had passed since that meeting in her office, followed by the latest call. Since then, Brant had seemed to shadow her even more closely, if that were possible. He had spoken to Thurmon several times, clearly frustrated because the pervert was still unknown and at large.

Jessica remained convinced it wasn't anyone she knew, certainly not any of the men at the top of Brant's list. Yet a stranger harassing her to such a degree didn't make any sense, either.

So here she was, in Switzerland, hoping to be free of her tormenter for a little while, and instead she was being subjected to torment of a different sort: Brant.

Every time he got near her, his cologne surrounded her like an aphrodisiac, bringing to mind their shared night of heady passion. Even though she'd noticed his hooded gaze filled with suppressed desire, he hadn't touched her again. She sensed his mind was filled with thoughts of Elliot and what to do about him.

Since the kid had appeared on her doorstep, Brant hadn't mentioned him again. She'd wanted to ask, but she hadn't wanted to intrude. Still, she worried about Elliot, knowing the agony he was most likely going through, having had an absentee father herself.

"You're awfully quiet," Brant said, after supervising the unloading of their baggage. They were now making their way to the registration desk of a small but gloriously renovated hotel with all of its old, unique features still intact.

"I guess I'm in awe, first that I'm here," Jessica said, quelling the urge to pinch herself. "And second, at the beauty of this country. Not only the snow on the mountains, even though it's summer, but the flowers. They're breathtaking. And everything is so clean."

"I know. This is my second trip here, and I'm just as impressed now as I was the first time."

Brant's gaze was indulgent, which heightened the flush already heating her cheeks. That was when it hit her that he seemed much looser, less uptight, *more human.* Not such a good thing.

Caring was foolish, crazy, *risky.*

Thank goodness Tony had been able to get them adjoining rooms. If not... Jessica shut down that thought, because they had arrived at the front desk, where an attractive young attendant greeted them with a smile.

Jessica gave the woman her credit card. While that was being processed, she gazed about, trying to ignore what Brant was doing to her pulse rate, standing as he was within touching distance of her.

Once again, the smell of him made her nerves sizzle. She shifted positions. When she did, she accidentally caught his eye. He was staring at her with discomforting intensity.

"Ma'am?"

The clerk's soft voice claimed her attention. A frown marred her face. "I'm afraid there's a problem. Actually, two."

Jessica answered her frown. "I don't understand."

The young lady was clearly embarrassed. "Your credit card registers as invalid."

"What?" Jessica was appalled. "But that can't be. I mean, I haven't used it..." Her voice played out, and she turned to Brant, whose eyes were narrowed on the woman.

"Check again, won't you?" he said. "I'm sure it's a computer error."

"No, sir, there's been no error. The card has been canceled."

"That's impossible," Jessica stressed, her voice pitched higher than normal. "I didn't cancel my card."

"What was the other problem?" Brant put in, his tone polite but hard.

"The rooms. We only have the one. An adjoining room was never available."

Jessica sucked in her breath as shock pumped through her.

Brant muttered a curse, then said, "Maybe we should just go to another hotel."

"I'm sorry, sir, but you won't fare any better elsewhere, I'm afraid. With several conventions in town, all the luxury hotels are booked."

Jessica's heart thudded. *They couldn't share a room.* That just wasn't possible. She didn't dare look at Brant for fear of what she would see mirrored in his eyes. She hoped she camouflaged the shiver that went through her. What she had thought would be a dream trip was fast turning into another nightmare.

"Let's deal with the credit card foul-up first," Brant said, his voice crisp as a chilly fall morning.

"Please run it through again," Jessica insisted. "I'm positive there's been a mistake." She couldn't believe this was happening. Her credit card canceled? No way. She had paid it off in full last month and hadn't used it since.

As far as the room went—well, she wouldn't stand for that, either. Somewhere in this hotel, there had to be another room for Brant. If it wasn't near her, then so be it.

As she'd told him all along, she didn't need a bodyguard in Switzerland.

"I'm sorry, Mrs. Kincaid, but there's been no mistake." The clerk shifted her gaze. "I'd be happy to take another card."

"But—" Flabbergasted, Jessica didn't know quite what to say.

"Does anyone else have access to your card?" Brant asked, his eyes piercing.

Jessica shook her head. "No, absolutely not."

"Well, someone's managed to get it," Brant said, not bothering to mask the fury in his tone. "And I bet I know who that someone is."

"You mean—" Her throat closed, robbing her of speech.

"That's right."

"Oh, my God." She felt suddenly light-headed, as if the rug had been yanked out from under her. "Is that really possible?" Of course it was. Hadn't she seen countless horror stories on TV and read in the paper about others who had been victims of illegal computer tampering? Lives had been shattered by such a vindictive act.

What about her bank account? Jessica's light-headedness increased, and if she hadn't clutched the desk, her knees might have buckled. As if he sensed her distress, Brant's features softened. "Hey, it's going to be okay. I have my credit card. Once we get settled, I'll call Thurmon."

Swallowing hard, Jessica nodded, feeling a wave of relief wash through her. At that particular moment she was glad Brant was there, although if she'd had to, she was perfectly capable of handling this dilemma on her own.

Still, in a strange country, it was nice to have him around to take charge, especially under the circumstances.

But only temporarily, Jessica cautioned herself, suddenly regaining her focus.

"About the room situation?" Brant asked, his outrage visibly lined in his face.

"I told you, sir, there's only one available, and that's Mrs. Kincaid's."

Though the young lady was obviously troubled and uneasy, she wasn't about to budge on her position. "That's totally unacceptable," Jessica said in a firm but polite tone.

"I'm sorry, ma'am, but—"

"Call the manager," Brant demanded in a low, even voice.

Jessica knew he was seething as she watched the muscle tick overtime in his jaw.

Following a shuddering breath, she waited while the manager approached, only to learn that his position was just as staunch as the clerk's.

Brant turned to her. "It's your choice. We can leave and take a chance on finding someplace else, or we can—" He paused deliberately. "Or we can tough it out," he added in a terse voice.

Out of the corner of her eye, she saw the curiosity burning in both the clerk's and the manager's eyes. Her anger almost got the better of her. If Tony was responsible for this mistake, she would fire him.

A stiff silence followed while Brant's eyes continued to drill her, the tension in him hard to miss. That was when she realized he wasn't overjoyed with the situation either. But what choice did they have? She was dead tired, having been unable to sleep on the plane. Tomorrow she was due to preside at a reception. The following day was her keynote speech, followed by the series of workshops.

She had to rest in order to function and do what she had come here to do. Yet the idea of sharing a room with him was overwhelming. Her blood chilled. She would have to shower, then parade around in her gown and robe in front of him.

"Jessica?"

Brant's impatient voice forced her to face him. "Fine." She swallowed her rage. "We'll make the best of it."

Brant didn't know how much longer he could take this "togetherness." Only one more night, he reminded himself. At the moment, that seemed an eternity.

The days hadn't been a problem. Jessica's schedule had been grueling, and it had started soon after they had been shown to the room.

Forcing himself not to react when he'd seen the king-size bed had taken more willpower than he thought he had. He couldn't possibly share that bed with her and keep his hands to himself. That was when he'd spied the alternative.

"Not to worry," he'd said, seeing the sick, pale look on her face. "I'll take the love seat."

Her eyes had followed his. "That's not an option. Two people can barely sit on that, and no one could possibly sleep on it, especially a man."

"I inquired about a cot," Brant fired back. "None were available. If you have another suggestion I'm all ears."

A stone-cold silence invaded the room.

Jessica swallowed a strangled sob. "No. I'm fresh out."

"The sofa it is."

"You won't sleep a wink."

"So?"

"That's crazy."

"Well, I don't see any other choice," Brant pointed out flatly. "Unless I sleep out in the hall."

Jessica pursed her mouth, which made him suddenly ache to draw that lower, pouting lip between his teeth and suck on it. He cleared his throat and strode to the window. The view was incredible, and he tried to concentrate on that while he took long, deep breaths.

"It's a huge bed."

He swung around and stared at her, slack-jawed. "You mean—"

"Yes," she said in a thin voice. "Since we're neither one a heavy weight, we can manage." She paused. "Besides, I trust you."

Big mistake.

"I trust you, too."

His attempt at humor hit its mark. Jessica's features lightened considerably, and she gave him a weak smile. "Right now, I'm more worried about my credit card than you pouncing on me."

Another mistake.

Brant watched color replace the paleness in her cheeks as though she were embarrassed by what she'd said.

He let it slide, turning his back once more before she noticed the bulge in his slacks.

On the heels of that disturbing conversation, he'd called Thurmon and brought him up-to-date.

Thereafter, almost every minute had been taken up at the large adjacent hotel where the conference was being held, or taking in the sights of Lugano, a picturesque city an hour's drive from Zurich, which they also explored.

Lugano was spectacular. The city was ablaze with gorgeous flowers, snow-covered mountains, crystal clear lakes and, according to Jessica, the best shopping ever in the quaint cobblestoned market jam-packed with avant-garde shops and restaurants featuring wonderful cuisine.

Back at work, Jessica had continued to dazzle them with her speeches and workshops. No doubt about it, she had found her calling. She definitely had the right stuff.

That was why the nights had been intolerable.

Neither of them had gotten any sleep to speak of, especially him. Although he hadn't been able to see through her gown and robe, it hadn't mattered. Hell, he was already aware of the curves hidden beneath the flimsy material. He'd touched and tongued every square inch of that succulent flesh.

Every time she moved, which was almost never, as if fearful of disturbing him, he'd gotten an erection. Her smell had enveloped him, making not only his dick ache, but every bone and muscle in his body, because he had to hold it so rigid.

Before he'd married Marsha, he'd had a lot of women. But never, Marsha included, had he craved one the way he craved Jessica Kincaid.

He couldn't define the reason, nor did he want to, knowing he would be wasting his time. When this assignment was over, he would never see her again.

Now, as he waited for her to return from the gift shop, Brant felt at loose ends. He hadn't wanted her to go alone, but she'd insisted.

"For heaven's sake, Brant, you know I'm safe. I'll be right back. I just need to get some toothpaste."

"You can use mine."

"I'd rather not," she'd said in a husky voice, swerving her gaze.

He'd conceded then, though he wasn't happy about it. She wasn't in any danger; his instinct told him that. So why was he pacing the floor when she'd only been gone for fifteen minutes? How bloody long could it take to buy a tube of toothpaste?

Cool it, Harding. You're making something out of nothing.

That was when he heard the knock on the door. With his heart thudding, he crossed to it and jerked it open. It was hotel security.

"I'm afraid we have a problem, sir."

His gut clenched, his worst fears staring him in the face. "Has something happened to Mrs. Kincaid?"

"Uh, yes, sir," the man said, stepping back as though to distance himself from Brant's looming presence and fierce expression.

"Where is she? If anything's happened to her, there's going to be hell to pay."

"Her elevator stalled, sir. She's trapped between floors."

Thirty

Brant tore out of the room as if the hotel was on fire, his heart lodged in his throat. What the hell else was going to happen? Trapped in an elevator. He could imagine how frightened Jessica must be about now, how helpless she must feel.

Dammit, he shouldn't have let her go out alone. At least he would have been with her. But how did you overcome a hardheaded female who was used to doing things her own way and in her own time?

Thank God his bum leg wasn't hampering his mobility. "Which elevator?" he demanded, feeling his adrenaline kick in, becoming the agent of old. On high alert. Ready for battle, regardless of the situation or the odds.

"The one at the end of this hall," the guard said, huffing and puffing. Once there, the man added, "She's halfway up, as you can see."

Brant paused long enough to notice the light indicating where the elevator had stopped. Swallowing a curse, he turned to the man and said, "Take me to the basement."

"Yes, sir. Follow me."

Brant practically flew down the stairs until he reached a huddled crew of electricians and several hotel employees, all of whom began immediately apologizing.

He ignored the apologies, immediately firing questions at the electricians.

At least they appeared to know what they were doing, Brant told himself, though that didn't lessen his building anxiety. The problem seemed to lie with the switch.

Although the old hotel had been refurbished, it hadn't been entirely updated, despite its five star rating. The elevators, or lifts, as the Swiss referred to them, remained as they'd been, antiquated by American standards, yet perfectly serviceable. Until now.

As Brant watched the workers, he was tempted to shove them aside and take over the operation, positive that, with his expertise in electronics, he could repair the problem in nothing flat. But then, he wasn't in the good old U.S. of A. where he felt comfortable throwing his weight around. If he had been, he wouldn't be nearly as frantic.

"Is there any way I can speak to her?" Brant demanded, watching carefully as one of the men worked on the tiny wires, his hands fumbling much more than they should.

If all mechanical endeavors failed, he would get her out even if he had to crawl up the guts of the lift himself.

"No, sir, there isn't."

"Is anyone else in there with her?" Brant asked, close to losing what little patience he'd had to begin with.

"Not that we know of," the manager said.

"Great," Brant muttered. "Just great."

"We're doing all we can, sir. It won't be long and we'll have the matter corrected."

Not with that idiot electrician working on it, you won't, Brant responded silently. Finally, when the man continued to fumble, Brant's patience ended. "Look, let me have a shot at it."

All eyes riveted on him, followed by a stark silence. Then the manager spoke again. "That's against hotel policy, sir."

"I don't give a shit about policy," Brant lashed back. "I want Mrs. Kincaid out of that elevator ASAP. So I suggest you take some help where it's offered." *Or I'll sue your ass,* he was tempted to add.

He didn't have to. The man obviously got the message. The electrician looked at his boss, who nodded his consent. Shrugging, the electrician moved aside and handed Brant his tools.

Although there was nothing wrong with the hotel's air-conditioning, Brant sweated profusely as he worked on the tiny wiring in the switch. Finally he flipped the switch and waited. The lift buzzed and coughed to life.

He pushed the basement button and waited, his heart in his throat. If he'd screwed up and it didn't work... It *would* work, dammit. *It had to.*

Though it seemed like an eternity, his task was completed, and the elevator finally whirred to the bottom, the doors sliding open. Jessica, pale and trembling, stepped straight off into his waiting arms.

Brant held her as though he would never let her go.

"I can't thank you enough." Jessica heard the husky edge to her voice, which made her sound like she was a heavy smoker.

Instead she'd been crying, something she rarely did. Only when her father had left and Porter had died had she shed so many tears.

"You've already thanked me," Brant pointed out in a gentle tone, his eyes holding hers. "Countless times."

"I know, but—" Jessica broke off and bit down on her lower lip. She wouldn't allow herself to cry again, though her nerves were shot. The experience in the elevator had taken her to her limit. Her emotions had taken too many blows.

Though the incident had happened several hours ago, she was still rattled, though she hated to admit that. While confinement in the small place had been terrifying in itself, walking off into Brant's arms had been even more so.

That particular terror was what was haunting her now. His strong arms, his hard body, had been a haven to her battered spirits. He'd clutched her so closely that she had felt every ribbed muscle and bone. She hadn't cared. The fact that her breasts were crushed against his chest and his lips buried in her neck was all that counted.

Once they reached the room, she had locked herself in the bath and soaked in the tub, willing herself to relax. That had helped, but it hadn't relieved her anxiety completely, especially after she was dressed in her night attire and returned to the room.

Sanity and reality had returned with a vengeance.

Now, as she looked at Brant, sitting on the sofa, one booted foot crossed over the other, his eyes closed, her heart raced much like it had when she was trapped in that elevator. He appeared so relaxed, but she knew better. As he had been so many times before, he was coiled tighter than a rattlesnake, prepared to strike at any time.

Jessica drew in a shuddery breath, then sat on the side of the bed and removed her robe.

"Are you okay?" he asked in a deep, thick tone.

Chills feathered her skin, especially when she realized the lamp beside the bed exposed her bare shoulders. Swinging around, she stared at him. Sure enough, his gaze was fixed on her. The heat lighting his eyes claimed her next breath.

"I'm...just tired," she whispered, licking her stiff, dry lips.

He groaned, then stood and began removing his shirt. Feeling color rush into her face, Jessica averted her gaze, then turned off the lamp.

Although she knew he slept bare-chested and in his cutoffs, she had made it a point not to look at him when he was partially undressed. Tonight, however, her eyes seemed to have a will of their own. They watched him unbutton each button, which seemed to take him an unusually long time.

Her heart clamored to get out of her chest as she finally got under the sheet and lay rigid. In a moment his side of the bed gave way under his weight. She held her breath, hoping he wouldn't say another word or make another move.

Her hope died instantly.

"He hasn't followed you over here."

She knew exactly who Brant was referring to. "I keep telling myself that, but it's hard."

"I'm so sorry that elevator shit happened." His voice sounded tight and strained. "You've been through too much."

His sympathy proved her undoing. Tears seeped from under her eyes at the same time that another sob escaped her lips. She felt his head turn, felt his eyes on her.

"Don't cry, please."

"I'm not crying," she denied.

"Come here," he muttered savagely, then reached for her.

At first she resisted. But when he ignored that resistance and circled her body with the comforting warmth and shelter of his arms, her insides turned loose and she sagged into him. Instantly, his erection pressed against her.

Jessica's senses swam, while her mind revolted, demanding she break his hold and move to the other side of the bed, where she belonged.

She couldn't move a muscle. In that moment she thought she couldn't live another second if he didn't hold her. *If he didn't make love to her.* She wanted to crawl inside his skin.

That truth shook her to the core, though not nearly as much as his lips claiming hers in a moist, sucking kiss that literally took her next breath. Her mind emptied of everything except him. Only him. With the same reckless abandon as before, she let her feelings take over. All rational thought was expunged.

"Oh, God, Jessica," he said, tearing his mouth off hers, "this is what I've wanted, what I've ached for." He paused, his breathing so ragged he could barely talk. "To hold you again, to love you again."

"Me too," she admitted brokenly and without shame.

His lips were everywhere, on her eyes, on her cheeks, her neck, both breasts, leaving a trail of fiery heat in their wake.

She moaned under the onslaught, especially when he pulled back so that he brought her breasts close enough together that he could almost suck both swollen nipples simultaneously.

"Oh, Brant, Brant," she murmured, wet and aching between her legs.

"Don't hold back," he told her, as though he sensed she was about to climax.

That was when she ran her hands brazenly down his back to his buttocks, then squeezed those firm cheeks of flesh.

Brant groaned out loud and stared at her out of glazed eyes before burying his tongue in her naval. There he laved, stroked in and out, purposely using his tongue as though it was between her legs.

Jessica's inside turned to mush, though she managed to find the strength to part her legs, giving him access to all of her. Wordlessly he reached down with one hand and gently parted that delicate seam and rubbed, all the while watching her.

She moaned, another orgasm striking her.

"You're even more beautiful when you come," he rasped, then shoved his hardness inside her softness.

She gasped, feeling him fill her to capacity and then some. For a timeless moment he didn't move; then he rolled over, taking her with him.

"Ride me," he begged, his breath hot against her ear.

"Brant, I—" She couldn't go on, especially after he tenderly eased her into a sitting position so that she straddled him, his throbbing penis like a stake, high and hard inside her.

"You've never been on top before, have you?" he ground out, his eyes glazed.

"No," she whispered, thinking about all the times she and Porter had made love, and never once had he changed or varied their positions. With Brant, a whole new sexual world was emerging.

Then he began to move her hips, slow, then faster, until she was indeed riding him fast and furiously until orgasms pounded them, their satisfied moans puncturing the silence.

* * *

This time, when she awakened, the place beside her wasn't empty, as it had been every other morning. Brant had used an elbow to prop his head up and was staring at her.

Unwittingly she smiled. The troubled look that darkened his features disappeared. Smiling in return, he ran the back of a knuckle down one side of her cheek.

"You know this is insanity in its highest degree."

"I know," she responded in a breathy tone.

"But I'm not sorry." His expression had turned fierce.

"Me either."

He smiled again, though it was short-lived. "So where does that leave us?"

Her features clouded. "In the here and now."

"I'm making no promises to keep my hands off of you in the tomorrows to come. I feel I have to tell you that."

"Fair enough," she said, swallowing hard, realizing she had taken another step toward digging her own emotional grave.

"Do you still love him?"

Brant's out of the blue question stunned her. "No," she finally answered. "I'm not sure I ever loved Porter, at least not passionately."

"I guessed that." Brant's finger grazed her cheek again.

"I didn't realize how inexperienced I was..." Her voice faded on an embarrassed note.

"Hey, you were perfect." His eyes were warm and tender. "I'm humbled I was the first to indoctrinate you into the world of sexual pleasures."

"No man has ever touched me like..." Again her voice faded.

"Like this," he said huskily, a hand parting her legs and cupping her mound.

The breath swished out of her. "Like...that."

He didn't work that hand, though; he just left it there. "I don't think I ever really loved Marsha, either, though I thought I did." He paused, his eyes filled with pain. "After Elliot was born, I was the happiest man on the earth. I had a son."

"What happened to change that?"

"I wish to God I knew. I guess I was so busy trying to keep Marsha in the style of living I knew she wanted that I sacrificed the most important thing—my son."

"What about your marriage?"

"I've never really missed her, only Elliot." Brant paused, then added, "What about you?"

"What about me?"

"Why did you marry a man old enough to be your father?"

Jessica gave him a troubled look. "A shrink would say it was because my dad deserted us at an early age."

"I know that must've been the pits."

"It was. It broke my heart, and for years I was never able to glue it back together."

As if feeling her pain, he clutched her tighter. "But Porter glued it back together, right?"

"In many ways," she admitted with an audible sigh. "Though I never let him get inside my heart. I've never let anyone do that, especially when it came to—" She stopped, unable to go on.

"Your sexual needs," he said, reading her mind.

She nodded.

"Like I said, I'm glad," he said thickly.

"What about you? Was Marsha your one and only?"

"As far as a relationship went, she was, though it was Elliot who proved to be my one and only love."

"How is he? Have you talked to him since you took him home?"

"Once, but he still wasn't receptive, I'm sorry to say."

"He's just going to need more time."

"Something I don't have," Brant said bleakly.

The same fact suddenly and brutally slapped her in the face, launching her back to reality, back to the indisputable fact he would soon walk out of her life, never to return. Even so, she was reluctant to break the delicate euphoria of the moment.

As if he read her mind again, Brant's probing gaze sought hers, and he groaned before lowering his head and reclaiming her lips. "Enough of this soul-searching talk."

Sighing, she parted her lips and circled her arms around him.

Thirty-one

"Have you made a decision yet?"

Brant's direct question concerning the chief's job forced her to face him, something she had been avoiding. Following their return from Europe two weeks ago, the tension between them had escalated.

Even now, in the spacious limo, she felt cramped, claustrophobic. The added anxiety resulted from that last night in Switzerland, even though he hadn't touched her once since arriving home.

The first few days she had wondered if he would attempt to kiss her, touch her, make love to her. He hadn't. Once they boarded the plane, Brant had reverted back to his old, controlled self.

She didn't know if she was affronted or relieved by his standoffishness. However, she wasn't fooled by it. She'd caught him staring at her with hungry eyes. And while those looks had reduced her insides to a quivering mass, she had purposely not met his gaze, fearing the repercussions.

Her work had been her only salvation. With so much going on in the office, she'd felt caught in a whirlwind. Included in that whirlwind had been the daylong budget retreat, which had been even more successful than she'd hoped.

In addition, she'd worked with several other mayors

concerning the proposed interstate highway. And by far the most important, she and the city manager had begun interviewing for a chief of police.

And during those hard-driving days, the e-mails and phone calls kept on coming, had escalated. That in itself had had an effect on her work and her temper. She knew Brant felt the same way, driving Thurmon relentlessly to come up with something, anything, that would point to a culprit.

Her only saving grace was that she'd been spared another disaster akin to the credit card debacle. But in the scheme of things, and under the heavy burden she carried, that now seemed a small mercy.

She was no longer in control of her life or her time, and she resented that. Would it ever end? She'd begun to fear Brant was destined to become permanently attached to her.

"Jessica?" Brant said, shattering the lengthy silence.

"Sorry," she said a trifle breathlessly. "My mind was a million miles away."

"That's an understatement." His eyes were narrowed on her.

"To answer your question, yes, I've made my decision."

"It's obviously not Forrester, the acting chief."

"You're right, it's not."

"So when do you break the news to the council?"

"At the next meeting." She paused. "I guess we'll see how strong a leader I am."

"And nothing's changed on the land deal."

"Absolutely not." Jessica paused again, tightening her lips. "Nor am I budging on my decision to seek reelection."

"A woman who knows what she wants and goes after it."

Somehow, she didn't think Brant meant those words as complimentary, and that stung. "You don't agree?"

"I didn't say that," he countered easily. "You're good at what you do, and I admire that."

She still wasn't convinced of his sincerity, but it didn't matter. *He* didn't matter. He would soon leave her and Elliot, and return to the wilds of Arkansas.

Thinking of his son made her ask, "How's Elliot?"

Brant sighed audibly. "Still struggling."

"It's not easy being torn between your mother and father."

"Do you think I did a bad thing? Coming back into his life, that is?" Brant's voice was riddled with guilt.

Jessica chose her words carefully. "No. As his father, you have that right. Still…" She hesitated, unsure how to venture further, since she was stepping into foreign territory.

"Still, what?" he pressed. "I value your opinion. Hell, you've been on that side. Would you have wanted your father to come back?"

Even though she didn't want to revisit that dark place in her heart again so soon, expose the pain to the light of day, she answered with honesty. "Yes, though I'm not sure it would have been the best thing."

Brant expelled a breath.

"I know that wasn't exactly the answer you wanted," she said softly. "But that's a hard call."

"To say nothing of putting you in a hard place."

"I'm used to that," she said with a resigned smile.

His lips twisted bitterly. "It's just that with Marsha's hatred of me, I don't see much changing."

"You're not giving up, are you?"

"Not as long as I'm upright and breathing."

"Do you think Elliot would like to go for a boat ride and do a little fishing?" Once she'd issued that invitation, Jessica knew she'd made a mistake. She had no idea what had prompted her to take such a bold step, involve herself to such an extent. Perhaps it was that pain again, that frustration Brant wore like a second skin when he talked about his son.

Now, however, he looked as stunned as she felt. "Probably," he said, his eyes piercing, and his tone cautious. "Why do you ask?"

She looked away, then back; swallowing a sigh, she blurted out, "You know I have a boat. It's time it was either sold or driven or something." She spread her hands. "Oh, just forget I asked. I—"

"We'll go, or we will if Elliot's game, that is. I think it's a great idea." Brant paused and angled his head. "Unless you weren't serious."

"Uh, no," Jessica said, wetting her lower lip, feeling like she'd just been tossed in the ocean without a life jacket. "I was serious."

"I'll call him, then."

Had she lost her mind for further involving herself in Brant's personal life when it wasn't necessary? And a pleasure outing with him and Elliot was definitely *not* necessary. Trying to mask her trepidation and shaking hands, Jessica saw her bag on the floorboard as a lifeline.

She reached for it, and so did Brant.

Their fingers touched, and they both froze. Faces as close as hands, they stared at each other. She saw his eyes focus on her parted, moist lips. She knew he was going to kiss her. She ached for him to kiss her.

He licked his own lips, then jerked back, cursing profusely.

Feeling color sting her cheeks, Jessica turned away, her heart threatening to burst.

"Dammit, Jessica," Brant spat in a tormented voice.

"You don't have to say anything."

Suddenly he leaned across, clutched her chin and brought her face back around. "Don't think for one second I don't want you." He grabbed her hand and placed it on the throbbing hardness between his legs.

Oh, dear Lord, she cried silently. "Brant, please," she whispered, feeling a new surge of raw desire spread through her.

"If I went with my gut, I'd press you back into that plush seat, hike up that designer skirt, jerk your hose down and take you right here." His voice sounded strained to the breaking point, even as he placed her hand back in her lap.

Then why don't you?

"But the next time I make love to you, I don't want it to be under these circumstances, when you're stressed or frightened. I want you to want me because of who I am, dammit, not because you need a warm, comforting body."

Jessica didn't say a word. She simply didn't know what to say. Her heart was too full.

"I'm so glad to see you."

After exchanging hugs with Veronica, Jessica echoed, "Me too. It seems like forever since we've gotten together."

"And done lunch," Veronica said with a grin.

Jessica pulled out her chair. "Well, let's sit. I don't have a lot of time."

"Oh, pooh," Veronica countered in a huffy tone. "You and your schedule. Don't you ever want to just chuck that fancy watch of yours and say to hell with it?"

Jessica smiled. "More often than you know."

"Then I suggest you just do it."

The waitress appeared and took their orders. Alone again, they faced each other. Veronica was the first to speak, cocking her head toward a table several yards from them. "You could've asked Brant to join us, you know. I wouldn't have minded."

"But I would."

Veronica's eyes widened. "Ouch!"

Jessica rolled hers at her friend's dramatic antics. "Don't try to make something out of nothing."

"Who, me?" Veronica asked with a grin. "I guess you do need a little space, huh?"

Jessica frowned. "It's not only him, it's the whole mess. I'm getting tired of living my life in turmoil."

"I'm sure." Veronica's eyes clouded. "It seems like you've had a long run of bad luck. But you're not thinking about abandoning thoughts of reelection, are you?"

"Heavens no."

"Good, because I've come up with some great ideas for slogans and logos."

"Actually I can't wait to really knuckle down and work on my campaign plans, but for the next few weeks, I have too much on my agenda."

"Thurmon, too," Veronica said. "Mostly busting his buns trying to nail that sicko's butt."

"And I appreciate it, too. It's just that it's taking so much longer than I expected."

"I feel the same." Veronica paused. "So tell me about the trip. Except the credit card nightmare. My better half's already told me about that. I bet that sent you into a tizzy.''

"I was furious and frustrated, to put it mildly." Jessica paused while the waitress placed their veggie wraps and fruit plates in front of them, then refilled their iced tea glasses.

A short time later, she added, "But that was nothing compared to the elevator incident."

"Elevator incident?" Veronica looked dumbfounded. "Whatever are you talking about?"

Jessica told her the horror of being trapped and how Brant had come to her rescue. What she didn't mention, of course, was their long night of lovemaking that had followed. She still couldn't share that secret, not even with her best friend.

"My gosh, how awful. I bet Brant was beside himself."

"He was that, and I was shaken to the core." Jessica shivered. "It seems I'm developing claustrophobia in my old age."

"Hell's bells, age has nothing to do with it. If that happened to me, I'd freakin' freak out."

Jessica's sober features cleared, and she smiled. "As far as the speeches and everything else, the trip was a dream come true."

"I'm glad," Veronica said warmly, then took another mouthful of food.

Jessica followed suit, and for a while they munched in companionable silence. Jessica even felt herself begin to relax only to catch a glimpse of Brant, who was eating alone. Suddenly her food tasted like sawdust.

"What's wrong?" Veronica asked. "Don't you like yours?"

"Oh, it's delicious," Jessica said, forcing a lightness back into her tone.

"So what's the latest on Roy-boy? Has he pulled any of his shenanigans lately?"

"No, and that worries me. I'm convinced he hasn't given up on getting more money out of me. In fact, he won't be satisfied until he gets his hands on all his trust."

"That's not likely to happen, is it?"

"No, not unless he has a better attorney than I do."

"Don't worry, if he acts like a fool again, Brant'll take care of him."

Jessica frowned. "Let us hope it won't come to that."

"Moving on to Curtis." Veronica grinned. "Has he still got a hard-on about the land?"

Jessica grinned back. "Of course, though I haven't heard from him since I've been back, either. I'm sure he's working the councilmembers, rallying them around his flagpole."

"A pole that would like to get inside your panties."

"Veronica!"

Her friend shrugged. "I'm serious. And hey, when the dust settles and Brant's no longer shadowing you, you really ought to think about having a fling with Curtis. Like I told you before, it'll do you good. And you could do worse."

"No, I couldn't," Jessica countered, sure her face was high red, only not for the reason Veronica thought. More hot sex was the last thing she needed right now.

"Okay, I'll keep my mouth shut," Veronica said with a contagious smile.

"No, you won't, but that's all right."

Veronica chuckled out loud. However, Jessica remained sober, dreading the moment when she would have to climb back in the car with Brant, especially after this morning's episode. Instead of seeing a light at the end of the tunnel, she saw another freight train heading her way.

"It's time for you to go, right?" Veronica asked, as though she'd picked up on Jessica's edginess.

"Yes, though I have to go to the ladies' room first. Would you mind telling Brant?"

"Of course not, silly. I need to give him a hug, anyway, and find out how things stand between him and Elliot."

Now was the perfect opportunity to tell her about the upcoming outing, but Jessica couldn't bring herself to divulge that, either. That admission would also bring on a lot of questions she wasn't prepared to answer.

"I'll tell him you'll be along shortly," Veronica said, after they took care of the check, stood, then hugged.

"Thanks. I'll be in touch."

"Me too."

Ten minutes later, Jessica walked out of the bathroom. But instead of heading back into the restaurant proper, she caught a glimpse of the small shopping area connected to the café.

Should she?

Her heart pumped overtime. Why not? What could it hurt if she strolled through the unique shops for a few minutes? Nothing, she told herself.

She had been gone only a few minutes and was poised in front of a bath shop, perusing all the pretties displayed in the window, when a strong hand clamped down on her shoulder. Fright ripped through her.

"What the hell do you think you're doing?"

She swung around and stared into Brant's fierce features.

Thirty-two

"Neato! This is really neat."

Jessica hid a smile, wondering how many times she'd heard that word since they left her town house and picked up Elliot. He had been excited then and was even more so now that they had arrived at the lake and she had pointed out the fancy boating rig that had been dear to Porter's heart.

Elliot's eyes lit like firecrackers, and he began to fidget, itching to get out and get the day started.

"Is that big one really yours?" he asked in awe, craning his neck while Brant parked the SUV.

"It's actually my husband's," Jessica responded, smiling openly at Elliot's unabashed enthusiasm. "Or was," she qualified in a soft voice.

"So it's yours now," Elliot countered logically.

"I guess it's safe to say it meets with your approval, son," Brant drawled, finally easing into the conversation now that the vehicle was stationary.

"Oh, man, it's cool. I can't believe I'm going to get to spend the day on it."

As though his gaze was drawing her, Jessica's and Brant's eyes met, and they both smiled.

Jessica finally looked away, her pulse skyrocketing. She couldn't recall ever having seen Brant smile such a genuine smile, as if he was really enjoying himself.

Maybe he'd decided to give this day his best, for both his and Elliot's sake. She hoped so. If the two were ever going to have a chance to bond, it was now.

"Come on, let's get out," the teenager demanded.

"How about you and your dad taking care of readying the boat while I unload the car?"

Brant raised quizzical eyebrows. "You okay with that?"

"Absolutely, especially since I don't know what I'm doing."

"Well, I do," Elliot chimed in with adult self-confidence. "Come on, Dad, let's show her how it's done."

Jessica laughed, then did something totally out of character for her. She reached out and ruffled Elliot's hair. "I like your style, kid."

Brant's intense gaze both caressed her and thanked her, which sent added color rushing into her cheeks. "You sure you can handle the picnic basket?"

"With ease," she assured him, squinting through her dark lenses, glad of their protective shield. Already she had exposed too much of herself, and the day was just starting.

"All right," Brant said with a lingering gaze. "We'll see you shortly."

After the vehicle was unloaded, Jessica made her way to the dock, close to the boat's slip. Elliot grinned and waved to her. "We're about ready to cast off."

"Just say the word and I'll come aboard."

"We're not quite ready for you yet," Elliot said, not bothering to look at his dad.

Brant's laid-back but concealed smile took her breath. Good thing he didn't turn that high-wattage beam on often, or she would be in even more danger than she already was.

Suddenly it hit Jessica how insane she was for opening her heart to this kind of abuse. But then, after the incident at the restaurant, she'd had no idea this trip would actually come about. In fact, she'd been sure it wouldn't.

Brant had been absolutely livid with her for giving him the slip in the restaurant.

His fury had in turn incited hers. "What does it look like I'm doing?" she'd said through clenched teeth, deliberately keeping her voice down, aware they were in a public place. "I'm window shopping."

"Dammit, Jessica, you know it's not safe for you to be alone." He rammed his hands into his pockets.

To keep from shaking her, she suspected. "I wasn't alone," she pointed out logically, cooling her own anger, hoping to diffuse the volatile situation. "As you can see, people are milling around everywhere."

"And that's my point," he retorted, then took a shuddering breath. "Look, you scared the bloody hell out of me. I thought—" He broke off with a noise that was akin to a tormented growl.

"I'm okay, Brant," she said, swerving her gaze, suddenly feeling contrite, as if she had indeed done something awful. Perhaps she had, by deliberately escaping and strolling through the shops. But she had needed the time alone, away from his all-knowing eyes, his smothering presence.

The fear of losing herself, her identity, had driven her to take such a bold step, and she had ignored the rational part of her brain that told her she was acting foolishly.

Too, she'd known Brant would be furious if he found

out. Had that been at the back of her mind? Had she wanted to rile him? If so, why?

"You're okay—through no fault of your own," he was saying, his voice now sounding weary.

Again Jessica felt awful, like a child who had been scolded and who deserved it. But she wasn't a child. She was a grown woman who had choices, choices she was free to make. And if there were unfavorable consequences, then so be it.

"Look, nothing happened, so let's just drop it, okay?"

"Only if you won't pull such a stunt again."

"I'm not a child, Brant, and I refuse to let you treat me like one."

"Then by damn stop acting like one."

"Go to hell," she snapped, then was appalled by her words and her loss of temper.

"That's where I've been ever since I came here."

Her eyes widened in horror, and an unbidden cry tore through her lips. She tried to skirt around him, but he grabbed her arm, his features contorted. "I'm sorry. That was uncalled for."

"Yes, it was," she said, breathing heavily, trying to gather her scattered wits and realizing they were probably creating a scene, which didn't bode well for the mayor of the city.

"Truce?"

She took another deep breath, then stepped back, though she kept her gaze averted. "Truce."

"Promise you won't do anything like this again."

"Don't push your luck," she responded shortly, turning and heading to the car.

An explosive silence remained between them the entire way back to the office. Just at they were about to get out, Brant said, "Is your invitation still good for the outing?"

He didn't give a rip about himself, she knew. It was Elliot. He wanted a day with his son, and only her co-operation could make that happen. While she had wished more than once that she'd kept her mouth shut, she couldn't renege, not when his eyes had a pleading glint in them.

"Of course, if Elliot wants to go."

"Of course," he said, a smirk tightening his lips.

Refusing to let him know his barb had stuck, she got out and went inside. Since then their relationship had taken another turn—for the worse.

Now, however, with the sun bright in the sky and the water crystal clear, all seemed right with the world. Even she felt a sense of freedom at being out of the city, away from the daily drudgery of responsibilities, realizing that she needed this day as much as Brant and Elliot.

At the moment all she cared about was feasting her eyes on Brant as he skillfully maneuvered the boat toward her, feeling a thrill dart through her as her gaze traveled up and down his body.

He had on a white T-shirt minus the sleeves, sleeves that he'd obviously removed with a pair of scissors. The edges were jagged and raveled. His legs, muscular and tanned, with just the right amount of hair sprinkling them, were highly visible in a pair of cutoffs that had suffered the same fate as the shirt. His tennis shoes fared no better; holey and stained, they were tied with fraying laces.

A perfect specimen of manhood, standing like a Greek god. The sight captured her breath.

Jessica swallowed, fighting off a choking sensation.

What was she going to do? she asked herself, alarm turning her stomach topsy turvy.

Still, her gaze held steady, settling on his hands. Strong hands that had touched every inch of her flesh. Hands whose fingers had invaded her most private place.

Wobbly-kneed, she forced herself to move toward the boat, secretly recoiling from taking that outstretched hand, yet finding herself doing just that. As she'd feared, a spark shot through her, though she did her best to camouflage any visible reaction.

Brant showed no reaction, either, which didn't surprise her. Even if he hadn't had on sunglasses himself, he was a master at hiding his thoughts and emotions, something she should become more adept at.

"What a super rig," Elliot said, smiling broadly at her. "If I owned her, I'd take her out every weekend."

"You would, huh?" Brant asked, his smile indulgent. "Well, if you get your education, then maybe one day you'll become the proud owner of one of these babies."

A slight frown crossed Elliot's face. "That's what Mom says."

"Your mom's right."

Elliot switched his attention to Jessica. "What do you think, Mrs. Kincaid?"

"Suppose you call me Jessica?" she said, giving him an indulgent smile.

"Okay, Jessica," Elliot said.

"Don't put her on the spot like that," Brant suggested with ease. "You know what you should do. But let's don't discuss that today. Let's just concentrate on catching some big bass or crappie."

"All right!" Elliot said, turning and digging into the cooler for a cold drink.

"You okay?" Brant asked Jessica, removing his shades and exposing his warm gaze as it wandered over her.

Her breath faltered. "I'm...fine."

"Me too," he mouthed over Elliot's bent head, his gaze continuing to stroke her.

And he was. In fact, he didn't know when he'd felt so good, so content. Not in years, that was for sure. And for the first time in years, he felt unburdened, as if a tremendous weight had been lifted off him.

Hell, he was living his fantasies. He was with the two people he cared about most in the world. *Two* people? Where had that come from? Seemingly out of nowhere, blindsiding him.

He didn't love Jessica. He only wanted to make love to her. And when the chips were down, she was just a job, like the First Lady and so many others he'd protected.

Sweat poured off Brant. Crazy thoughts like that could get a man in big trouble, especially when his libido was on fire. He had to admit, though, he'd never had such good sex.

Regardless of the fact that she'd been married, Jessica had been an inexperienced lover, which had delighted him, especially since she was a quick learner and avid participant. Thinking about their time in bed sent the blood thundering through him, settling in his groin, making him ache with need.

Since they had returned from Europe, it had taken every ounce of willpower he could muster not to sneak into her bed, and to hell with the consequences. But he hadn't. He'd kept his head and his dick where they belonged and done his job.

He didn't like it, though, especially on such a perfect day, when she looked incredibly young and adorable, dressed in shorts, a skimpy top and sandals. Her hair, kissed by the sun and swept by the wind, was more tousled than usual, accentuating her bed-head persona. The gentle breeze was also doing a number on her body, molding her shirt to her breasts, giving his gaze free access to the jutting nipples her bra failed to disguise.

The very idea that she was the mayor of one of this country's most prestigious cities was mind-boggling.

He had never seen her so relaxed, so carefree, so breathtakingly lovely. And the fact that she had recognized his bold and warm look and actually returned it had his insides twisted in knots.

"Hey, Dad, I studied a map of the lake."

"And?" Brant said absently, still tying to get his mind off Jessica, whom he could never have, and back on track.

"I know all the best places to fish."

He turned and grinned at his son, feeling pride sweep through him. At this moment, his son's animated face, his son's acceptance, were all that was important to him. The only things in his life that mattered. So savor this time, he told himself. Don't waste a precious second.

"Then haul your butt over here, son, and take the wheel."

Elliot made a mad dash to the bow. "I'll show you how it's supposed to be done."

"Cocky little shit, aren't you?" As he spoke, Brant sought Jessica's eyes, and they burst out laughing.

Thirty-three

Jessica stared at the pile on her desk and wanted to turn around, get back in the car, change clothes and return to Lake Ray Roberts. That out-of-the-blue thought took her by surprise.

When Porter had been alive, she had rarely accompanied him on an outing. The times she had, she couldn't recall particularly enjoying it. But then, she didn't think he especially liked to take her, either, preferring the company of some of his male friends.

Yesterday, however, had been different. She had loved every minute they'd spent on the water, inhaling the fresh breeze, feeling it ruffle her hair and caress her skin. She had felt free, free from hateful phone calls, e-mails and prying eyes. In fact, on that Sunday, it had seemed her life was normal, like any other woman who was benefitting from a day spent in the company of loved ones.

Loved ones?

Had she lost her mind? She wasn't in love with Brant. And she barely knew Elliot, though she had to concede that when he didn't have that sullen twist to his mouth, he was an okay kid. Quite charming, in fact. Like father, like son, except that on average Brant was charming even less often than Elliot was.

Yesterday, however, throughout the entire adventure,

she'd seen a different side of that complicated, private man who had been part of her life for nearly a month. He had seemed to revel in every second of the day, laughing spontaneously at whenever she or Elliot would say something amusing. But he'd really come to life when she tried to catch a fish.

"Hey, hold tighter!" Brant had exclaimed at one point, dashing to her side. She'd apparently hooked a big one and was wrestling like crazy with it.

"Better hurry, Dad," Elliot said with unabashed laughter. "Or Jessica's going to go overboard and be bait for the fish."

"Funny, kiddo," Jessica quipped. Then she followed Brant's advice and got a firmer hold on her rod. "Don't worry, this sucker's not going to get the best of me."

About that time, the rod flew out of her hand. She just stood there, stunned, her mouth gaping. Then was when Brant tossed back his head and laughed, along with Elliot.

Jessica stiffened, pretending to be affronted. "Just wait. Next time I'll get the better of that sucker, and the joke will be on you two."

Brant's warm eyes roamed over her, sending her pulse into a tizzy. "Maybe it's time to take a break. How 'bout we pull over and have our picnic? I'm famished."

Jessica was, too, only not for food. She wanted to feast on him. And if the sudden glint in Brant's eyes was anything to judge by, he was thinking the very same thing.

For a long moment their eyes held, and the world around them ceased to exist.

"Hey, Dad, look!" Elliot cried.

The spell shattered, they whipped around and

watched as Elliot struggled with a big bass. Brant jumped to help him. "Way to go, son."

The remainder of the day was filled with the same relaxed fun and enthusiasm. For Brant's sake, Jessica couldn't have been more pleased. She now had hope father and son would eventually heal the breach completely.

If so, she would take joy in knowing she'd played a small part in bringing that about. For now, though, having heard Brant's laughter and watched the harsh lines ease in his face was enough. She would remember that day always.

That last thought making her sad, Jessica grabbed her pen and forced herself to add to her upcoming council meeting notes. That was when a knock on her door interrupted her. It was Brant. Another surprise. He rarely disturbed her.

"Come in," she said, trying not to stare at him.

"I know you're busy," he said in a rough voice.

"I should be, but my mind keeps wandering," she admitted in a faltering voice. All he had to do was get anywhere near her and...

Cutting that thought off, she watched him walk to the window, look out, then turn and prop himself against the wall. He was obviously still feeling caged, more restless than usual.

Back to his normal self.

Not a bad thing, she assured herself. The euphoria of yesterday couldn't last, at least not between them. Brant at his best was highly lethal.

Her first clue that his mood had swung had been the way he walked into the kitchen this morning. He hadn't spoken, except to mutter good morning. She'd pretended to focus on breakfast, taking her cue from him.

"Is something wrong?" she asked now, forcing her thoughts back to the moment at hand.

"I just wanted to thank you again for yesterday," he said, not looking at her. "You were a real trooper."

"You've already thanked me. More than once, actually." Her tone was soft. "But hey, I had a great time myself."

"I did, too," he said deliberately and thickly.

The air seemed to be sucked out of the room, forcing her to struggle for a decent breath. "It was good for me."

"I couldn't agree more. You should indulge yourself more often."

"I'll keep that in mind," she said lightly, struggling for composure.

He looked at her with shuttered eyes, then changed the subject. "Do you think I made progress? With Elliot, I mean."

"Don't you?"

A white line defined his lips. "Yes and no."

She almost smiled, only it wasn't a smiling matter. "Elliot seemed to have a ball."

"Oh, he did. But it was the boat, the lake and the fish that excited him, not me."

"I don't know so much about that," Jessica said hesitantly, not wanting to discourage him, but not wanting to give him false hope, either. Right now, she went for the hope, realizing how torn he was. "I saw Elliot looking at you with real admiration."

Brant shook his head. "I'd like to believe that, but I'm realistic enough to know that one outing isn't going to make up for a lifetime of neglect from me."

"You're right, it isn't. But it's a start. And you have

to know that, hold on to that. Elliot was neither disagreeable or disrespectful.''

"I know, which is part of the problem. The thought of calling him and hearing that old sullen anger again..." Brant's voice dissolved, and he gestured impatiently with his hands.

The pain and fear were eating him up, and there wasn't one thing she could do about it. It wasn't her concern, and besides, she was at a loss as to how to console him. But she had to try. She couldn't stand to see him hurting so badly.

"He invited you to come watch him play ball," she reminded him.

"I have you to thank for that, too." A smile suddenly toyed with his lips. "The truth of the matter is, he invited you."

"Well, he knows I can't come without you, so there."

His eyebrows arched. "That's really reaching."

She shrugged. "It's another start. That's the way you should look at it."

"Oh, believe me, I'm going to take the invitation and run." He paused again, his eyes drilling her. "If you want to go."

"Of course I'm going." She was offended and let it show. "I don't make promises I don't intend to keep."

"With your busy schedule, you never know."

"Well, this is one time I know," she declared, snapping outright.

A twinkle suddenly appeared in Brant's eyes. "Didn't mean to get you stirred."

You keep me stirred. And you know it.

"Yes, you did," she countered hotly.

He looked at her for another long moment, then said abruptly, "I'm here if you need me," and strode out of the room.

Brant paced the wood floor in his room. "To hell with it," he finally muttered, then picked up his cell phone and flipped the lid, only to slam it shut. He wanted to call Elliot, but like he'd told Jessica that morning, he was leery.

Nothing particular was on his mind except that he just wanted to talk to his son, to rehash the fishing trip that had thrilled him far beyond his expectations. Most of his thanks really was due to Jessica. She had indeed been a real trooper, especially when it came to the fishing, having admitted she'd never baited a hook in her life.

"And there's another verse to that," she'd added, "I'm not going to."

"Then how you gonna fish?"

Elliot's teasing question seemed to have caught her off guard for a second. "Well, uh," she sputtered, "I guess I just won't."

Brant smiled. "If you'll ask nicely, maybe I'll help you out."

She cut him a look, though he saw the twinkle in her eyes. It was in that moment he gripped the rod for all it was worth, squelching the urge to toss it, grab her and kiss her until they were both crazy with lust.

His son's laughter brought him back to reality. *Forget her. She's poison.* Elliot was what he was all about, what his future was all about, not some designer-clad career woman.

Still, she was awfully fetching in her casual attire on this gorgeous, sunny day.

"Ah, come on, Dad, give her a break."

Dad.

Brant didn't think he would ever tire of hearing that word. It had been so long. He had to make this day count for him and Elliot. It had to be a turning point, but he was scared shitless that he would blow it.

Thanks to Jessica, he hadn't. But now he was back in the real world and he had to go forward, desperate to keep that fragile line of communication open between him and his son.

Jessica had unselfishly done her part. Now the rest was up to him.

He finally punched out Elliot's number. Marsha answered.

"Is Elliot around?"

"No, he's not."

"Will you tell him I called?"

She paused, which sent his blood pressure soaring.

"I just wish to God you'd leave him alone."

"Marsha, please, don't start. We have got to make peace between us, if for no other reason than Elliot. I don't want to battle with you over him. It's not necessary."

"Goodbye, Brant," she said coldly.

"Dammit, Marsha!"

He smelled her scent before he saw her. Swinging around, Brant stared into Jessica's troubled face. "I'm sorry to bother you—"

"It's my job to be bothered," he responded, trying to get his temper under control. "Is something wrong?" Of course, it was. Otherwise, she wouldn't have come to his room.

Her face seemed to grow paler. "I just got a call. Roy's in the hospital."

"What happened?"

"He's...he's been severely beaten."

They made it to the hospital in record time.

When they reached the cubicle where her stepson was being treated, Brant gently touched her arm. "Are you sure you're up to this?"

Jessica swallowed the lump in her throat. "No, I'm not sure at all."

"He's not going to be a pretty sight."

"I know," she said in a shaky voice. "But this is something I have to do."

And it was, though she was loathe to walk into that room. The officer who had found Roy's bruised and battered body in a dark alley had called the chief of detectives, who had in turn called her. Detective Reeves had told her Roy's attack might have been drug-related. Beyond that, little else was known, since Roy was unconscious.

"Want me to go in first?"

Brant's voice broke into her thoughts. Jessica shook her head. "No, I need to be with him."

"Want me to stay out here, then?"

Her eyes widened. "No. Please come with me. If you don't mind."

"I wouldn't have it any other way."

Brant's tone was gentle, which made it much easier to open the door. Then she gasped and covered her mouth.

Her stepson was almost unrecognizable. His eyes were swollen shut, and his face was cut and bruised. She shuddered to think what the rest of his body looked like. Was he going to die?

The short, squatty E.R. doctor stepped forward and extended his hand to Jessica, then Brant. "Clyde Temple," he said in a deep voice. "I'm sorry about this, Mayor."

"Thank you, Doctor. Me too. Is he going to be all right?"

"Only time will tell. We're getting ready to transfer him to ICU."

Jessica swallowed hard again, thankful for Brant's presence, though he kept his distance. "Thank you for all you've done." Tears threatened, but she held them at bay. If Porter had been alive, such a vile act would never have happened. Suddenly she felt like a miserable failure.

As though he read her thoughts, Brant stepped closer. "This is not your fault. He's a grown man who's responsible for his choices and the consequences of those choices."

"You're right," she whispered. "But it breaks my heart to see him like this, to know he's wasting his life."

"If he survives, maybe he'll clean up his act."

Jessica prayed that would be the case, though she didn't verbalize that. Instead, she looked at Brant and asked, "Would you check at the nurses' station for Roy's personal items? I didn't think to ask the detective about them."

"No problem."

Moments later, Brant returned with keys and a billfold, handing them to her.

"I'd like to stop by his apartment and pick up a few things for him and bring them back here," she said.

"Suits me. I'd like to take a look around and see if there's any clue as to who might have done this to him."

Shortly thereafter Brant parked the SUV in Roy's

driveway. Once inside, Jessica was appalled at how messy the place was, though she knew it hadn't been ransacked.

With grim expressions, they assessed the situation; then Jessica headed for Roy's bedroom. "I'll grab a few things," she said, feeling worse by the second. How had Roy stooped so low?

"You know he has to get treatment," Brant said flatly.

"That goes without saying." Jessica turned then, and went about her business.

It wasn't long until Brant appeared in the bedroom door, his eyes as cold as steel. A shiver darted through her. "What now?"

"At least one question has been answered."

She frowned her confusion.

"Roy-boy's the one who tampered with your credit card."

Aghast, Jessica opened her mouth, then shut it.

"Yep, he sure as hell did. Found the evidence on his computer."

"How could he?" Mixed emotions charged through Jessica. She was sad, but she was also mad.

"There's more."

Her hand went to her chest. "More?" she mimicked.

"Yeah, your stepson's been a busy boy. I found a credit card, in *your* name, on his desk and another one in his billfold."

"Oh, no!" Jessica exclaimed, horrified.

"There's still more. He's making plans to tamper with your bank account. Or maybe he already has. Are you missing any money?"

Thirty-four

"I hope you have something."

Only Thurmon's lips smiled. "I do, but it's not exactly what you want to hear."

Since Roy had gotten the stuffing beaten out of him, Brant hadn't had the opportunity to meet personally with Thurmon, though he had kept him updated by phone. Thurmon had reciprocated. Still, they had wanted to meet. This morning, here in Jessica's private coffee room, had been the appointed time and place.

"Hell, man, at this point in the investigation," Brant said in an edgy tone, "I'll take anything I can get." He paused and took a drink of his coffee, then shoved it aside. "I still wish I could hit the pavement," he added in a mutter, a dark scowl clouding his features.

"Are you suggesting my men aren't doing their job?"

"Yeah, that's exactly what I'm suggesting," Brant said, though a smile tweaked his lips.

Thurmon grinned openly. "That's another thing I've always liked about you, you bastard. Your honesty."

Brant merely shrugged.

"Look, you know I've taken an active role in this thing with Jessie." Thurmon's face and tone took a serious turn. "Especially after her skull was nearly crushed. Veronica insisted, though I would've anyway."

"I appreciate your efforts, too," Brant responded on a sigh. "And I know you're on top of the situation, as much as you can be, with no evidence. So far this creep's just been smarter than us, and that gets my goat."

"But we're closing in, narrowing the field."

Brant straightened. "Oh?"

"Yep." Thurmon leaned in closer. "It looks like Roy's been ruled out."

Brant felt his adrenaline kick in and was about to speak when Thurmon held up his hand. "Hold your horses. Hear me out. Roy was in jail on a traffic violation that day."

"My gut's been telling me all along that Roy-boy wasn't the one. Even though he hacked around with Jessica's credit, I saw no signs of him having e-mailed her from his house. Of course, that doesn't necessarily mean anything, considering it's impossible to pinpoint the exact source of the e-mails or calls."

Brant paused. "Still, Roy doesn't have the balls for the heavy stuff. He's a spoiled, overgrown kid who's just interested in getting the money he thinks he deserves."

"But with her out of the way," Thurmon posed, "wouldn't it be clear sailing on his trust?"

"I don't think so, not the way Kincaid had it set up. His attorney would take over. And I don't figure he'd be nearly as lenient as Jessica."

"So we'll scratch Roy."

Brant rubbed his jaw. "Yep. Let's just narrow our focus on the cops and Curtis Riley."

"Anything new on Riley from your end?" Thurmon asked.

"I don't think he's our man, either. He's much too smart to dirty his hands that way. Also, I suspect he may have political ambitions of his own."

"He could've hired someone to handle his dirty laundry," Thurmon pointed out.

"Well, that's certainly more his style. Still, he doesn't get my nod, though I'm not totally ruling him out. Not quite yet." Brant got up and reached for the coffeepot, then raised it toward his friend.

Thurmon shook his head, covering his cup. "No more for me, thanks. As it is, I'm barely hitting the ground."

"I bet you'll be as glad as I will when this is all over." After having said that, Brant felt his stomach clench. While he sorely missed his home and his solitude, the idea of distancing himself from his son again was something he didn't want to think about.

And Jessica. He shuddered inwardly. He didn't want to think about leaving *her,* either.

"What's wrong?"

"Nothing," Brant replied darkly.

"Yeah, right." Thurmon's tone was sarcastic. "You know better than to try and outshit a shitter."

"None of your business, then. How's that?"

Thurmon laughed. "I'm gonna miss you, you know, although I haven't given up on keeping your ugly ass here."

"You're wasting your time." Brant's tone brooked no argument.

"I'm not so sure," Thurmon said with a display of outward confidence. "It's going to be tough to leave Elliot, especially after you two have made peace."

"Whoa! Hold on. We haven't made peace, at least not in the sense you mean."

Thurmon's big features scrunched into a frown. "Ronnie said the outing went great. And even you said—"

"What I said was that Elliot had a great time. We didn't get to talk personally about anything."

"Oh, I see. Anyhow, you shouldn't look a gift horse in the mouth, my friend. The fact that Elliot even went is a plus."

"Jessica gets the credit. She's terrific with him."

"Ah." Thurmon's eyes took on a glint. "Now that's interesting."

The second Brant mentioned Jessica in a personal light, he knew he'd let his mouth overload his ass, something he didn't make a habit of. But when he did, it was wholeheartedly.

"So is something going on between you two? Ronnie's suspected that for a while now, only she hasn't had the nerve to ask Jessica. I'm not nearly as tactful."

"No shit."

Thurmon chuckled. "Hit a sore spot, huh?"

"No," Brant said harshly. "So don't go getting any ideas."

"You could do a lot worse, you know."

A scowl darkened Brant's face. "You're really meddling now."

"Well, I'll be damned. So Ronnie's right." Thurmon grinned. "You two are sharing sheets."

Brant forced himself not to react, not be conned into saying something else he would regret. Thurmon's investigative nature had a way of doing that to unsuspecting people. But he wasn't just anybody, and he sure as hell wasn't unsuspecting.

Thurmon stood, that grin still in place. "You're a piece of work, old buddy, to be able to pull that off."

"Get outta here," Brant muttered, getting to his feet.

Thurmon's grin broadened, then faded abruptly. "Just so we're on the same page, is anything coming up with Jessica's schedule that I need to know about?"

Glad to be back on solid ground, Brant felt his stiff posture ease somewhat. "Tons of meetings, as usual. Plus the all-important council meeting. It's looming. And there's Roy. We've been back and forth to the hospital."

"Is Jessica going to file charges on the little bastard for credit card fraud?"

"Oh, I doubt that. She's planning on getting him into a treatment center. If he makes it, that is."

"Do they have any leads yet on who might've worked him over?"

"The woman he's been shacking up with, the one who supposedly got him hooked on the stuff, is being questioned. The detective who's handling the case is keeping Jessica updated."

"Hopefully they'll find the bastard and Roy will have learned a valuable lesson."

"For Jessica's sake, I hope you're right. But I'm not holding my breath."

Thurmon headed for the door, then turned around. "Oh, before I go, I meant to ask if you'd talked to Elliot since the outing. I don't think you ever said."

"I tried, but Marsha said he was out."

"She's not about to cut you any slack, is she?"

"Not one ounce. If Elliot and I patch things up, it won't be with my ex's blessing, that's for sure." Brant's tone was as bleak as his features.

"Well, feel your kid out, and if he can fit it in around

his ball schedule, I'd like the three of you to come over for hamburgers one evening soon. I'll have Ronnie mention it to Jessica."

"I'd like that, but we'll have to wait and see how things go."

"Later, then," Thurmon said and walked out.

Brant took care of their cups, then headed toward Jessica's office proper. Seeing that it had emptied, he turned to Tony, who was conversing with Millie. "Is the mayor free for a few minutes?"

Tony flicked his wrist, exposing his Rolex watch, then said in his prim tone, "She has thirty minutes."

"Thanks," Brant mumbled, walking toward Jessica's open door, all the while feeling Tony's eyes shooting daggers in his back. Brant smiled to himself. Jessica wasn't the only one who would be glad to see him go. Hovering Tony hadn't liked him from day one.

"What did Thurmon have to say?" Jessica asked without mincing words.

Brant thought she looked tired, even though the dark circles under her eyes added to the sheer beauty of her skin. Of course, the peach-colored suit that hugged her slender frame enhanced the entire package.

He was going to miss her. Jerking his thoughts out of that dangerous mode, he answered her question, updating her.

Brant was about to feel her out about Thurmon's invitation when her phone jangled. Jessica punched the intercom button. "Who is it, Millie?"

When Jessica hesitated, Brant asked, "Is it our guy?"

"No."

"You want me to leave, then?"

Shaking her head Jessica lifted the receiver. "Hello, Curtis."

Instantly Brant felt his hackles rise. He averted his head so she wouldn't see his reaction. Wonder what that bastard wanted? Probably to beef up the pressure on her about the land. No matter. Besides the fact that Riley hadn't yet been dropped from the suspect list, he just plain rubbed Brant the wrong way. Ever since he'd grabbed Jessica and kissed her, Brant had wanted to hurt him.

Actually he'd wanted to do that the second after the man had walked into her house.

"Thanks, but I think it's best if I just see you there." Jessica listened a few seconds longer; then she said goodbye and hung up.

"Where is 'there'?" Brant asked before she could say anything.

"A charity ball to raise money for The Children's Hospital."

"And he wanted you to go with him." A flat statement of fact.

"Yes."

She angled her head and peered at him through unreadable eyes. Dammit, did she want to go with Riley or not? He couldn't tell.

"Do you have a tux?"

That question took him aback for a second. "Not on me," he said with dark humor.

"Then I suggest you rent one."

He suppressed a groan, breaking into a premature sweat. The last place he wanted to be was in a ballroom full of people with overstuffed egos that rivaled their overstuffed pocketbooks.

Great. Just fucking great.

The ball had been in full swing for an hour before Curtis made his appearance. Jessica looked on from a distance and watched him smile and greet several of the councilmembers who were present.

She had been moving from person to person, group to group, herself, doing her job, which was to shmooze with the contributors and thank them for their patronage.

An easy task, as The Children's Hospital was a pet cause of hers, and she chose to visit it often. She'd also done work behind the scenes for Hospice, another of her favorite charitable endeavors.

Curtis, however, had a far different motive, a hidden agenda, trying desperately to swing the council vote in his favor. He just might pull it off, she forced herself to keep in mind. If so, then she would have no choice but to concede defeat.

But not yet. Anything could happen between now and the all-important vote, especially as Curtis remained on Brant's suspect list.

Unwittingly her gaze went to Brant, who was leaning against the wall nearest her. When she moved, he moved. His constant shadowing should have been comforting.

Only it wasn't.

Every time she looked his way, which was often, her breathing turned ragged. He looked so ruggedly gorgeous, but so uncomfortable. But then, he'd told her up front that he hated wearing monkey suits.

If he only knew how well that monkey suit suited him, he wouldn't have griped. She noticed more than one woman giving him the eye. She couldn't imagine his wife letting go of him so easily.

Suddenly Jessica tore her gaze off him and moved it onto Curtis, who was striding toward her.

"Good evening," he said in his smooth voice, his eyes trailing over her. "You're stunning in that dress."

"Thank you," she said with a forced smile. And while she knew she was at her best, having chosen a plain, but backless, long black dress, that showed off her creamy skin and slender figure, Curtis' compliment didn't set well with her.

"Will you dance with me?" he asked.

"I'd rather—"

"Come on. I refuse to take no for an answer."

In order not to make a scene, Jessica let him lead her onto the ballroom floor, which was shy of dancers, she noted with dismay. Out of the corner of her eye, she saw Brant straighten and narrow his eyes.

He wasn't happy. Although she hated having Curtis' arms around her, she sensed that Brant hated it even more. Was he jealous? Crazy as it was, that thought brightened her spirits.

It seemed like forever since they'd made love. God, she ached to know those feelings he'd evoked in her again.

"So how are you, my dear?" Curtis asked, guiding her smoothly across the floor.

At least he was a good dancer. "I'm fine."

"Looking forward to the showdown, I imagine."

"Aren't you?" she threw back at him, her eyes meeting the challenge in his.

"There's nothing I can do to make you change your mind?"

"No, Curtis. And though you want to take my stance personally, it's not meant that way. What I'm doing is for the good of Dallas. No ulterior motives exist."

"I wish I could believe that," he said bitterly, a strange glint appearing in his eyes.

Unbidden fear rose in Jessica, and she stiffened. Underneath that smooth facade of charm and flirtation, danger lurked. "Look—"

Her word was slammed back down her throat by Brant. He planted himself next to Curtis and said in a brusque, unyielding tone, "I need to speak with Mrs. Kincaid. So I'm cutting in."

For a second Jessica stood paralyzed, watching as another mutinous expression darkened Curtis' face. Please don't make a scene, she cried silently, struggling for a way to diffuse the flammable situation.

No way was Brant going to back down. So that left only one alternative. Miraculously Curtis complied with a shrug, and a smirk, before letting go of her. "She's all yours."

Brant didn't respond. Instead, he circled her trembling body with his arms and stared down at her. "I hope you don't mind."

"And if I did?" she asked, a trifle breathlessly.

"It wouldn't matter," he muttered in a guttural tone. "I can't stand seeing that bastard's arms around you another second."

Jessica's stomach bottomed out.

Thirty-five

"Hey, son, how's it going?"

"Okay."

Brant tried not to be disappointed at Elliot's aloofness, but he was. He hadn't talked to him since the outing, though he'd tried, leaving several messages. His son had returned none of them.

"When will you be leaving?"

The question took Brant by surprise. "I'm not sure. As soon as we find out who's trying to harm Jessica."

"Man, that boat's super. I've been telling my friends all about it."

"Maybe next time you might ask a couple of them to come with us," Brant said, knowing he was speaking way out of turn. First off, he could be gone at any time. And second, Jessica had made no mention of a repeat outing.

But he hadn't wanted to dampen Elliot's enthusiasm; he was too excited at carrying on a conversation with him that wasn't one-sided. "You know, I have a similar boat at my place."

"You do?" Elliot sounded astonished.

"Yep. I take her out just about every day, too."

"Do you catch a lot of fish?"

"Most days, then I go up to the cabin and fry them for supper."

"That sounds like lots of fun."

Elliot's tone had taken on a bleak note, which tore at Brant. That was when he took another chance on speaking out of turn. "How would you like to come stay with me for a few weeks when ball season's over?"

A silence followed his invitation. Oh great, Brant thought, here comes the hatchet job.

"Mom wouldn't let me."

Though he sounded cautious, he hadn't said no outright. Hope flared anew. "Is that the only thing that would stop you?"

"Guess so."

Brant felt his heart swell. "I bet your mom wouldn't mind as long as the visit didn't interfere with ball or school."

"Want me to ask her?"

Brant could hardly contain his excitement. "Why don't you let me take care of that?"

"What about Jessica?"

Brant's breath left him. "What about her?"

"Would she come to Arkansas, too?"

Not in this lifetime. "I doubt that, son."

"Oh."

"But we can talk about that later, okay? Right now, I called to see when your next game is."

"This coming Friday. We have the early one." Elliot paused. "You coming?"

"If it's at all possible."

"You bringing Jessica?"

"It's more like she'll be bringing me. That's the way it works in this business." Somehow Jessica had touched a chord in Elliot, which was fine, but he wanted his son to feel that way about him, too. Patience, he told himself. Patience.

"I know she'd like to come." Now Brant used caution, realizing if something happened and he couldn't go, then he would have lost the ground he'd gained. He'd made too many promises in the past that he hadn't kept. Somehow, some way, he had to make it to this game.

"Well, guess I'll see you, then," Elliot said in a matter-of-fact tone.

"Sure hope so. I'm looking forward to it. Until then, you take care of yourself, you hear?"

"Okay."

Once his cell phone was back in its case, Brant sat down, feeling like all the blood had been drained from his body. This emotional shit was for the birds. He hated feeling as though his heart was in a vise, something that was totally foreign to him.

But God, he cared about that kid. Seeing Elliot, again, being around him, had made him realize the precious gift he'd sacrificed for his job. He wouldn't let him go again. He swore he wouldn't.

What about Jessica? He tried to ignore the little voice deep inside him, but it wouldn't stop taunting him. He didn't want her. Not for keeps, anyway. He just wanted to make love to her whenever he wanted, then walk out with no strings attached.

No big deal.

Only it was a big deal, especially when he couldn't stop thinking about her. Ever. Even when she was behind closed doors, out of sight, for hours, she filled his thoughts. Worse, she haunted his dreams. She haunted him, period.

After they had come home from that charity shindig, two days ago, he should have made love to her. He should have said to hell with doing what was right and satisfied his own lust. He'd never had a conscience before. Why now?

Holding her graceful, flowing body swaying in his arms while her breasts poked his chest and his crotch rubbed against her had set him on fire.

In that timeless moment, he'd sensed she felt the same way. For several heartbeats, she'd melted against him, giving herself up to the blatant sexual ritual of heated bodies connecting.

"God, you smell good enough to eat," he'd whispered into her ear, stifling the urge to take a bite of her delicious skin.

"Don't, Brant, please. Not here," she countered in a muffled whisper of her own.

"I can't help it. It's been too damn long since I've held you."

He felt her heart pounding against him, and for a second longer, she let him hold her tightly. Then she pulled away and walked out of his arms.

Later, on the way home, she had ignored him, though the tension inside the limo had been thick and pulsating. The fire she'd started inside him still burned. He'd almost reached for her several times, but hadn't. Her standoffish attitude had kept him at bay. And pissed him off, too.

And he was still pissed, more at himself than her.

Muttering an expletive, he strode out of his room and made his way to the kitchen to get a beer, only to pull up short. She was sitting in the living room, her feet curled under her, staring into space.

"Jessica?"

She swung around, her eyes startled.

He cleared his throat, noticing that she had on a flowing robe of some sort. He would bet she was naked underneath. "Sorry, didn't mean to frighten you."

She licked her lips, which he also tried to ignore. "It's okay."

"Are *you* okay?"

"I'm fine. My mind wouldn't slow down enough to let me sleep, so I just got up."

"You didn't get another e-mail or call, did you?"

"No, thank God. For now, the sicko seems to be laying low."

"Mind if I grab a beer and join you? I'd like to talk to you about something."

She hesitated, but only for a second. "Actually I want to talk to you, too."

A feeling of unease shot through him. After that dance floor incident, had she had it? Was she finally sending him packing? "Want anything from the kitchen?" he asked in a raw-edged tone.

"Maybe a glass of milk. Thanks."

Moments later, he made his way back into the living room. When he handed her the glass, he made sure he didn't make contact with her hand. That would be his undoing.

"So what's on your mind?" he asked, following several swigs of beer.

"You first."

"Why?"

A brief smile softened her lips. "Just because."

A bit of humor was a good sign, he told himself. "I spoke to Elliot, and he wants us to come to his game Friday night." He paused, on the pretense of taking another sip of his beer. "Does that conflict with your schedule in any way?"

"If it does, I'll change it."

"You will?" He didn't know why he was surprised by her quick decision, but he was. He was thrilled, too.

"Elliot really wants you to come."

"And I want to. It'll be fun. Besides that, it'll be good for me. I can't tell you the last time I saw a ball game."

"Me either, I'm sorry to say."

"It'll all work out," she said in a gentle tone. "You and Elliot, that is."

"It just has to," he replied fiercely, then switched the subject. "So what's on your mind?"

"The all-important council meeting is coming up."

"How soon?"

"Monday night."

"You're right. That's soon. Are you ready?"

"As ready as I'll ever be. Both issues, the land and the chief's position, are up for a vote."

"But you're sticking to your guns on both, right?"

"Absolutely, though I might not win. Curtis doesn't seem the least bit worried, which worries *me*."

"If he's behind this crap, he'd best get worried."

"It's not him. I'm convinced of that. He's too smart, too political, for that."

"I told Thurmon the same thing, though I'd love to nail him for something." Brant sneered. "His attitude, for one thing."

Another smile teased her mouth, which stirred his loins anew. When she smiled, her entire face shone. And without makeup, she was even lovelier, breathtakingly so.

"You just don't like him."

Brant grunted.

"But that's beside the point. Ultimately the councilmembers have the final say on both deals. At least the city manager's on my side, so that's a plus.''

''What about the interim chief? Does he go?''

''Yes. I don't trust him. He's close friends with Wells and Stokes, so I know he'd have them back in uniform in a heartbeat.''

''Do you have someone else in mind?''

''Several, another plus. However, the council seems to be split down the middle, and if I cast the deciding vote, that's not good.''

''It could cost you reelection.''

''That it could.''

''Would that be the end of the world?''

Jessica's expressive eyes clouded. ''Yes, it would. My work is all I have.''

She sounded so forlorn, so desperate, that he wanted to grab her and shake her, tell her that wasn't true, that it was a mistake to live for her work. Of all the people who could make a life for themselves, she was the one who would succeed. With her intelligence, personality and enthusiasm, she deserved so much more.

However, he kept his mouth shut, knowing she would laugh in his face, since putting his job first was exactly what he'd done, and what had landed him in the mess he was in.

But he had regrets, deep regrets that had scarred his heart. If he could live those years of his life over again, he wouldn't make that same mistake. His family would come first. He wanted Jessica to escape that pitfall, but it was really none of his business.

Only you'd like to make it your business, because you're in love with her.

Trying to disguise the feeling that he'd been suddenly kicked in the gut, Brant leaned his head back and downed the last of his beer. When he righted his head, he couldn't look at her. This couldn't be happening to him. Surely what he felt for her was only lust, not love. But he knew better. His gut was telling him better.

Panic crippled him, and for another long moment, words failed him. What was he going to do? A permanent relationship with her was impossible, *not* going to happen. And yet he had done what he'd feared. He'd put his heart in jeopardy one more time.

Would he ever learn?

"It might not only prove deadly to your reelection," he finally said in a rushed, brusque voice, "but to you personally, especially if the cops are behind your troubles."

"You think they'll become bolder in their attacks?" Her voice was both weary and unsteady.

"Yes, though I don't want to give you cause for more worry."

She sighed and stared at him through suddenly vulnerable eyes. "What do we do?"

"We wait," he said with grim firmness, "then make *our* move."

Jessica cast a tentative glance at Brant, whose eyes were on the road ahead. They had been to Elliot's game and were on the way home. Dusk was settling around them.

What a treat the evening had been, despite the smothering heat and humidity. She'd had a great time, especially because Elliot had had a great game. He'd pitched a no-hitter and gotten two hits himself. Brant had been beside himself with pride and excitement. But then, so had she, jumping up and cheering right along with the rest of the crowd.

Although she had known his ex-wife and her husband were among the crowd of parents and fans, it hadn't dampened Brant's spirits or hers. For those stolen hours, she'd felt totally carefree, much like she'd felt on that Sunday outing.

Afterward, she and Brant had stood aside and waited until Elliot spotted them. She had kept her fingers crossed that he wouldn't slight his dad, that he would acknowledge his presence. She didn't give a damn about herself.

Elliot hadn't disappointed her.

"Hey, I'm glad y'all came," he said, bounding up to them, sweat dripping off him.

Brant grinned, then slapped him on the back. "You made me proud, son, real proud."

Hearing the choking sound in Brant's voice got to her, though she didn't let on. "Me too," she said, smiling broadly. "Am I allowed to give the hero a hug?"

Elliot looked embarrassed for a second, then shrugged. "Sure, why not?"

Brant looked on in stunned amazement before asking, "Do you have any plans?"

"Mom told me to invite a bunch of friends over. She's got all kinds of snacks and stuff." He paused. "You wanna come?"

Jessica didn't move a muscle, fearing Brant's response.

"Not this time, son."

"Okay," Elliot responded, apparently taking no offense. "Gotta go. Thanks for coming, Jessica. You, too, Dad."

Now, as she continued to watch Brant, she could still see the pride in his profile, in his posture, in the way his hands were relaxed on the steering wheel, hands that had loved her body.

She sucked in her breath and looked down.

"Thanks for going," he said huskily.

Feeling his probing gaze on her, she raised her head.

"You were a real trooper, especially for hugging him. I bet you can't wait to take a shower."

"I wouldn't have missed it for anything."

"Really?"

"Really," she echoed in a breathy voice.

It was in that second, with his eyes caressing her, that she faced the truth. She had fallen in love with Brant Harding. And his son. In a matter of a few weeks, her feelings for him had gone from lust to love.

And though he had never hinted that he returned that love, she sensed he cared for her, as well. However, nothing had changed to make her think they had a future. As soon as he was done guarding her, he would return to his life and she would remain in hers. Yet she loved him so much. Wanted him so much.

While that thought filled her with deep despair and incredible pain, she was helpless to do anything about it.

"Jessica, please," Brant said in a thick, grating tone, "don't look at me like that unless you mean it."

Silence drummed around them.

"Mean...what?" she stammered, mortified that she might have revealed her heart.

"You know what," he rasped.

Jessica opened her mouth to respond when it happened, when the vehicle seemed to appear out of nowhere and crash into her side of the SUV.

"Oh, my God, Brant!" she cried, terror filling her.

Thirty-six

Jessica screamed as the dark vehicle slammed into the passenger side once again.

"Dammit!" Brant lashed out, frantic about Jessica while trying to keep his SUV from turning over, severely injuring them—or worse. Finally one quick swerve sent his truck into the nearest ditch, but it remained upright.

Once they had come to a halt, he turned frantic eyes toward Jessica. "Are you all right?" he asked, his heart racing, his eyes examining her entire body.

"I'm…okay," she stammered.

Brant unhooked his seat belt and bounded out. By then, the van was past them, though not traveling all that fast. That enabled him to memorize a portion of the license number.

Then, whipping around, Brant dashed back to Jessica, who was still buckled in, though her head was back against the seat. Under the glare of the truck's interior light, he noticed that her eyes were closed, and she looked ghostly white.

For a second his heart completely stopped. Was she hurt after all? Was she dead? Suddenly he saw her chest move up and down. Relief stampeded through him.

He unbuckled her seat belt and grabbed her. "It's over. We're alone."

Jessica sank against him, her strangled sobs dampening his chest at the same time she began to shake. "Don't," he pleaded. "You're fine now. I've got you." While he was soothing her, his hands were busy gently roaming her slender frame to make sure she was indeed all right, that the bastard hadn't caused her any physical damage.

Emotionally—now that was a different matter. Just in the weeks he'd been a part of her life, she'd suffered more than her share of mental and emotional bruises.

This incident, however, should never have happened. He should have seen the other vehicle. He should have been watching for the unexpected. After all, that was his job. His mind had been on Jessica and not on business.

Beating up on himself at this juncture wouldn't solve the problem. At least, with the partial license number, he had a solid lead. With that, Thurmon could find who owned the van.

Then he would take over. Whoever was liable was going to wish he'd never been born.

"Brant?"

The whispered use of his name regained his attention. He clutched her tighter. "I'm right here, darling." That last word just slipped out, but he didn't care. She was his darling and would be for the rest of his life.

The idea that he could have lost her made him realize just how much he loved her. If anything had happened to her, especially on his watch, he never would have forgiven himself.

"Are you all right?" she asked.

"Physically yes. Mentally no. I'm about to blow a fuse."

Slowly Jessica lifted her head and stared at him

through tearstained eyes. "What happened? That...that tank seemed to come out of nowhere."

If the circumstances had been different, her use of the word "tank" would have garnered a smile. But these days, smiles were at a premium. What had just happened was deadly business. And he aimed to put a stop to this menace, even if he had to lock Jessica behind bars in order to keep her safe while he hit the streets himself.

It wasn't that he didn't trust Thurmon, but he himself had had it. This was the last straw. Whoever had rammed them, intending to hurt them—or kill them—had pissed him off one time too many and was going to pay. Simple as that.

"You're right, that tank appeared out of nowhere," he said roughly. "Still, I should've seen it."

"What are we going to do?"

A jolt of adrenaline shot through Brant. "First off, I'm going to take care of you. Then I'm going to find the bastard."

"Let's go home," she whispered.

Home. Was that ever music to his ears.

Yet he couldn't quite let himself believe Jessica could love him. He was afraid to let his mind even touch on that mind-boggling gift for fear he was setting himself up for a major fall.

"Are you sure you're okay?" he asked, hearing that raw, anxious note back in his voice. "Maybe I should take you by the emergency room and get you checked over."

"No," she stressed. "I'm just shaken and rattled, but otherwise, I'm all right."

Reluctantly Brant removed his arms. After they were both buckled up, he paused a moment longer, reached for his cell phone and made two calls—one to the detective who was working the last incident, then Thurmon, offering no explanation to his friend, except to tell him to meet them at Jessica's.

A short time later Brant found himself anxiously pacing the floor, waiting for her to get back downstairs. He'd made sure she'd gotten in and out of the shower without mishap, waiting in her room until she'd actually walked out of the bathroom, smelling like she'd dipped in a tub of fresh flowers.

It was all he could do not to grab her again, and not because of a sexual urge but rather a nurturing one. He wanted to soothe her troubled mind and heart. But he wanted her to make the first move. At the time she'd seemed in a daze.

Dammit, where the devil was Thurmon? he asked himself, peering at his watch. His friend had had ample time to show up, though he knew the owner of the van and the van itself were long out of sight. Most likely the vehicle had been driven straight to a secure and hidden place.

"Hey," a husky voice said from behind him.

He swung around and stared at Jessica, who had paused in the door dressed in a loose-fitting pair of white jeans and a lavender T-shirt. Her hair was still damp from the shower, and her face, devoid of makeup, made her appear younger and much more vulnerable.

Gone was the sophisticated, in-charge career woman, Brant thought with a wince. Uncertainty now lurked behind those lovely blue eyes, and when she spoke again, that same uncertainty thickened her voice. "Thanks again for saving my life."

"Don't thank me." Brant's lips took on a sarcastic,

bitter twist. "Under my watch, you've almost been killed, not once but twice."

"But I wasn't, thanks to you. It's the bottom line that counts."

"Thanks," he muttered in a raw, husky tone, his eyes holding hers.

She lowered her head, then lifted it. "I know we have a lot to talk about personally, but—"

He groaned, then stepped toward her. The chiming of the doorbell froze him midstride. Cursing, he crossed to the front door and jerked it open.

"It's about time you got your sorry ass here." Brant knew his face must look like a thunder cloud about to erupt.

Thurmon merely grinned, as if he'd expected that kind of comradely abuse from Brant. "What's up? From your tone, I figured it must be urgent."

"It is. The bastard tried to run us off the road this evening."

Thurmon let go of an expletive, then asked, "Is Jessie okay?"

"Believe it or not, she is." Brant angled his head. "Come on in. It's nut-cutting time."

When they returned to the living area, a tray with coffee and cookies sat on a table. "There's iced tea if either of you would rather have it," Jessica offered.

"Thanks, honey, this is fine," Thurmon said, crossing to her and giving her a hug. "Want me to call Ronnie to come over?"

Jessica shook her head mutely.

Watching her, Brant sensed that another onslaught of tears was close, which showed how distraught she was. Mayor Jessica Kincaid was not a crybaby. What she'd been through, however, was enough to undermine any-one's strength and courage.

"I'll give her a call later," Jessica finally said.

Thurmon nodded, then faced Brant. "Have you got anything?"

Brant gave him the partial plate number, as well as a description of the van. Thurmon immediately picked up the phone, dialed, then barked orders into the receiver.

"I also called Detective Reeves at headquarters," Brant added. "He's also on it. Even as we speak, I suspect he and his men are combing the site. But it's a waste of time, except maybe for the tire prints."

"You're right. Your skid marks will probably be all that's visible. And there may be some paint from the car on the SUV."

"I'm tired of this shit, Thurmon."

Thurmon rubbed his jaw, his grim features mirroring Brant's. "We should be hearing something shortly."

Jessica and Thurmon had just sat down, ignoring the goody tray, when Jessica's phone rang. "I'm sure it's Reeves." She reached for it, only to slam it back down seconds later, her face stark white. "It was…him."

"Dammit," Brant muttered. "What did he say?"

Jessica's breath seemed to flutter through her lips. "Next time I won't be so lucky."

Brant and Thurmon's cursing ripped through the air simultaneously.

"I think he's trying to kill me." This time Jessica's voice was barely above a whisper, and every ounce of color had drained from her face.

Brant crossed to her side and, without thought, pulled her into his arms. When he felt her relax against him, his hold tightened, even though Thurmon was staring at him with raised eyebrows and a stunned expression.

Offering no explanation, Brant gave Jessica one last squeeze, then gently released her. "We'll get the sonofabitch. He *won't* hurt you."

Her eyes were wide and frightened. "I know that."

With that vote of confidence, Brant put distance between them, though he loathed letting Jessica out of his arms for one second.

Thurmon's cell phone rang, which refocused all their attention. He said in a jubilant tone, "Got it. Thanks."

Brant didn't waste time or words. "You got a name?"

"Wesley Stokes. The bastard was driving his father-in-law's van."

Brant rammed a fist into his palm. "Paydirt."

"So the cops are responsible after all," Jessica murmured in a somewhat dazed tone.

"That's right, honey," Thurmon said, though his eyes were on Brant.

"Since it's not Wesley's own vehicle, we still don't have proof enough to arrest the bastard."

Thurmon smoothed his mustache. "Right, but we'll get it."

"Damn straight we will," Brant said in a deadly tone.

"Do you think Dick Wells was in the van with him?" Jessica asked.

"Absolutely," Brant said.

Thurmon stood. "I'm outta here for now so Jessie can get some rest. Meanwhile, I'll be devising a plan to nail these bastards before they carry out their threat and have another go at you." His gaze had fallen on Jessica.

Brant nodded. "I'll call you later, then."

"I'll see myself out."

Once they were alone, Brant concentrated on Jessica, who looked ready to collapse, though there was a stubborn lift to her head.

"What are you thinking?"

"I think you know," she declared with a spark in her voice.

"Yeah, a way to beat them at their own game."

"Right."

"And they *will* make another attempt, especially with the council meeting looming. Apparently they know their ass is grass. That's why they're willing to go for broke." Brant paused, clenching his jaw and staring into space. "Only this time, I'll be waiting."

"No, *I* will."

Although Jessica's tone was soft, she might as well have shouted. The effect on him was the same. He flinched visibly. "Have you lost your mind?" Then, realizing how angry that question sounded, he toned down his voice. "Look, I know where you're coming from on this, how you feel, but—"

Jessica cut him off. "I'm going to be the bait."

"That's not going to happen."

She stood, her eyes suddenly sparking to life. "I'm the one with everything to lose if they aren't stopped. Besides, you work for me, which means I get my way."

Though he showed no outward response to her crazy idea, Brant was furious and offended. "It's because you hired me that I have the right to make that call. And that call is no."

Jessica bowed her head, then said flatly, "My decision is nonnegotiable."

Thirty-seven

"Is everything in place?" Brant asked, his features set and grim.

Thurmon nodded. "I still don't like this."

"Neither do I, but it's the only way."

Thurmon shifted his holster belt. "You're the boss."

"Actually, Jessica's the boss." Brant spoke with a mixture of sarcasm and humor.

"That goes without saying. Hell, man, the sooner you figure that out, the better you'll make it in this old world."

"Is that a fact?"

"Yep," Thurmon said.

"What makes you such an authority?" Brant asked, purposely killing time by stringing out this inane conversation.

"Years of marital bliss," Thurmon answered arrogantly.

Brant smirked. "The verdict's still out until I ask Veronica."

"Be my guest," Thurmon responded with a nonchalant grin.

"Oh, believe me, I will."

Thurmon was silent for a moment; then he cocked his head. "What's with you and Jessie? Don't you think it's time you leveled with me?"

"No."

Thurmon barreled on. "You took her in your arms like you had every right, like you made a habit of it. And don't tell me that's none of my business, either."

"It's none of your business," Brant said blandly.

"You're a first class…" Thurman's voice trailed off.

Ignoring him, Brant glanced at his watch, then back up at Thurmon, his features once again set and determined. "Let's do it."

Wesley Stokes reached for a toothpick and dug around his crooked teeth. "How much longer are we gonna sit here?"

"As long as it takes," Dick Wells said in a hard voice. "I'm tired of this shit. *Her* shit, to be exact."

They were parked down the street from Jessica's town house, having chosen a spot that allowed them to see her whether she left through the gate or through the front door. It was after dark, and they were trying to decide when to make their move. A desperate move.

Stokes dug some food out from between two teeth, wiped it on his jeans, then cut his companion a look. "It's about damn time you got pissed."

"Oh, I've been that way a long time, I just have a different way of showing it."

Wesley snorted. "Whatever."

"She's one hard-nosed bitch," Wells said. "At first, I thought she'd soften, or that Forrester would soften her, convince her to hire him. If that had happened, it would've been a no-brainer for us. We'd be off suspension before a cat could lick his tail."

"Could still happen, you know," Wesley said, continuing to pick his teeth. "The council meeting ain't happened yet, even though she's been interviewing all those other big city dudes with more social skills than street skills.''

"Word has it that she's chosen one of those dudes, too," Wells said. "Which means she'll be calling Forrester soon and giving him his walking papers.''

Stokes cut Wells another glance. "You think that's really the way it's gonna come down?''

"I'd bet my mother's life on that.''

Stokes snorted again. "Hell, Wells, you ain't got no mother. You were hatched.''

"Funny," Wells responded sarcastically. "Anyway, you know she doesn't like Forrester. He's told us that all along. Neither does the city manager.''

"If something doesn't happen soon," Stokes said, tossing the used toothpick out the window, "my old lady's gonna kick my ass out and probably send the kids with me.''

"God help those kids.''

"What about me?" Stokes snarled. "I ain't got no other place to go.''

"Grace isn't going to kick you out," Wells said coldly. "So stop bellyaching. That's why we're here. We're going to put ourselves out of our misery once and for all. You're not the only one with a heavy note to grind each month. I got a wife and kid, too, you know.''

Stokes rubbed his distended gut. "Hell, as much grief as we've dealt that bitch, you'd think she would've wised up by now and figured out she couldn't mess with the police force and get by with it, bodyguard or no bodyguard.''

He shifted his hand from his stomach to his grizzled chin, narrowing his eyes. "Especially after she found that dead rose on her pillow, not to mention all those calls. I made them as threatening as possible, without giving myself away.''

''What do you think about the e-mails? I busted my balls writing those, thinking she'd finally get it and shape up. At least hire Mayfield back, if nothing else.''

''What about the chunk of concrete?'' Stokes demanded. ''Are you forgettin' that?''

Wells scowled. ''Of course not.''

''Even if the calls and e-mails failed,'' Stokes continued in a coarse voice, ''that alone should've done the trick. Hell, if that guy who's sucking up to her hadn't knocked her out of the way, it's a good possibility she'd be six feet under right now.''

''In light of our screwup in the van, I wish it had.'' Wells' breath was shallow while he slapped at a mosquito buzzing around his head. ''These damn things are starting to chew on my flesh.''

''Mine, too,'' Stokes said, also slapping at one. ''That's why I ask how much longer we're gonna sit here in this heat, waiting for something to happen.''

''Until it happens, I guess,'' Wells said wearily. Then, with more force, ''You got any better ideas, Einstein?''

''Me?'' Stokes bared his crooked teeth. ''Hey, you're supposedly the brains behind this operation. What with all them computer skills you got, I thought you would've figured something else out by now.''

''You figure something out,'' Wells challenged in a nasty tone. ''You're the one who's always wanting to put the hurt on her.''

''You think I'm blowin' hot air, don't you?''

''I don't give a shit about it,'' Wells said savagely. ''I just want my job back—and now.''

"Then suck it up and let's break in. We did it once. We can do it again."

"I don't think so." Wells' voice held contempt. "We just got lucky that time. Caught her in a senior moment when she forgot to set her alarm. And what about Harding? You want to come up against him? I don't think so."

"You're right," Stokes agreed, disgust sharpening his voice. "He's never out of her sight, always sniffing around her like a dog in heat." He paused and let go of a belly chuckle. "Ever wonder what it'd be like to get between those legs?"

"Like dipping your wick in a glass of ice water, most likely," Wells muttered. "I'll pass, thank you."

"Not me. That's my fantasy, making love to her before I wring her scrawny neck."

Wells' lips turned up in a snarl, his gaze settling on Stokes. "You're sick."

Stokes shrugged. "Some might say that's just what being a man's all about."

This time Wells snorted, his features distorted with contempt.

"Hey, would you just look at this?"

Wells swung his head around, his mouth dropping open. "Am I seeing what I think I'm seeing? Or am *I* having a senior moment?"

"That you ain't," Stokes said, scratching his chin again and literally licking his chops. "That's her stud, Harding, all right, leaving the house."

"And without her, too."

"What a stroke of luck," Stokes said, sounding amazed as he leaned forward and peered through the windshield. "Ain't no mistake, either. It's Harding, all right, in the flesh."

"Thank God for streetlights," Wells muttered, sitting straight up.

"We're outta here."

Wells checked his gun. "I'm ready. But before we go, is this it?"

"Are you asking if we're going to kill the bitch?"

Wells swallowed. "I guess so."

"Whatta you think?"

Wells swallowed again. "She's left us no choice, right?"

"Just keep tellin' yourself that, and you'll be just fine and dandy."

"I'm ready as I'll ever be," Wells said in a resigned tone. "Even though Harding drove off, my guess is he won't be gone long."

"So let's haul ass and get this over with. My wife's got grub waitin' on the table, and it's gettin' cold."

Wells merely rolled his eyes at the same time he rolled out of the truck and followed Stokes into the darkness.

A short time later, both men were sweating profusely, but Wells had managed to disengage the alarm system.

"Are you ready?" Stokes asked, mopping his brow with the back of his beefy hand. "That took longer than I thought it would."

"That's your opinion," Wells shot back. "I made record time, actually."

"We're lucky Harding's not back."

"He isn't, and that's what counts."

They crept onto the deck, then, with ease, tripped the lock on the French doors and walked into the frigid air-conditioning. Stokes motioned for Wells to follow him.

Tiptoeing, they made their way toward the hall, into the bedroom.

It was empty.

Stokes tilted his head toward the stairs.

Wells nodded. With gun in hand, he led the way, treading cautiously up the stairs. Together, their hearts gonged in time with the grandfather clock.

Following a check of one small bedroom, which was also empty, they made their way toward the third one, assured of finding their target. Once there, Stokes nodded for Wells to stand aside. Wells followed the silent order, widening his gaze and lifting his gun slightly higher.

Stokes eased the door open, ever so gingerly, until the large master suite was visible. Luck was still with them.

Jessica was in that great big bed.

All alone.

They crept inside, guns poised. Suddenly the room was flooded with light. They stopped in their tracks, a double barreled shotgun pointed at them.

"Drop those guns," Brant ordered. "Or I'll drop you both in your tracks."

Thirty-eight

The ordeal was over.

Free at last.

Jessica, however, was having difficulty realizing she no longer had to worry about answering the phone, checking her e-mail or looking over her shoulder. She had lived under fear's umbrella for so long, she found it hard to reclaim her life.

But then, her life wasn't the same and never would be. Brant had changed that. He had changed *her*. Just thinking about him this morning weakened her all over, especially after what he'd done to apprehend Stokes and Wells and put them behind bars.

She rolled over in the bed, her sixth sense telling her she was alone. She was right. But she didn't panic. She knew Brant was somewhere in the house, that he hadn't left her. Not yet, anyway.

He had truly placed himself in jeopardy to save her. She couldn't rid her mind of the image of him facing down the two cops with their guns pointed at his heart, a heart that belonged to her.

Since things had turned out the way they had, she owed her life to Brant. Thank God he hadn't given in to her foolish demand to be the decoy. It appeared she had underestimated the desperation of the men. More than likely she wouldn't have survived, because they had been prepared to kill her. Even now, she couldn't quite comprehend that horror.

A shiver darted through Jessica, and she crossed her arms over her chest. When she had posed that ridiculous idea to him, she had thought she would be able to get out of harm's way in time for him to step in. Brant, of course, hadn't seen it that way.

"No, Jessica," he'd told her again, his jaw clenched. "That's not an option."

"And I told you, it's not your decision."

"Look, I'm not going to argue with you about this. It's my way or no way. And my way is no. What is there about that you don't understand?"

When she didn't respond, he charged on. "If Stokes and Wells make their move tonight, then they'll be out for blood. Your blood, dammit. And I won't have it on my conscience."

"What about yours on mine?"

"That's not going to happen," he said with steely confidence.

"You're that sure?"

"I'm that sure. I know what I'm doing. And you don't. Have you ever fired a pistol?"

The question caught her off guard. Jessica frowned. "No, but—"

"I don't even want to discuss this anymore. I'm taking over. Otherwise…"

She knew he purposely left the sentence unfinished, but she got the message loud and clear. He had reverted back to a hard-nosed, impersonal stranger, hell-bent on doing his job.

And if she didn't relent, he would walk. She had no doubt about that. "All right," she said with as much dignity as she could muster, "we'll do it your way."

"Good. Now let's get down to business."

The plan had then been that, with Thurmon as his backup positioned in the closet, Brant would pretend to be asleep in her bed. She, in turn, would remain in the complex, safely tucked away at a neighbor's with Veronica and two detectives, who were there as a precaution.

Once Stokes and Wells had been arrested and hauled off in cuffs, Brant had come after her, and the four of them had celebrated. During the remainder of the night, Brant had simply held her in his arms, reassuring her that he was all right, that there wasn't a scratch on him.

"All in a day's work," he'd quipped; then, noticing she was trembling, he'd groaned and clutched her tighter. But he hadn't made love to her or touched on anything personal. It was as if he sensed that she simply needed to be held, and he'd been sensitive to that need.

Now, however, in the light of day, she realized they couldn't ignore what was between them, especially since Brant no longer had a reason to remain.

Except for his son.

Instantly Jessica's rigid body relaxed and she could breathe, though not for long. She had the all-important city council meeting today. While that was going on, Brant hoped to spend time with Elliot.

"Whatever it takes," Brant had said before she fell asleep in his arms, "I'm going to see my kid and get some things straight, Marsha or no Marsha."

"You'll be fighting your dragon at the same time I'm fighting mine," she had told him, snuggling closer in his warm arms.

"Now that your mind is free, I'm confident you'll win your battle."

"Not necessarily," Jessica countered. "At this point, the vote could go either way."

"If it does, you'll survive. You're a strong woman."

"I'm not so sure," she said with a tremor. "Nonetheless, I'm holding to my convictions. I'll see what the fallout is, then I'll go from there."

Brant had brushed her forehead with his lips. "It's going to be all right. I just know it is. But right now, I want you to sleep."

"You'll stay with me?"

"I'm always with you," he said in a husky but rugged voice. "Now sleep."

And sleep she had, only to wake alone. She just prayed that today would be Brant's lucky day, as well, that he wouldn't come away from his son with his heart still broken.

Pushing that disturbing possibility to the back of her mind, Jessica peered at her watch. She had to get up and face her own lion—the council. If she failed, then her life could take another drastic turn.

She could lose her beloved job.

Dare he indulge himself with the thought that she loved him?

But how could she love him—a washed-up recluse with a troubled teenager and the ex-wife from hell?

Of course, she doesn't love you, you idiot.

What if she really did?

Love was the answer to everything, right?

Bullshit.

He doubted love could overcome all the obstacles in front of them. Still, the thought of returning to his world and leaving her in hers was something he couldn't imagine.

Just like he couldn't imagine leaving his son again.

So if it came down to choosing...

No. He couldn't afford to think about Jessica now, not when he was waiting for his son to join him.

Brant knew he would have another chance to see Jessica. His son was a different matter. He never knew about Elliot and his mood swings. And his time here had run out. It truly was now or never.

He no longer had a valid reason to hang around. With that in mind, he'd called Elliot and asked to see him. Miraculously he'd said okay. Now, as Brant waited in the drive for him to appear, he wiped the sweat off his brow, having opted to let the windows down and kill the engine. He should have known better; the heat and his mood were an explosive combination.

Just as he was about to crank the engine again, Elliot came bounding out of the house, dressed in a pair of baggy shorts, a T-shirt and tennis shoes.

"Hey, it's good to see you," Brant said when his son was in the vehicle.

"Uh, you, too."

Brant hid a smile, thinking how uncomfortable most kids were with small talk. He remembered he had been. And still was, he reminded himself. He had just looked down the barrel of two guns pointed at him, and he hadn't been this nervous.

But this was different. Elliot wasn't a job. But then, neither was Jessica, at least not anymore. Still, there was a difference. Maybe that difference stemmed from desperation, knowing he would be leaving town soon.

"Name the place you want to eat breakfast, son," Brant said, trying to force his clenched stomach muscles to relax.

Elliot did, and soon they were seated and their orders

placed. While it was on the tip of his tongue to blurt out his feelings, Brant held back. He wanted the kid to enjoy his food, and he needed more time to come up with the right words to convey what was in his heart.

Hell, he wasn't sure there were any right words.

"So how many more games do you have to play?"

"One more, then we start the playoffs."

"So what are your chances of winning it all?"

"Good," Elliot said with confidence. "You saw us play."

"That I did. And you're right. As a team, you guys are real solid."

"If I just don't blow it this time," Elliot said, down-in-the-mouth.

"So you got the nod to pitch the first game?"

"I got it last year, too, and I blew it."

"What happened?"

Elliot shrugged, his eyes narrowed. "I just couldn't get it across the plate. They used me for batting practice."

"We all have days like that, when nothing goes right."

"Mom doesn't," Elliot said seriously. "Except now."

Brant's good humor fled, and he bit back a retort. Marsha was one person he didn't want entering this conversation, but it seemed there was no way around it.

"You've got her all messed up."

Now Elliot was smiling, which didn't set too well with Brant. "Look, son, I've told you this before, causing a row between you and your mother was never my intention. She should always come first. But that doesn't mean we can't have our time together. But most of all,

I—'' He paused, trying to come up with the words that would convey his soul.

"It's okay, Dad," Elliot said.

Brant blinked. "Uh, what's okay?"

"I don't think I'm mad at you anymore."

Brant opened his mouth, but no words came out. Too easy. Something was wrong. He didn't deserve this good fortune. His throat suddenly tightened again, and he swallowed. He couldn't cry. But that was exactly what he felt like doing. He felt like grabbing his son and hugging him, too. But he didn't do that, either.

He simply sat there for a moment and fought back tears.

"Are you all right, Dad?" Elliot asked.

Brant made himself smile. "Actually I'm fine, son, just fine. So when can you come to visit me?"

Suddenly a wary expression crossed Elliot's features. That was the catch. Elliot still didn't trust him and his good intentions. And only time would take care of that, which meant he still had his work cut out for him.

"Maybe at the end of the summer," Elliot said.

Brant's hope was reborn. "Any time is fine with me," he said eagerly. "And I'll talk to your mother."

"No, Dad, I'll tell Mom."

Brant's heart swelled with added pride. Was his son maturing in front of his eyes? It sounded like it, especially with Elliot assuming the daunting task of crossing Marsha.

With that in mind, Brant asked, "Are you sure? Your mother's not going to be happy."

"I know," Elliot said. "But it'll be all right."

"Would you mind if I gave you a hug?"

"Here?" Elliot looked panicked.

Brant laughed out loud. "No, not here. Later."

Elliot sort of smiled. "Uh, I guess so. I mean sure."

Walking out of the restaurant, Brant's feet barely touched the ground.

Thirty-nine

"Well, you stuck to your guns and won."

Jessica was careful to keep her emotional shield in place. "I did what I believed was the right thing to do."

Councilman Lance Saxon let go of a heavy sigh that set his jowls and girth in motion. "I still think you're wrong on both the chief and the land, but I don't aim to be a sore loser."

That remained to be seen, Jessica thought with a twist of hidden sarcasm. "I was hoping I wouldn't have to break the tie. Unfortunately I did."

The council meeting had just ended. And while several members had hung around to chat, especially since the outcome was so controversial, others had already gone, seemingly tired of the uproar.

"For now, you're in the driver's seat, which means you wield the power," Saxon said.

Jessica ignored his remark, realizing he was indeed expressing sour grapes, despite his claim to the contrary. "The man I have in mind for the chief's position will do the city a fine job. I'm convinced of that. And I'm also convinced the annexation of the land will be a windfall for the city."

Saxon rubbed his jowls, than said in an oily voice, "We'll see. Until all the dust settles, the verdict's still out."

His meaning was clear. She was up for reelection soon. If she lost, Saxon and his cohorts would try to undo all that she had done.

She hadn't lost yet, she reminded herself, though she knew the fight would be much tougher than before.

"Though I'm willing to give the new man a chance," Saxon added quickly, and in a more conciliatory tone.

Jessica wasn't fooled by his shift in attitude. If she didn't lose the election, then he would have some backtracking to do. And that didn't set well with him, either. Too bad. At this point, she didn't care. Saxon was the least of her worries.

"I'd appreciate your cooperation," Jessica said, smiling politely.

He nodded. "Have a good evening, Mayor."

A short time later, Jessica was alone in her office except for her assistant, who was flittering around nervously and talking incessantly.

"Tony, you're driving me nuts."

He pulled up short and gave her a shocked look. "I am?"

"Yes," she said, tempering her tone. "You are."

"Sorry," he said, wide-eyed. "I guess I'm letting off steam now that those goons have been arrested and you came through the meeting a winner."

"Let us hope," Jessica said, her tone subdued.

Tony cut her a sharp look. "What does that mean?"

"My refusal to compromise made a lot of enemies."

"You're not having second thoughts, are you?"

Jessica straightened. "No."

"There you are. You fought for what you thought was right, and you won on both fronts. All's fair in love and war. And someone has to lose. Remember that. Saxon and his allies will just have to suck it up."

Jessica smiled. "You and Veronica. Both of you are good for me. Besides, I don't know what's wrong with me. I should be ecstatic. I made great strides today in proving that a woman can successfully hold her own in this office."

"Sure you did. But you've been through hell lately. Don't forget that."

"I won't ever forget that," Jessica said in a flat tone.

"You haven't had any time to adjust to having your life back. The cops were arrested one day and you had this meeting the next. Give yourself a break. After all, those idiots tried to kill you. That in itself is mind-boggling."

"You're right, it is, and I am exhausted."

"By the way, has he-man gone?"

Jessica chose her words carefully. "No, no, he hasn't."

"You mean he's still hanging around? Whatever for?"

"He has a son here."

"But he's no longer underfoot?" Tony halted and narrowed his gaze on her. "Under *your* feet, that is."

The intercom on her phone chose that moment to sound. Saved by the bell, Jessica thought, literally, feeling her stomach uncoil. She couldn't think about Brant rationally, though she would have to face him again this evening. Meanwhile, she was grappling with the possibility that she might lose him.

"Oh brother," Tony mumbled, after answering the call.

"What?" Jessica demanded, slipping back into her old guarded mode, forgetting for a moment she was free.

Tony made a distasteful face. "Of all times for him to make an appearance."

"Who?"

"Curtis Riley."

"I don't want to see him."

"Didn't think so. I'll get rid of him."

Jessica massaged her temple. "Thanks. I'll owe you."

"I like it when you owe me." Tony chuckled, then headed for the door, only to halt midstride.

"Hope I'm not intruding," Curtis said, all but thrusting Tony aside as he crossed the threshold.

"Actually, you are," her assistant countered in a huff.

"It's okay, Tony," Jessica said. "I'll talk to you later."

Tony glared at the unwelcome visitor, his lips stretched in a tight line. "If you need me, I'll be in my office."

"Thanks," Jessica said, standing rod-straight while giving in to the fury charging through her.

"I just wanted to be the first to congratulate you," Curtis said when they were alone.

"Oh really?" Jessica didn't believe that for a second, but she played it cool and gave him a fixed smile.

"Yes, really. However, I still think you're wrong and that you'll regret your move."

"I guess that means you're not going to vote for me in the next election."

His brows shot up. "Did you expect me to?"

"No."

He shrugged, his eyes taking on a glint. "You could make me change my mind, you know."

Inwardly recoiling, Jessica stepped back. "I'm comfortable with things the way they are."

The glint in his eye turned to cold anger. "I make a formidable enemy."

"I'm aware of that," she said with matching coldness.

If she had seen this side of Curtis before the cops had been caught red-handed trying to harm her, she might have agreed with Brant and cast her vote for Curtis. When thwarted, he was not above playing down and dirty.

"I might even run against you for mayor."

Ah, so that was what this little visit was all about. He figured he would get her one way or the other. Well, let him try. She would gladly take him on, or anyone else who chose to run against her. She would do her best, and let the chips fall where they may.

That thought shocked her. When had she become so blasé about the career that had once meant everything to her, that was her life? Brant. He was responsible for those careless thoughts. Panic kept her silent.

"Jessica."

Curtis' tone was abrupt, as though he resented her lack of attention. "I'm glad the cops were arrested and won't be dealing you any more misery. I hope you know I'm sincere about that."

"Thanks, Curtis."

"So I guess we'll see what happens when election time rolls around."

Jessica didn't so much as flinch. "Guess we will."

He smiled without warmth. "May the best man win." His mouth took on a smirk. "No offense intended, of course."

Jessica met his gaze head-on. "None taken."

"Good luck."

"Goodbye, Curtis."

His lips tightened in another smirk before he turned and left the room.

Jessica didn't realize how rigidly she'd held herself until he was gone. Following several deep breaths, she felt her muscles unknot. Thank God this day was nearly over. The meeting had lasted nine hours. Besides the crucial votes, there had been other business on the agenda.

Easing down in her desk chair, she rubbed her temple, then peered at the clock. She was free to go home. And alone, too.

Her adrenaline kicked in. Would Brant be waiting? Yes. She was confident of that. She suspected he was eager to settle the unfinished business between them.

But was she? Was she up to facing him, dealing with this emotional crossroads in her life?

Jessica stood and loaded her briefcase. After bidding Tony and Millie good-night, she headed for home with both anticipation and dread.

She knew he was there.

The scent of his cologne instantly sharpened her senses and sent her pulses soaring. She paused in the foyer, her heart pounding like a drum inside her chest. At least she didn't see any luggage, which might or might not mean anything. At this point, she simply didn't know what to expect.

"Hey."

"Hey, yourself," she said huskily, then made her way into the living room. He was standing by the fireplace, facing her.

She stopped, and their eyes met. Then, swallowing

around the sudden lump in her throat, Jessica crossed deeper into the room. He looked tired, like he hadn't slept in days. Apparently this new twist in their relationship had taken its toll on him, as well. Or maybe his exhaustion had to do with his son. She had no idea how Brant had fared with him.

"Would you like a drink?" he asked, breaking the tense silence.

"Thanks," she responded, pulling her eyes off him. "A glass of Chardonnay would be nice."

"Chardonnay it is." He crossed to the bar area, then returned shortly with glass in hand. While there, he'd also helped himself to a beer.

"You won, right?"

She was taken aback. "How did you know?"

He smiled. "I just did."

"No, you didn't. You just took a wild guess."

"Whatever," he countered, his smile fading into another silence.

It was obvious they were both reluctant to make the first move, even though the tension continued to mount. When it became so thick that Jessica couldn't stand it, she asked, "How did your meeting go with Elliot?"

"Better than I ever thought possible." He gave her a detailed accounting.

"Oh, Brant, that's wonderful. I'm thrilled for you both." She sat in the nearest chair and took a sip of her wine, feeling it hit the bottom of her empty stomach with a thud. Food had been the farthest thing from her mind all day. She didn't recall having eaten a thing.

"Me too, or at least, I think so," Brant added, blowing out his breath. "With kids, you never know."

"When will you see him again?"

"He's coming to Arkansas. And believe it or not, he's going to square it with his mother himself."

"Which obviously won't be easy."

Brant's features darkened. "Marsha might as well accept the fact. It's going to happen, with or without her blessing."

"Good for you."

Another silence fell.

"This is bullshit, you know." Brant's harsh tone hit the silence like shattering glass. "We're acting like strangers, or uptight teenagers. Take your pick."

Jessica flinched without meaning to. "Why don't you say what's on your mind, then?"

"I just did." His tone grew harsher.

She sucked in her lower lip and turned away.

"Jessica, look at me. Please."

Now his tone was pleading. She couldn't ignore that. Yet it was all she could do to face him again, an unnamed fear threatening to choke her. God, she wasn't ready for this showdown. She needed more time to collect her thoughts, to search her soul. She swallowed her mounting apprehension.

"I love you, Jessica, and I don't want to leave you."

He loved her!

Suddenly her thoughts were clear as the rarest of crystal. "And I love you, too," she whispered, her heart leaping with joy and her eyes brimming with tears. "So now you have no reason to leave me. You can stay here, with me, forever."

His eyes burned into her. "I have a better idea. Marry me and come to Arkansas."

Shock rendered her speechless. To admit to herself and him that she loved him had been a giant leap of faith. But marriage... Ice-cold fear numbed her. Too much, too soon. She wasn't ready to step that far out of her previous life. How could she tell him that? How could she unpack her heart with the right words?

She couldn't. There were no right words.

"And give up my job as mayor?"

"Yes," he said without hesitation.

Her nerves clenched. How could he ask that of her?

"Do you love me?" he went on.

"Yes," she whispered. "But—" Her voice broke.

Brant crossed to the sofa and sat beside her, though he didn't touch her. "I can't stand the thought of you in such a high-profile job, a job that will always have the potential for danger. If anything had happened to you—" This time his voice broke.

"I find that reasoning a bit ironic, don't you?" Jessica paused, grappling with her tangled emotions. "Aren't you forgetting all those years you lived in danger?"

"I won't deny my words smack of a double standard, but if I had it to do all over again, I'd walk away. That job contributed to the breakup of my marriage and the loss of my son. I can't stand the thought of that happening to us."

"But you're asking the impossible," Jessica responded in a disbelieving voice. "I love you, but I love my job as mayor, too, and it's important."

"More important than me?"

"That's not fair, Brant, and you know it."

He stood and walked back to the fireplace.

"What if I put you on the hot-seat?" Jessica said. "And asked you to stay in Dallas, to consider going into partnership with Thurmon?"

He swung around. "Are you asking me that?"

She hesitated, but only briefly. "No. I would never ask you to make that kind of choice."

His features closed down. "Good, because I never want to return to security work. Like my Secret Service work, it's too demanding." He paused and searched her face. "Anyhow, our relationship should be top priority, not our jobs."

"And you think I'm putting my job before us?"

"Aren't you?"

"You're twisting things, Brant, and trying to make me into something I'm not."

"What you're saying, then, is we have no future." His tone was sharp-edged and blunt.

Feeling her heart crumble, she whispered, "Perhaps what we need is time. Apart."

His features remained closed. "Perhaps you're right." He strode to the door, then turned around. "Take care of yourself, Jessica."

Forty

"I'm okay, Ronnie. Really I am."

"I just don't understand how Brant could just walk out and leave you high and dry."

Veronica had dropped by to check on her after she had learned Brant had returned to Arkansas.

"His job was over," Jessica pointed out softly, careful to keep her voice as normal as possible.

"Still, I think he's a rat for just up and hauling out, not even bothering to say goodbye to Thurmon and me."

"He was eager to get back home. You should understand that, knowing him."

Veronica's gaze homed in on her. "Don't you think it's time you told me the truth?"

Jessica averted her gaze. Tell her, a little voice whispered. Tell her the truth. It will do you good.

"You two had a thing," Veronica said in a matter-of-fact tone.

Jessica swung around, widening her eyes. "How did you know?"

"Actually it was pretty obvious, more so to Thurmon than me, actually."

"Did Brant say anything to him?" Jessica found that hard to believe. That wasn't Brant's style.

"No, he didn't have to. Thurmon figured it out on

his own.'' Veronica paused. ''And you've changed, Jessie. There's something different about you, something softer—'' She broke off with a shrug. ''Hell, I didn't mean that the way it came out. It's just that I can't put my intuition into words, if that makes sense.''

Jessica bit down on her lower lip to stop it from trembling. ''It…does.''

''You want to talk about it?''

''There's not really that much to talk about,'' Jessica said, continuing to hedge and not knowing why.

''Sure there is. The truth.''

''We…love each other.''

This time Veronica's eyes widened. ''Well, I'll be damned. And to think you two managed to keep it a secret.''

Jessica smiled, though it didn't reach her eyes. ''Crazy, isn't it? Me, who swore she'd never fall head over heels in love.''

Veronica waved a hand. ''I know what you mean, honey. You loved Porter, but you weren't in love with him. As for you and Brant, I think it's great.'' Her features sobered. ''If you do, that is.''

''Right now, I'm so confused.''

''What happened? Something not good, obviously, or Brant would still be here.''

''He asked me to marry him and go to Arkansas with him.''

''Surely not,'' Veronica responded in an astounded tone. ''What about your job? I mean—'' She broke off on a splutter.

''Exactly.'' Jessica stood, suddenly feeling too jumpy inside to sit still for another second.

''And he wouldn't even consider staying here and working with Thurmon?''

"No," Jessica said in an unsteady voice.

Veronica stretched her lips into a thin line and shook her head. "I thought for sure Elliot might lure him out of those woods, but I guess I was wrong."

Jessica didn't respond. She couldn't. Her whole body seemed to have shut down, leaving her feeling empty.

Veronica scrunched her face in anxiety. "Oh, honey, I'm so sorry. It's just not fair. You've been through so much, you deserve a break. You deserve to love and be loved. Damn Brant and his bullheadedness."

"I've never felt this way before, Ronnie. Like you said, I never loved Porter with all my heart. I never let him get that close. I was too afraid." Jessica swallowed around the lump lodged in her throat. She refused to cry in front of her friend, but that was exactly what she felt like doing.

"Do you think there's any way you and Brant—" Veronica's words faded out as if she was on uncharted seas.

"Right now, I'm so mixed up, I don't know what to think about anything, especially the direction of my life."

Veronica walked over and gave Jessica a hug. "Things will work out the way they're supposed to. You have to believe that. And you know I'm here for you anytime, day or night."

Jessica could only nod, tears replacing the lump.

"I'll call you tomorrow."

What was she going to do about Brant?

How was she going to purge him from her heart when he refused to budge? More important, why did she want to? He was the best thing that had ever happened to her and surely worth fighting for.

Passion.

Family.

Love.

He represented all those things and more. In the few short weeks he'd been with her, he'd entrenched himself in her life as no one ever had. So how could she just have let him walk out the door, knowing he would never come back?

Fear.

And lack of trust.

But love and trust went hand-in-hand. One was no good without the other. Neither could stand alone. Yet she had to admit she didn't trust him, and she was afraid.

Whole-hog love demanded that you trusted the other person enough to let go, to lose control and know they were going to catch you if you fell. She had always been afraid to take that ultimate risk. Instead, she'd taken the safe, acceptable path and married a man who was no threat to her emotional security.

Because Porter hadn't touched her soul, he could never destroy her the way her daddy had done so long ago. But Brant wasn't her father, and she was no longer a child. She was a grown, self-confident woman.

A chill ran through Jessica, and she cloaked her upper body in the security of folded arms. From the beginning, she had feared Brant. He'd tapped into her emotions, and that had freaked her out.

Until now she had trusted only in herself, in her ability to manage her life, happy to remain within the confines of her box. Now she realized what an empty life that was. Brant's loving warmth and protection had shown her that.

Risk.

Wasn't that what life was all about? That was certainly what her career was all about, and she thrived on that aspect of it. She was always the first one to jump in headfirst.

So why not take that plunge when it came to love, something much more substantial and rewarding in the long run than a career? Any woman could have a career. Not just any woman was lucky enough to find someone to love from the heart and who loved her in the same way.

So could she give up her career and move to Arkansas? Make the ultimate sacrifice?

Even though she loved Brant desperately and was finally willing to trust him with her heart and soul, she didn't think she could be cut off from civilization, from her friends, her work.

While she would always need Brant, she needed others, as well. Yet she couldn't ask him to become something he wasn't, either. The city represented pain and heartache for him. He was content to bask in the peace and quiet of the woods.

Letting the fresh tears flow, Jessica stared out the window into the inky blackness and prayed for a miracle.

The sky was perfect—azure-blue, without so much as a cloud to mar it. His boat was also full of fish. And solitude surrounded him. Only the sounds of nature's critters cut into that silence. He was doing exactly what he had longed to do for so many weeks.

So why was he one miserable sonofabitch?

He missed the two people he loved most in the world—Jessica and Elliot, though he had the promise of a strengthening bond with Elliot to hold on to. Not so with Jessica. It was over.

His heart wrenched, which surprised him. He had thought he was numb to the pain, that the biggest chunk of his heart had remained with Jessica. God, he ached for her—her smell, her touch, her laughter. He missed everything about her.

Yet here he was, back in the woods, back where he belonged. The thought of resuming a normal life in normal surroundings was too terrifying to contemplate. Even the thought made him break out in a cold sweat in the glaring heat of the day.

But the thought of never seeing Jessica again was more terrifying.

He watched his line jerk in the water. So what if the fish took the rod and all? He didn't give a damn. Actually he didn't give a damn about anything but Jessica.

So what was the solution?

He couldn't live without her. Yet he couldn't live in the city, either.

Or could he?

Brant froze. Had he lost his mind? Or had her love healed him enough to make the impossible possible? With Jessica's love and strength behind him, anything—hell, everything—was possible.

Realizing he was shaking like a wet dog in the wintertime, Brant jerked in his rod, cranked the motor and headed for shore. Once there, he forced his unsteady limbs to move, though it seemed his mind and body weren't properly connected.

When he reached the cabin and walked inside, he knew. He had to try, for his own sake. He couldn't bear to remain in that dark pit any longer. He had no choice but to return to Dallas.

To Jessica.

"Thank God your life has finally settled back into a routine, even though you really don't seem excited about that."

Jessica scarcely paid attention to Tony's words, especially since he'd been in her office for over an hour. As much as she continued to depend on him and his efficiency, he was stepping on her nerves.

But then, of late, everything and everyone did that.

"I'm not so sure my routine is that good anymore," Jessica mused out loud, then regretted that lapse in judgment.

Tony's mouth fell open. "Surely you don't mean that?"

Jessica kept her silence.

"Why, I thought when the cops were arrested and he-man exited your life, you'd be over the moon. And well you should be, too. Your election campaign is off the ground and gaining steam."

Tony began pacing the floor. "And despite the fact that Curtis Riley's running against you, I think you're a shoo-in. He's just a big bag of hot air with an ax to grind. He won't get to first base with the voters."

Tony hammered on. "Besides, the preelection polls have you ahead. And you've managed to get your stepson in a drug treatment program that seems to be helping him. And since the big council vote, the office itself is running like clockwork. What more could you ask for?"

Brant.

She hadn't heard a word from him. And while she hadn't expected to, his silence was killing her. Sleepless nights and long desperate hours bore testimony to that.

"Are you sick or something?"

That question jolted Jessica. "You know better than that," she replied in an irritated tone.

Tony shrugged, his gaze shrewd. "I noticed you've lost more weight."

"It's just the fallout from the cops," she said, removing her gaze.

"Hope that's all, since you're busier than a cranberry merchant at Christmas and will be until the election's over."

"Trust me, Tony, everything will be all right," she said, stretching the truth again. At the moment, she didn't think anything in her life would ever be right again.

That thought still haunted her as she sat in the lonely comfort of her home, with only her sadness as her companion. Was this evening a pattern for the future? Would this gaping hole inside her continue to zap her energy and her enthusiasm?

The doorbell must have rung several times before she realized she had a visitor, even though whoever it was seemed to be sitting on the button. If it was Curtis Riley, she swore she wouldn't let him cross the threshold. He seemed to think he could court her and challenge her at the same time. He had more gall than anyone she'd ever known.

"Yes?" she asked, not even bothering to place her hand on the knob.

"Jessica, it's Brant."

Her legs turned to water. Blindly she reached for the wall and leaned against it, trying to quiet her runaway heart.

"May I come in?"

"Of course," Jessica whispered, though she knew he couldn't hear her. With trembling, uncoordinated fingers, she unbolted the door and swung it open, knowing her heart was in her eyes and not caring.

She loved him. She would make no apologies for that.

He had one hand propped against the doorframe, and he looked haggard and vulnerable under the glare of the porch light.

"Jessica," he rasped, his eyes devouring her. "I couldn't stay away."

With a cry, she flung herself into his open arms and soaked up the love she felt emanating from him.

Even though his penis was no longer rock-hard, it remained nestled inside her warmth following hours of making love.

After holding on to her for the longest time, he'd scooped her up in his arms and taken her into the bedroom, where clothes were dispensed with in record time. He'd kissed her fiercely on the lips but hadn't stopped there. He'd taken those kisses down her body all the way to her toes.

During those magic hours, her body had been his slave, and his hers. She wasn't ashamed. In fact, she had reveled in every moment his naked flesh had been adhered to hers, especially when he'd sensed she was about to climax under the sweet assault of his hands and mouth. He'd spread her legs and pierced that moist heat between them with his tongue, sending her over the edge.

She'd writhed in blissful agony. Unwilling to slight him, she'd push him on his back, bent over and taken him in her mouth, using her lips to bathe his entire penis, finally concentrating on the soft tip, sucking there until she tasted him.

"Jessica, Jessica," he'd moaned before grabbing a leg and pulling it across him, which enabled him to thrust high and strong in her. Then, clutching the sides of her buttocks, he'd moved her back and forward, creating a friction that had nearly taken both their heads off.

Now, facing each other, Jessica tried to concentrate on Brant himself. But that was difficult with him still inside her. She knew it would only take one unplanned move and he would harden instantly and go off like a rocket.

But they needed to talk. They had so much to decide.

"I love you," he whispered, continuing to devour her with heated eyes.

"And I love you."

"Marry me."

"Today?"

He chuckled. "Today's not soon enough."

"It's the best we can do," she responded in a sassy but breathless tone.

His features turned serious. "I've decided to stay, to try things your way."

"Oh, Brant," she whispered. "I don't want you to do something you don't, can't do."

"I want to be with you, my darling, and if joining the real world again is what it takes, then I'm willing to give it my best shot. Besides, there's Elliot. I miss him, too."

"Do you think he'll mind about us, especially since your relationship is so new and fragile?"

"Are you kidding? He'll be delighted. Like I've always said, he likes you better than me anyway."

Jessica poked him in the ribs and felt him spring to life inside her. She caught her breath.

He chuckled. "Better watch it."

She felt her face grow hot, which escalated his chuckle into full laughter. "God, I love you. You're the best thing that ever happened to me."

"I feel the same way."

"I guess I should call Thurmon and make his day."

"And I'll make Ronnie's at the same time."

Brant leaned down and kissed a distended nipple, causing her to lose her next breath. "You're not playing fair."

He grinned. "I know."

"How about Elliot?"

"We'll tell him together."

"What do you think about him being your best man?"

He grinned. "Hey, that's a great idea."

His features sobered. "What about Roy? How's he doing?"

"He's responding to treatment. For now, that's all I can hope for."

Brant held her still closer, then said, "I'll help you with your reelection campaign."

Jessica pulled back and stared at him. "You will?"

"Don't sound so surprised," he said in a gruff but teasing tone. "You don't have to beat me over the head with a bat. I've come to terms with how much your career means to you."

She kissed him long and hard. "Thanks for saying that, my darling."

"Although I know you'll win, will you be devastated if you don't?"

"Not at all. Now that I have you, my job is no longer the most important thing in my life."

Brant stared at her for a long moment. "What if you're pregnant? Have you thought about that?"

She didn't know what she had expected him to say, but it wasn't that. She made a strangled sound while trying to clear her throat. "What on earth made you ask that?"

"Because it's not impossible, is it?"

"No, no, it isn't," she said, licking her lips.

He groaned, and that was when she felt him expand to full strength. "Would you mind having my child?"

"Oh, Brant, I never thought I'd want children, but I can't think of anything I'd like more."

"Thank God, because I feel like we've made a baby tonight."

As though that thought was contagious, she whispered, "Me too."

His eyes darkened. "I'll never leave you again. Ever."

"It wouldn't work, anyway," she said with a catch in her voice. "I'd just follow you."

He laughed, then shifted over her and began loving her again.

Forevermore.

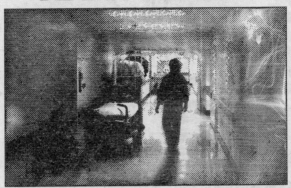

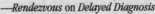

If you enjoyed what you just read,
then we've got an offer you can't resist!

Take 2
bestselling novels FREE!
Plus get a FREE surprise gift!

Clip this page and mail it to The Best of the Best™

IN U.S.A.
3010 Walden Ave.
P.O. Box 1867
Buffalo, N.Y. 14240-1867

IN CANADA
P.O. Box 609
Fort Erie, Ontario
L2A 5X3

YES! Please send me 2 free Best of the Best™ novels and my free surprise gift. After receiving them, if I don't wish to receive anymore, I can return the shipping statement marked cancel. If I don't cancel, I will receive 4 brand-new novels every month, before they're available in stores! In the U.S.A., bill me at the bargain price of $4.74 plus 25¢ shipping and handling per book and applicable sales tax, if any*. In Canada, bill me at the bargain price of $5.24 plus 25¢ shipping and handling per book and applicable taxes**. That's the complete price and a savings of over 20% off the cover prices—what a great deal! I understand that accepting the 2 free books and gift places me under no obligation ever to buy any books. I can always return a shipment and cancel at any time. Even if I never buy another The Best of the Best™ book, the 2 free books and gift are mine to keep forever.

185 MDN DNWF
385 MDN DNWG

Name	(PLEASE PRINT)	
Address	Apt.#	
City	State/Prov.	Zip/Postal Code

* Terms and prices subject to change without notice. Sales tax applicable in N.Y.
** Canadian residents will be charged applicable provincial taxes and GST.
  All orders subject to approval. Offer limited to one per household and not valid to
  current The Best of the Best™ subscribers.
  ® are registered trademarks of Harlequin Enterprises Limited.

BOB02-R   ©1998 Harlequin Enterprises Limited

MARY LYNN BAXTER

66902 LIKE SILK	___ $6.50 U.S.	___ $7.99 CAN.
66809 TEMPTING JANEY	___ $5.99 U.S.	___ $6.99 CAN.
66588 SULTRY	___ $5.99 U.S.	___ $6.99 CAN.
66523 ONE SUMMER EVENING	___ $5.99 U.S.	___ $6.99 CAN.
66440 HARD CANDY	___ $5.99 U.S.	___ $6.99 CAN.
66417 TEARS OF YESTERDAY	___ $5.50 U.S.	___ $6.50 CAN.
66300 AUTUMN AWAKENING	___ $5.50 U.S.	___ $6.50 CAN.
66289 LONE STAR HEAT	___ $5.99 U.S.	___ $6.99 CAN.
66165 A DAY IN APRIL	___ $5.99 U.S.	___ $6.99 CAN.

(limited quantities available)

TOTAL AMOUNT	$_____
POSTAGE & HANDLING	$_____
($1.00 for one book; 50¢ for each additional)	
APPLICABLE TAXES*	$_____
<u>TOTAL PAYABLE</u>	$_____

(check or money order—please do not send cash)

To order, complete this form and send it, along with a check or money order for the total above, payable to MIRA® Books, to: **In the U.S.:** 3010 Walden Avenue, P.O. Box 9077, Buffalo, NY 14269-9077; **In Canada:** P.O. Box 636, Fort Erie, Ontario, L2A 5X3.

Name:_____
Address:_____ City:_____
State/Prov.:_____ Zip/Postal Code:_____
Account Number (if applicable):_____
075 CSAS

*New York residents remit applicable sales taxes.
 Canadian residents remit applicable
 GST and provincial taxes.

MIRA®

MMLB0203BL